"You have brought Ethel Smyth an
to life, given us a window onto he
The historical novel – it's so much
life punctuated by some amazing
Emmeline), by Ethel's sense of he
subordinate herself in ways that were expected of women, and
by her music – her very raison d'être."

Helen Pankhurst, activist, academic, granddaughter of
Sylvia and great granddaughter of Emmeline Pankhurst

"A fascinating, highly readable novel, based on the life and times
of composer Ethel Smyth, from the drawing rooms of Victorian
London to the opera houses of Europe and the grim walls of
Holloway prison. What a defiant, gifted, big-hearted woman,
totally committed to her craft and determined to weather the
constant obstacles put in her way."

Caitlin Davies, author of
Bad Girls: Rebels and Renegades Of Holloway Prison

"A wonderful insight into how life may have been for a woman
composer fighting for her music and talent to be acknowledged
in a male-dominated world. This imaginative piece underlines
the difficulty Dame Ethel Smyth had in gaining recognition and
opportunities as an outlier in musical society. Her never-ending
determination to have her music heard and to carve a path for
other women following in her footsteps shines through. This well-
researched book gives a vivid insight into what Smyth's personal
life may have been like, traces her development as a musician, and
presents her as human, flawed, rather than portraying a perfect
but unrealistic image we sometimes form of a famous composer.
A thoroughly enjoyable and enlightening read."

Nicola Hands,
Tailleferre Ensemble

SHINING
THREADS

Joy Bounds

The Book Guild Ltd

First published in Great Britain in 2023 by
The Book Guild Ltd
Unit E2 Airfield Business Park,
Harrison Road, Market Harborough,
Leicestershire. LE16 7UL
Tel: 0116 2792299
www.bookguild.co.uk
Email: info@bookguild.co.uk
Twitter: @bookguild

Typeset in 11pt Minion Pro

Printed on FSC accredited paper
Printed and bound in Great Britain by 4edge Limited

ISBN 978 1915603 791

British Library Cataloguing in Publication Data.
A catalogue record for this book is available from the British Library.

For Lynne

1

ENGLAND 1876

Ethel clapped wildly, gasping at the women's poise, their colourful dresses, their bright hair as they stepped to the front of the stage. She could feel the wide grin on her face. Already, sitting there amongst the buzzing crowd in the huge concert hall with its bright chandeliers and back-to-back gleaming pianos, she had found it necessary to thrust her fist into her mouth to stem her excitement. Now the hall quietened, ready to listen.

The perfect clarity of the soprano's singing vibrated in her ears, whilst the men's voices weaved in and out beneath, all at one with the pianos. She leant out of the box where she sat with Mrs Sinclair and her friends, reaching for the stage, so far that if Ralph had not grabbed hold of her jacket, she might well have gone over.

'Hang on there, Ethel,' he muttered, trying to draw her closer to him. She shrugged him off impatiently. How they all wanted to keep hold of her. If she was too outrageous, however, she might not be invited again, and she sank back into her seat, forcing herself to smile at him.

Ethel guessed her mother's plan. She hoped that if Ethel was invited to an occasional concert, she would stop talking about becoming a composer. She might even meet a handsome young man (like Ralph) and decide to settle down. Ethel only complied so she could come and hear music.

She found herself leaning forward again. She wanted to be as near as possible to this sound that swelled from the women's throats, and from the deep chests of the tenor and baritone. The roaring wind, birdsong, the voices of lovers, a mother crooning over her child, the to and fro of the sea, the steps of the dancer, the rustle of the grass on the dunes, a gentle waterfall – all the experiences of life were caught in the songs. She glanced at her programme again – *Songs of Love*.

At the end, Ethel stood and clapped loud and long, sometimes pressing her hands to her mouth or chest in disbelief, sometimes cheering. She wanted the concert to go on for ever. Ralph pulled at her dress. She looked around irritably; everyone else in the box was clapping firmly but gently, nodding their approval of a fine performance. They thought her exuberance vulgar, she knew that, but she continued until the performers left the stage.

She sat back in her seat. She had no desire to start chatting with her companions, who were already seeing to their shawls and jackets, and talking about supper, but at last she must go.

Mrs Sinclair put her arm around Ethel's shoulders as they swished through the curtains into the corridor. 'You mustn't feel it so, my dear,' she said. 'The music is for us to enjoy; we mustn't let it stir us too much.'

'It was beautiful beyond belief,' said Ethel, pushing back tears. 'He must be a great man to write such things.'

'Who, Johannes Brahms?' said Mrs Sinclair. 'A strange and dull man, they say, though I've not met him. Now, I've got to go backstage to remind some of the violinists about my garden party. Come with me. You may get the chance to speak to the two ladies, if you want to.'

Ethel wanted to, of course; to breathe the same air as those two singers for a few minutes and talk with them...

She followed Mrs Sinclair to the stage door whilst the others went to find their supper table. How strange backstage was. Gone were the red velvet drapes and embossed wallpaper, the shining glass lamps and gleaming panelling. Instead she saw rough wood partitioning and bare floors, stacked chairs and music stands. Yet the Artists' Room was bright and comfortable, and full of all the performers of the evening's programme receiving the congratulations of their families and friends.

Ethel looked from face to face. Five minutes ago they had been plunging the depth of human experience with their music. Now they were talking about the weather and where they might get a hot meal nearby.

Mrs Sinclair introduced Ethel to the two women, who were sitting on the sofa sipping glasses of wine. They greeted her politely and received her thanks for their wonderful performance. She looked from one to the other in admiration, Fraülein Friedlander in her kingfisher blue dress, and Fraülein Redke, her braids wound tightly around her head, fastened with silver clasps.

'I loved that bit in the sixth song,' she said at last. 'The bird's flight. So powerful! Brilliant!'

'That's one of my favourite songs, too. Here, come and squeeze in. I'm Thekla, by the way, and this is Gustchen. Please don't call us Fraülein this and Fraülein that.'

They made way for her on the sofa by pulling in their large, stiffened skirts, and laughed at the unstoppable questions that gushed out of her about their tour, and about the songs on the programme.

'It's a life of unbelievable glamour,' said Ethel. 'Great music and people adoring you for what you do.'

'It's not glamorous,' said Gustchen. 'But we do love our audience, especially people like you who are so enthusiastic.'

The women chatted on, mentioning slight mistakes that they or the men had made. Ethel wanted to pinch herself. She was sitting on a sofa with two of the most feted singers in the world.

'And what about you? Do you sing?'

'Not really,' said Ethel. 'I play the piano quite well, and compose a bit, too.'

'Compose, eh?' said Gustchen. 'I'm impressed.'

'I'm going to study at the Leipzig conservatoire as soon as I can persuade my father to let me go.' She hesitated. She would have liked to tell them about the bitter arguments at home, confide her fear that she might never get to fulfil her dream.

'How exciting,' the woman called Thekla said. 'We live near there. Maybe we can help.'

'Ethel.' It was Mrs Sinclair. 'We must go and join the others if we are to have any supper.'

Ethel wanted to say she did not care about supper or her friends or anything but these women and the music they made.

'Why don't you call on us in the morning?' said Thekla. 'We can continue our conversation over a bowl of chocolate. We're staying quite close to here.'

Ethel looked up at Mrs Sinclair. 'Could I do that before I get my train home?'

Ethel had imagined that the women might rent a room in a fashionable part of London a bit like Mrs Sinclair's, but the carriage was going where the houses were small and the streets narrow.

'Are you sure this is the place?' called the coachman as he stopped in front of one of the cramped little houses. The street was dirty and as Ethel stepped down she had to lift her skirts a little to keep them out of the stinking water and the rubbish lying about. People were getting on with the work of their day, with children holding on to horses' bridles as the drivers delivered their load.

Mustering up her courage, she said briskly, 'Yes, this is it all right. Now, I'll see you in an hour or so.'

She banged on the knocker and was let into the house by a woman who introduced herself as the landlady. Ethel thought her clothes were more like what the scullery maid at home wore and, as she was led upstairs, she noticed the worn treads and the dull, stained walls.

'I don't think the ladies are properly up yet,' the landlady said. 'They work so late, poor things, and by the time they've talked to everyone and had something to eat the night's half over. I did take their breakfast in a little while ago, and they said to bring you straight up.'

On the third floor, she knocked at a door and beckoned Ethel to follow. 'Here's your guest, ladies,' she said, going to pick up the breakfast tray. 'I'll bring you some hot chocolate shortly.'

'Ethel,' said Thekla, coming to kiss her, 'I'm sorry we're not ready for the day yet. But if you don't mind, come on in.'

Ethel felt her face flush. The women weren't dressed yet, and had various silky shawls draped around their shoulders. Their hair was undone, and their faces seemed pale and ordinary without any make-up. Their feet were bare. The room smelt stuffy, of night-time smells, and the curtains were only slightly open. The bed at the back of the room was unmade, and the glamorous dresses they had worn the night before were slung over the back of a chair.

'You are shocked,' said Gustchen, looking at her face. 'We're very different creatures in the day. This is how artists live, I'm afraid, cramped in small rooms in second-rate lodging houses, with no space to put anything. Here, take your hat off and come and sit here.' She threw bits of underwear off the chair by the fire, and kicked several pairs of boots out of the way.

'Nevertheless we like it here, and we adore being in London again,' said Thekla. 'Now Mrs whatever-your-name-is, let's be having that chocolate.'

Ethel looked around, unsure where to put her hat on surfaces which were crammed with gloves and combs and bits of jewellery and music scores. Eventually she sat down, keeping it on her lap.

Gustchen had got a bottle in her hand. 'Darling, have you seen a clean glass anywhere? A little spirit would work wonders.'

The two women poked around the room, but no glass was to be found.

'I guess we could use this,' said Thekla, holding up an eggcup which had been left behind on the breakfast table.

Gustchen giggled. 'Needs must, it seems.'

'Ethel, will you have a drop?' she said, holding out the tiny cup.

Ethel nodded. She could imagine her father's face as he surveyed the scene. It would be full of anger, of loathing. It would confirm everything he believed about artists. Poor Mrs Sinclair would be shocked that she had allowed her to come to such a place.

'Why not?' she said, accepting the little glass of clear liquid. 'Now, please, tell me all about Leipzig.'

~

Ethel stayed in her bedroom. Several weeks had passed since she said that she would not join in family life again until they allowed her to go to Leipzig. Once or twice, when her parents were out, she had run across the fields to the station and taken a train to London on money she had persuaded local tradesmen to give her on her father's account. How glorious it was to sit and listen to the full sound of the orchestra playing a symphony.

Her bedroom was a lonely place. Until recently, it had been full of her big sisters, Mary and Alice. All their lives they had spent under the covers talking, giggling, making fun, smirking at the misfortunes of their neighbours, devising punishments for their governesses, imitating foolish visitors, complaining about the restrictions and punishments of their father.

Then they had left, just like that. Got married, gone away with a respectable bishop and a rich businessman, made their parents

6

happy. How bleak it was: the shelves empty, the wardrobe hardly half full, the bed large and silent.

They were different when they visited now, sharing their beds with those men rather than with her. That's what Mother and Father were trying to do to her; they had presented her at court, arranged countless parties and engineered invitations to others. It was humiliating to find some man pressing himself against her under cover of a dance. Still, it was only temporary. She was going to be a composer, and that was that.

She sat at her table, writing a song. As she struck out for the third time a line that was wrong but she could not see how, a splurge of anger shot through her. Not only would Father not let her go and study music; he had dismissed her teacher. She hated him.

She longed for the music room in Mr Ewing's untidy wooden house at the barracks where she had spent so many hours, studying the harmonies of his compositions and learning how to apply them to her own songs. He had taught her how to control her intense excitement as ideas gripped her, until something emerged as black notes on lined paper – notes that she or anyone else who could read them could transform into sound, song, rhythm, beauty.

After the lesson, she would hang over his tinny old piano whilst he played arias from Wagner's operas, which they sang with gusto; or he might choose a snippet of some new Brahms symphony. Later, whilst Mrs Ewing laid out lunch, she would browse through the piles of music books and scores from which she could freely select.

Father hadn't liked a letter Mr Ewing sent her. *These other people slope calmly through their narrow, restricted lives,* he had written. *Their joys and their sorrows are feeble and dim... but ours flash and blaze.*

He had gone, but his words were scorched into her mind. Flash and blaze.

There was a knocking on her door, a fierce knocking. 'Ethel, let me in, I want to talk to you.'

'Not unless you want to talk about me going to Leipzig,' she said. The song was beginning to take shape at last.

'For heaven's sake, unlock the door.' He rattled the handle. She said nothing. 'You are not to go into the kitchen and ask the servants to give you food. You eat with the rest of us or not at all. D'you hear me? Now come on, open up. It's time to put an end to this.'

She sensed his fury through the door. Was he actually going to kick the door down and come in and hit her again? She drew another set of quavers on the line, black dots with their intriguing tails, and hummed the tune hovering between her mind and the page.

~

Ethel walked into the dining room where the brigadier and his wife and brother, the local bishop, and Mrs Sinclair were already settling down to dinner. She had not washed for days or changed out of her grubby day dress.

'Ethel,' said her father, signalling to Teddy to pour out some of the fine wine that was to accompany the fish course, 'please go and get dressed properly if you wish to join us for dinner.'

'It's all right, John,' said Mother. 'She can sit by me. Teddy, bring a chair for Ethel, and tell Mabel to set another place.'

Ethel sat down but turned away from her mother's embarrassed smile.

'Don't worry about me,' she said. 'I'm not eating anyway.'

The others started to eat, and her father resumed the conversation.

'In my time, he would have been court-martialled,' he said. 'Such a blatant disregard for the rules.'

'I agree, Major-General,' said the brigadier. 'They are becoming very soft on discipline now. They'll regret it when there's another crisis, you mark my words.'

Ethel interrupted loudly. 'You and your rules,' she said. 'Doesn't a soldier have any freedoms in your blessed army?'

'Ethel, please,' said her mother.

'It's a shame we can't put you in the army for a bit, my girl,' said her father, trying to make a joke of it. 'They'd teach you how to behave. Wouldn't they, Brigadier?'

Ethel put as much contempt into her laugh as she could, but before she could say more, the bishop's wife cut in with a story she had heard about a neighbour's nursemaid. Ethel let the guests voice their opinions before wondering loudly how sad it was that women had nothing to do except gossip over tea and a piece of cake. Mother flushed and put her head down.

Ethel enjoyed her success in making everyone uncomfortable. They had begun to eat very quickly, and even the brigadier refused any further helpings. Then the smell of the desserts hit her nose. Cook was renowned throughout the neighbourhood for her meringues and stiff-whipped creams, and tonight they were combined with the last soft fruits of the year into an elaborate tower. She greedily demanded several helpings.

'You know I've been going up to concerts in London,' she said generally to the table. 'Last week I heard a man playing the violin with an orchestra. Oh my goodness, it was wonderful. Joachim, I think he was called. The bow was like an extension of his arm.'

'Don't be silly, Ethel,' said her mother. 'You've been stuck in your room for weeks. Quite unnecessarily, I might add.'

Ethel ignored her, and raised her voice so she was almost shouting. 'I think I've been three times now, or maybe four. Gosh, it's a bit scary coming home now the nights are drawing in. I was sure last week a man was following me when I got off the omnibus, but I managed to run for the train.'

'You're just making up ridiculous stories now,' said her father, signalling for the dessert to be taken away.

'No, I'm not,' said Ethel. 'You just check your butcher's account. The tradesmen are very generous, letting me have money for the train.'

Ethel looked around the table, smiling broadly. Everyone was flushed with embarrassment, but Father's shocked face was red with anger and shame. Mother's restraining hand on her knee was trembling.

'Shall the ladies withdraw?' said the brigadier to fill the silence.

'Yes, thank you,' said Father, and the women got up quickly, making as much noise as possible.

In the drawing room, Mother asked her to play the piano. Ethel sat and looked at the beautiful keys, waiting for her touch to bring Mozart alive for everyone. How she would have loved to enclose herself in that tight little world, delight everyone with her playing. That's what Mother was hoping for. Instead, she banged out a tune, made numerous mistakes and sang in a harsh, tuneless voice.

Father came into the room and shut the piano lid so sharply that she had to pull her fingers back to prevent them getting trapped. 'That's enough. Go to your room.'

'But I thought you wanted me to.'

She braced herself in case he hit her as he had before, but he merely wrenched her arm, forcing her to stand.

'Go to your room. That's quite enough. Go.'

~

The house fell silent. Her little sisters and Bob were sent off to stay with Mary. There were no more calls for her to come out and play with them, or have foolish conversations through the window. Mother spent the whole day in her room. Father no longer kicked the door or shouted orders through the keyhole. Ethel stopped eating, and wandered the empty rooms at night, restless. She was becoming a ghost in the house.

Just one thing kept her from despair; she held in her hand the map to her future. Waiting one evening for the train back to Farnborough after a concert, she had asked the railway clerk about the journey to Leipzig. On a piece of paper, he had written several times and place names. She looked them up in her old school atlas: London, Brussels, Liège, Düsseldorf, Dresden, Leipzig. She delighted in the undulating black line they made across Europe. They were shining beacons, their very names a song, creating her path to the conservatoire. She hugged the paper to her as she wandered the moonlit house, weeping tears of frustration.

She worked out from the times the clerk had noted down how long it would take to get there: twenty-nine hours and thirty-three minutes.

~

The moon shone bright through the window, and in the half-light her fingers found the soothing rhythms of the *Moonlight Sonata*. She remembered how she had first heard her governess play it after dinner one evening, years ago, how it had rung in her brain, vibrated through her body, awoken feelings she had never experienced before. She had known then that she must understand how such music had been written, must try and write it herself. The governess, before she was dismissed, had told her stories of the Leipzig conservatoire where she had studied, where hundreds of music-loving students learnt and played and practised.

Thekla and Gustchen, too. So many had gone there, and she must go too.

'Ethel, my darling,' said Mother, coming into the room, pulling a shawl around her shoulders. 'It's two in the morning. Why don't you go to bed?'

'I'm so... so... Mother, I just want to learn about all of this so much.' She got up and began pacing the room in agitation. 'It's torture, this, it really is.'

'Don't be so dramatic. There are so many other good things for you to enjoy, musical things too.'

Ethel went to the piano, and carefully closed the lid. 'I'll go to bed now,' she said.

~

Father knocked at her door. 'Ethel, come downstairs. I want to talk to you.'

His tone was different. Ethel brushed her hair and tied it up. It was so stringy and lank that she pinned a cap over it. When she put on one of her best day dresses, she was shocked at how baggy it had become. She felt sick as she entered his study. Wayward daughters were sometimes sent away to institutions.

She stood in front of his desk.

'I had hoped you would give up this ridiculous idea, but it's obvious you won't stop until you have brought us all down. I can't allow that, but you are fortunate to have friends who support your musical ambitions. Your sisters too. You may go to Leipzig.'

Ethel's hands flew up to her mouth to prevent the shrieks and joy that wanted to escape.

'Thank you,' she said, as if he had done no more than offer her the price of a new hat. 'When may I go?'

'When you can reassure your mother that you have somewhere suitable to live, with proper protection. You must promise that you will put aside this impetuous behaviour and bring some respect back to our family. You will have to manage on the small allowance I make for you.'

'Of course, of course. Yes, anything.'

'And when it is satisfactorily arranged, Alice's husband will escort you there, and ensure that you are safe.'

'I understand. This is wonderful. Thank you.'

He stood up and started to tidy his papers. 'Now, I'm sure you have plenty to do.'

2

LEIPZIG 1877

Ethel savoured the city. Just the market itself could take days to poke around. She wanted to take time to examine the different stalls, smell the bread and flowers and hams and spices and cheeses, and listen to the exchanges of conversation in a dialect so thick it could hardly be the same language she had learned from her governess. She would have liked to linger by the Thomaskirche where, apparently, Bach had written his glorious music, and where there was a concert several times a week. A concert, many concerts, less than ten minutes' walk from her lodgings!

Thekla would not allow any of it. 'There'll be plenty of time for all that. Come on, I want to show you something.'

Ethel followed her friend through the doorway of one of the merchant houses which lined the streets of Leipzig, and found herself in a plain little lobby, chilly after the warmth outside, whose only feature was a set of ascending wooden stairs.

'Where are you taking me now?' she asked.

'Up we go,' said Thekla.

Ethel hitched up her skirt and started climbing, stopping at each little landing to look out of the window as more of the city revealed itself below. Thekla pointed out the town hall with its row of gabled windows, the striking angular tower of St Nicolai church, the names of the streets, where the horses and carts grew smaller as they climbed.

At the fourth landing, Thekla said. 'Shut your eyes, Ethel. And when I ask you to open them you will see something exquisite.'

Ethel was pulled through a door into a room where all she could hear was the sharp sound of their boots on the floor.

'Where on earth are we?' she said. She was surprised how tiny her voice sounded, how silent this place was, how big it must be. It was not the apartment of one of Thekla's friends, where she had assumed she was being taken for tea.

She was pushed down gently onto a hard, wooden bench.

'You're going to love this. All right. You can open your eyes.'

She was in a hall, an enormous concert hall under the sloping roof of what must have been several houses. It was empty, and although there was very little light, she could see the wooden seats running across and along, and the stage at the front. A shaft of light coming through a half-open shutter showed ornate balcony grills, moulded cornices and golden light brackets.

'Oh my goodness. It's the Gwondhouse, isn't it? It's amazing.'

'The Geh-vant-hows,' said Thekla. 'Yes, this is where it all happens, Beethoven, Mozart, Clara Schumann, you name it.'

'You're going to tell me you've sung here.' Ethel got up and began to walk slowly down towards the stage.

'I did, yes. Last year. Gustchen and I sang the Brahms songs here – just like when you heard us in London. It was the best. The sound is incredible.' She ran up onto the stage, composed herself and sang a few lines. Her voice, pure and true, filled the large, empty space.

'Oh, that's lovely. How does one voice make that huge sound? Those songs sent me into raptures,' said Ethel. 'I'd never heard anything like it. What's that one called?'

'They don't really have names, but it's about the breeze in the trees. Goodness knows how such a brute of a man wrote a delicate thing like that.'

Ethel's head went up in shock. 'No,' she said. 'Brahms, a brute of a man?'

Thekla laughed. 'You'll see. He comes to Leipzig often enough. He'll stand right here, conducting.' She stamped her foot on the front of the stage.

Ethel couldn't believe that might happen, and yet here she was, standing with a renowned singer on the stage of the world-famous Gewandhaus.

'When's the next concert? I want to come.'

'Not for a while. Everyone's on holiday just now.'

They walked down the steps into the seated area again.

'You see up there?' Thekla was pointing to a box right above the stage. 'Old Frau Frege pretty much runs the show from there. She keeps an eye out for young musicians. We'll get you an introduction.'

'What a great place to sit.'

'You'll love her, she's a dear.'

'Is the conservatoire near here? I've got to find out when my studies begin.'

'It's very near. Come on, let's go and see.'

They jumped down the stairs and out into the street. Ethel's heart leapt at the sign on the corner: *Conservatorium der Musik.* An imposing set of doors marked the entrance. They were all locked.

Thekla led the way up the alley at the side of the building, dark and cool after the hot, noisy street behind them, and they came into a courtyard. At one side, horses were stabled, waiting for their owners to finish their business in town. Ethel breathed deep of their smell, surprised by a sudden longing for home.

'Ah, good,' said Thekla. 'An open door.'

They went along a dark corridor, calling as they went. The first open door led into a hall, where men were standing on ladders with paint and brushes in hand.

Thekla called up, and one of the men shimmied down the ladder. Ethel could hardly catch one word of their conversation.

'As I thought,' said Thekla, leading the way out, 'the conservatoire is shut until the beginning of September.'

'September? That's weeks away. I suppose I must have it in a letter somewhere.' She had left as soon as Father said she could come, for fear he might change his mind. She didn't care, it would give her plenty of time to explore the city and improve her German.

'Come with us to Thuringia,' said Thekla. 'Gustchen and I are going next week.'

'Thuringia? Is that part of Leipzig?'

'No, it's not far away, though. My mother has a little cottage by the lake. She wants to meet you. Georg is coming too.'

'Georg?'

'You know, Georg Henschel? George, as he likes to be called. He sang with Gustchen and me in London. We've got some new songs to learn.'

A church clock struck four nearby.

'We'd better hurry,' said Thekla, before Ethel had chance to reply. 'Tante Heimbach's a bit of a stickler; she won't like it if we're late for tea.'

'Your aunt has made me so welcome,' said Ethel. 'I can't thank you both enough. I'd love to come.'

~

Ethel woke up to bright light streaming in through the gap in the curtains. She could see the leaves moving slightly on the tree outside. There was the rustle of the wind, and the sound of birds calling to one another high above. That was surely the baking of bread she could smell, too. She jumped out of bed and threw the curtains open.

'Oh, there you are,' came Thekla's voice from below. 'Time for your early morning swim. I've got a towel for you.'

Ethel leant out and could see Thekla and Gustchen outside the back door beneath her. They had very little on, just their chemise and drawers, and were drinking water from the well.

'Where are you going?'

'To the lake,' said Thekla. 'Come on.'

Ethel threw off her long nightdress and put on some underwear, drew a shawl around her shoulders, and within a minute was running down the stairs.

'I can't swim very well,' she said, catching up with them as they started walking into the trees.

'I'm surprised,' said Gustchen, putting her arm across Ethel's shoulders. 'Look at you, you're so strong. Isn't she, Thekla, not like us arty town folk?'

Ethel laughed. She would have liked to stroke Gustchen's flowing yellow hair, normally severely plaited, but didn't dare.

The trees gave way to reveal a small lake, with two or three rickety jetties where small rowing boats were tied.

'Might others come down to the water?' she said, conscious of her lack of clothing.

'It's too early for most of the people here,' said Thekla. 'Come on, in we go.'

The two women ran down the little sloping beach and screamed as they entered the water without stopping, striking out strongly to where it was deeper.

'Come on, Ethel,' shouted Thekla when they paused for breath. 'No breakfast for the wary.'

'Oh, oh, oh! Be brave,' muttered Ethel to herself as the water lapped around her thighs and then her waist. It was exhilarating how the cold water found and enfolded every inch of her body.

By the time they were getting cold and talking about breakfast, she had begun to strike out more confidently. Wading out, she covered herself with her arms, afraid of anyone seeing her in her wet underwear. The others had no such worries. They swung towels around their shoulders and raced each other towards the cottage. Bread rolls, bright butter and jams were laid on the table by the back door.

'I'm starving,' shouted Gustchen, running into the house, the other two hot on her heels. 'Let's get some clothes on quick.'

~

It was nearly dark when Ethel sat at the piano in Thekla's tiny lounge and looked at the music on the rest in front of her. Her hands were trembling, sweaty. How stupid she was to have offered to sing her own songs. It had been the greatest fun accompanying the others, but now they were sitting quietly waiting for her to start on her own work – singers who were used to receiving new songs straight from the imaginations of the greatest composers of the day.

Not to mention Herr Henschel – no, George, as he insisted she call him as if he were English. He was so young, so handsome, so full of music. The four of them had sung and played favourite Schubert and Schumann songs, George's own songs too.

It was unfair to expect her to follow that.

'Come on, darling,' said Thekla. 'No need to be shy. Don't forget when you start at the conservatoire you'll be playing your work to others all the time.'

Ethel smoothed her skirt over her knees, trying to dry the sweat on her hands.

'It is daunting at first,' said Gustchen. 'But we are your friends, and we just want to hear what you've written.'

As Ethel played and sang, first choosing her familiar *Schön Rohtraut*, confidence and hope surged through her. If they didn't like it, she was here to learn how to do it properly after all. By the quieter section in the middle, she had forgotten to be nervous, and she carefully shaped the phrases before moving on to the tempestuous end. She followed up with *Bei einer Linde*.

'Bravo! Bravo!' they called when she had finished, clapping enthusiastically.

'Look, George,' said Thekla, 'for once we are showing you a new talent.'

'You really can do this,' said Gustchen.

'Please don't sound so surprised.' Ethel laughed, longing to hear what George would say.

'I'm not surprised,' went on Gustchen. 'I'm a mere performer of other people's work, but you're actually creating it. Well done!'

'That's so good,' said George. 'I enjoyed it. And you say you've had very little tuition so far? Is your family musical?'

'Not at all.' Ethel blushed at how little music meant back home. 'No, I have everything to learn.'

'Goodness. What else have you got?'

He was probably just being kind and polite to a fellow guest, one from another country too.

'A few more songs, and a mostly finished piano sonata.'

'I would like to see your sonata,' he said.

'Not now,' said Thekla. 'You can take her sonata home to look at. No more talking. Sing on! Don't you think so, George, darling?'

'Indeed I do,' said George. 'Come to my house tomorrow, and we'll talk some more. Now sing us another of your songs.'

~

George was already sitting at the piano when Ethel arrived, puffing heavily. His lodgings were on the hill above the lake, and she had run most of the way there. Her sonata stood on the stand. After the briefest greeting, he gestured to her to sit down.

'It's good,' he said. 'Better than I expected. The melody is very strong and I like the powerful, slow section. Now just tell me what made you end that movement on such an unusual chord.' He played the last few notes.

Ethel felt her face burn red. She had not expected such questions.

'I don't really know,' she said. 'It just felt the right thing to do.'

'It's unusual, so you must have had some reason for finishing it that way, instead of what would have been more normal.' He struck a series of notes. 'Like that.'

'No, no, I didn't want that,' she said. She looked round the room for inspiration. It reminded her of Mr Ewing's room with its piles of music everywhere. She had no words to describe what she had done.

That was not the end of it. He went through page after page of her manuscript, asking for reasons, suggesting alternatives and often using words she did not understand. She had to bite back her disappointment and the desire to burst into tears and run out of the room. She might as well go and drown herself in the lake, because it was clear that she was no composer, and the life she longed for was over before it had begun.

'I'm so sorry, Fraülein Ethel,' said George. 'I can see you're upset. I'm treating you like one of my pupils who's been studying for years. Have I been too harsh? Forgive me.'

'You've made me realise how little I know.'

'How little you know? No, no. You have not had much teaching – yet you produce this. It is extraordinary. If your piece had been merely charming, our conversation would have lasted no more than two minutes, I assure you. Please, do not be down-hearted.'

'I've got so much to learn, everything.'

'I should have said more about what I thought was good, as well as what needs more thought. This phrase, for example…'

He began to play some passages from her sonata, talking between times, until she felt quite dizzy. She had never heard her music played before.

'I can see what a thirst you have,' he said at last. 'There are many good things in here. You are going to write a lot of very interesting music, that much is already clear.'

Ethel took the path back to the cottage through the forest. She felt like a flower bulb whose life has lain dormant during a long winter, and blossoms richly and rapidly in the sunlight. Every now and then she stopped and breathed in the warm smells of summer. Trees creaked in the breeze, their leaves rustling to their own rhythm. The forest floor crunched under her feet, soft with decomposing leaves, twigs, flowers, grasses. She moved into a little patch of sun and raised her face to take in its warmth.

She sat on a log, thinking of what George had said. She would change that, and of course that wasn't quite right, she should have been able to see that for herself. Then she put her hands over her face, laughing, pulling her cheeks down with her fingers so that her eyes stared wide. She wanted to shout out the joy within her. Instead she started to run, away from the path, thrusting into the wildness of the deeper-set trees, enjoying the wind and ripping off her hat the better to feel its power. She scrunched up her skirt, almost tut-tutting to herself on her mother's behalf as she did so, and as she came into a clearing she jumped over fallen logs and stray brambles, and did half a dozen cartwheels where the ground was smooth with moss.

~

'Only three more weeks now until the conservatoire opens up. How wonderful it's going to be. I'm going to absorb skill and knowledge just by walking along the corridors,' Ethel said. She looked at George, expecting him to laugh at her foolishness. Instead he put his fork down and examined the inside of his bread roll.

'You know, Ethel,' he said, 'you are going to be part of the wonderful musical world of Leipzig, with all its traditions. But you must look forward, not dwell on the greatness of the past. I say that because the conservatoire is not necessarily as great a place as you think.'

Again she looked at him, expecting the broad smile that would show that he was teasing her or just giving a slight prick to the golden bubble of her dreams. Instead, he looked concerned.

'I suppose it's possible,' she said slowly, 'that having longed to go there for so many years, I might be a bit unrealistic about it?'

'It's not just that,' he said, 'though it's true that the Hall of Music in Paradise itself couldn't possibly provide everything you are wishing for.' Now he did smile gently at her. 'But music is moving on very fast, leaping ahead with new ideas and forms. The conservatoire is no longer at the forefront of such innovation, not like it was in Mendelssohn's day.'

'Is that going to matter? Just learning the basics is going to take me years.'

'We don't want you to be disappointed.' He included Thekla and Gustchen in his glance. They were sitting quietly, sipping beer.

Ethel hunched over the fish which one of the villagers had caught in the lake that morning and brought over for them. It no longer smelt as fragrant as it had five minutes ago, and when she raised a forkful to her lips, she found she could not eat it.

'Surely you don't mean it's poor. Just a bit old-fashioned?'

'It's still good, of course. I worry that it will not be as inspiring as you hope.'

'But, but...' She was starting to lose control of her voice, and coughed. 'Excuse me. I need a little air.'

She had to get away from these people; how foolish to think of them as her friends. She ran down to the lake and threw stones across the water before wandering distracted through the trees. She sat on a boulder and rubbed her face, then stared without seeing anything but the forest floor. Six years, she kept saying to herself. Six years I've been waiting for this. Six long years since her governess had played that sonata, and wakened from nowhere the desire to write something similar. And now they were spoiling it.

She vomited onto the ground.

After a while, she heard Thekla calling. At first she thought to flee further into the forest, away from everyone, but when her friend came into the clearing, she jumped up and ran into her outstretched arms.

'Poor darling,' said Thekla. 'George has said too much. Even if the conservatoire has become a bit fuddy-duddy, you're still going to have a great time. Your future's bright, we can all see that.'

'It was so unexpected,' said Ethel. They began to walk back, their arms around each other. 'But if it's terrible, how shall I learn to compose?'

'You're going to be fine,' said Thekla. 'George just wanted to make sure you don't expect too much. You will soon see who can offer what you need. And there's much more to musical Leipzig than the conservatoire. You'll see.'

'I'm not going home, no matter what happens,' said Ethel.

'Absolutely not. Now come on, let's run. There's some lovely fresh cheese from the farm on the table, and I've told those greedy friends of ours not to touch it until we get back.'

3

Ethel woke early, her stomach fluttering. She leapt out of bed and began to lay out her clothes. She had paid out a fair bit of her allowance to have made for her the plain, dark grey skirt and jacket, which she now gently brushed. She considered whether to wear the white shirt or the creamy one that Thekla and Gustchen had given her. She checked once more that manuscript books, pencils and paper were in George's present of a little leather case. She had no idea of what was suitable for the conservatoire, and had been happy to be guided by her landlady who, after years of students living in her house, knew.

She knocked and came into her room now with a breakfast tray. Ethel waved it away.

'Come on, dear,' Frau Heimbach said, 'you must eat a little. It's a big day for you. Remember how proud your parents are, thinking of you this morning.'

'I can't eat anything. I've waited so long for this day, but I don't know what to expect.'

Under Frau Heimbach's gentle insistence, she cracked off the top of the eggs and ate them with surprising relish. Unexpectedly, she chewed her way through the fresh breakfast roll smeared in bright yellow butter.

'I'll bring your hot water in, and then I'll leave you to finish up,' the old lady said, laying out the towel. 'Come and say goodbye when you're ready to go. I want to see you in those fine clothes.'

Ethel leant over and gave her a hug. 'Thank you,' she said. 'Thanks for everything.'

She pulled on the clothes one by one, enjoying the feel and smell of the new fabric. When she squinted in the mirror to pin the new hat over her flyaway hair, she thought she looked every inch the serious student.

The courtyard was buzzing with young people, all moving towards the open doors of the conservatoire. Many were chatting to others, but there were several who, like Ethel, were walking on their own. Her breath came short as she stepped inside.

Following the others, she came into a large hall with a raised area at the front, on which was a fine-looking piano. The dark panelling on the walls gave the room a solemn air, and there were busts that she assumed were of musicians, perhaps previous students, on plinths around the walls. Young people, more than she had ever seen before in one place, were talking, sometimes getting to their feet and shouting greetings across the hall.

Ethel delighted in every one of the formalities that took up the morning. Registers were called, tutors introduced, welcome speeches made, rules and customs explained. She was part of it, not observing, not dreaming; she was actually one of these students being addressed in words she could more or less understand. When she was allocated to a group to be shown around, what excited her most was the number of small rooms in which a piano stood. Some also had violins and trumpets, oboes and bassoons stacked on shelves, or cellos and harps backed up against the wall. The idea that anyone could go and play as loud and as long as they wished was something entirely new. She would not have to fight to play music, nor was it a trivial matter to be fitted in amongst other lessons; it would not cause rolling of the eyes or protests. The thought that she might be criticised for doing too little music rather than too much made her want to laugh out loud.

At the break, Ethel found a quiet spot and studied the folder she had been given. It contained a list of lectures for the next eight weeks. There would be one each day, given by one of the conservatoire lecturers or by a visiting musician. She scanned the list – yes, there was George's name, coming to talk about Schubert's *Winterreise* song cycle. Otherwise she recognised no-one, but just by looking at the list of topics she was amazed to discover what there was to learn.

Following the general drift of students, Ethel found herself in a crowd in front of the noticeboard. It was alarming to be in the middle of a group of students, all men, who were talking so rapidly and loudly that she could hardly understand a word; but with a bit of jostling and poking she managed to get to the front. Long lists were up on the board – they must be the specialist sessions she had chosen in earlier correspondence. Ah, there was her name. Her name! She would learn piano with Herr Maas, counterpoint with Herr Jadassohn and composition with Herr Reinecke.

'I don't know those names,' she ventured to the young man standing by her who was also noting down his tutors. 'Herr Reinecke? I thought he was the conductor of the Gewandhaus orchestra.'

'He is,' he said. 'And he teaches here too. He's not too bad.'

'You know him?' said Ethel, amazed.

'A little. My father plays in the orchestra. I'm Peter Röntgen, by the way.'

They shook hands. 'Ethel Smyth.'

'I thought you must be when I heard your accent. Look,' he 'd, pointing at the lists, 'I can only see a few other ladies' names ' on the singing and piano list.'

Ethel looked around but could not see them.

'You're studying composition, too,' she said.

'Yes, and violin.'

Ethel moved along to look at other notices, and when she next turned round to comment, he had gone.

~

Ethel looked around the table, smiling. There were six young people of various ages – she wasn't sure if they were all brothers and sisters of Peter Röntgen – and though they talked over each other too fast for her to understand anything much, the volume, the laughter, the shouts of outrage, the games, the foolishness, the teasing were all utterly familiar to her. For once, she felt more at home than did Thekla, who was sitting opposite and struggling to make herself heard.

'I'm so happy to meet you. Please make yourself at home,' Frau Röntgen had said as she came forward to greet her. 'I told Peter to bring you round as soon as possible – we've never had a woman composer student at the conservatoire before. Well done. I do hope it's not too horrible with all those strapping lads.'

The similarities to her own family were superficial. Music filled the minds and lives of all the Röntgens; they talked about little else. Ethel gathered that one of the older boys played viola in the Gewandhaus orchestra, and that the quiet, white-haired, smiling man at the head of the table was its leader.

As soon as the noisy lunch was over, she was ushered into the music room. Music stands and instruments stood everywhere, and sheet music was piled up on every available surface, except that of the grand piano. All the children had their own instruments. After a great deal of arguing, Peter shouted until they all settled down.

'Would you like to play the piano?' asked Frau Röntgen. 'Peter said you play beautifully. I'm generally the accompanist, but I really need to finish this dress for Grete before tomorrow.'

'Absolutely,' said Ethel. 'I'd love to.'

'All right,' said their father. 'What shall it be?'

'Clara Schumann,' said Johanna, one of Peter's sisters. 'In honour of Fraülein Ethel and women composers everywhere. We could do her piano trio.'

Ethel counted eight people, all poised with their instruments. Thekla had sat herself down with a piccolo.

'Don't worry,' said Peter. 'It's meant to be a trio, but we always play with as many people as are in the room.'

'Have you met her yet?' Johanna asked Ethel. 'Clara?'

'Goodness, no,' said Ethel. 'She was born in Leipzig, wasn't she?'

'Yes, she often comes back. You're bound to meet her before long.'

Ethel had got used to this sort of talk from Thekla, as if meeting someone who was a legend to the whole of musical Europe was an everyday occurrence.

'Are we all ready?' said their father, raising his bow.

The trio was a fiery affair and certainly different from the composer's intention when reproduced on so many instruments, but to Ethel, happily struggling with the difficult piano part, it sounded beautiful. All laughter, teasing and shouting had ceased entirely, as even the youngest applied themselves to the score.

When it had finished, they all clapped and shouted, 'Bravo, bravo.'

Frau Röntgen put down the dress she was hemming. 'Now,' she said to Ethel, 'Thekla tells me that you spent a few days with our darling George Henschel, so I expect you know the new songs he's written?'

'Yes,' said Ethel, 'we sang them numerous times in Thuringia. At least Thekla and Gustchen did. I love them.'

'Good, we've got some copies here.' She started flicking through music on the shelves. 'Somewhere.'

'They're over there,' said Peter, pointing to the piano. 'I made some more copies for us, and a recorder part for Grete.'

'Will you sing, Thekla? And you stay at the piano, my dear.'

The songs, which had sounded so simple when played in the little country summer house with just the upright piano for accompaniment, were fuller now but still pure. Thekla's voice soared above the strings, with the recorder in the hands of the little girl pricking out its own melody.

'It's getting dark, already,' said Ethel at the end, surprised that the light had faded. A lunch invitation had spread throughout the autumn afternoon.

'You must bring your own work next time,' said Herr Röntgen. 'We are always looking for new music to play.'

'I'm not sure about that,' said Ethel, wondering how she would ever be brave enough.

'I doubt poor Ethel has recovered from George's criticisms,' said Thekla.

Ethel flushed.

'An excellent recommendation,' said Papa Röntgen, smiling. 'If George Henschel has put you through your paces, it shows you are writing music of some substance.'

'He was quite harsh,' said Ethel, smiling. 'I learnt a lot.'

Ethel and Thekla were helped into their coats and hats, and after many farewells and promises to return went out into the evening air. The gas lights brightened, and as they walked arm in arm through the streets Ethel coughed from the smoky fumes of fires now being lit against the cold.

'They're wonderful,' said Ethel. 'Thank you for arranging for me to meet them.'

'Oh, I think young Peter already had that sorted,' said Thekla. 'But I'm so glad you like them, because even if it is total chaos in their house, they are very kind.'

'I like that sort of chaos,' said Ethel. 'And I'm beginning to see what a musical life might look like.'

'I'm sure they'll invite you to join them often,' said Thekla. 'Meanwhile Gustchen and I have to live in cheap lodgings and earn our living.'

'How could you talk of it like that?' said Ethel. 'You are feted wherever you go. You meet fabulous conductors and pianists and musicians of all kinds. After all, you are going to sing in an opera in Berlin.'

'It's not as glamorous as you think,' said Thekla. 'But we are doing pretty much as we like, and that counts for a lot.'

They had come to the corner where they would part.

'I'm going to miss you terribly.' Ethel said. 'Who's going to look out for me?'

'You're going to look out for yourself. And write to us, and tell us everything.'

'Well, don't keep wandering around Europe for ever,' said Ethel childishly. 'Come back soon.'

Thekla laughed and gave her a big hug. 'You're the one who's going to have the big adventure.'

~

All Ethel's letters home were wildly enthusiastic. She told her parents and sisters at length about her tutors, and all the different things she was learning; about the other students and the Röntgen family; the concerts she was able to go to; the occasional invitations to dinner.

She did not tell them how sometimes, on a Saturday afternoon when it was raining and there was nothing to do, she went to bed and sobbed under the covers, cried for lack of her sisters and Bob, their joyful games, arguments and foolishness, or longed with all her restless body to gallop across the fields on one of her father's horses. The hunting season was starting, and she was not there. She did not tell them how she still found the conservatoire strange and confusing, and how lonely she was now that Thekla and the others had gone off on their European tours.

'I must be going down with something,' she said to Frau Heimbach, pushing away once again her uneaten plate of food.

'It's all very new, my dear, and you're far from everything you know. I don't suppose every single thing is just as you expected. It's no wonder if you feel a bit homesick now and then.'

'Is that what it is? I'm homesick?'

'It'll go, you'll see. You'll soon be used to everything. Come on, just try a little of this soup.'

Ethel straightened her back. So it wasn't that she was unsuited to this new life she'd been planning for so long. Homesick. Of course. She could deal with that. She stretched for the steaming bowl.

4

LEIPZIG 1879

Ethel could hardly contain her excitement at all the people so
beautifully dressed making their way up the stairs to the concert
hall, chattering and calling to each other. Thekla leaned over to
straighten the little bolero Frau Heimbach had lent her.

'You look gorgeous,' she said as they came towards the top
of the stairs leading to the upper boxes. 'Where did you get that
dress?'

'Mother sent it to me for Christmas,' said Ethel, smoothing
down the shimmery silver fabric.

'You wouldn't get one like that in Leipzig,' said Thekla.

'Come in, come in,' said Frau Frege, greeting them at the
door to her box. 'It's time I had some young people in here. It gets
wearisome being with these old folk all the time.'

Ethel curtsied, overwhelmed by this elegant old woman,
her grey hair dressed with silver and rubies. She had been an
international singing star years ago, Thekla had told her, but had
been forced to give it up on her marriage to a rich merchant. Now,
she devoted herself to the musical life of the city.

'It's such a romantic story,' Thekla had said.

'Hardly,' said Ethel. 'How many brilliant women have to give up their careers because they get married?'

'That's the way it is,' said Thekla. 'Apart from Clara, of course.'

'Clara Schumann? I'm longing to meet that woman; she's my shining example.'

'You wait till some young man sweeps you off your feet,' said Thekla.

'That will never happen.'

They followed Frau Frege into her box, and Ethel was directed to the front. As she settled into her seat, she looked down to the stage, where the orchestra were beginning to tune their instruments, and into the main auditorium, which was rapidly filling up. Ethel had never seen such an array of evening dresses as met her eyes now, jewellery glittering in the light of the many candles flickering in their sconces on the walls, and of the chandeliers raised to the ceiling.

'No knitting tonight,' she muttered to Thekla beside her.

Thekla suppressed a giggle. At an afternoon concert, Ethel had been amused to see many of the townswomen knitting their way through the programme. The orchestra began to file onto the stage.

'Look,' said Thekla, 'George is waving at us.'

'Where?'

'There, in the box almost opposite. He's with the von Herzogenbergs.'

Ethel waved madly. She hadn't seen George since their return from Thuringia. 'Everyone's in town tonight.'

'Look, here comes Herr Brahms.'

Ethel put her hand over Thekla's and squeezed it. 'Pinch me,' she whispered. 'I am dreaming, aren't I?'

The audience clapped wildly as a portly, middle-aged man strode onto the stage, and instantly raised his arm and started the orchestra. The players seemed reluctant, and although Ethel had been to so few symphony performances, she could see that there was a lack of harmony on the stage. Sometimes Herr Brahms himself seemed confused; his arm that was meant to be keeping a regular beat would jerk and vary the tempo, some of the orchestra trying to follow, some continuing with their own idea of what the rhythm should be. All the time she could see Papa Röntgen playing his violin fiercely, trying to keep everything together.

Ethel closed her eyes. Despite the difficulties, the generous warmth of the music shone through so the rest was easily forgotten. She began to be able to pick out the various melodies, how they came back again, more and more varied, in the voices of the different instruments, now deeper and now more bird-like, until eventually she forgot to analyse it and allowed it to glow within her.

With the last notes played, in a grand climax in which all the instruments of the orchestra managed at last to blend themselves, Ethel and Thekla were on their feet, cheering and clapping as loud as they could, as were many others in the hall. As Herr Brahms took his bow, accepting the applause with the slightest of smiles, Ethel hoped he was pleased. Thekla had warned her that he would only turn up at Frau Frege's supper if he thought the performance had been reasonable.

George's hand tugged at her arm. They had eaten supper and were being ushered into Frau Frege's drawing room for the entertainment. 'Come on, my favourite English person,' he said. 'I want to introduce you to Frau von Herzogenberg. I've told her all about you, and she's dying to meet you.'

'Sit with me here,' said the woman with a warm smile after they had been introduced. She shifted up on the sofa, gathering her heavy skirts to make space, whilst George and Thekla went off to get ready to sing. 'How are you finding all our strange German ways?'

'I'm having the most wonderful time,' said Ethel. She had never seen a bodice with so many sequins. She thought the woman wearing it must be about thirty, beautiful too, with her golden, elaborate hair and grey, warm eyes. 'I'm getting to know people slowly.'

'I'll introduce you to my husband shortly. I think he and Papa Röntgen are going to play something.'

'He's a composer, too, isn't he? I would love to meet him. There are more composers in this room than I've ever met in my whole life before.'

'Well, they're clever people, of course, but not all are worth meeting. For example, that man talking to my husband keeps trying to get him to recommend him, but his music is pure rubbish.'

Ethel laughed. She hoped she wouldn't be dismissed so casually. Frau von Herzogenberg continued to point out different people in the room, often adding a slightly arch comment to her description, which made Ethel laugh out loud.

She sat in awe as artistes who performed in the largest concert halls in Europe filled the room with fine singing and playing. She thought how much her mother would love it, and how her father would hate it, and blinked at her good fortune.

After the music finished, Herr von Herzogenberg came over. 'I was wondering who that was sitting with my wife, laughing at all our foolish ways. I suspected it might be a person I've wanted to meet for a while. Fraülein Smyth, isn't it? A very Happy New Year to you.' He bent low over her hand. Looking at his thinning hair, Ethel guessed he was a few years older than his wife.

She stood up quickly. 'I'm so honoured to meet you,' she said. 'I heard some of your music at a chamber concert a couple of weeks ago. I loved it. There are so many things I would like to ask you about it.'

'I'm so glad you enjoyed it. I hear you are quite an accomplished composer yourself, from what Herr Reinecke says.'

'Herr Reinecke?' Ethel had not thought that her tutor rated her at all. 'He's very kind.'

'There's no time to talk this evening,' he said. 'But please come and have dinner with us soon. What do you think, Lisl?'

'That would be lovely. Come on Wednesday. There'll just be us, so we'll have plenty of time.'

'Thank you. Do you play or sing yourself?' Ethel asked her.

'I do, yes. Not as well as these people here, unfortunately. I like to arrange evenings like this one in my house. But tell me how you are finding us all in Leipzig, and how it compares with where you come from.'

'It doesn't compare,' said Ethel slowly. 'Here it seems everyone is connected with the world of music or the arts. But back home, in Farnborough, everyone is connected with the army. They are all majors and generals, major-generals sometimes.' They laughed. 'Music is just what polite people do to pass the time after dinner.'

'There's a certain amount of that goes on here, too, believe me. Look, there's Herr Brahms.'

George Henschel appeared to be bringing the conductor straight over to where they sat.

'Fraülein Ethel,' he said. 'I want to introduce you to Herr Brahms.'

Ethel got to her feet. In a moment she would wake up from this glorious dream.

'Good evening,' said Herr Brahms, bowing slightly towards her. 'I hear you are the young woman who composes sonatas without ever having studied music.'

Ethel looked up and almost flinched under the intensity of his gaze and of his piercing blue eyes. There was little warmth or friendliness in his voice. She could hardly call a German word to mind to answer him.

'I try,' was the best she could do.

'You must carry on, carry on, keep learning,' he said vaguely, turning away.

Ethel sank back onto the sofa. She felt her face redden. At the biggest moment of her life, she had found no words.

'Don't worry,' said Frau von Herzogenberg. 'Conversation's not his forte. That's a compliment.'

'Did George, I mean, Herr Henschel, show him my music, do you think? He said he might.'

'I'm sure he did. People are trying to help you, my dear, not just because you're a bit of a novelty in town but because you obviously have talent.'

Ethel looked at her in amazement. 'You're scaring me.'

'Herr Brahms always stays with us when he's in Leipzig. Next time, we'll make sure you meet him properly.'

People were beginning to take their leave, and Thekla came over to see if Ethel was ready to go.

'Until Wednesday,' said Frau von Herzogenberg.

~

Ethel thought of little but Lisl von Herzogenberg and the warmth of her regard in the next few days, longing for Wednesday to come. When she got a letter affectionately reminding her of the dinner invitation, she felt a thrill of excitement. She loved the sound of that name in her mouth, her teeth and lips getting around the many syllables. It was a song in itself.

She did not forget that the purpose of the invitation was to talk with her husband about her music, and she popped into her bag her unfinished string quartet.

It was only a few minutes' walk to their apartment, which was in a wealthy part of Leipzig. She admired the smart exterior with its gabled windows that looked out over the fields marking the boundary of the city.

'Come on in, dear child.' Frau von Herzogenberg fussed over her as she took her into her sitting room. 'It's so cold out there, come and sit by the fire and get warm.'

They chatted about their sisters, Ethel's lodgings, and where might be the best place to go for a warmer winter coat now that the snowy weather had set in.

Soon there was a tap on the door, and Herr von Herzogenberg came in. He greeted Ethel warmly and bent over to kiss his wife.

'I hope you don't mind, darling,' she said, 'but I've asked for supper to be laid in the library. It's just the three of us tonight.'

'Excellent. I shall change out of these formal clothes. If you don't mind waiting a few minutes, Fraülein?'

'Hurry up, then,' said his wife. 'We're going to fade away for lack of food in a minute. Come on, Ethel, we'll go through anyway.'

The large, airy space was as much a music room as a library, and at one end of it was a grand piano of the darkest wood, its lid open in an invitation to sit and play. Ethel was shown rows and rows of music scores, mainly written by Bach, as well as by other familiar and unfamiliar names.

'Heinrich founded the Bach Society here in Leipzig,' said Lisl, as Ethel had now been instructed to call her. 'It seems to be his mission to collect everything the man ever wrote. Which was a lot.'

'We sing in the Thomaskirche,' said Herr von Herzogenberg, coming up behind them. 'You must come and hear us.'

'I will,' said Ethel. 'I've heard a lot about Bach since I came to Leipzig, and some of his music too. He's hardly mentioned in England.'

'He was one of the very best. And we're discovering how much he wrote too. Can you imagine? The poor man had to produce new music for the choristers every single Sunday of the year, and even more at festival times. Amazingly, almost all of it is glorious.'

'That's enough, Heinrich,' said Lisl. 'We're meant to be having supper, not a Bach lecture. Come on, Ethel. Food awaits.'

As Ethel swallowed the last of the chewy, creamy meringues, Herr Heinrich asked her about the conservatoire. This was a question that Ethel had come to dread. It seemed that everyone in Leipzig had their own opinion on their beloved music school. The vaguest criticism might meet with a vigorous defence, and perhaps the politely expressed suggestion that such comments were not welcome from a young foreigner. Others were critical, like George Henschel had been on that disappointing day in the summer, believing that it was resting on past glory and not moving forward.

'I'm enjoying myself tremendously,' she said cautiously.

'Do you feel,' said Herr Heinrich, 'you are learning what you need to?'

'I don't know. I just don't have the background of most of the students, so it's hard to judge. I'd never even heard of counterpoint six months ago!'

'I'm not surprised if you're struggling,' said Lisl.

'I do find quite a lot confusing. I probably need more basic tuition than I'm getting, especially the technical aspects. But I'm also writing music I could never have imagined writing.'

Lisl got up from the table. 'Come on, let's go and sit on the sofa. Heinrich, make yourself useful by getting us a little port.'

Herr Heinrich bought them a drink, and then sat at the piano and started to play. Some of the pieces Ethel knew, some she did not, but they were soothing and beautiful. She swished the red liquor around in the glass and sipped its warmth.

'Shall I tell you what happened the other day?' Immediately Ethel wished she had not said that. She had not intended to.

'Go on,' said Lisl.

'I went to Herr Reinecke's study – you know he teaches me composition. It was only the second time I'd seen him. I had handed in the second movement of my quartet a few days before for him to look at. He didn't seem to remember that he had got it, and spent ages looking for it on his table.'

'Did he find it?'

'Eventually. He sat there turning the pages, occasionally saying that wasn't bad, or I'd got that chord wrong. I found it difficult to understand him, he spoke so fast, and I discovered afterwards that there are no markings on my copy.'

'Oh dear,' said Herr Heinrich. 'That's not good.' Ethel had not noticed he had stopped playing. She hoped the two men were not good friends.

'I've heard this sort of thing about him before,' said Lisl. 'What happened then?'

'After about ten minutes, less maybe, he closed it and said, "You're doing very well, Fraülein. Put a note in my office when it's finished and we'll arrange another meeting." I was so disappointed. I still don't know what I need to work on.'

Ethel's voice started to break, and Lisl put her arm round her. 'Poor child,' she said. 'You poor child.'

'I'm sorry,' said Ethel. 'It's so frustrating.'

'I would be very happy to look at your workbooks, if that might help?' said Herr Heinrich. 'I'm not a teacher, but perhaps I can give you a few tips.'

'No, no, I couldn't possibly,' said Ethel, wiping her eyes. 'You have so many commitments. I'm sure it will all become clear to me in time.'

'You've come to Leipzig to learn,' said Lisl. 'Everyone can see how talented you are – you're causing a bit of a sensation here, I might say.'

'You are kind. If you're sure. I did bring a bit of my string quartet tonight, but nothing else.'

'Oh, good. Leave the quartet with me for a couple of days. Why not drop your notebooks off tomorrow and come back for supper again very soon?'

~

Ethel had three days to wait. She thought about her music, and what Herr Heinrich might be thinking about it. A quartet was much more complicated than a song or a sonata, and she worried it might be dreadful.

It was Lisl, however, who was mainly in her mind. She

imagined running her fingers through that soft, golden hair, loosely tied back. She remembered the luxuriously soft bosom when Lisl had held her close to comfort her, her flowery perfume, her gentle hands.

Often, when Ethel was at her desk working, she would find that she was sitting there turning the end of her pen round and round within her lips, longing for the moment when she would step once more into the warm light that was Lisl.

~

'I'm quite shocked,' Herr Heinrich said, flicking over the pages of her notebooks. 'The marking's not good at all. Look, that's quite an elementary error you've made there, and he hasn't even put a correction for you.'

Ethel looked at the carpet and screwed up her eyes. Did that mean all her work was rubbish?

'Really,' he went on, 'there are virtually no remarks, and those few are ill-considered. I would say that was a very sound piece of counterpoint, but you would never know, because nothing has been put. I'm afraid it seems to be true that the teaching at the conservatoire is not as good as it was, or as it should be.'

'I was warned by George,' said Ethel, 'but I don't know enough to make that judgement myself.' She put a hand over her mouth to try and keep the disappointment inside her.

Lisl put her arm around her. 'Heinrich, there must be something we can do.'

'Of course,' he said. 'You can't come all this way to learn music and go away feeling Leipzig has failed you. If you like, I can offer some help, especially how to apply the theory to your work, and of course I can pass on my own ideas about composition. We could have a couple of sessions and see how it goes.'

'I shall join you and learn too,' said Lisl. 'I'll never be a composer like you, Ethel, but I'd like to know more. What do you say?'

'I don't know what to say,' she said, looking from one to the other. 'I can't believe you would be so generous when you have so much to do.'

'Let's give it a go,' said Heinrich. 'I've just finished my concerto, so a new challenge will be good for me.'

5

LEIPZIG 1881

Ethel breathed in deep of the various scents that were released as she dismantled Lisl's hair. Pulling out the pins and slides and jewels that held together the intricate arrangement, she could detect the last hint of the perfume that had been sprayed on it earlier in the evening. The thick hair was also redolent of the busy evening – food and smoke and a slight aroma of sweat. As Ethel brushed it, long, deep strokes from the scalp, spreading the soft hair across the width of her back, teasing out the little tangles, all those smells dispersed, leaving a scent that was just plain Lisl.

She bent over and kissed her head.

'I love you,' she wanted to say from the depths of the strong whirling within her. She held back, however. Any such expression in the past had been met with a laugh and a light, 'You know I love you too. Heinrich and me, we both do.' It must be enough to be so near to her.

'Thank you so much for this evening,' she said instead. 'I never had such an amazing birthday party.'

'I shall have to stop calling you "dear child" now you're so grown up,' said Lisl. 'Even though you still are our dear child, of course.'

Ethel laughed. 'I should hope so.'

'Do you like Herr Grieg?'

'Who wouldn't? He is so pleasant, and his music so different. I wish I could work out quite how.'

'Cold lakes and mountains,' said Lisl.

'Icy and clear. Yet he is so warm.'

'What did you enjoy the most?'

Ethel paused a moment, wondering what to say. The fact that Lisl had arranged such a wonderful evening for her was enough, with all the Leipzig friends who had become so dear to her over the last few years invited.

'Do you mean apart from the glorious cake? Not to mention everyone toasting me?' Cook had worked wonders with her icing bag, decorating the cake like a music score, with 'A Violin Sonata by Ethel Smyth' piped onto it. 'It was seeing my old teacher again, I think.'

'Mr Ewing? What a stroke of luck he happened to be passing through Leipzig.'

'I used to worship him. My father was a brute to him, sacked him for encouraging me. The musical world hasn't been kind to him either.'

'Has life in general been kind to him?' said Lisl, taking off her rings and bracelets. 'He looked poorly to me.'

'He always looks like that. He hates army life, but he hasn't any other living.'

'That was a lovely piece he played, anyway. And he was so proud of you. We're all proud to be part of your future. Now, I must get to bed. We'll have a quiet day tomorrow. Will you be all right? I've asked Helga to make sure there are lamps lit upstairs.'

Lisl stood up and put her arm round Ethel as they went to the door.

'It's been the best evening, thank you so much, Lisl. My life in Leipzig would be dull indeed without you.'

'I don't think so,' said Lisl. 'I don't think your life will ever be dull.'

In no time at all Ethel had unpinned her own hair, which she found mousy and dull in comparison, taken off her new blue dress and prepared for bed. She looked around the tiny attic room with its sloping roof and inadequate bed. How lovely it was to stay over sometimes, to see the evening out, not to have to go out into the chill air; not to be a guest but a friend, a part of the household, learning so much from Heinrich and helping Lisl with her elaborate soirées and evening entertainments. She would go back to her lodgings tomorrow and get on with her work, but she knew already that after a day or two she would no longer be able to resist the longing to be with Lisl.

~

Normally, Ethel loved this walk from the centre of Leipzig to her new lodgings a couple of miles out. The fields were covered in beautiful summer flowers, and the river ran clear and silver alongside the path. But today it might have been a sea of mud for all that she noticed. Every few steps a horrible cough racked her. Her head was pounding, and she had to keep stopping to get her breath and blow her endlessly running nose.

Her old lodgings would have been much more convenient. She had not wanted to move, but one day, returning to her room, there had been no lunch on the table. A scrawled message said that Frau Heimbach had tumbled down the stairs and had been taken to her sister's to be cared for. She never recovered properly, and Ethel had been forced to find a couple of rooms to rent. For a while, she missed the kindly woman with her delicious meals and unexpected nuggets of gossip, but now she relished her greater independence.

She could go in and out as early or late as she wished. She could sit and compose all night long if she wanted. There was only the servant, who brought up firewood and did a little washing for her, to complain at her irregular schedule. If she was not invited to Lisl's, she ate at a restaurant in the town. There was no-one to remind her it wasn't quite proper for a young woman to do that. On evenings when she had no invitation elsewhere, she fended for herself. She had hung a little bird cage out of the window, which served as a larder for her ham and cheese.

Ethel blew her sore nose again and pushed open the door. She stumbled up the stairs and fell on the bed. She must have slept for a while before getting into her nightgown and crawling under the covers, moaning at the effort. The room was hot and she was hot, very hot, so hot she couldn't bear it. She fought off the covers weakly, coughing the while, taking a sip of water. A little while later, she did not know how long, she was pulling up the covers again, shivering.

For the first time in a while, she thought longingly of home, of her mother's hot, pungent possets, and how one of her sisters would sit and read to her if she was ill.

She asked the servant to send a message to Lisl.

Time passed and she did not come. She was not going to inconvenience herself by coming into a sick room. She was happy for Ethel to go to her house, to help her with her parties and musical evenings, to study and chat together, but she would not put herself out and come now.

'My poor child,' said Lisl, bending over her. 'Why did you not send for me earlier? Look, you're so pale and thin.'

'I feel ghastly. I've got a terrible fever,' said Ethel. Relief flooded through her. 'I thought it would just go if I rested up, but it hasn't.'

'We'll soon get you well again,' she said, stroking back Ethel's hair.

'I don't think I'll ever feel well again.'

Another wave of fever came over her, and she started to shake and sweat. Lisl got a cold cloth and pressed it to her forehead until she was calmer.

When she woke up, Lisl was sitting by her bed, reading a book. Ethel stretched out a hand to her.

'Helga brought over a little of her famous broth for you,' said Lisl. 'She always makes this whenever Heinrich or I are ill, and it's never failed to cure us!'

Lisl bent over her and helped her sit up a little, manoeuvring pillows and cushions to support her back. 'Goodness knows when last you ate. Come on, darling, try a little.'

Ethel managed to swallow a few spoonfuls before exhaustion overcame her again. 'I feel like I've walked up a mountain with a great weight on my head,' she murmured.

Next time she looked around, Helga was sitting at her bedside. 'Hello, Fraülein. Frau Lisl had to go home. Her parents are staying for a couple of days, and they're entertaining some government colleagues.'

'I'm causing everyone a lot of trouble, I'm afraid.'

Ethel pictured Lisl's mother, a stern, strong woman, always dressed in black since her husband lost his title and position after some political upheaval. The older woman did not return that admiration. In fact, she hated any sign of affection that Lisl might show to Ethel, and seemed exasperated that they spent so much time together. Until Lisl decided to keep them apart, Ethel had felt the full chill of her icy politeness. She was not going to tolerate Lisl coming over to look after her now.

'I'm to make sure you're comfortable for the night. Herr Heinrich has asked the doctor to call and see you in the morning. We'll have you better in no time.'

She started to draw some water from the little kettle on the fire and looked round for a washcloth.

'Thank you, Helga. I feel a lot better already,' she said, trying to smell the lavender of the soap.

'There. Now, try to sleep. You'll probably feel a bit feverish in the night again, but try not to worry. We'll see what the doctor has to say.'

~

The influenza was persistent. No sooner did Ethel begin to feel a bit stronger, more able to sit up for a while, even talk and read a book, than she was thrown back into bed, sweating and coughing.

Helga took over her tiny household, chasing the servant to make sure that there was always wood for the fire, food and drink, clean laundry, warm water. Lisl spent several hours a day with Ethel, reading to her, or talking. Sometimes, she lay on the bed with her. Ethel breathed in the particular perfume of her clothes and of her hair.

~

'We've decided to put off our holiday,' said Lisl on a day when Ethel had managed to get dressed and sit by the fire. 'I can't leave you like this and travel off to Vienna as if I didn't have a care in the world.'

'What about Heinrich?'

'He's happy. He's in the middle of revising his new violin concerto, and he doesn't admit it, but the delay suits him perfectly. Even if it didn't, he knows I wouldn't leave my darling child like this.'

'I wish I was revising my music,' said Ethel wistfully. 'I'm so behind.'

'Shh, you must not think like that. When you're better, you'll soon catch up. Everyone is starting to go off on holiday, so you're missing very little. Leipzig is becoming a ghost city.'

'And I have to go home when I'm better,' said Ethel. 'I shall miss you.'

'We're not going to think about all those weeks apart. Now, you sit quietly and I shall play for you. Even on this crusty old piano, you'll recognise this.'

She started to play a Mozart sonata. Ethel drifted away, but every time she came to, Lisl was still playing – some Beethoven, perhaps, a little Haydn, maybe something of Heinrich's. It didn't matter who had written it. It was the very blood in her body, the pulse of her heart, and the steadiness of the in and out of her breath. That Lisl played in this small room that had become her sanctuary, overlaid it with tenderness.

~

Lisl was there again.

'I'm so excited,' she said, pulling something out of her bag. 'You'll never guess what I've got here.'

'Something new?'

'Oh yes, yes indeed. So very brand new and yet you've already heard it.'

'I haven't a clue.'

'Come on, get up, and then I'll tell you.'

'It's a manuscript, isn't it?' Ethel pulled her wrap around her and sat in the chair.

'I shall play you a little,' teased Lisl, starting to play from the huge hand-written pages. 'Don't look.'

Ethel closed her eyes as the music emerged from beneath Lisl's fingers. It was big music, bigger than a piano was meant to hold.

'Herr Brahms,' she said.

Lisl played on for a while. 'What is it? Have a guess.'

'His new symphony? His disastrous new symphony?'

'Or his wonderful new symphony that had a disastrous premier?'

The two women laughed. Herr Brahms had demanded his coach straight after the performance, and left Leipzig with a sullen expression on his face.

'Has he forgiven us, then, if he's sent you the piano reduction?'

Lisl played on. Ethel sat half listening, half dozing. Scraps of writing she had been working on before she became ill ran through her mind. She could see how they might fit together in a rather different way, using some of the same techniques as Brahms to give intensity and richness. Perhaps she could write her main theme in various ways and create very different effects.

She felt herself being shaken. 'Ethel, my darling, are you all right? Wake up.'

'Variations,' she said. She sat up straight and started to get up off the chair.

Lisl pushed her back down. 'Herr Brahms has transported you to a different country. Look how pale you are. It's too intense for you just now.'

'I must write it down,' said Ethel.

'No,' said Lisl. 'You must not. Here, have a drink of water.'

Slowly, Ethel relaxed. 'It's a force raging in my head.'

'Heinrich speaks like that sometimes, of a wildness that must be tamed. Now we're going to do something a bit more ordinary until I can be sure your mind is properly with me.' She took some cards off the shelf and began to deal.

~

Ethel felt energy flowing through her body again, an impatience to be up and about. She would soon be strong enough to travel to England. And yet, part of her wanted to stay in this room where Lisl cared for her, told her what to do, fed her with appetising dishes, fussed over her, lay on the bed with her, held her.

'I'm going to miss you so much,' she said the night before they were to part. They were sitting on the bed, since Ethel's half-packed clothes covered every chair.

'Don't think about it. It's only for a few weeks, and then you'll be back again, we both will.'

'You will write to me, won't you?' said Ethel.

Lisl put her arm around her. 'There won't be many days I don't write, and I shall look for your letters too. And you must write your Variations, so we can play them at a grand party when you come back.'

'It's been such a lovely time, just you and me.' She put her head on Lisl's shoulder.

'It has,' said Lisl, kissing Ethel. 'We shall have lots more lovely times together.'

Their kisses grew in intensity, and Ethel fell backwards onto the bed, pulling Lisl on top of her.

'I love you,' said Ethel, kissing Lisl more fiercely.

'And I, you.'

Ethel felt a surge through her body as Lisl pressed kisses onto her throat, her hands pulling back the top of her dress a little to kiss the softness above her breast.

Ethel reached down to lift up Lisl's skirt so that she could caress the skin of her leg, but all at once, Lisl pulled away and stood up.

'Oh my goodness,' she said. 'What am I doing? That never happened, Ethel. I must go.'

Ethel turned over so she did not have to see Lisl leave the room.

6

ENGLAND 1881

'I can't wait to saddle up Starlight and go bolting across the meadow,' Ethel said to Violet, who with Bob had come with the carriage to meet her. 'All the horses are still there, aren't they? And the dogs? Father hasn't got rid of any of them in the house renovations, has he?'

'No, they're still there, all right – probably more than when you left. There's new stables now, everything's very splendid, or it will be when it's finished. The servants' quarters are in the old stables. Believe me, you were lucky to be away. Father's been the most bad-tempered ever throughout, not to mention the noise and dust. He talks about nothing but the cost. Still, we have got a bathroom now.'

'I laid some of the bricks for the new stable myself,' chimed in Bob.

'Oh dear. That won't last very long then.'

'Believe me, Ethel, apart from the chaos in the house, everything is just as usual. Boring and predictable.'

'Except that you have now become an elegant young woman, and this scrubby boy almost passes for a human being.'

The carriage had hardly drawn to a halt when Ethel saw her mother rushing out of the front door with Nell and Nina right behind her. The dogs leapt into the carriage barking and jumping whilst Bob shouted and tried to intervene.

'Molly, Rufus. Come here!' shouted Mother. 'Bob, stop it. Our darling Ethel will be smothered before I even have chance to say hello to her. Now, come on.'

Ethel extracted herself from the dogs, with their snuffly noses and heavy paws, and got out of the carriage.

'You look pale,' said her mother, hugging her tight. 'We shall have to feed you up and get some good sunshine on you.'

'What's all this noise in front of the house?' A loud, stern voice overrode all the chatter and shouting. Ethel turned towards her father walking round from the stables. She waited until his face broke into a smile, then ran to him and hugged and kissed him.

'The wanderer returns,' he announced, pulling Ethel's arm into his own. 'Welcome home.'

'From what I've heard, I might not recognise it.'

'I shall show you around. When you're rested, of course,' he said, as Ethel's mother started to protest. 'And we'll have dinner early so this wretched boy can eat with us before his bedtime.' Bob ran with the dogs in circles around them as they went up the steps into the house.

~

Ethel rode fast, her face turned up to the rushing wind, across the fields away from the village, and along the bridleways through the woods. The powerful horse needed little prompting to avoid any obstacles. Her body was drinking in warmth and sun, fresh air and the wide expanse of the downs, the sounds of the birds, the smells of the animal. She had missed it, the exuberance, the danger. The last of her sickness vaporised into the crisp air.

How weak she had been. The first game of lawn tennis with Violet had sent her sprawling, unable to run fast enough to hit the ball. When she tried to climb trees with Bob that she had mastered at least ten years ago, she had no pull in her arms. But now, at last, she had enough strength in her legs to control the horse, and she brought him to a halt, jumping off without stumbling. She fed him one of the apples in her pocket, stroking his nose and putting her cheek against the toss of his head. The horse was hot and steaming, deliciously musky. She took the other apple out of her pocket and sat with her back against the tree, munching, looking out across the hills, checking out the tiny villages alongside the river below, the sheep grazing, the little knots of trees. It was beautiful, as familiar as the furniture in her bedroom.

A big fuss had been made of her. Ethel relished the fact that when she had something witty or pithy or complicated to say, she no longer had to look for the German words, find grammatical constructions, or fail to come up with her exact meaning. Mother wanted to hear all she had to tell. It might be about her fellow students, or Johannes Brahms arguing with Herr Röntgen, or the box she sat in at the Gewandhaus with all the bejewelled gentry of Leipzig around her, the different foods served up at dinner parties or the way their dances were ordered.

Ethel led the horse over to a fallen tree which she could use to help her climb back on. Rubbing her face against his head, she felt the pull of Lisl, and wondered for the millionth time what she might be thinking.

~

There had been few of the letters that Lisl had promised. Of course, that promise had been made before… Ethel did not know what words to use for that passionate embrace. The letters that did come were affectionate enough, full of detail about Vienna, the music she was hearing, the people they were meeting, the rides out into the countryside, the oppressive heat. But she had hoped for so much more. The kisses, the caresses, had they been forgotten?

Every night she would think of those times, not just the kisses but the times Lisl lay with her on her bed. Her hands lingered on her breasts, on parts of her body for which she had no name, touching where she had felt that deliciousness.

Ethel kept her own letters factual, not knowing if they might be shared with Heinrich, merely saying that she longed for the days to pass until she was back.

~

The whole family were with Ethel at Mary and Charlie's garden party weekend, riding by day and partying by night. That evening a sweet little quartet had played, whilst they danced quadrilles and minuets and gigs in the glowing candles of the terrace.

Finally, when all the guests had gone to bed, Ethel sat out on the balcony sipping a last glass of port with Mary. She breathed in the rich, cool air of the warm night.

'I hadn't heard you talk about Leipzig like you did at dinner,' said Mary.

'What d'you mean, darling? I thought I'd told you every blessed thing about my life there.'

'You have. Your letters are always full of wonderful details. Mother and Alice and I always share your letters when we meet.'

'That's probably because I don't write often enough.' Ethel laughed.

'No, I meant I've always thought of you as my little sister learning a lot, being a student, meeting interesting people, having great experiences.'

'That's precisely what I've been doing.'

'No, it's more than that.' Mary sat up, searching for words. 'You've become part of that world. You're not just a child or young person on the edges, admiring and learning and looking in. You're a part of it. You belong in it. I know you're not going to come back.'

Ethel laughed and stretched for the bottle.

'I'm certainly enjoying it,' she said.

'And you're so grown up. Even Charlie remarked on your poise.'

Ethel burst out laughing. 'I can still trip over a bit of fluff on the carpet.'

Mary was not to be deterred. 'You were right to fight so hard to go. I'm proud of you. That's what I wanted to say. It sounds like you're going to be successful.'

'Thank you, darling,' she said. It was the first time anyone in the family had ever said anything like that. 'You must never think that because I fought so hard to go, I don't love you a great deal.'

~

Ethel found her mother in the garden, dead-heading flowers in the hope of encouraging some autumn blooms.

'I need to think about going back to Leipzig,' she said. 'I could do with a couple of new dresses and a warmer coat. It's much colder in winter than here.'

'Oh, surely you're not going back there.'

'Of course I am. I've got to get on with my studies.'

'But I thought you were enjoying yourself here. We've had a lovely summer, haven't we? And the season will begin soon.'

'I don't care about that,' said Ethel. 'I have enjoyed the summer, very much, but of course I have to get on with my work now. You must know that.'

Ethel looked into her mother's face. Of course, she knew that.

'I don't want you so far away,' said her mother slowly. Ethel hated the querulous tone of her voice. 'It's not right. Time's moving on, and you must give up all this independence.'

So nothing had changed, after all. She could have kicked every bloom off the flowers in the border.

'I thought you'd come round to supporting me,' she said bitterly.

'The children miss you too,' said her mother, pleading.

Ethel turned away. Anger heated her whole body.

'Does Father think this too?'

'You'll have to speak to him.'

Ethel started looking for him. Eventually, she found him down the drive examining one of the ash trees that had got damaged in a recent storm.

'It's time I was planning my journey back to Leipzig,' she said. 'My studies start again in a couple of weeks.'

'You won't be going back,' said her father, beginning to walk back up the drive. 'You've had I don't know how many years there. Now it's time to settle down. It's not as if there aren't musical people here. You'll stay with your mother until you find a suitable husband.'

Despite the warmth of the sun, Ethel felt cold. Very cold. She breathed in sharply.

'You've been very generous, and I'm grateful,' she said. 'But it was never time limited. I've kept to my allowance and done everything you said.'

'Goodness me, girl, how long do you expect me to go on paying? Look at all the expense I've had this year with the house and everything. Now, I'm going to talk to Samuel about that tree, so let's hear no more about it.' He turned off along one of the paths that led to the back of the house.

All the magic of the summer disappeared. What had seemed a pleasant interlude at home was actually a trap from which she was going to have to fight once more to escape.

'Just a minute, Father,' she called.

'I don't want to hear your arguments,' he said, when she caught him up. 'It's time, more than time, you gave this up. You're upsetting your mother. Now stop it.'

'There's no need for me to upset anyone,' said Ethel. 'Surely you can see that I'm not wasting the wonderful opportunity you've given me.'

He stepped nearer to her. She felt the weight of her dependence on him.

'You're very headstrong,' he said. 'Even so, there's no reason why you shouldn't find a good man to marry. But you can't afford to leave it much longer, so you must be here when the season starts.'

'I'm not interested in marriage. I'm creating a different sort of life for myself, as you well know. Why make me fight so hard?'

'I'm not making you fight. You're not going, that's it.'

'I am going, Father. I shall go anyway. I'll manage somehow, I don't know how. But you are not going to stop me.'

Ethel gasped at what she had said. Her father turned sharply away and walked rapidly along the path to the stables.

Mother came in and sat on the edge of the bed, watching Ethel packing her books into the trunk.

'Are you sure this is what you want?' she said.

'You know it is, Mother. It's all I want,' said Ethel.

'Isn't there anything we can do to make you stay?'

'No. I'm sorry, but I just don't want the life that you would like me to have. I shall find some way of supporting myself.'

'That wouldn't be right. Father and I have discussed it, and he will continue with your allowance.'

'You don't have to, really. I don't want to face this every time I come home.'

'It's not what we want for you, but you can't live unsupported out there.'

Ethel went over and hugged her. 'Thank you,' she said. 'So much.'

'You don't know how much I miss you,' Mother whispered. She stood up. 'Now, stop packing and come down for tea. We'll go up to London tomorrow and buy that coat.'

7

LEIPZIG 1881

Ethel rushed through the busy streets. She did not even have time to study the poster she spotted advertising the concert season at the Gewandhaus. She wove her way impatiently through the people picking up a last-minute bargain at the closing market, ran down Humboldtstrasse and arrived quite out of breath at Lisl's apartment.

She paused for just a moment after making her way round to the back, then ran lightly up the steps and knocked on the kitchen door.

'Grüss, Helga,' she said, smiling broadly at the maid who answered the door.

'Fraülein Ethel, you're back. How lovely. Come on in. I'll let Frau Lisl know that you are here. We hadn't expected you today.'

'It's a surprise.' Ethel laughed.

Ethel wanted to push past Helga and run along the corridor to Lisl's little sitting room. Instead, she paced the hallway, waiting to hear Lisl's door open.

Helga reappeared. 'Fraülein,' she said, 'please come into the drawing room. Frau Lisl will be with you directly.'

'The drawing room?' said Ethel, following Helga into the large, formal room. 'Shall I not go along to her room?'

'Come and sit by the fire,' the maid said, pulling a chair forward. 'It's getting a little chilly now, isn't it? I noticed the trees were just beginning to turn when I was out this morning.'

Ethel sat on the edge of her chair, fiddling with the string around the little present she had brought for Lisl, waiting for the door to open.

'Lisl,' she cried, moving towards her as soon as it did. 'Lisl, I'm back. I wanted to surprise you.'

Instead of the squeals of delight, the warm hug that Ethel had expected and dreamt of, Lisl merely offered her cheeks to be kissed.

'Lisl?' said Ethel, trying to look her in the face. 'Are you well? It's so lovely to see you.' She leaned forward, into the sweet perfume that was so familiar to her, but Lisl drew back.

'I knew you must be due back soon,' she said, going to the hearth to ring the bell. 'Please sit down and we'll have some tea.'

The joy of anticipation drained away. As they waited for Helga to bring in the tea, Lisl asked about her journey, polite questions about trains such as she might have asked anyone just returned from another country.

They drank tea and ate the little cakes, and Ethel asked about Leipzig and who was expected when the new season began. Lisl asked about England and the family, but all the stories that Ethel had stored inside her about Bob, and the horses and her father's ridiculous military friends, remained untold.

There were awkward silences. Then Ethel's hand fell on the book of poetry she had selected so carefully.

'Oh, Lisl, I brought you a little present. I know how much you like Christina Rossetti – here is her latest collection.'

She stood up and held the present out to Lisl, waiting for the smile, the gladness with which she would surely receive it.

'Thank you, Ethel, that's very kind,' Lisl said, taking it from her and putting it on the table. 'I shall enjoy looking at it later.'

There was a silence.

'Well, I've still got my unpacking to do, so I'd better go.' Ethel was sure that Lisl would tell her to stay a while longer.

'Very well,' said Lisl. 'I'll let Heinrich know you're back. I'm sure he'll want to arrange a time for your next lesson.'

Ethel began to walk towards the door. There were no farewell kisses or expressions of delight as she was ushered out. No invitation. No doubt the door was closed behind her in the normal way, but it set up a clamorous vibration in Ethel's body as she went slowly down the steps and into the street.

~

Ethel caught the sound of the church clock striking in the middle of the night – was that three or four times? She put her pen down and looked around her. Surely she had not been working all these hours, yet the candles burnt low, very low, and the fire was dead. She poked her head out of the window. There was only the silence of the time before dawn, before anyone, even the earliest tradesman, was up and about.

The sky was still black, with dark grey clouds scudding over on a breeze that soon chilled her cheeks. She leant further out and twisted her head up to see if any blurred moon might show behind the clouds, but there was none.

Shivering a little, she drew back into the room and shut the window. She pulled a light blanket off the bed and threw it round her shoulders as she returned to her desk. The manuscript was covered in crossings-out and corrections, some almost written on top of others. She could not get the cello and the viola to sound harmonious yet diverse. She could not see what was wrong yet, but the solution would emerge; she must be patient and trust that it would. Now that the magic of Lisl's household had dispelled, it was less easy to ask Heinrich for help. She must solve her own problems.

There was still so much to be done. In ten days, or maybe it was nine already, Julius, Peter, Johanna and Papa Röntgen were going to play her string quartet, not just in the sitting room with the whole family playing whatever instrument was to hand, but properly with almost all her Leipzig musical friends invited. Her first semi-public performance.

She took up her pen and dipped it into the ink. She could not afford to be diverted by thoughts of Lisl. She had worn herself out thinking of her, cried for hours about her, puzzled until she thought her brain would burst. Every time she went to the apartment, she couldn't help hoping that Lisl would gather her into her arms again, commiserate with how cold 'her little one' had become, fuss over whether she had eaten that day, call Helga to make her some hot broth.

None of that happened. Lisl was kind and polite with her as with all of her friends. She would even invite her to help out at her soirées as if she wanted everything to look the same. But it was not the same. She was always kept at arms' length. Just occasionally, Ethel caught Lisl's glance off guard, and there was the old smile and a flash of the eyes, just for her, rapidly masked.

~

Ethel hardly recognised the Röntgen music room. It had been cleared of all its piles of music; instruments had been put elsewhere and the furniture re-arranged. Now the piano stood at the far end, its lid open ready for the stars of the afternoon to perform. Four chairs and music stands stood nearby ready to be put in place for Ethel's quartet. Every other straight-back chair in the house, and surely some from neighbours too, had been commandeered and stood in rows waiting for the guests.

Ethel could hardly stop shaking when Peter showed her. 'It's a good job I don't have to play anything myself,' she said. 'Is it true, my name is actually on the same programme with Clara Schumann and Julius Röntgen?'

'Believe me, we are very happy to have your quartet to play,' said Peter. 'These pianists get all the glory. Did mother tell you about the surprise?'

'The whole thing is a surprise to me,' said Ethel. 'What?'

'You'll be happy,' said Peter, taking off his glasses and wiping them.

'Go on.'

'Thekla and Georg are in town for a few days and are going to sing.'

'Ah! Even more brilliant musicians to criticise my work,' said Ethel happily.

'Ethel, Peter.' It was Frau Röntgen shouting. 'Come and have a bit of lunch before the hordes arrive. We're in the kitchen.'

Ethel did not mind at all that her name was by far the most insignificant on the programme. To see Frau Schumann scrapping with Julius over her share of the keyboard in one of Liszt's thunderous Hungarian Rhapsodies was excitement enough. She followed that by passing from one Mozart sonata to another in thirty minutes of brilliance and precision. And when Frau Röntgen sat at the piano to accompany Thekla and George singing songs by Fanny Mendelssohn and her brother, the whole room held its breath in wonder.

Yet it didn't seem to Ethel that her quartet was totally out of place in that room, though of course Papa Röntgen, leading on his mellow old violin, shone it to its absolute best. As her nerves gave way to intent listening, to hearing for the first time the whole work performed without interruption, she could see that, yes, that bit in the middle was chunky still, and heaven only knows why she had given the cello that strange key change; but it was fine. It was quite good, actually, very much as she had heard it in her mind before writing a note. She was called to the front to take a bow and was almost overwhelmed as she shook hands with the performers, Peter looking as proud as if he had written it himself.

She felt she might drown in the praise at tea afterwards.

'This is just the first of many successes, I'm sure,' said Heinrich. 'Really good work.'

'Thank you, Heinrich, so much of it was down to you.'

George swept her off her feet in a massive, improper hug. Lisl was warm and generous, of course, but there was still no invitation to tea, just the two of them, at her house. Years of love had, it seemed, been wiped out by those few passionate kisses.

~

'Why don't you join me in Italy?' said Thekla.

Ethel followed her as she slid away down the frozen river. The whole of Leipzig, it seemed, was enjoying the first thick ice of the winter, and conversation was sporadic.

'That's a good idea,' said Ethel as she caught up with her. 'A couple of weeks in Florence would be lovely. Warmer than here.'

'No,' said Thekla, linking arms with Ethel and skating more gently. 'Why not stay in Florence for a few months? From what you've told me, the other day at the Röntgens was a bright one in a dull winter.'

'Yes, Leipzig doesn't feel the same at all this year. I don't feel I'm learning so much anymore. Perhaps a break would be good.'

Ethel longed to tell Thekla about Lisl, their kisses and embraces, share her misery and confusion, but drew back every time. She had no idea what Thekla might think. She did not know what to think herself, what she had felt. She did not know what words to use.

'Perhaps you need some new musical influences,' said Thekla.

'What do you mean?'

'Leipzig is wonderful, and we all love it. But it's not the only place. In fact, you say yourself how conservative it is. Even Frau Frege's box empties out the minute a Wagner overture appears on the programme. If you're feeling less settled here, go and get a taste of something else – in a place where Brahms is not necessarily God.'

'Thekla Friedlander, really! There is no such place.'

Thekla guided her to a little cart on the bank, where a heavily wrapped old woman was serving hot chocolate from a little brazier.

'Ooh,' said Ethel, sipping the thick liquid from the cup that Thekla handed to her, 'this is the best. Thank you.'

'You'd be surprised. At the very least, it'll give you something new to think about.'

'Possibly. I'm certainly a bit stuck at the moment.'

'You were brave enough to come here in the first place, now you can surely move on to somewhere new.'

Ethel put her head back to drain the last of the chocolate. '*Danke*,' she said, giving the cup back to the old woman. '*Danke. Es war wunderschön.*'

Ethel left Thekla standing as she sped away on the ice.

'I think I might,' she shouted. 'Catch me if you can.'

She leant forward dangerously to pick up speed, digging her blades deep into the ice.

8

FLORENCE 1882

Ethel paced around the three sides of the bed, across to the chair and through the narrow gap alongside the fireplace. Her path took her into the centre of the room where manuscripts and books were piled haphazardly on the table, where she could almost touch the piano before turning round and doing it all again in reverse. And again. She was chewing her knuckles. The candle flickered, low.

She found herself by the window and opened it to the sounds of the start of the Florence day; the wheels of the carts juddered along the cobbles and tradesmen greeted each other cheerily and shouted at their horses. The street was still shadowy in the grey of dawn, and people scurried along pulling their jackets tight against its chill. A horse and cart stopped at the osteria opposite, and men hoisted huge baskets of fresh bread onto their shoulders. She turned back into the room. She must remember exactly what had happened.

It had been after supper at Frau Hildebrand's house. The other guests had gone back into the house out of the cooling evening air, but Harry Brewster had put out a hand and detained her.

'You are so beautiful,' he had said, holding her hands, drawing her close, his eyes warm, inviting. 'Please, let us find time to talk very soon.'

She hadn't broken free immediately, as she should have done. She had allowed herself to be locked inside his intense gaze, to relish the feel of his hands grasping hers.

'I've been fighting against it since you first arrived,' he had said. 'I want to know you better.'

'But you're Julia's husband,' she said, surprised, confused, reaching for something to say.

He laughed. 'That's true. Ever since you started coming to our home, I've wanted to spend time with you alone.'

He had leaned forward and brushed his lips over her fingers, causing her to step back sharply.

Watching a wine merchant unloading barrels of wine below, whilst the horse snorted and burrowed into its nosebag, Ethel shivered at his audacity.

Until last night, Harry had been merely a part of the richness of her winter here in Florence, a half of the enigma that was him and Julia. Her only interest in him had been as husband of Lisl's sister and father of those lovely children.

'I want to get to know you better,' he had said, in his perfect English with its slight European accent. 'You have brought life and energy into my drab existence. Please don't send me away.'

He was standing very close, too close. She would have liked him to put his arms right around her.

She stepped back. 'But… but what about Julia?'

'This need not affect your friendship with her.'

Ethel found herself in the middle of her room, hugging herself. She couldn't remember what her reply had been, or even if she had given one. All she could recall was asking for her coat and hurrying away, away from Harry and from the villa and down the dark lane home.

She put the fingers to her mouth where his lips had brushed, wanting to feel that tender sweetness again. Her hands intertwined restlessly, seeking to remember his touch.

That momentary pleasure, this night of confused longing, must be abandoned, resisted completely. She went to her table and pushed everything aside to make herself a little space. She pulled out a piece of writing paper and dipped her pen in the inkwell. She would write to Lisl, try to make sense of it.

Coming away from Leipzig had slowly melted away the awkwardness with Lisl. Almost every day they wrote warm, detailed letters to each other. Now, however, she paused in her writing. Then in one swift motion, she tore the pages in two and dropped them on the fire. She wasn't sure what Lisl would think. She did not know what to think herself. She was probably making too much of an unguarded moment. Yes, of course, it was just a man amusing himself in one of Florence's endless flirtations.

It was fully morning when she crept into bed.

Ethel was determined to spend the rest of the day working. Often on free days like this, she would walk over to Julia's for tea, and for energetic games with the children. She couldn't do that today. She tapped on the table, wondering that those few short moments yesterday, however enticing, had already changed something.

Now she must focus on the music she was writing for Clara, or it would not be ready for Frau Hildebrand's soirée. Ethel loved to hear all the stories about Clara Schumann – a powerful and beautiful woman with total mastery of the piano, touring European concert halls. She admired the fact that she had continued her musical life throughout her marriage, and her widowhood, into her old age. That's what she was now, an old woman, short and round, with white hair and poor sight, yet still commanding huge audiences when she gave the occasional concert recital.

Ethel smiled as she began to work at the music on the page. It was a humorous piece with the ironical title 'Prelude and Fugue for Thin People'. In its earliest draft, back in Leipzig, long before it

was anything other than a clever musical exercise, she had asked
Clara to play it. They had laughed long and hard at how difficult
it was for Clara to get her plump arms to cross over to play the
complicated variations.

'I will do it,' she had kept on saying. 'It is not so hard, after all.'

She had congratulated Ethel on writing a piece that for such
unexpected reasons was so difficult for her to play.

Ethel was near to finishing it. The task of making the various
musical lines come together was painstaking and detailed, and
today she was happy to be absorbed in a musical challenge. Even
so, with the slightest distraction her thoughts would turn to
Harry, his intense brown eyes, the soft fair hair, the way his lips
had lingered over her hand. At the same time, whenever a line
of the fugue fell into place, she felt energetic and enthused. This
is what she did. Nothing and no-one was going to turn her from
this. Next thing, the bell was going for dinner. She yawned and
stretched her stiff arms and legs. She was hungry.

~

*I waited for you all day yesterday and you did not come.
In the evening I went to the Hildebrand's hoping you might
be there with Clara, and then to the opera. Dismal, dismal
emptiness. Can we not talk, at least? Harry.*

Ethel did not reply. She did not know what to say. She knew no-
one in Florence well enough to confide in. Thekla was on tour
now and she did not know where a letter might find her. She
continued with the painstaking detail of Clara's piece, and walked
over to give it to Antonio, who was to play it at the soirée.

She felt like a prisoner. She had never spent so much time
alone. There had always been places to go, people to visit, concerts
to attend, invitations to tea or lawn tennis or some other activity
– now she turned everything down. She was terrified of bumping

into Harry, and confined herself to brief walks at dusk along the riverbank.

~

On the evening of the soirée, Ethel began to write a note of apology to Frau Hildebrand that she was not well enough to come, then stopped. She had stayed at the San Francesco di Paola villa for a few days on her arrival in Florence with Thekla, and the Hildebrands had become fond of her. Herr Hildebrand liked her to sit with him in his studio whilst he sculpted, and Frau Hildebrand was keen to help her with her music, introducing her to the many composers and conductors who came to Florence. Certainly, someone would be sent down the hill to see what was wrong. There would be fuss. She put the blank piece of paper back on the pile. It was an important evening; she must take every opportunity to showcase her music.

She practised what she had promised to sing that night, two of Robert Schumann's lesser-known songs, together with a couple of her own, and began to dress carefully. For once, she felt the need to fit in, not to look in any way different from the other women there. Normally, she made only the slightest concession to what was required at an informal musical evening with supper, but tonight she was meticulous. She discarded her plain, panelled skirt with blouse and jacket, and wore instead a long, grey, high-necked dress in soft wool, with a darker bolero in a lacy pattern her mother had sent her at Christmas time. She wore no jewellery or ornament in her pinned-back hair but dressed it carefully. The only exceptional thing about her would be her music.

She scanned the drawing room quickly. Good, no Harry or Julia. She hurried over and sat by Frau Hildebrand on the sofa as usual. They kissed fondly.

'Are you better, dear? Someone said you had a bit of a cold.'

'Yes, thanks,' replied Ethel. 'It was just enough to keep me at home for a few days. I've been working hard on Clara's piece.'

'She'll love it, I know.'

The sofa was placed so that Frau Hildebrand could see people as they were announced, and they would naturally come and greet her and exchange any bits of news or gossip. In this way, Ethel was introduced to everyone too, and was free to join in their conversations as the evening wore on.

Ethel looked up just as Harry and Julia were coming in. Her eyes locked with his, lasting seconds longer than any casual or even friendly glance or greeting across the room. She got to her feet as agitation and excitement pounded in her body.

'What is it, my dear?' said Frau Hildebrand, looking up at her.

'I do beg your pardon,' said Ethel, trying to cover her confusion. 'Could you excuse me a moment? I just spotted Clara, and I need to mention something to her. I won't be a minute.'

She was hot, breathless, surprised she could make any reasonable excuse to flee. She headed over to where Clara stood with her daughters and a group of admirers.

'I can't regret my career as a concert pianist,' she was saying to Antonio. 'But I wish I'd been brave enough to compose more. Brave and studious.' She put her arm around Ethel's shoulders. 'Like my young friend here.'

'And I wish I could play so wonderfully,' said Ethel. 'I could make what I write sound so much better.'

'No, no,' said Clara. 'Anyone can play. You are a composer first and last.'

'Have you seen Herr Hildebrand's new sculpture?' said the voice she was dreading.

The group parted slightly to let Harry in.

'I certainly have,' said one of Clara's daughters. 'As usual, it's completely incomprehensible but very beautiful.'

'I shall see it at supper,' said Clara. 'I believe that's when it's to be unveiled.'

'Have you seen it?' said Harry, looking at Ethel.

She addressed the whole group, rather than look at him. 'I saw it a couple of times when it was in the workshop. I'm looking forward to seeing the finished work. Some sort of black marble, I think.'

They were being called to take their places in the music room. Ethel felt Harry's hand gentle on her back as they turned towards the door. She felt stiff and awkward.

'Come on, Ethel,' said Clara, linking arms with her on the other side. 'At last, music.' As she helped Clara cross the hall, Harry melted away.

The rows of ornate, upholstered chairs and the huge mahogany piano which gleamed under the heavy candelabras gave her courage. Here she could forget the tricky world of manners and conventions. She was the artist, the composer, the professional. She sat at the piano, quietly playing a couple of Robert Schumann's *Scenes from Childhood* as the audience settled. Thoughts of Harry, his almost irresistible gaze, the sensations in her body as he touched her, fell away.

Ethel walked across the piazza, leaving the old villa behind, and started down the hill towards the city. The pressures of the evening, which on the surface had been such a success, began to fade. She had said nothing but the truth to Frau Hildebrand when she excused herself, saying the evening had over-taxed her. Now, there was only the sounds of her footsteps and those of the servant who had been sent to make sure she got home safely.

She pulled her cloak around her. Her music had been applauded and praised. Herr Hildebrand had teased her that his salon had become fuller with people who could not wait to hear her music. He was flattering her; it was Clara whom people had come to see, combined with the unveiling of his new sculpture. Despite the success of the evening, and the acclaim awarded to her, she had remained nervous throughout. She had kept an eye on Harry, afraid of being embarrassed by him, scared to come face to face with Julia.

The clatter of a passing carriage shook her out of her self-absorption. She had come to the via dei Serragli, and she turned and told Frau Hildebrand's servant he could go back, since she was nearly home now.

Too restless to go indoors, she walked on towards the Ponte Vecchio, breathing in the river's night-time smells as she crossed. How mysterious the thick, black water was.

Beyond the bridge, the squares and alleyways and closed stone buildings were beautiful and silent, without their daytime bustle and incessant noise. The city's art and splendour was scattered carelessly about, so different from Leipzig. Ethel had a pang of longing for her old rooms, the little bird-cage larder hanging outside her window, and the big fireplace with its boiling kettle. She didn't have to stay; she could go back to Leipzig tomorrow if she chose; there was nothing to hold her here. She could make her excuses to her new friends, and allow the routine of her life in Leipzig to swallow her up again. Or perhaps she would go back to England. Mary had just had a baby, and wanted her to come and see her. Yes, that's what she would do.

9

'I've missed you so much,' said Harry. 'So many long, dreary summer months.'

Ethel flushed. 'It's lovely to be back and see everyone again.'

She looked around the coffee shop for someone she could go and sit with, but everyone she knew had gone. How foolish to be here still, when the others had finished their drink and gone home to dress for dinner or whatever they might be doing next. Harry waved to the waiter to bring them some more coffee.

'You have been constantly in my mind. Nothing has changed since I first saw you. Please, say something to me.'

'You're a married man,' she said finally, hot and flushed. 'Julia is my friend, as you are. That is all that needs to be said.'

Ethel began to smooth on her gloves for something to do.

'Don't go,' he said, leaning closer towards her. 'I won't bother you any more if you tell me you don't feel something real for me. Please, look at me.'

She could not look at him, or think clearly about anything, or find any words. Her heart was racing. She had not expected to still feel this excitement. She got up and hurried out into the dark city. Breathless with shock, she only slowed her pace when she was sure that he had not come after her. She leaned on the parapet of the bridge and let her gaze rest on the water flowing beneath whilst her thoughts churned. It was her fault. She should have left before they were alone. She was just a diversion for him, with his lovely townhouse, and his family and his philosophy and books.

Her feet took her across the bridge and around the narrow streets and squares near her lodgings, where she walked until her restlessness calmed and she went in and dressed for dinner.

~

Ethel worked at her table and at the piano, hour after hour, trying out different harmonies in fierce concentration. After dinner, she took out again the letter she had received from Lisl the day before.

Heinrich is as happy as can be, she wrote. *He has got a post at the new School of Music at the university in Berlin. We would like you to come and be with us there when we move next year. There's not so much music going on in Berlin as in Leipzig (or Florence), but that can be changed. Please come, how I would love that.*

Ethel did not know what to say; she had no idea what Berlin would be like. It was never mentioned as a musical city. Leipzig was home. It was where she had found her feet. The Röntgens were there, and Frau Frege in her box above the stage, not to mention all the musicians who passed through the town. And she was always welcome backstage at the Gewandhaus. Any performance of her music was likely to be there.

Yet it was Lisl who made it home, who had made so much happen for her. If she stayed after they left, everything would be different, pointless.

She looked at the letter again. Perhaps Lisl had forgotten

their kisses; Ethel hoped so, since it had caused such a change, although she never would. How foolish of her to hesitate. No, she would be sad to leave Leipzig behind, but of course Berlin was full of new opportunities as well, which they would help her to realise.

Thank you, she said, *thank you so much for inviting me to come with you. I would love to, of course.*

Ethel had said very little to Lisl about Harry. Now she found herself writing about how he seemed to have fallen for her, and she couldn't help but find him very attractive, more than any other man she had ever met, and how well they got on together.

Lisl's reply came as quickly as a letter between Leipzig and Florence could travel. Harry could certainly be very charming and gallant, she wrote, even if he was a bit odd in some ways, but he had never looked at another woman in all the fifteen years of his marriage to Julia. They were famous for their closeness. She was mistaken if she thought it was more than just a flirtation.

~

Ethel and Harry saw a lot of each other. The coffee house was a favourite place, where they could enjoy lively conversations with other artists and writers and, sometimes, find themselves alone at a table when others had left. Then they would talk about every aspect of their past lives, their knees touching under the table. At dining tables, or in salons, or at concerts he was utterly correct, and yet they would always manage some small conversation, even if it was only when he turned the pages for her at the piano.

~

Ethel dressed carefully for her visit to Frau Hildebrand's. Afternoon tea in Florence was a formal occasion. Wealthy women from well-connected German or English families were often there, whose views were not that different from the wives of the military top brass whom her mother had to tea. Ethel was happy enough to have tea with them and help Frau Hildebrand with the cups and pastries. It might result in an invitation to play at a party or supper, when she could include some of her own compositions, or to accept a seat in a box at the opera or the concert hall.

Sometimes, she would go early and spend an hour with Herr Hildebrand in his studio, arguing with him whilst he worked his sculpture, giggling sometimes when he teased her and giving him a hand if needed.

But today, to Ethel's surprise, tea was set just for herself and her host.

'Come and sit with me here,' said Frau Hildebrand, patting the sofa. 'I thought we should have a little chat. Sometimes weeks go by without us really talking. There are always far too many people around.'

'You are very hospitable,' said Ethel. 'And people love to come here. Especially to this incredible old convent. I always expect a ghostly nun to appear from the shadows.'

'Yes, but you are very special to us. We loved having you to stay last year with dear Thekla, and I miss our conversations. When you were home in the summer, poor Hildebrand began to pine. You know how stupid he is about you.'

'He's a wonderful man,' said Ethel. 'He always makes me laugh with his jokes and observations. And I never saw a sculptor at work before.'

'Don't mention sculptures to me. The house is becoming not just a workshop but a warehouse. I haven't got room for one more, as I keep saying to him. He takes no notice, of course.'

Ethel laughed. The issue of the sculptures and where they should go was the subject of daily arguments between them. The maid brought in the tea tray.

'You played quite beautifully last week at my soirée,' she continued, as Ethel got up to pour the tea. 'We haven't had so much great music this year, and we've missed Thekla terribly. I think her voice gets better, don't you? Thank you. Help yourself to some cake.'

Ethel stirred sugar into her tea. 'I think she's in Madrid now, singing in Gounod's *Faust*.'

'She does it all so well,' said Frau Hildebrand. 'Now, tell me about dear Heinrich and Lisl. Do they talk about visiting Florence at all?'

'Heinrich is very happy. He's been asked to go to work at the new Berlin conservatoire next year. They've asked me to move with them.'

'That's a good place for a young musician to be, though it is an awful long way from us all here.'

Ethel dug her little fork into the chocolate gateau. 'Mm,' she said. 'Mother would love to have a cook who could bake a cake like this. It's delicious. She's talked about coming to Leipzig for a few days next summer.'

'How lovely for you. I don't suppose her travels would bring her as far south as Florence, would they? I would love to meet her.'

'I doubt it; her health isn't that good. I'd be surprised if she makes it as far as Leipzig. I hope she will.' She leant forward to put down her plate and pick up her tea.

'And what would your dear mother say about your friendship with Harry Brewster?'

The jolt that went through Ethel's body caused her cup to jump in its saucer, and she felt herself flush.

'Mother's glad I have so many good friends,' she managed to say.

'You know what I mean, Ethel,' said Frau Hildebrand. 'I'm not going to say any more, except that a young woman in your position must always take care. It is never good if there is gossip. You know what is expected. Now, we've had some wonderful news this morning. Pyotr Tchaikovsky is coming here in a couple of weeks on his way to Rome. He's got his public performances, of course, but he's always happy to fit in a musical evening here. There'll be quite a few musicians involved, and we wondered if you would like to have some of your instrumental music performed, as a change from your songs?'

Ethel's heart, which hadn't stopped thudding from the warning she had received, almost stopped.

'You mean, here, in front of your guests?'

'Yes, we're going to invite as many as we can fit in. Can you have something ready for rehearsal in ten days?'

'I certainly can. Goodness, what shall I choose? Thank you, Frau Hildebrand, that is a wonderful opportunity.'

'Well, Thekla told me that Herr Tchaikovsky is curious to hear your music. He heard about you in Leipzig, apparently. Antonio will organise everything. Now, if you've finished your tea, we'll go and see if that husband of mine is back. He will never forgive me if he knows you were here but didn't come and say hello.'

Ethel wrote a short letter to Harry that evening:

Maybe there's gossip about us, I don't know, but Frau Hildebrand warned me to be careful. I ought to go back to Leipzig after what's been said, but she's helping me with my music.

His reply was there when she went down for breakfast:

Meet me at the coffee shop this afternoon.

Ethel struggled to keep on her hat and scarf as the chilly wind blew her along the pavement. Autumn seemed to have crept into Florence. The coffee shop was crowded with the people of the city who loved to sit for hours discussing the finer points of art or politics or philosophy. They greeted Ethel warmly and made space for her to sit down and ordered her coffee. It was as far from drawing-room life as could be, full of smoke and the occasional profanity and sharp, irreverent conversation. She knew Harry had come in because everyone shifted around to make room for him to sit by her. With these people, Harry threw off some of his shyness, and became animated and witty. Ethel found her own opinions properly considered, and felt her intellect being honed on their clever insights.

Today, however, she could not make any sense of the conversation. She was waiting for people to drift away, as they usually did, so she and Harry could talk, but no-one was moving. As the afternoon turned into evening, she stood up pleading an oncoming cold. Harry immediately offered to escort her home.

It was getting dark now, and the streets were full of the bustle of people who wanted to buy what they needed in the shops as quickly as possible and get home.

'This is too busy,' said Harry. 'Let's walk along by the river. It will be quiet there.'

He led her down the steps by the bridge, and after a few minutes of brisk walking, the town was left behind. Without the lights of the streets, it was dark. Ethel felt afraid. It would not be easy to explain if she was recognised.

'Don't worry,' he said quietly. 'No-one will see us here. Come, put your arm through mine and then we can talk.'

Ethel threw back the hood on her cape and enjoyed the wind on her face, speckled as it was with rain. The river was dark at their side. There was little light for it to reflect, and yet its flow was full of shade and sudden glimmers.

'Now,' said Harry, 'what did that dragon say that scared you so much?'

'She has noticed that we like to be together.'

'That's probably not difficult, if anyone is looking.'

'I hope she's the only one,' said Ethel anxiously.

'Go on,' said Harry. 'What did she say?'

'It was over in an instant. A five-second lesson in how to behave.'

'Well, you know how these people live on gossip. But we haven't done anything that we need to worry about.'

'If it wasn't for the Tchaikovsky evening, I'd be thinking it might be better to go away.'

'No, no! Even on this muddy path, I'd get down on my knees and beg you not to. The very thought invokes such grey days ahead.'

'It's too complicated,' said Ethel.

'Please don't start to think that,' said Harry. 'For the moment, all we can do is relish what we are feeling.'

'But I'm so dependent on them for my music.'

He stopped and turned her towards him. 'You are strong and powerful, and your music will be successful. Don't let them decide how you'll behave.' He bent and kissed her lightly.

'We should go back.'

'Very well. When I get home I shall write a poem – Ethel and Harry walk by the Arno on a dark, wet night.'

'And I shall set it to music.' She laughed. 'Should it be a quiet, thoughtful piece or full of drama and risk?'

'You choose,' he said. He started to declaim, and she started to hum, and the rain started to pour down. Harry put his arm round her until the lights of the town began to glimmer ahead.

'We have stolen a rare hour tonight,' said Ethel, drawing away from him.

'We have. A most glorious hour. And now we must return to the selves the world expects of us. You need not worry that I shall do anything to make Frau Hildebrand and her ilk think badly of you.'

That night Ethel wrote to Lisl. How she wanted to tell her about that walk with Harry along the river, about the hot pulsing in her body, even now, and the feel of his lips, so brief, on hers. But she must not. Instead, afraid that Lisl would find out anyway, she told her about Frau Hildebrand's warning to her. She reassured her that there was nothing to worry about.

She put the letter on the post tray in the hall when she went down for breakfast. It was only when she lifted her head from a page of her quartet that she was re-copying ahead of rehearsals, that she wondered if she had been wise. She couldn't remember exactly what she had said, but she had certainly forgotten that Harry's wife was Lisl's sister. She walked round her room, then dashed downstairs to check if the letter had gone. It had, of course. Now she would have to wait days for a reply. In the meantime, she would write long, newsy letters which would reassure Lisl that all was well.

~

From the very first sentence, Lisl's fury bounced off the page. She simply couldn't understand what was happening. If Frau Hildebrand had taken the embarrassing step of mentioning it, then there was more than some little flirtation going on. What on earth was she thinking of, playing around with a married man, one who, moreover, was devoted to his wife, her sister? Ethel put her hands over her eyes, but not before she had seen the last couple of sentences. *You could bring shame on us all. You must come away from Florence NOW.*

She did not reply but focussed on the rapidly approaching performance. The musicians had their copies of her work, and every couple of days she would meet with them. It was exhilarating to work with people who knew their trade so thoroughly and were happy to share their thoughts with her. Just like Ethel herself, they were daunted, and ridiculously excited, by the fact that Herr Tchaikovsky would be there listening to them. Not since playing with the Röntgens had Ethel felt such pleasure at what she had created with a mere pen on paper.

Ethel knew her quartet was merely to gain everyone's attention before Herr Tchaikovsky's piano trio, but nevertheless she enjoyed every minute. The four musicians did her proud, very proud, and when she joined them on the stage at the end of the performance, the applause was protracted and genuine. She looked round at the guests, perfectly dressed in their rich evening clothes, for whom this kind of evening was quite a normal event. It was similar to the old days of court patronage, she thought. She was utterly dependent on these clapping people, and those like them, to hear her work and put the word around that there was an interesting new composer here. Only in that way would anyone ever think to include her music in their concert programmes.

She spotted Harry, sitting near the back, and looked away quickly. She hoped no-one else was looking at him because his face was animated, smiling and proud. How she would have liked to go and sit with him, feel his arm brushing hers. Instead, she returned to her seat at the side so she could see the musicians and the dark, brooding face of Herr Tchaikovsky, and be swept away by the tempestuous trio.

10

Ethel hurried through the squares and streets of Florence, past the cathedral, up the narrow passageways, until she reached the station. She had told friends that she was going to Sienna to spend a few days with friends of her parents. She had not told them that she had invited Harry to escort her there.

Now spring was here, she had been making train journeys to the little towns and villages of Tuscany – partly to absorb the rich colours and textures of the countryside, which she hoped would suffuse her music, and partly to distract herself from persistent thoughts of Harry. Just a few words alone with him, or even a discreet touch could make her fizz with energy, become witty and talkative in the ways that were so attractive to him. She had started to look forward too much to their snatched walks along the night-time river.

Harry, she had written, *would you travel to Sienna with me? I'm not due there until evening and perhaps we could spend a little time together.*

How bold, came his reply. *Yes. Leave it to me.*

A porter took her to her reserved seat in the first-class

carriage. She admired the comfortable seats and luxurious fittings. Normally she could only afford to travel third-class and sit on hard wooden benches; now she was being treated to coffee and pastries. Just as she was wondering if Harry had failed to get away, he jumped onto the train, which was already beginning to whistle and belch its steam in preparation for departure. He surprised her by kissing her heartily, like a friend or relative.

As the train got underway, she snuggled up to him as he sat looking at the newspaper the attendant brought to him. He kissed the top of her head.

'This is pleasant,' she murmured, watching as the train emerged from a tunnel into the green countryside. 'I do hope the people who built the railway understood what a tremendous gift they were giving to us.'

'I love it,' he said. 'I miss my travelling days. It's only since the children arrived that we've settled at all. I always envy you when you go back to Leipzig, or across to England.'

'It gets very boring to make the same journey again and again. Did you know that I learnt when I was little more than a child exactly how long it would take to get from Farnborough to Leipzig?'

'Why did you need to know that?'

'I had my journey all planned, ready to leave as soon as Father gave way.'

'What an extraordinary child you must have been. All determination and tempestuousness. Not so different from now, really.'

At Sienna they stepped into the hired carriage and rode into the countryside for lunch. Ethel leaned out of the window, exclaiming at the river they were following, its little crossings where cattle were drinking and the spring flowers that covered the grass.

'I'm a country girl at heart,' she said. 'I have to be in the town for my music, but nothing is so good as this.'

Harry looked up from his newspaper and glanced out of the window. 'It's just one field after the other,' he said, ducking to avoid her outrage.

'These few days will be so good,' she said. 'What do you think English people do on a country weekend near Sienna?'

'The same boring things as elsewhere, I expect. Dogs, horses, walking, shooting probably, cards, gossip and poorly played music in the evenings.'

'Sounds wonderful,' said Ethel, settling back down. 'Not the poor music, of course.' She snuggled against him as he folded his newspaper away and took her hand.

The carriage drew in at the inn – little more than a farmhouse with its scuttling hens and barking dogs – where Harry had booked a private room for their lunch. The table was covered by a white, lace cloth, and no sooner had they sat down than a bowl of thick vegetable soup was served, with chunks of bread stirred in. A dish of simply cooked chicken in a creamy sauce followed, with a jug of local wine from the vineyards nearby. Afterwards, they sat on the sofa by the fire, sipping the wine and nibbling at the chocolate dessert.

'I wish I could whisk you off upstairs,' Harry said, putting his arm around her. 'I'm sure they would have a room to give us.'

Ethel lay against him, her head on his shoulder. She listened to the strange play of sensations in her body. What might it be like, to go to a room with a man, and what exactly would then happen? She would have liked to roll over onto him, feel his body against hers.

She looked out of the window, at the rutted lane outside the inn with its farm on the opposite side, the washing on the line to the side of the house, and a woman hoeing the rows between the small plants.

'Shall we walk?' she said.

As they passed out of the village and took a path across the meadow, Harry said, 'Perhaps we should give up art and come and live here.'

'I could give up the pursuit of success.'

'We could keep chickens and live the simple life.'

Ethel laughed. 'Have you ever been near a chicken? Except the one on your plate? You are the most city-bred creature I've ever met. At least I know about plants and animals. The main problem is, there aren't many shiny big pianos in these cottages.'

'You won't need one. You'll be too busy chopping the vegetables from the garden for our midday soup to worry about that.'

Ethel reached up and put her hand over Harry's mouth. 'No more dreaming. Now come on, let's run.'

Harry groaned. 'Walking is perfectly lovely,' he said. 'Next time, I must remember to fall in love with a pale, drawing-room sort of woman.'

'Love is a forbidden word.'

Ethel maintained that he had hardly run more than a few steps since he was a boy, as was obvious when he had tried to keep up with her games with his children in the days when she had been able to visit his villa. She left him far behind, then ran in smaller and smaller circles around him, and let him catch her as she ran past.

'How unseemly. You are so delightful,' he said, pushing escaped strands of hair back from her face. He put his arms around her. 'Now run from me if you wish.'

She did not wish.

'We must go back,' he said at last. 'If you are to be delivered to your weekend party.'

'I shall lock this day away in a special place,' said Ethel as they wandered slowly back.

'Have you been happy? That's all I wanted for today.'

'It's been exquisite.'

11

GERMANY 1883

'Promise me,' said Lisl. 'Promise me you won't see him again or have anything more to do with him.'

There was a sick churning in Ethel's stomach. She had decided, when she stopped off at Lisl and Heinrich's summer house on her way back to England, to tell Lisl everything. Now things had gone so far with Harry, and the desire to be together one day had been voiced, she had no option.

Ethel could feel the warmth, smell the perfume of Lisl, sitting so close to her on the window seat. They were both as near to tears as could be.

'Don't cry, Lisl,' said Ethel. 'I don't see how any of this needs to hurt you.'

'I forget how young you are, Ethel. You can't see that this silly thing you and Harry have started could affect so many people. What must my poor sister be feeling? It hurts me because I thought you belonged with me and Heinrich. You do still want to be with us in Berlin, don't you?'

'You know I do.' It was true. From the moment that Lisl came running out to greet her, she had felt safe, happy, at home. How wonderful to be with Lisl, beautiful Lisl who had hugged her so close, and told her how much she had missed her. It had been so familiar to talk over lunch with Heinrich about Florence's music and Leipzig's music and her music before he went to spend the afternoon on the lake fishing. She found a handkerchief and wiped her face.

'Harry has all these ideas about free love,' continued Lisl. 'It doesn't work like that. Please end it before any harm is done. In time, you'll wonder at how foolish you were. Irene Hildebrand always likes to stick her nose into any bit of gossip, but I'm glad she warned you. You must have been indiscreet, which doesn't surprise me because you're not good at hiding things. You need the support of those people if your music is to succeed.'

Ethel looked at the mantelpiece with its delicate porcelain ornaments and gold-framed mirror, at how the sun flooded the pretty room with light.

'I'm so sorry,' she said. 'I never wanted to make you sad. I would really like everything to be as it was before. I probably shouldn't go back to Florence.'

'Stay with us for a little while before you go on to England. You'll love the funicular and we can go walking in the mountains. Even the air up there is different. Or we can take a boat out on the lake. Let's forget the world of music and drawing rooms. Then in the autumn, we'll start serious study again. Please, promise me that you won't have anything more to do with him.'

Ethel could see, now that she was away from him, how impossible the situation was.

'You're right,' she said. 'I promise.'

Lisl had twisted around to look out over the lake. Ethel could see how upset she was.

'What is it?'

'You can't imagine how tedious life is when you aren't here. Sometimes I think I can't stand it. Heinrich and I look at each other over the lunch table and wonder where our darling is.'

'Oh, Lisl, please don't cry.'

Ethel put her arms around her, and they sat hugging each other, wiping the tears from each other's eyes.

12

LEIPZIG 1883

It was so good to be back in Leipzig with its markets and its concerts and its well-known faces and its endless stream of musicians; back where there were people rooting for her to get her music ready to be performed. It was a thrill to be back here in her old room, with its rickety piano and bird-cage larder.

Ethel looked up from the desk, rubbing her tired eyes. She was battling with the third movement of her string quintet. People were going to pay – well, she hoped they would – to come and hear her music performed in the beautiful chamber-music room at the new Gewandhaus. The String Quintet in E by Ethel Smyth. In her mind, the words glowed on the front of the programme, even though she knew it would be hidden amongst other items, better known. For the first time, there would be people she knew and didn't know who would buy a ticket to come and hear it; there would be newspaper journalists to review it.

'Come on, Ethel,' she muttered. 'Keep your mind on it, or there will be nothing for those people to hear.'

~

As Christmas approached, she started to meet with the members of the string quintet, led by Papa Röntgen himself. There were discussions about why this and why that, perhaps she might consider a different combination in that place there? Sometimes she became angry; it took her a while to see that the instrumentalists had their own knowledge, different but no less valid. She began to view her quintet as a quilt – it was hers, all hers, and yet many people were working to make it beautiful.

~

It was a cold, January evening, but the hall was full. Friends old and new, including Edvard and Nina Grieg and Frau Frege, sat near to where she was between Lisl and Heinrich. Exhausted and overwrought, she took in very little. The sound in the brand-new hall was bright and clear, frighteningly so in some places. Surely, she had not written that. It was terrible. No, it wasn't; it was amazing. All too soon, it was over.

Everyone was clapping. The applause was loud and long. She stumbled onto the stage when the audience shouted for the composer, looking out over the smiling faces, shocked.

Afterwards, she heard a lot of congratulations, and had a wonderful supper with a proud Lisl presiding, with many people coming and praising her.

'Am I launched, Heinrich?' she said, taking refuge in the corner where he sat.

'You've had a wonderful debut,' he said. 'I'm sure it will be followed up by many more performances. When we are in Berlin, there will be another musical world for you to storm.'

'I can't wait,' she said.

'There's nothing straightforward or predictable about this. Hard work and a lot of luck are needed.'

'And more counterpoint lessons?'

'Of course.'

~

Ethel turned the letter from Harry over in her hands. Since making her promise to Lisl in the summer, she had discarded all his letters unread, and not written to him either. It had not been easy. She opened it.

I was so thrilled to hear from Frau Hildebrand about your debut. Oh, I would have so much loved to be there, to steal even a few seconds alone with you to share your delight. Dearest Ethel, our separation is intolerable. I wonder, I just wonder... if by any chance you do read this, please take pity on me. I'm going to be passing through Germany soon on my way to some lectures in Frankfurt – might we not meet, however briefly?

The idea of meeting with him began to take root in her mind. It would just be for a day, after all. It was only fair to explain to him that she could not return to Florence, that she needed to be with Lisl and would go with them when they moved to Berlin in the summer; that now she must follow up on her success to further her musical career. Her future could not include him.

~

When she saw him waiting for her at Halle, far enough away from Leipzig not to be seen, she hoped, a surge of excitement pulsed through her. As his eyes sought hers, she felt a secret, unexpected delight. She ran to him and put her arms around him and pushed into his body, feeling his hands press her close. The feel of him, the smell of him, the murmuring in her ear – how had she thought she could do without that? She made herself pull away from him; the station might be thick with smoke and grime, but it was also full of daylight.

They walked through the streets of the little town, admired its cathedral and castle and the run-down house where Handel was said to have been born, and had luncheon in a pleasant little hotel near the market. They talked about all the people they knew, discussed music and philosophy and politics, and touched arms and hands whenever possible.

They began to walk through the woods that surrounded the town.

'Julia has told me that she would not be unhappy for us to meet now and then,' said Harry, drawing Ethel's arm through his.

Ethel took her hat off so she could look more easily into his face as they walked.

'I promised Lisl that I wouldn't be in contact with you anymore,' she said.

'And yet, here we are,' he murmured. 'May we not decide ourselves on this, if Julia is in agreement?'

'You know how much I love Lisl,' said Ethel. 'And I must be with people who can help me musically. It's the right thing for me to go with them to Berlin.'

'I hate the thought of you moving there. It's so far away. You're just beginning to try out other styles, but from what I hear, there is no comparable music world in Berlin. It is very conservative, not really welcoming European influences. Please think again.'

'I would much prefer it if they were staying in Leipzig, but they aren't. I have to go with them.'

'I can live if I have the hope of us meeting now and again. Lisl can trust us to be entirely discreet. Maybe with that reassurance, she might not be so opposed?'

'I'll talk to her again when I can,' said Ethel. 'I'm not sure what her reaction will be. There's nothing straightforward about this.'

'I don't want you to have to choose. You shouldn't have to,' said Harry. 'We must be able to find a way forward. But let's not spoil the few hours we have. Isn't this just the very best day?'

'The best since Sienna,' she said, pulling her arm out and picking up some fir cones from beneath the trees. 'How far can you throw these?'

'No, no! Not more of your sporty contests. As soon as we get comfortable, you start running or throwing things. You'll be pleased to know that I can sometimes beat Christopher at lawn tennis.'

'Well done,' said Ethel. 'You can take on a six-year-old. Very impressive.'

He put his arms around her. 'Now, let's see how strong you are.'

'Perhaps not so strong,' she said, laying her head on his shoulder whilst he stroked back her hair.

~

Ethel sat in the kitchen with Frau Röntgen, drawing up a list of the people they wanted to invite to her final musical evening in Leipzig. The family wanted to play her quintet, as well as try out one of Julius's new compositions.

'It will be lovely for us, too,' said Frau Röntgen. 'The house is horribly quiet now we just have Grete at home.'

'Does Peter like Dresden?'

'Yes, thank goodness. He was so disappointed not to get into the Gewandhaus orchestra. He's fine where he is. I had to calm poor Johanna down. She shouted at him, "I'd give my back teeth to play at Dresden, or with any other orchestra for that matter, so stop complaining. It's not fair." It's not, is it?'

'Absolutely not. She plays at least as well as Peter.'

'And yet she will never have that opportunity.'

'We have to hope these things will change in time.'

'Anyway, enough of our woes. Husband and babies are keeping her busy. How are things in the von Herzogenberg household?'

'Everything is focussed on the move,' said Ethel. 'Heinrich is in Berlin a lot, talking to professors about his new duties, and looking for a suitable house, and Lisl and I are doing nothing but pack up the library.'

'It's probably best to do that when Heinrich is away. Knowing him, he probably doesn't want to discard a single thing.'

'I'm going to miss you all dreadfully,' said Ethel. 'You helped me so much when I arrived, and I don't think I will ever find another family where it's as natural for someone to pick up a violin as to make a cup of tea.'

'We shall miss you, too. But travel gets easier all the time, so I hope we will see each other often. And of course Papa will continue to press for your new music to be performed at the Gewandhaus.'

As Ethel walked through the streets to go home, she found herself naming the different buildings – Thomaskirche, the town hall, the market, Clara Schumann's birth house, the now-abandoned conservatoire and Gewandhaus. She was beginning to say goodbye.

There was a grey envelope in Lisl's elegant writing on the table by the entrance to her room. Ethel took it inside, lit the lamps and sat by the window to read it.

We don't want you to come with us to Berlin. Ethel rocked back in her chair, and blood rushed to her face. What was that? *You've let me down, Ethel, me and Heinrich. We're disappointed. You didn't keep to our agreement about not seeing Harry, so we can't trust you. It would be best if we never see each other again, or have any contact.*

Ethel folded the letter and pushed it roughly back into its envelope. Twice she brought it out again to re-read parts of it. Surely it must be some sort of joke. The words were running together on the page, and it was impossible, in the waves of panic that were beginning to rise through her body, to take in what she was reading. Don't come to Berlin. Is that what she'd read? She must make sure.

Her head felt heavy, and her mouth opened as if she had seen something terrible. How, when they had so happily shared the tasks of the last few days, could Lisl say she never wanted to see her again? Never!

Ethel read the letter again, in case she was wrong. But no, the words seemed already engraved on her mind. Never. Yes, that word was there. She scrunched up the letter and threw it towards the bin.

She leapt on the letter again, which was lying amongst other rubbish that had spilled out under the table. They'd been talking about Berlin for months, about who they knew there, the musical evenings they would start up immediately to meet new friends. They would make sure her lodgings were very near as well. All that couldn't have come to nothing, could it?

'No, Lisl, no!' she shouted.

We don't want you, the letter as good as said. Heinrich and I have decided. So don't come.

Ethel rubbed her face, which had become wet with tears. She must go out. Out of this horrible little room with its bad news and smashed future. Out, not into the town; no, away from the streets so there would be just her running along the paths through the fields with no-one to bother her.

~

Ethel sat at the window looking out at the street, hoping that one of Lisl's servants or a message-boy might come by with another letter, an apologetic one saying how silly she had been, of course she didn't mean for her not to come to Berlin. She'd just been having a dull day. Hour after hour, no-one came.

Ethel's head was nothing but a persistent ache. She had no memory of whether she had eaten any breakfast. There was no coffee in the jug, or bread rolls in the cupboard. She pulled a skirt out of her wardrobe, and put on the jacket and hat she had thrown on the chair the evening before, not caring to re-pin her hair or look in the mirror.

She walked without looking right or left, through the fields and alongside the river, making herself breathless and hot in the April sun.

Down past the university she marched, paying no attention to the old Gewandhaus and conservatoire buildings, or looking around to see who else out walking she might recognise. She barely noticed the dark grey stone church on her right, with its ornate tower, where she had sat on so many Saturday afternoons listening to boys singing in the clearest tones the pure music of Bach.

Panting a little now, she crossed the road which encircled the old town and entered the network of wider, residential streets. Her heart pounding, impervious to the fine new houses she had so often paused to admire in the past, she was almost running by the time she reached the back steps to Lisl's apartment. She raced up, knocked as she opened the back door and popped her head into the kitchen. Cook and one of the drivers were standing by the table talking. The kitchen had that quiet feel of mid-afternoon, before dinner preparations begin.

'Hello, it's only me. I'm just popping in to see Lisl,' said Ethel, 'presuming she's at home.'

The two servants looked at each other. 'I'm not sure that she's available, Fraülein,' said Hans. 'I'll find Helga for you. Would you like to wait in the hall?'

They looked at her as if embarrassed. She went through to the hall until he came back with Helga.

'I'm sorry, Fraülein Ethel,' she said. 'Frau von Herzogenberg is unable to see you. She is indisposed this afternoon.'

'Indisposed?' said Ethel. 'That no problem. I'll just make my way along to her sitting room.'

She could see how awkward this was for the servants, people she had known for years who were fond of her. It had been Helga who had nursed her in her lodgings, and looked after her when she stayed in the little attic room, and Hans had driven her dozens of miles in the horse and carriage.

'It's all right,' she said lightly. 'I'll tell your mistress that I forced you to let me through.'

She brushed past them, ran along the passage and burst into Lisl's sitting room.

'Hello, Lisl. Hello, I'm here,' she said, pretending that everything was as usual. Lisl would get up and come towards her, and they would embrace and kiss, cry over their silly upset and sit on the little sofa talking of all they had seen, thought and felt since last being together.

As Ethel's eyes adjusted to the bright room, however, she knew it would not be like that. Lisl, pale and distraught, stood close to her mother, who looked more severe than usual.

'Don't bother closing the door,' Frau von Stockhausen said to Helga, who had followed Ethel into the room. 'Fraülein Smyth is leaving immediately.'

Ethel put her hand to her mouth to stop the sound of terror escaping from her throat.

'Lisl?' she forced out, ignoring the older woman. Lisl's hands were clenched beneath her chin. 'Lisl? Aren't you going to invite me in?'

'She is not,' said Frau von Stockhausen. 'She does not want to talk to you, or see you, ever again.'

'I'm sure that Lisl is able to tell me herself what she wants.'

Ethel was afraid of the tall, determined older woman in her dark gown. Once she had admired her, courted her affection, but Frau von Stockhausen had never allowed herself for a minute to be relaxed or friendly. She took a deep breath and made herself take a step towards Lisl.

'Can't we talk?' she said. 'I know I need to apologise.' She hated how her voice trembled.

'You've let us down, Ethel,' said Lisl. Her voice was small and sad. 'Me and Heinrich. You promised you wouldn't have any more contact with him, but you did. You were with him in Halle.'

Frau von Stockhausen looked even more furious.

'Leave the house now. I won't see my daughter upset like this. Neither of my daughters deserve the pain you have caused, when they have shown nothing but kindness to you.'

Lisl's sad face was unbearable. Ethel started to walk towards her, holding her hands out. Lisl turned away, and her mother stepped in front so Ethel could no longer see her.

'If you don't leave the house this minute, I will have you removed.'

Ethel stood for a moment, bearing the older woman's hostile glare. She looked for a word or gesture from Lisl. There was none. Ethel dropped her gaze and turned to go out of the room, walking slowly, head down.

At the door she looked back and, putting what strength she could into her voice, said, 'I will always love you, Lisl. More than anyone else in the world. Please do not ever forget that.'

She passed along the corridor and across the hall to the front door, which Hans opened and then closed behind her without looking at her or offering any farewell.

13

FRIMLEY 1884

Ethel rushed into the hall when the post came. Just as on the last hundred days, she waited like a child until her father received it, looked at each envelope and dispensed it. She ran up the stairs to her room, looking at the envelopes – as always, there were letters from her friends or sisters. Sometimes, though not today, there might be a letter in the tiny, precise hand of Harry, which she threw unread into the waste-bin. There was never the pale grey envelope she longed to see, sporting a Berlin postmark.

She could no longer hold on to the hope that had sustained her throughout the summer. Lisl remained silent. Ethel's eyes were sore with the pain of hope once more dashed. How long would it take, she wondered hundreds of times a day, for Lisl to come round? She had surely had time to settle in Berlin now and get her new apartment furnished to her satisfaction. She must have begun to miss her. Lisl must know, because Ethel had written to her every single week and told her, that she was not in touch with Harry anymore, as she had promised, and did not intend to be.

Lisl was punishing her for her deceit, that was all, just making her wait a little longer. Previously, when they had been cool with each other and not written or spoken for a while, it had blown over eventually. She must just wait.

~

Ethel had written to tell Thekla that she would be returning to Leipzig after all, since it seemed unlikely that she would be going to Berlin just yet. Here was her reply at last:

> *I've talked with George and some of your friends, Ethel, and we're thinking it would be unwise for you to come back right now. It will remind people that there's a rift between you and the von Herzogenbergs, since you haven't gone to Berlin with them, which might give rise to those silly rumours again. Also, their departure has left a terrible musical gap in the city. That gap will close in time, but it will be harder for you to meet the people you need to meet here just now. Why not stay away, just for this year, since neither George nor I will be here to help you? If this is where you come next autumn, everything will be forgotten, a new normality will exist and everyone will be so delighted to see you again.*

Ethel sat in her room, angry, bereft. The door to Europe had slammed shut, preventing her from the excitement of that boat, that train journey which she had taken so many times. She wasn't welcome in Berlin. She couldn't go to Florence where the Hildebrands knew – had perhaps spread – the gossip about herself and Harry. And anyway, she mustn't be anywhere near him if she hoped to earn Lisl's forgiveness. And now Leipzig, dear bustling city with its churches and markets and traders, and its continuous, rich musical life, was closed to her too.

As the room darkened and she lit the lamps, she declared the summer at an end. Despite her sadness, she had enjoyed its activities, the big weekend parties at her sisters' homes, the Cornwall holiday with Violet and her new husband, the rounds of socialising and the limited after-dinner music, the quieter times at home with the horses and the dogs, and her parents with all their grumbles and ailments. Throughout it all had run the thread of hope of a life in Berlin, or the comfort of Leipzig if that failed. She must stamp on that now. She must look to see what England could offer.

~

Ethel wrote to everyone she knew who was a recognised musician: Hubert Parry, George Stainer, Arthur Sullivan, Peter Barnsdale, Walter Parratt. Several of these had studied at Leipzig themselves in the past. She included pieces of her music and asked for their comments, and any help they could give with getting it performed. She wrote to family friends, people who had helped her years ago when embarking on her music career, and solicited their help again. There were a couple of meetings, some useful comments, tickets to concerts, but there was no opening into anything that might be called a musical circle that encouraged young composers. There was no-one like Lisl von Herzogenberg, it seemed, who could introduce her, vouch for her musicianship, create opportunities; no offers from anyone like Heinrich to mentor her, teach her, take her under their wing; not a family like the Röntgens to invite her to play.

~

At Alice's lunch, Ethel was surrounded by church high-ups. She had become more used to it since her sister had married her ambitious bishop. They were much the same as the military top brass, she thought, obsessed with social status and talking their own arcane language. She did not try to make any impression.

She did not think that any of these people could help her, and she sat at Alice's side joining in the chit-chat around her.

'Who is that?' she whispered to Alice, indicating a woman sitting opposite, who was keeping up a fascinating, critical commentary on church matters. Ethel couldn't stop watching her animated face and hands as she talked.

'Mrs Benson, the archbishop's wife.'

'I thought you said he wasn't coming?'

'He's not, but she came anyway. Mrs Benson!' Alice called to the woman across the table. 'Have you met my sister, Ethel?'

'I thought that might be you,' she said. 'I'm so happy to meet you. Alice has told me about you, and I want to hear all about your fantastic adventures abroad.'

Ethel found herself drawn into answering questions about Germany. Mrs Benson knew everyone, it seemed, or about everyone, even some of Ethel's friends in Leipzig, though she confessed she had little knowledge of music. Ethel found herself recalling incidents of her time there that she had almost forgotten, amusing the dinner guests with anecdotes about Brahms and Grieg, the quirks of their personalities and stories of German life in general.

When the conversation moved on, Ethel found herself upset and sad. To hide it, she ate more of the ice-cream concoction in the middle of the table and allowed the talk to go by her. She didn't want to be remembering Germany as if it was an exciting part of her past, especially not to amuse people at the dinner table.

'Miss Smyth,' said Mrs Benson from across the table. 'I have to go in a few minutes as I have a committee later this afternoon to attend. Can I give you a lift somewhere in my carriage?'

'That would be lovely, thank you. I'm going to head back to Frimley. Mother wasn't well enough to come today, so I should get back to her. Is that all right with you, Alice?'

'What a lovely lunch,' said Mrs Benson, standing up. 'I do apologise that I have to leave for my meeting. I'll drop Miss Smyth off at the station. We'll see you all again soon.'

Alice signalled to the servant to have Mrs Benson's carriage brought round, and walked with them to the door.

'Tell Mother I'll come down at the weekend,' she said to Ethel.

Ethel bent to kiss her. 'That would be good,' she said. 'You know how irritated I get with her when she's ill.'

Then she was out in the fresh air, being helped into Mrs Benson's capacious carriage. They smiled at each other.

'Now then, my dear,' said Mrs Benson, settling back, 'when you're next in London I want you to come and see me. My daughters will love you, I know that. Ellie has your spirit of adventure.'

'My life is very dull at the moment,' said Ethel. 'I can't seem to make any progress with my music.'

'I'm not sure I can help with that. Forgive me if I'm being impertinent, but obviously you spent some good years in Leipzig, all the people you met. Why didn't you go back?'

'I didn't mention Heinrich and Lisl von Herzogenberg much,' said Ethel after a moment. 'They were the centre of the musical life there. He taught me nearly everything I know about composition, and Lisl and I were the closest of friends.' Ethel had intended merely to say that things had gone a bit wrong, and anyway, they had moved to Berlin, but instead she found her eyes full of tears. It was impossible to say more.

She found herself being held closely by Mrs Benson, who had come to sit by her.

'You poor thing,' she said, gently taking Ethel's hat off and stroking her hair. 'I knew there was some sadness there. Tell me about it.'

Ethel found herself telling Mrs Benson about how much she loved Lisl, about the attraction between herself and Harry Brewster, the strangeness of his marriage to Julia, and how their mother had dismissed her. Once started, she seemed unable to stop. Lisl's silence, unbroken over six months, her own refusal to be in touch with Harry, her hope that even now she and Lisl would be reconciled – the whole story was told as they rumbled along the London streets. Mrs Benson hugged her and murmured comfort and understanding.

'You can rely on my discretion, Ethel. Things have stalled for you at the moment, but that doesn't mean they have to stay stalled. You will find another path for yourself, I'm sure. It's not easy to leave such pain behind.'

'I would cope a lot better if I could get a musical opening.' She coughed as if choking.

'You will, my dear. Don't let these events put you off. We have to live in this world of right and wrong, and yet our feelings don't always fit into those restrictions.'

Ethel grasped Mrs Benson's hand gratefully. She had not heard that said before.

At the station, the carriage came to a stop.

'Thank you so much,' said Ethel as the driver opened the door. 'I've talked too much, I'm afraid.'

'Talking is what helps,' she said. 'You're not alone. Do let me know when you're next in London, and we can talk some more.'

~

Ethel forced herself into the discipline of writing music. She tried to lay the persistent ache aside by focussing on the sonata for violin and piano that she had started in Italy, when she was so happy and confident. It was hard. After a few bars, inspiration fell away. She shouted and slammed her hand on the table in frustration. Just when she most needed the joy of creativity, the total absorption of composition, the affirmation of note following on after note with their funny symbolic tails and sharp or flat signifiers, the hope that one day skilled musicians might perform it – there was nothing. There was just the hollow, sickly feeling in her stomach, a turmoil of grief and anger, a fear of what was to come next. Yet, if she was to return to Leipzig, she must have something new to offer.

Ethel thought of Lisl, who was enjoying a new life in a great city, while she sat here in her parents' home, no longer a young woman, with no prospects. Lisl was creating, or was already part of, a world where musicians met and talked and performed, whilst she was here in Frimley, on the edge of nowhere. She pushed her music aside, and stretched for a piece of paper and pen to write to her; surely if she expressed just a little better, a little more strongly, her grief and loneliness and longing… But she had done that already, so many times. Lisl did not care.

She must stop this now. She must not let what had happened prevent her from writing. She tried to focus on her work, screwing up her face to keep those thoughts at bay, ignoring the voices that said that the music inside her had died the minute Lisl rejected her. Before, there had been promise; now she must work to turn that into success, even without her help.

When it all got too much, she wrote to Mrs Benson to ask if she could come and see her. She would pour out to her the plight she was in and take some comfort from being held in those arms, even if they were not the arms of Lisl.

14

LEIPZIG 1885

Ethel's heels clicked on the stony streets of Leipzig. She could have shouted her happiness. The year of exile was over. The city was so gloriously familiar to her. The sounds and smells of the market proclaimed that it was Tuesday long before she had finished walking up the Katherinstrasse. She looked up, admiring all over again the ornate merchants' houses that lined the street, and paused briefly at No 11 to see if she might spot Frau Frege at a window. It was too early, and anyway, Ethel did not want to surprise her, nor risk seeing a hesitancy in her face as she wondered whether to greet her or not.

She shrugged off the worry. Thekla had assured her that any shadows on her reputation had passed, and she would be made welcome. She must hope to be as dear to the old lady as ever, to sit with her in her box and exchange caustic comments about the musicians below. Ah yes, here was the town hall, with its proud clock tower presiding over the cows and pigs being auctioned on the market square below, over the stalls with their vegetables and trussed chickens and exotic spices, fresh bread and cakes. She breathed in a sound and smell so special, so essentially Leipzig, and felt the happiness of coming home.

At the end of the market, she stopped. Left or right? The churches on either side pulled at her. She was meeting Thekla in The Coffee Tree in ten minutes, so there was hardly time for both. She must check that all was as usual at the Thomaskirche. There were ladders and crazy, dangerous arrangements of steps and platforms both inside and out, as stonemasons, builders and carpenters continued the never-ending work. She wasn't allowed in but was reassured by a notice on the door that Bach cantatas would be sung as usual on Friday.

A couple of minutes later she was hugging Thekla tight.

'Look who's here too,' said Thekla.

'Gustchen,' said Ethel, when she could breathe, 'it's been so long. What are you doing here?'

'I'm staying for a few days with Thekla and her mother,' she said. 'We've been practising some songs already for you to hear.'

'Yes, and we're hoping you've brought something new with you,' broke in Thekla. 'We're not tired of the old favourites, of course, but we do crave some different songs.'

'I thought you'd given up singing,' said Ethel to Gustchen.

'In the concert hall, of course. But my mother is looking after the babies for a few days, so my husband said I could come to Leipzig to see Thekla. My voice shrieks like a rusty hinge.'

'That rust is dissolving fast.' Thekla laughed. 'We knew you'd be tired today, Ethel, so we'll just have a little rehearsal later, ready for tomorrow.'

'Tomorrow?'

'Yes, our welcome-back-Ethel party.'

'Party?'

'Yes, for you, and all of us who haven't been in Leipzig for a while. Someone else will be there too.'

For a brief moment, Ethel thought she might mean Lisl. 'Who?'

'George Henschel. And his new wife, Lilian.'

'Oh my goodness. I thought he was staying in America.'

'Who can resist the concert halls of Europe?' said Gustchen, pausing whilst the waiter put bowls of steaming coffee on the table. Ethel leant back, looking at the portraits of Schumann and Mendelssohn on the walls, allowing herself to be enveloped in the rich aroma.

'We've found you a place to live,' Thekla said. 'If you like it, you can move in whenever you want, though Mother will be very upset if you don't stay for a day or two with us first.'

'What a lovely friend you are,' said Ethel. 'Where is it?'

'Not far from the centre of the city.'

'In the new streets?'

'Yes. It's small, but nice. If you still insist on walking home alone late at night, you will feel perfectly safe.'

'Thank you so much. This is entirely unexpected.'

Thekla stretched out her hand to her. 'It's going to be fine. Plenty of people are glad you've come back. You'll see.'

~

The new Gewandhaus was less familiar, and yet somehow not strange at all. There was Papa Röntgen at the leader's desk, waving cheerfully at her as she leant precariously out of Frau Frege's box – a beautiful box, of course, and more spacious, but not quite so well-positioned as in the old concert hall.

'It's a wonderful space, isn't it?' she said to Thekla, waving her arms to indicate the size and splendour of the new hall.

'I miss the quirkiness of the old one,' said Thekla. 'The sound isn't as perfect here.'

'Have you sung here yet?'

'In the spring, when we're touring, we're sure to come here.'

'I'm going to miss you so much,' said Ethel. 'Everyone is going away now the season's starting again.'

Ethel turned to Frau Frege who from her stately chair was watching critically as the orchestra filed in, tutting at any untidiness or lack of order. 'Thank you,' she said, stretching out her hand to her. 'It's wonderful to be here again.'

'We're glad to have our little Engländerin back,' the old woman said, smiling. 'My box hasn't been the same without you. It was very quiet without your enthusiastic outbursts.'

'Oh dear, I'm sorry if I spoiled anything for you.'

'Not at all. It was a delight.'

~

Ethel crossed out, re-wrote and added new phrases, and the sonata for violin and piano began to take more of the shape intended. The finale, which she had failed so many times at Frimhurst to complete, sat more solidly on the page. She worked on through the day. Only when her eyes were sore and she needed to light the lamps did she remember that she had no invitation for dinner, and no Lisl to chat with or Heinrich to get advice from. Then she went out and walked, despite the darkness, across the fields and along the river nearby, or through the dark, dimly lit streets; walked and walked, until she turned back towards home and collapsed on her bed, exhausted.

~

The Röntgen house was full of babies and dogs.

'Where have all these come from?' said Ethel, trying to calm a complaining baby, while Frau Röntgen made some coffee.

'What, babies or dogs?'

'Both, maybe.'

'These are Johanna's twins. She's not well today, so I'm looking after them. And Grete has decided that since all her brothers and sisters have left home, she'll fill the house with stray dogs. Of course, when she's at the conservatoire, it's me who has to see to them. Papa was unimpressed when this massive creature appeared the other day.'

'Oh, he's lovely,' said Ethel, stroking the nose of a dog that was threatening to push her off her feet. 'Perhaps I could help by taking him for a walk?'

'That would be wonderful. The garden really isn't big enough for him. In fact, you can borrow him if you want.'

'What, you mean I can take him home? What is he?'

'We don't know. A bit of Saint Bernard, I think, with a lot of other big dog things as well. You don't need to say now – he'll need a lot of care.'

Ethel stroked the dog's huge head. 'He's beautiful,' she said.

'He needs an awful lot of exercise.'

'That's no problem. Oh, look at him. I love him already.'

'See how you get on. If all goes well, and your landlady's happy, you can have him. We've been calling him Marco. You can let me know when you come on Saturday. And don't forget your music. We're all dying to see what you've written now.'

~

Lunch finished, Ethel took out of her bag her new sonata. The whole family clapped, and went through to the music room.

'If Ethel agrees, I shall play the piano,' said Frau Röntgen, looking at the score. 'You must fight between you for the violin part.'

'I'm going to play it,' said Peter.

'No, you're not,' said Johanna, coming in after making sure the babies were settled. 'I'm by far the better violinist, aren't I, Papa?'

'No fighting. We don't often have the honour of a completely new work. Let's see – you can start us off, Johanna, and you can take on the Scherzo and Romanze, Peter. If Fraülein Ethel is happy, I would very much like to play the final movement myself.'

Ethel was dizzy with delight, as well as nerves, grinning at how Peter and Johanna jostled for position just as they had when they were much younger. The room resounded with the movement of music stands, the tuning of the violins against the piano, and the scraping of the chairs for the tiny audience. Finally, everything was ready.

It didn't matter that none of them had seen the sonata before. They could all read the music on sight just as easily as if it were a novel. Ethel's anxiety began to settle. She listened and took copious notes.

There was a slight pause after each movement as the violin part changed hands, but no-one spoke until the last note was played and its sound had died quite away. Then there was clapping, and loud cries of, 'Well done, Ethel,' and big smiles on everyone's faces.

'As usual,' said Papa Röntgen, 'you have given us a real treat, something both unique and recognisable.'

Peter continued to pick out small sections to play, saying things like, 'This is good, Papa, isn't it? That bit went so well with the piano.'

'I enjoyed playing it, my dear,' said Frau Röntgen. 'Excellent. It's so good to have you back, and for you to bring us some new music.'

'Thank you so much for playing it,' said Ethel. 'You are always very generous with your comments. I've noticed several different problems as you played, and I would welcome your criticisms.'

Such invitations, as she had found more than once in the past, could be dangerous. It was much safer to pick up the score and go home, happy that her music had sounded much as she had intended. By inviting comment, she knew that they would delve into the heart of the piece, analyse its structure and inner workings, argue about it, and emerge with a host of technical and artistic suggestions. At first she had got angry, defended her work, hurried home cross and sore. Then she had come to trust them; they knew about music, all of them, loved to argue about it, and wished her well.

'What do you think, Papa,' said Frau Röntgen at the tea table, cutting huge slices of apple cake for everyone, 'about suggesting

Ethel's sonata for the next programme at the Kammersaal? After all, it was built with the idea of encouraging and developing composers and performers, though there's been precious little sign of that so far.'

'Good idea,' said Papa Röntgen. 'Would you like that, my dear? What is it – two or three years since your Quintet?'

Ethel flushed. She put her hand down and ruffled Marco's ears. He was coming home with her. 'I'd be honoured,' she said. 'If you think it will be good enough.'

~

Ethel huddled into her wool scarf and pulled her hat closer around her ears. There had been no snow, perhaps it was too cold for that, but the pavements were slippery with unseen ice. The merchants were doing business as usual, of course, and everywhere the breath of horses sent clouds of vapour into the air. The tradesmen, wrapped in their biggest coats and muffled up with scarves, loaded or unloaded the heavy rolls of cloth through the open doors of the houses, their shouts loud in the clear air. None of this was of the slightest concern to Marco, who trotted by Ethel's side, picking his way through the debris of the streets. He loved the cold, as if some dog memory of frozen mountain trails woke in him.

She was making her way to Herr Brodsky's rehearsal room. Papa Röntgen had been as good as his word and her Violin Sonata was listed in the winter chamber music programme. Herr Brodsky was going to play the violin part and had called for the score.

Only when they got to the market where the usual stalls were punctuated by great braziers of fire did Marco show any excitement. The air was full of smoke, undispersed on this still day, and the smell of seared meat and roasting sausage. He barked briefly and looked at Ethel. She added a fat, hot sausage to the bags of bones she had learnt to get whenever she passed through the market. Keeping this dog fed was neither cheap nor easy.

'Here you go, old boy,' said the butcher, throwing him some pieces of discarded fat.

Herr Brodsky was, it seemed, hard at work when she arrived at the address given. From the pavement, she could hear the piano stopping and starting, a violin joining in and, in the pauses, voices debating.

'Marco, my darling,' Ethel said, tying the dog's lead to the scraper by the front door, 'I can't take you in there. Now you lie here until I come back. I won't be long.'

As always, he looked at her as if he understood, and settled down to enjoy the bone she gave him.

As she entered the room, Ethel felt her face go red with surprise and heat coursed through her body. Johannes Brahms was coming to greet her. She had not seen him since the break with Lisl.

'Well, here's our little English composer,' he said coolly, aloof as ever, making the slightest bow over her hand. 'Welcome, Fraülein Ethel. Here, let me introduce you to Adolph Brodsky, who has not had the pleasure of your company before.'

'I've brought you my score,' she said, as soon as introductions were done, fumbling with the clasp on her bag and hoping to make a quick escape. 'I'm so glad you are going to be playing it.'

'Thank you,' said Herr Brodsky. 'I shall be in touch just as soon as I have had a chance to play it through.'

'We're just running through some bits of my quintet before it is performed this evening,' said Herr Brahms. 'Come and give me a hand.'

'Of course,' said Ethel, still trying to recover herself. 'What can I do?' At least he had not snubbed her.

The stop-start of the rehearsal resumed. Often at Lisl's, she had sat and turned the pages whilst he played the piano, but today it seemed particularly sweet to be asked. She was even included in one or two of the discussions about tempo or how softly the violin could risk being played if it were still to be heard.

Just as they were starting the final section, there was a banging on the stairs, and Ethel could hear Marco barking. Before she could get up, the door burst open and the dog sprang into the room. Panicked, impervious to any obstacle, he jumped over the players to where Ethel sat, knocking over a couple of music stands with his trailing leg and coming to a slithering halt on the polished floor.

'Oh my goodness. Marco, whatever is the matter?' said Ethel, bending down to quieten the dog who stopped barking now he had found her.

'Very droll,' said Herr Brahms, going over to help Brodsky, who was too scared to move, holding his threatened violin in the air. 'I presume this creature is a new acquisition of yours, Fraülein?'

'I do beg your pardon,' she said. 'I left him tied up at the front door. He obviously wasn't happy.'

Herr Brodsky, recovering from his shock, started to laugh, running his bow up and down the strings. 'Leaping dog,' he said. 'There's a challenge for you, Johannes. Try and write that into your next concerto. What a magnificent beast.'

Herr Brahms gave a laugh that was not unlike a bark.

'You have always had the capacity to surprise, Fraülein,' he said drily.

'We should probably go,' she said. She didn't know Marco well enough yet to guarantee his behaviour in a small room full of precious instruments.

'I'm glad we've met,' said Herr Brodsky. 'I shall be seeing Miss Davies later this month, and we will get together in the days before the performance.'

'Shall you be at the Gewandhaus tonight?' asked Herr Brahms, holding the door for her.

'Of course,' said Ethel.

'Without the dog, I trust,' he said, leaning over her hand.

Ethel did not answer. Marco had already been to several concerts with her and lain peacefully at her feet. Tonight, though, she might ask her landlady to look after him.

~

On the day of the performance Ethel woke early, very early. She had met with Fanny Davies and Adolph Brodsky a couple of times, and been delighted to hear them treat her music seriously. The fact that they made such a great partnership, however, made her even more nervous. Her mistakes would not be hidden behind a fumbled violin part or a poorly executed passage on the piano. They would play her sonata well, and the music must stand or fall on its own terms.

Moreover, there were several musicians in town just now, spending a few weeks in Leipzig on their way to Milan or Rome. Ethel was especially happy that Herr and Frau Grieg were here. They were such big favourites with the audience. He charmed them with his cold, northern songs, pared down to the bone, which his wife would sing with intense emotion. Ethel often went to their hotel, where she and Herr Grieg vigorously defended their different musical methods.

Ethel had invited Pyotr Tchaikovsky the moment she heard he had arrived. He was here to conduct one of his enormous dramatic symphonies. How she hoped he would remember her from Florence and come to her performance. Perhaps he would meet with her in the days afterwards to give her his comments.

Thekla had rushed in by train from Munich just for the evening and she sat with Ethel in the raised seating at the side of the hall, with all the Röntgens sitting behind. Ethel was too restless to concentrate on the other music in the programme, and was trembling all over by the time Fanny Davies and Adolph Brodsky took the stage. She stretched for Thekla's hand to calm herself. They looked so handsome: he in his formal suit, the black hair falling into his eyes as he tuned his violin; she at the piano in her long, flowing silver gown with a green bodice which matched the ribbon tying back her fair hair. The hall went quiet, and they began.

How amazing it was to travel with the musicians, so assured, efficient, inspired, through the journey of her music, along with the people in the hall. At each pause between the movements, the audience coughed and shuffled as they always did, and Ethel could tell that they were enjoying it, were happy to settle back into their seats for the next part. The players were perfect, but the music was less so. That bit was insipid, and, oh dear, wasn't that passage almost a carbon copy of a Brahms trio, when she had thought it sounded Italian? The scherzo was not as animated as she had intended, and the dramatic finale, which she had found so powerful in the rehearsal room, had far less impact in the hall. It was cold on this January evening, and yet sweat was pouring down her back.

Perhaps the audience did not share her view, for their applause was long and appreciative. After Miss Davies and Herr Brodsky had taken their bow, they turned towards her and clapped her. When she stood up to acknowledge them, there were calls for her to go up onto the stage. The applause and cheers terrified her.

Afterwards, Ethel was feted with all the others who had figured in the programme at a supper at the Hotel de Bavière. It was different, so very different, from the sumptuous parties hosted by Lisl and Heinrich, but nevertheless the musical conversation was pithy and constructive. There was a great deal of fun after Grete brought Marco in.

'Congratulations, dear Fraülein,' said Herr Tchaikovsky, leaning over her hand whilst trying to keep his distance from the dog. 'Your music is interesting, but there is more you could do. Come and see me tomorrow.'

As she walked the few streets to her rooms, Marco at her side, Ethel felt both exhausted and elated. Perhaps she could, despite the massive gap where Heinrich and Lisl had been, make Leipzig her home.

15

FRIMLEY, SURREY 1887

Ethel smoothed the paper out on the desk and bent to sniff its specific smell, its call to write music. She flicked through one or two of the books on the pile to her side. They were new books, some with exercises to highlight different aspects of orchestration, some full of theory and examples. For days, they had been shining like a beacon on her desk. The sort of beacon, Ethel would think as she passed by on the way to carry out another task for her sick mother, that was a herald of good things, that signalled a box of delights, a welcome rather than a warning.

She breathed in the rare quiet of the house. Mother had been encouraged to feel well enough at last to go to a friend's house for tea. Father was busy being a magistrate, and Marco lay fed and exercised at her feet. She had a little time to consider the challenge that Pyotr Tchaikovsky had thrown down so casually. 'You want to be dramatic in your work, orchestrate it.'

Up to now, she had only thought of composing music for small groups of instruments. It was hard enough, making those few parts hang together. Now he was suggesting that she do it with fifteen or twenty lines, for all the instruments of the orchestra, which had to contrast and support each other, work with and against. It challenged her even to think about it, but today she was going to start.

In her last weeks in Leipzig, as Ethel now thought of them, before the telegram had called her home to nurse Mother, she had got to know Pyotr quite well. He liked to tease her about her admiration for Johannes Brahms, whom he called stodgy and conservative. He would sit at the piano in her lodgings picking out phrases of his rival's work that were particularly banal. She was alternatively indignant and deeply amused.

'I suppose you never write anything mundane,' she said. In fact, she was so struck by the 'other-worldly Russian-ness', as she called it, and sheer power of his music, that she thought he probably did not.

'Let's just say I'm not so stuffy about it.'

Ethel felt a thrill run through her. Johannes Brahms was a musical colossus, but even so, it was delicious to poke fun at his arrogant, condescending attitude.

'Let's forget His Lordship JB for a moment,' she said. 'I want to ask you more about this orchestration idea.'

'Like?'

'Like everything! Like some basic principles, or just how to go about it.'

'Pfff, basic principles. Any old book will tell you those.' He continued to strum on the piano.

He could be very annoying, Ethel thought. How could she shake some of that gold dust out of him to transform her own music? She waited, hoping he would say something interesting.

'What instrument is your ghastly dog?' he said at last, trying to stop Marco from pushing at his legs under the piano.

Ethel let out a blast of laughter. 'Come here, Marco,' she called. 'A euphonium, perhaps? When he growls? All that low rumbling.'

'Exactly,' said Pyotr, smiling. 'And what am I?'

Ethel played with ideas in her mind. Not smooth or solid enough for a cello, she thought, too quicksilver for a double bass, too brooding for a bassoon.

'A French horn, maybe?' she said tentatively. 'Or an oboe.' That had a slight edginess to it that suited him. She laughed in the hope he would not think she was insulting him.

'That's more like it, Madame Trumpet. Think of orchestration like a group of friends in the room. They all have something to say, but each voice is a little different. They have their own timbre and style. Even in a loud room, you can recognise each one.'

'Right!' said Ethel. 'So it's not just a whole lot of instruments making a louder or gentler or wilder sound.'

'It can be, but go on.'

'Each is not only contributing its own voice, but its mood, which might be quiet, or animated or dominating or scarcely heard.'

'Very good,' he said condescendingly.

'How do you do that?' she said. 'Make something I've been puzzling about for ages so simple?'

He laughed. 'You're too attached to your German friends. They don't like things too simple. Listen out for it at concerts. Then you'll also see that various combinations can make a sound different from what you would expect.'

Ethel had started to go to every possible concert where a full orchestra was playing, be it opera, symphony, light music or song. She began to listen in a different way, hearing for the first time the colour, variation, subtlety and nuance of the instruments.

That was before she was called back to Frimhurst.

How Ethel wished Pyotr was sitting with her now, across the table from her in her room. She could do with a dose of his world-weariness, that touch of cynicism which masked his genius, that playfulness. What an exotic figure he would cut in the conventional Frimhurst day. Her father would hate his flowing hair and extravagant moods.

Such thoughts were a distraction. It was just her and her desk. She dipped her pen into the inkwell and began to draw on the music lines the various symbols that helped structure what she would write. She worked her way steadily through the exercises in the new books. There was nothing difficult about them; it was just a matter of doing more and more to bring all the concepts and tricks alive in her mind. Yes, yes, yes. That was clever. A few more days of this and she would be ready to apply it to her own music.

When the dinner bell rang, she ignored it. The set routine of the house threatened to destroy her concentration. Hours like this were rare. And yet Mother would be waiting to tell her about her afternoon, petulant if it had not gone well, and Father expected her to be there. Soon she would go down, soon. Marco, who had looked up hopefully at the sound of the bell, had a good shake, grumbled and lay down again on her feet.

~

Ethel turned out of the station towards Rustington. The sun was warm on her shoulders, and she breathed deeply of the perfume of the flowers on the verge as she walked along the lane. Marco hunted invisible prey in the nearby fields, returning every few minutes to her side.

She was looking forward to seeing Maeve Parry again, who she had got to know at a couple of tennis parties, and probably Agnes Garrett would be there too. She did hope they would not talk all the time about women having the vote, or rather not having the vote, as they usually did, or go on at length about what meeting, petition or lobbying they were involved with right now. Ethel could not raise a flicker of interest in this. How could women having a vote to elect those in parliament affect anything?

It was irrelevant to her struggle to be recognised, despite them trying to explain that it was not.

The invitation was enticing, however, because Maeve had said that Hubert would be there. So far, contact with him had led to very little, but now it looked like she was going to be in England for a while, she must press for more. He was becoming the most influential person in the country as far as music went – popular as a composer, and professor at the Royal College of Music. So far, when she had come across him, they had shared a few memories of the Leipzig conservatoire, where he had studied long before her, and that was about all.

She raised the enormous knocker on the door.

'Come in, come in,' said Maeve, answering the door herself and showing Ethel into the drawing room. Ethel kissed Agnes, whilst Maeve rang the bell. 'I'll have some tea brought in straight away. Will your dog be happy to go in the scullery? Agnes and I are just talking about Mrs Fawcett's meeting in London. I was wondering if you would come with us, but Agnes said you're bound to be back in Leipzig by then.'

'Thank you,' said Ethel, sitting on the sofa, smiling. She looked around the beautiful room, which she knew that Agnes had designed with her cousin Rhoda. It was light, bold, delightful – a long way from the airless rooms of Frimhurst or the many drawing rooms in which she normally took tea, with their over-stuffed chairs and heavy curtains. 'I won't, but thanks for the invitation.'

'What do you mean? You won't come, or you won't be in Leipzig?' said Agnes.

'Both. I've had some lovely years there, and successful ones. I'd come to think of it as my home, but it's not the same now Lisl has left. I'm not sure it's the best place to get on musically now. I have to try to put all that behind me, if I can.'

Ethel knew she was far from doing that.

'I understand how much you might miss her,' said Agnes. 'I've struggled a lot since Rhoda died. And I'm only just starting to get the business going again. It will be very different without her skills.'

'You must miss her terribly. Mother's not well either. She's got a morbid fear that as soon as Bob is posted to India in a few weeks' time, that'll be the last she sees of him. I can't leave her just now.'

'Does she have anyone left at home now? Your little sisters aren't little anymore, I'm sure?'

'No, even Nell got married this year.' Ethel caught herself sighing deeply. 'Another military marriage.'

'We're going to have a lovely couple of days,' said Maeve. 'Hubert said he would happily spend an hour with you talking music before dinner, and then tomorrow we're going to go for a long walk by the sea. Does that sound good?'

'Marco will certainly love that too,' said Ethel.

The maid brought in tea.

'I do hope you like chocolate cake,' said Maeve.

'Obviously you always think about composers,' said Hubert, when they sat down in his study, a room full of light and space, 'because they are the people who have taught you so much over the years. But surely it was not so different in Germany – in most instances, it's not composers who decide what is played at concerts. They sit and wait just as you are doing now.'

'So, who is it that decides?'

'Overall, it is controlled by those putting on the concerts. The concert halls have committees, who have a say in it. But the power really lies with the conductors.'

'Maeve and Agnes are always talking about where the power lies,' said Ethel.

'Aren't they just?' Hubert smiled. 'It sometimes helps to know. These people do tend to be quite conservative, I'm afraid.'

'You mean the idea of a woman composer is anathema?'

'Well, let's just say they've never considered it. You have

to remember too that the idea of English music is still quite a progressive one. What are you working on just now?'

Ethel pulled a few pieces of paper out of her bag. 'This is my *Serenade*. I'm having a first go at orchestration.'

Hubert stroked his luxurious moustache as he looked over the pages. 'That's interesting,' he said. 'Has someone taught you this?'

'I got to know Herr Tchaikovsky a bit in Leipzig last year. He inspired me to have a go.'

'I envy you. How I would love to meet that man.'

Hubert moved over to the piano. Ethel couldn't help but notice his fine, long fingers as he played a few lines from her score.

'That's very good. Honestly, I'm not sure I can add much to this. Well done. It's very ambitious. So, let's think where you could send your work. Being performed twice at the Gewandhaus will mean something.'

He began writing names and addresses on a piece of paper, occasionally getting up to check something. 'I've put a star by the ones I think most likely,' he said. 'You can mention to them that I recommended you write.'

~

Ethel worked on the list all week. Every day, if her mother was not too poorly to be left alone, if the house seemed to be running smoothly, if there were no invitations she must accept, she sat at her desk. She sighed with the tedium of it. Please, please, please, it seemed as if she was saying, help me, please help me. Every time she wrote to one of the people on Hubert's list, she must find the most persuasive words. She had to make a new copy of what she was going to send, a movement of the violin sonata, perhaps, or a couple of pages of her *Serenade*.

Replies trickled in. She would stand in the hallway, tapping the envelope with her finger, working up the courage to ease off the seal. What might be the reason to reject her today? No concert was planned that such a piece might fit into, programmes were already full for the foreseeable future, not taking any work unless specifically commissioned, audience not receptive to work by unknown composers…

Ethel crossed the names off on her list, noting briefly if it seemed worth following up in the future. She threw most of the letters into the bin – sometimes they were torn into shreds or screwed into the tightest of balls. Often she shouted. There was nothing useful in them. If the copy of her music was returned – and even that seemed very hit and miss – she would scour it for any suggestions for improvement, any comment at all. There was nothing. Nothing to show whether her work had been read and properly considered. Nothing to help her.

England is a funny country, wrote Thekla, trying to comfort her. *It's hardly had any of its own composers for centuries and doesn't know how to nurture new talent. Your public would prefer to bring in stars from other countries than find some of their own to make shine. But don't give up, or lose heart. By the way, my American tour is nearly finished. I've enjoyed it so much, and guess what? I've met a rather lovely man. I think I'm going to stay on a bit longer.*

~

Ethel was shown to the seat on the right-hand side of Archbishop Benson. She did not want to be sitting so near to him at the dinner table. Thank goodness his lively, witty son Fred was at the other side of her; perhaps she could chat to him and ignore the archbishop. The rows of gleaming silver cutlery and crystal glasses, which were laid so precisely on the starched white tablecloth, separated her from where Ben sat at the other end. When Ethel caught her eye, she smiled and shrugged slightly as if to say that she didn't know what had happened, or how Ethel came to be sitting so far away from her, by her husband too, or how an informal lunch had turned into something so formal.

It was not what Ethel had hoped for when she had set off in the bright sun from Frimley that morning. She had expected a day with Ben; a day when she would be able to talk about everything that was troubling her – her music, her mother, the endless silence from Lisl – and be comforted by the warm attention of the older woman, her arms, her embraces.

She had hoped to hear more of Ben's own stories – stories of how she had loved women. Yes, it was extraordinary that this archbishop's wife had felt that same attraction that Ethel had felt for Lisl. She had even gone away from her husband with another woman for a while, before being drawn back for the sake of her marriage. That morning, Ethel had heard the word 'Sapphist' for the first time.

She wanted to think about that word. She wanted to talk to Ben about what exactly it meant. Was it true that it was not so unusual for women to love women, something she had never heard talk of before? Could it be that there were people that did not find that unnatural, or impossible, that there were places where they went?

Yet here she was, so far from Ben and as close as could be to the archbishop. Perhaps she might have just got up and left, if he had not made her feel like an awkward, tongue-tied fifteen-year-old. He was so large and commanding, so much in control of all before him, of the way the dinner was served, of the people who served it as well as of the people who ate it.

Ethel tried to take no notice of him and chatted to Fred at her side. She knew the archbishop did not like her either, found her loud and opinionated. In fact, Ben often joked that he made himself scarce the minute she arrived at the house.

She looked round the table to see who else was there. Lovely Ellie, Ben's adventurous daughter, was opposite. That was good, and that must be Hugh, home from school for the holidays and sitting by his mother. Peter Barnsdale sat by Ellie on the other side of the table, a musician and cleric in the house whom she had met once before. He had not answered her letters asking for help with her music. Presumably those other men in black gowns were some of the archbishop's many priests. Servant-priests, she thought, mustering up a hint of disdain to help her through. She bent forward to smell the soup served out to her from the vast silver bowl. Asparagus, creamy, with a generous speckling of parsley, cut no doubt from the large kitchen garden where she and Ben liked to sit, away from the busy house and formal gardens.

Just as she was lifting the spoon to her mouth, the archbishop leant towards her as if to speak. She gulped at her soup and felt a warm splash fall on her dress. It was a small drop, easily dabbed away, even with the stiff, white serviette. Fred, sitting next to her, noticed and started poking fun at the Prime Minister's speech that day in parliament, and soon everyone was chatting and laughing.

'How's the *Serenade* coming along, Ethel?' asked Fred as the soup dishes were being cleared.

'It's hard work,' she said. 'I'm trying to write the orchestral parts.'

'That's amazing,' said Ellie. 'You mean you actually write out a part for the violin and one for the flute?'

'Yes, I do, or try to. And all the other instruments,' said Ethel.

'When I wrote my latest concerto,' said Peter Barnsdale, 'that was one of the trickiest parts.'

Ethel did not respond. He had, after all, ignored her letters.

'I love your music, Miss Smyth,' said Fred. 'It's unbelievably dramatic. May I ask, if you are doing the serenading or being serenaded?'

Ethel laughed. 'It's there for whatever is required.'

'I can't describe it,' Fred continued. 'Whenever I hear you play, it really is such a wonderful experience.'

She took a few mouthfuls of the delicate, fragrant salmon that had now appeared on her plate.

'Would I like it, Mother?' asked Hugh.

'I'm sure you would, darling,' said Ben. 'Everyone loves Ethel's music.'

'You must play some of it for us afterwards,' Fred said.

'I doubt it,' said Ellie. 'Ethel is a proper composer, not just someone who writes a little something for your after-dinner entertainment.'

Ethel laughed. 'I'd be very happy to play something for you.'

'And what might a proper composer be?' said their father. 'Are you attached to any musical institution, Miss Smyth?'

Ethel felt her face flush. His tone was not playful like the others.

'Well, I was when I studied in Germany. I would very much like to meet someone here who could help me get my music performed, as it was in Leipzig.'

'Do we know any women composers?' he asked the table at large. 'Are there any?'

'That's not the point,' said Ellie. 'You're being very old-fashioned now. Powerful people like yourself should offer more support.'

'The academy sometimes turns out women who can write the odd song,' said Peter Barnsdale. 'But I do wonder what the point is in training them.'

'Why?' asked Hugh, trying to join in the adult conversation.

'Well, they write a few songs and a simple prelude or nocturne for the piano, which is just about all they can do, and then they go off and get married, and that's the end of it.'

'They can do a great deal more than that, if only people like you would listen,' said Ethel.

'It doesn't really matter in the end whether they can compose or not,' said the archbishop. 'Nothing must hinder the duty of the woman to create a home for her husband and children.'

'That's exactly what is so absurd,' said Ethel angrily. She felt her face flush. 'All these conventions about what a woman may or may not do. I want people to take an interest in my work and give me an opportunity the same as men have, not just wonder if a woman can, or should, compose.'

'Well said,' Ben chipped in. 'Just because women rarely have doesn't mean they can't. Look at our Maggie, she's showing them at Cambridge that a woman can be just a clever as a man, even if they won't reward her with a degree.'

'Women are doing all sorts of things they were never thought suited for,' said Ellie. 'And when we get the vote, you'll see how things change. You need to get ready for it, Father.'

The archbishop did not answer but signalled for the plates to be cleared.

'You must come to our next special dinner for artists, Ethel,' said Ben. 'And then we'll see if we can link you up with someone who can help.'

'Those dinners are expressly for successful writers and artists,' said the archbishop.

'Well, perhaps we should also try and help those who need a leg up from a successful person,' said Ben. 'I like that idea.'

'Music has a way of working in this country,' he said. 'I'm sure Miss Smyth's music will be recognised eventually, if it is deemed fit.'

'How music works in this country has to change,' said Ethel, restraining herself from calling him a pompous ignoramus. 'It can't just rely on people who go to Oxford and Cambridge, who all know each other and are looking to promote the next person who is just like them.'

'Can't it? It's done pretty well so far.' His voice was cold. 'English music has been in the doldrums for centuries.'

'Surely you can agree that there are more successful English composers now than for a long time?' said Mr Barnsdale. 'People like myself, if I might say so, who are getting a foot on the ladder.'

Ethel bit her lip. 'You are very fortunate if that is so,' she said at last. 'Fortunate in your friends, perhaps. I agree that English music is having a revival. But surely it should be seeking out new talent from wherever it might be found.'

'And is that going to be found in women? I can't see it myself.'

'Stop it, Father. You're being rude as well as horribly conventional,' said Ellie. 'You don't seem to mind us having a go at cricket, so why not at music? Women are not going to be excluded from everything in the future. You're playing with us next week, aren't you, Ethel?'

'I certainly am.' She could have gone round the table and kissed her for changing the subject. Cricket was a new passion. She could almost feel the solid weight of the bat in her hand, and the thrill of stretching out in the hope of hitting the ball hurtling through the air. 'Thank goodness I'm in your team. You're famous for your bowling now. I certainly wouldn't want to face it. Have you any idea how good she is, sir? At cricket, up to now a man's sport?'

It was a deliberate and satisfying taunt. He ignored her, and Ethel smiled broadly at Ellie across the table.

~

All right, thought Ethel, turning the letter over and over in her hands. One more rejection wasn't going to upset her. She was used to this now, after all. She paused, then broke the seal and in one movement pulled the letter out of the envelope:

I've heard about your work from George Henschel, and enjoyed looking at your violin piece. Unfortunately, I'm only performing works for full orchestra in my next series. Let me know if you have anything.

Ethel laughed out loud. August Manns. The only bit of proper encouragement in this country so far came from a German. True, he'd been in England forever. She'd been to his concerts at Crystal Palace on Sunday afternoons and found him a good conductor.

She paced up and down and around the hallway, holding the letter, re-reading it, hugging and kissing it, giving a little whoop now and then. Marco came running in and started barking and jumping up.

'Look, Marco,' said Ethel, 'somebody likes my music. I'd bark myself if I could.'

She gave the dog a hug and, in trying to prevent him from eating the letter, fell over on top of him.

'Stop licking me,' she said, trying to stand up. 'You're a horrible mucky dog. Off you go. I'll take you for a walk soon.'

Back in her room, Ethel took a piece of paper from the bottom of her writing desk. She would let Herr Manns know immediately that she would send him an example of her part-orchestrated work in the next few days. It crossed her mind for a moment to wonder whether the letter might be a rejection, couched in the most encouraging terms. Even if it was, he should know that she had other types of work in the pipeline.

The letter written and put on the tray in the hall for posting, Ethel allowed herself to think of the task ahead. Her *Serenade* was half-finished, and *Antony and Cleopatra* only just started. She had no way of knowing how her attempts at orchestration sounded. She had not learned yet to think into the different natures of the many instruments, did not understand all the various blends and combinations, was unable to hold all the sounds in her mind.

She was far from being concert-ready. Very far. She did not know where she would find the help she needed.

16

MUNICH 1888

Ethel wondered if a person could reach musical saturation point.
It was such a wonderful time to be here. Every day there were
several performances of operas, of other music too. The musicians
of Europe were there – those that didn't utterly despise the music
of Wagner anyway – as were thousands of music lovers. Every
day Ethel came across some acquaintance with whom she could
discuss the music and the performers. If her hosts Conrad and
Magdi got sick of a continuous diet of music, she always had an
invitation to sit in some other box at the opera house or go to a
concert at another venue.

However, Ethel was going to have to wait for Hermann Levi
to help with her work.

Yes, do come, he had written, responding to her plea for help.
*I've been following your progress ever since my Leipzig days. We'll
have several orchestras here for the Wagner weeks, so if you send
me your Serenade, there will definitely be the opportunity to run
through it.*

When she wrote to say that she was here, and sent her
manuscript, his reply was perfunctory: *We're not as far forward as*

I'd hoped. Too much still to prepare for Festival. Hope we'll get the chance later. Be in touch. Here are some concert tickets.

'Oh no,' said Ethel. 'This is terrible.'

She was in Magdi's sitting room. They had been writing letters and chatting about their mutual acquaintances in Leipzig, where their lives had overlapped briefly. Now she paced the floor, his note in her hand. 'Just my luck that the one person who can help me with my music is so tied up in the Festival.'

'I know patience isn't your strong point, my dear,' said Magdi. 'But that's what's required here. It can't be such a terrible wait when there is so much wonderful music to hear.'

'I haven't got time,' said Ethel, stamping her foot. 'Herr Manns wants my music before Christmas if it is to be in his spring programme. I was so happy that Herr Levi agreed to give the piece a run-through, but maybe I was too optimistic. Perhaps I can find someone else.'

Ethel looked out of the window. Magdi came and stood with her, putting her arm around her.

'From what you've said, Herr Levi is just the man to help you. Even I know he is one of the best conductors in Europe just now, and he's clearly interested in your work. He hasn't said "no", has he?'

'When he has the time,' Ethel said. 'But I don't have time. If I have to make a lot of changes, rethink some bits, I shan't meet the deadline.'

'Come and sit down,' said Magdi. 'You look pale and shocked. This isn't like you. From what you've said, you're able to get through a lot of work very quickly if you need to.'

Ethel stared out ahead. 'I wonder if Lisl realised when she decided she didn't want me as a friend anymore, that she was also making it virtually impossible for me to succeed as a musician.' Discussing old times with Magdi and Conrad had brought Lisl close into her mind again.

Magdi took her hand. 'Come on, now. Don't be so downhearted. The split with Lisl caused you a lot of pain, but it's a few years ago now. You are just hurting yourself by hanging on to these feelings.'

'She has everything. I have nothing.'

'You can't say that. But even if it were true, are you going to let that defeat you? There are many others who can help you.'

'Maybe I'll still be feeling like this when I'm fifty.'

'Please make sure you don't,' said Magdi. 'We all suffer heartbreak, but eventually we must learn to treasure the wonderful years we had. We have to try and create something else – even if it's not quite so good.'

'You're right,' said Ethel after a few minutes. 'I hate myself when I think like this. It's just so damn hard.'

~

Ethel moved into lodgings nearby. They were scarcely adequate, just one small room that held little but the piano and the bed. After a couple of weeks, the routines of Conrad and Magdi's home had started to grate. There was still no word from Hermann Levi, but when the time came, she would not be able to do the work required as their guest. It was a house full of comings and goings, of strict routines and well-meant interventions. Marco was often a nuisance. She would need to be able to work flat out, with no interruptions or etiquettes to observe.

Another week drifted by.

There was work she could do, of course. Her bag was full of half-finished manuscripts, sketches of ideas for new music, the more substantial *Antony and Cleopatra*. She was too restless to work on them. The work she longed to do, on the *Serenade*, could not be done until she got the score back from Herr Levi.

Every day, a happy Marco at her side, Ethel would buy some bread and cheese and meat as they passed through the marketplace, and walk out of town into the nearby mountains.

Ethel breathed in the summery perfume of Pauline and edged closer to her in the box. Enthralled by the slow aria, feeling its turbulence through her whole body, she was forgetting for a moment to analyse how this or that effect was achieved. *But there you shine, loveliest of stars.* Ethel risked a glance towards her, felt the desire to place her cheek – no, her lips – on the breasts slightly swelling out of the top of her bodice, to undo the golden clasp that held up her dark hair, which in this semi-light had a red glow, and feel its silkiness fall into her hands.

There was no answering look. She had not expected one.

It must be about a week since she had met Pauline and her family in this self-same box. Herr Levi had sent her the ticket – to keep her from pestering him, Ethel thought – and she had found herself taking the last seat amongst a family that were chattering amongst themselves in English. They had included her in their conversation, and since then she had dined with them in their hotel, taken excursions to nearby spas and villages, and sat in the park with them, muffled up against the late autumn chill, to hear some of the Festival's daytime events.

From the start, Ethel loved Pauline's mother. She found an endless stream of adjectives to describe her – beautiful, gentle, witty, cultured, musical. No, that didn't do her justice; how about kind, sensitive, intelligent, elegant, solid. She liked that: solid and musical. Very involved with her three daughters, too, encouraging them in every way. She seemed happy to include Ethel in their activities, even arranging an evening of her music at their hotel, to which she invited all the English families in Munich.

Ethel looked on the daughters very much like she might her sisters. It was ages since she had enjoyed herself so much, boating down the river amongst the golden trees, hiking up nearby mountains, hiring horses to canter through the forest, enjoying laughter and fierce competition.

It had taken a while to realise it was Pauline's company she particularly sought.

The whole audience gasped as one when the axe fell, and Ethel felt Pauline's hand reach for hers. How she would have liked, here in the semi-darkness, to kiss the dark vein in her wrist, and feel with her lips the soft skin in the bend of her arm. She stroked Pauline's hand and looked at her. Pauline's expression was that of a friend sharing the horror of the grisly scene being enacted on the stage.

Ethel's body fizzed just like it had when Harry had kissed her in the darkness by the gleaming Arno, flowing slowly nearby. She wanted to share with Pauline the play of lips, the press of bodies. She was glad when the opera ended and she could stand up and clap wildly and shake away from her body the longing that had taken hold.

~

Ethel almost ran along the street, Marco beside her, clutching her bag, hardly noticing the coffee houses beginning to up their shutters, or the rain. She had received the note from Herr Levi at about ten o'clock the previous evening, asking her to join him for breakfast. How could it be such a rush when she had been waiting for the best part of five weeks? She gathered her skirts up in one hand to avoid the water running down the street and dashed into the hotel.

'Fraülein,' he said, bending over her hand and kissing it. 'So early. I do apologise, but I know how urgent your situation is, and soon I must get busy with clearing up all the loose ends of this exhausting Festival. Did you find much to enjoy?'

'Thank you so much. I loved the festival atmosphere, with so much to choose from, not to mention rubbing shoulders with the best musicians. I've enjoyed more events than I could have imagined, thanks to your generosity with the tickets. And learnt a lot, too.'

'Have you been in Leipzig recently?' he asked.

'Not for about eighteen months. My mother's not well, so I'm having to base myself in England at the moment.'

'Well, congratulations on getting this offer from August Manns. He's a fine conductor. We'll work while we eat,' he said, pointing to the breakfast trolley just a few feet from the piano. 'Please help yourself. Here, let me pour you some coffee.'

'One of the concerts I enjoyed most had nothing to do with Wagner,' said Ethel. 'I apologise for that, but the Beethoven Missa at the cathedral was truly one of the most amazing pieces of music I have heard.'

Herr Levi buttered a roll and took his plate to the piano. He started to play some phrases from the Kyrie. 'When I conduct this,' he said, 'all the hairs on the back of my neck stand up.'

'We were all enraptured. I haven't heard it before.'

'Have you written any oratorio? Or opera?'

Ethel laughed. 'Goodness, no. I hardly know how to orchestrate a tune, never mind add singing and drama to it.'

'Your music's going in that direction. You should try it sometime.'

As he came away from the piano and gestured for her to sit with him at the table, she could see how exhausted he was. There were heavy bags under his eyes and he appeared to have a bad cold. The table was covered in neat piles of music, some tied together with ribbon. He glanced over them and selected one. As he opened it, she could see a scattering of comments in the margins, and sometimes between the lines.

'Ah, here we are.'

'Thank you,' she said. 'I'm so glad you've had the chance to look at it.'

'You are being very bold with this,' he said. 'Herr Röntgen thought your chamber music was very strong, and now you've taken this big step. Well done.'

Ethel's hands were holding tight to the edge of the table,

and she forced them off and folded them in her lap. Herr Levi flicked over some of the pages, riffling through the individual instruments' parts too.

'As you can see, I ran it through with the orchestra. I must say it was one day when we were driven mad by an impenetrable chunk of opera. They found it very refreshing.'

'I'm honoured, thank you. I can see from the number of comments that I still have work to do.'

'The orchestra was impressed, Fraülein. I didn't tell them who the composer was – just that it was a first effort at orchestration and they should give me their opinion. They liked it. There was good contrast in it, both delicacy and drama. Some of their comments are purely technical – sometimes you have asked for something that a particular instrument can't do, and sometimes they suggest how a different instrument might achieve the effect better.'

Ethel breathed out, relieved. She wanted to get up and hug Herr Levi and dance around the room and bury her face in Marco's fur.

'That's just what I wanted. I'm so grateful,' she said. 'I shall have much more focus for my revisions.'

Herr Levi buttered himself another roll, poured coffee for them both and took his watch out of his waistcoat pocket. 'I have an hour,' he said, 'before I must go. We could go through a couple of things, if you have time.'

He moved to the piano and waved Ethel onto the seat beside him. 'I can't sing today,' he said, blowing his nose, 'so I'll play and you can sing whatever instrument has the most prominent role. I think you'll soon see what I mean.'

This was a lot easier with two people than one, thought Ethel as they went along. And more fun too; and more revealing. She squirmed a little at his comments, but he was right, every time.

'I can never repay you for this,' said Ethel, after a gruelling couple of hours.

'To know that a large audience will hear your work is enough reward,' he said. 'Thank you for letting me help. Do write and tell me how it goes.'

What a generous man, thought Ethel as she went out into the street, trying to restrain Marco, who was behaving as if he had been imprisoned for days. She didn't care about the pouring rain, the wintry turn to the weather, the splashes on her skirt. She pushed her bag beneath her coat. She couldn't wait to get back to her desk. She had four weeks until she must post the final copy to August Manns if he was to receive it before the New Year deadline.

~

Ethel was hard at work when the landlady put her head around the door.

'I apologise, Fraülein,' she said, 'but I'm afraid you will have to leave at the end of the week.'

Her accent was so strong that it took Ethel a while to understand what was meant.

'To leave? But why? I've always paid promptly. I know I've made a fuss about the amount of noise in the house in the evenings, but—'

'It is the rule of the town,' she said. 'Now the Festival is over, I can no longer rent out rooms to ladies living alone.'

'That's ridiculous. What do you mean?'

'It's a city law. You must have your own servants in your household or go into a boarding house.'

'Please,' she said, 'I'm at a crucial stage with my work. Please let me stay.'

'I give you one more week, then you must go.'

As soon as the door closed behind her, Ethel shuddered and turned back to her manuscript. Every few minutes, however, she found herself distracted. The beginning of December. She would still be busy with her revision; it would be at a most urgent stage.

It would be disrupted. Whenever she tried to concentrate, the thought of packing up and finding another place edged into her mind.

Mid-afternoon, nothing was being done, and she walked through the rain to Magdi's house.

'I've had a ghastly day,' she said, after the servant had taken her wet coat off her and shown her into the drawing room.

Magdi came over and kissed her. 'Come and have tea with us.'

Ethel became aware of other women in the room, smart, neat and dry, where she was wet and bedraggled, distracted.

She tried to sit down and join in the conversation. She could hardly grasp the meaning, but it would be utterly trivial, anyway. She kept getting up to wander around the room, cup and saucer in hand, looking at the pictures and humming to herself. Occasionally, she would go to the piano and try out a phrase or two.

'Will you play for us?' said one of the visitors. 'We have heard good things about your music.'

Ethel looked around. She wanted to shout at the woman, trying to be nice without the least understanding of what was happening.

'No,' she said.

'Ethel is not very well today,' intervened Magdi. 'We will have a musical tea another time.'

The guests left as soon as was decent.

'Was that really necessary?' said Magdi.

'I've embarrassed you. I'm so sorry,' said Ethel.

'Never mind. Here, come on, have another slice of this lovely torte. I don't expect you've eaten properly for days.'

'I've got to leave my lodgings,' Ethel burst out. 'Now. When all of this is going on. It's impossible.'

'Then you must come and stay here. I promise you, we will let you get on without any interruptions.'

Ethel knew what that meant. Magdi was a bit like Mother used to be: she loved her dinner parties and entertainments, and would find it difficult to have a guest in the house who did not join in.

Conrad would be delighted to have her back in the house to talk politics and history. Ethel would have to respect mealtimes, and certainly would be very nervous about trying music out on the piano at night.

'Thank you, Magdi. You are so kind, but I must try and find somewhere of my own. I would find all the interesting things that go on in your house too tempting. I know that from the past. I have to keep going flat out if I'm to get this done.'

She got up to go.

'Oh, please stay for dinner. Conrad will be sorry to have missed you.'

'No, thank you. Everything about this revision business takes masses more time than you think.'

'Have you got anything in for dinner? And what about Marco?'

'Knowing your kitchen, I'm sure they've fed him well already,' said Ethel.

Magdi rang the bell and asked the maid to bring a basket of food for her.

~

Ethel pulled her coat around her and settled her hat more firmly on her head. The cold was so intense that she had taken to wearing most of the clothes she had brought to Munich at the same time. She tucked her feet under Marco's body. Apart from the fire, which seemed to eat up scuttles of coal quicker than she could pay the girl to bring more, there was nothing to make this room warm. The upholstery was worn, the mat covering a few of the floorboards was threadbare and the curtains thin.

Ethel hadn't been able to buy anything to warm up the room or make it more cheerful, because the allowance from her father was diminishing fast. Munich was expensive. Even this terrible, sparse room was costing her a sum of money that made her angry even to think of it – she had bribed the landlady, basically, to allow her to live here with her students, all men. During the night, these students put her nerves on the tautest edge with their chattering on the landing, their drunken midnight entry.

Today it was cold, but quiet. She smoothed onto her hands her fine leather gloves – fingerless now because she had chopped off the ends so that she could keep her hands warm whilst she wrote. Her pen was flying over the five-line sets on the page. She was humming, singing, excited. Yes, that's right, that's what Herr Levi had meant, she'd got it at last. For that bit anyway. Now what – yes, the bassoon, that was the thing here, not the oboe, and hadn't he suggested a little harp might lighten the tone there? Oh, that was good, that was very good.

Ethel went out onto the landing and looked at the grandfather clock. Three o'clock. Surely not. Yet she knew it must be, because the light was already fading. She must stop. There was no meat for Marco, and she had eaten nothing all day herself. She must get to the market. Moreover, Pauline and her family were back from their travels and she was to spend the evening with them. Pauline, lovely Pauline. Ethel had promised herself a trip to the public baths so she could dress properly for dinner. She touched her tied-back hair. It was horrible.

She walked briskly through the streets to the family's hotel. Bathing and careful brushing of her dress and bolero had transformed her into a person fit to go out. She must have seen before, but not noticed, how the city was beginning to get ready for Christmas. Fires had been lit along the riverbank so that people could go ice-skating in the early evening, and there were stands where hot, spicy wine was sold along with sausage and sweet pies. The smell was intoxicating. When I've finished, not until I've finished, said Ethel. She mustn't be tempted, though her body longed for the freedom and joy of ice-skating, and poor Marco, who was running around as if drunk, needed relief from the dreary underside of the table in her room.

She wanted to hold Pauline, her mother too, and all the sisters, in a joyous hug, but forced herself to merely exchange suitable greetings. Dinner was already on the table in a private room, set for a dozen people, and soon everyone was eating the roast partridge with gusto and enjoying the dark gravy which covered the vegetables and potatoes. When she could, Ethel dropped slices of meat to where Marco was lying underneath the table.

The talk was of the family's travels in the wintry Alps and the effectiveness of the Spas' cures, whilst a visiting diplomat and his wife gave the news of Britain, where there was a furore about women being murdered in Whitechapel.

'And you, Ethel, my dear, how is your music going?' asked Pauline's mother.

'I'm living the life of a hermit in a bustling city,' said Ethel. 'Working all the time and resisting the many interesting things going on around me.' She signalled to the waiter to refill her plate. 'I don't think I've eaten a proper meal since you went away.'

'And?' said Pauline, her eyes warm and attentive.

'Oh, it's going very well. I'm almost ready to get the copyists in to help. Conrad has kindly found them for me.' She could never have afforded them herself.

'What does that mean?' asked the diplomat. 'Copyists?'

'All the parts have to be written out for each instrument of the orchestra,' said Ethel.

'You mean, each one individually done?'

'Indeed. There comes a point when I have to say, that's it, no more changes, and then the copies can be made.'

'And are you nearly there?'

'I have to be.' Ethel laughed. 'Time has almost run out. In ten days, they must all be on their way to England.'

'We shall be gone by then,' said Pauline.

'Gone? I thought you were going to stay in Munich for Christmas.' Ethel bent her head over her empty plate.

'We've changed our plans,' said Pauline's mother. 'We'll be going home next week.'

'Shall I tell everyone?' said Pauline to her mother.

'Why not? We're all close friends here.'

'I'm to be married in the spring. We're all going to spend Christmas with my fiancé and his family.'

'That's wonderful,' said the other visitors. 'May we ask who the fortunate man is?'

Ethel hung her head, her stomach as empty as if she had eaten nothing. All this time she had been thinking about Pauline, but Pauline had been thinking about someone else.

~

Time passed, faster and faster. Every couple of days, Ethel would take the fair copy of the next section of the *Serenade* to Conrad and Magdi's home, and they would give it to the young students they had found to write out the parts for her. At first, this arrangement went well. She would have a quick lunch or early dinner with one or both of her friends, Marco would be fed, they would get a little exercise walking through the streets, now thick with snow, and the work was getting done.

Ethel knew she was beginning to create difficulties, but she couldn't stop. Whenever she read over what she had done, which might already have been distilled into ten parts and copied, she could see how it might be improved. She would alter the manuscript, even re-write chunks, and then ask if the copyists could make some new parts for her.

'Ethel, I'm afraid your willing helpers are rebelling,' said Conrad one day.

'Rebelling? For heaven's sake, why?'

'They're enjoying the work. And believe me, one or two of them are learning useful things about music.'

'But?'

'They are dispirited when they do their best copying, and then there are changes, and they have to do it all again. I'm not sure how long we can keep them.'

'You have been so generous,' she said. There was no time for the angry argument welling inside her. 'I'm very grateful and please apologise to them if I have been harsh. I can do the last bits myself.'

Ethel couldn't concern herself with uncertainties, arguments or debates. Day and night she sat at her table, falling into bed for a few hours whenever she had to. She went out only to buy food and let Marco run alongside the river, making herself deaf to the winter fun around her. She ignored the letters, invitations and messages that piled up on the little table by her door. Her only visitor was the maid, bringing her the scuttle of coal she had ordered, or a jug of hot water to throw over her face and hands. The time had nearly run away. She could only make the tiniest changes now.

Four days before Christmas, she parcelled up *Serenade* and sent it off to August Manns in London.

~

Ethel looked at the letter in disbelief.

I'm so sorry, my dear. Magdi has become very unwell the last few days and I am going to take her to our daughter's in Köln to have a change and a rest. This means that we will not be home at Christmas. We were so looking forward to having you with us, but I'm afraid that won't be possible. We will be away for a few days, and look forward to seeing you again on our return.

The bruise within her, that had been pulsing with pain since Pauline left, took another pounding. It was Christmas Eve, and there wasn't anyone she knew well enough to ask for a last-minute Christmas invitation. She was stuck here, alone.

She looked around the tiny room, with its poor furnishings and greedy fire. This was no place to celebrate Christmas, yet that was what she would have to do. She started to get dressed, sniffing and coughing as she pulled her clothes on. She must get out to the shops. She would have to hunt through the market for foodstuffs she could cook in the pot balanced on her grate. Even if she had the money for it, the restaurants would be closing for the holiday.

'Marco, Marco,' she said. 'It's just you and me.' He licked the hand she held out to him. The grand German Christmas and New Year she had looked forward to, was not to be.

She reached for the bedside table as she stood up, and paused a moment whilst she found her balance. Her head felt heavy and her brain slow as she gave herself a cursory wash. She found her wallet hidden at the back of the cupboard and counted her money carefully. Without the hospitality of Magdi and Conrad, she had hardly enough.

'We'll have to go home,' she muttered. There was a little relief in that thought. She made three small piles of money, one for her train ticket back to England, one for coal from the landlady and one for food. Most would be needed for Marco.

The streets were full of people, happy people. The markets were making the best of Christmas Eve to sell out. The smell of grilled meat and hot wine hung in the still, cold air. The shouting of children, the laughter of young families, the call of the market traders, the food, the general excitement – it was all muffled and distant to Ethel. It belonged to a world from which she was excluded, through which she could only pass slowly, sniffing with cold, alone except for the dog at her side.

At the river, she let him go and leant against a tree whilst he raced up and down, investigating anything that caught his attention, children, smells, patches of snow, rabbit holes.

Occasionally, he brought a stick and looked at Ethel wistfully, hoping she might throw it. She was too weak and preoccupied to give him more than a pat and an automatic, 'Good boy, off you go.'

Stall-holders were beginning to pack up as she returned, everyone thinking of the Christmas Eve celebrations that would start soon in their homes. It was a good time to pick up a few bargains – food that would spoil if it were not sold, meat, bread and fruit. It was hardly a festive dinner.

'Happy Christmas, Fraülein,' rang in her ears.

Ethel only got up when Marco made it very clear that he needed to go out, and go out now. She had been dozing on and off for a while, unwilling to wake up fully and face the day. A Christmas Day alone.

The feverish cold was still in her head and her chest, creating a foul taste in her mouth. The house was strangely quiet; all the other lodgers had gone to their families.

She couldn't stand her room. After she had drunk a little tea and toasted a piece of bread on the fire, and forced herself to eat it, she dressed and went out with Marco into the street. She walked slowly through the near-deserted streets to the little English church. There was no-one there she knew. She found nothing of the magic and comfort she had experienced when she had gone with Pauline.

The day was interminable. Its only pleasure lay in packing her bags ready to take the early train back to England the next day.

~

Numerous families – parents, children, grannies and old grandads – had decided, it seemed, to get on the train to go visiting, with their skates, their luggage, their Christmas presents, their toys, their food and their drink. The third-class carriage, all Ethel could afford, was unheated and bare. It lacked any comfort and almost steamed with the mass of bodies. The smell of wintry, damp clothes clashed with food odours, and the talking, the shouting, the crying of babies and the clattering of the train on its rails was deafening.

Ethel had hoped to find a quiet corner where she could sit and snuffle in peace, where she could try and contain her shivering and coughing by dozing away the long hours of travel. Instead, she was perched on the end of a hard, overfull bench. Luggage and baskets of food were crammed underneath. There was no room for Marco, and he started to turn in circles trying to create a larger space where he could lie down. Ethel tried to soothe him, patting him gently and talking to him. His size, discomfort and occasional barks were making the people nearby nervous. The children who had wanted to play with the huge, friendly dog began to be scared.

Ethel knew she should get up, move her luggage somewhere else – she could not immediately see where – and make sure Marco had enough space. Her head was pounding, and his barks were adding to the pain. Suddenly, he snapped at a small boy who was getting too close and poking fingers at his face. The boy screamed and ran to his mother. Ethel pulled Marco's head onto her lap and tried to quiet his barking.

'Fraülein.' A commanding voice disturbed her feeble efforts to calm him. 'The dog must come with me.'

'I'm sorry,' said Ethel. 'He'll settle down in a minute. He'd never harm anyone. Come on, Marco, behave yourself.' She stroked and patted his head, and he began to relax against her.

'No, Fraülein,' said the guard. 'The train is very full and I cannot risk an accident.'

Marco could be unpredictable if panicked, Ethel knew that, and they had a long journey ahead. She could not guarantee his behaviour in the packed carriage if one of these small children annoyed him, or if he took a fancy to the strong-smelling food.

'Do you have somewhere he could go, at least until the train becomes less full?'

'Yes, come with me and I'll show you.'

Ethel held tight to Marco's lead as she followed the official along the train, every bit of which was full and noisy. The guard's van at the back was a haven of peace in comparison. Sacks of mail stood around the floor, together with trunks and a couple of baby carriages, as well as a large bath chair. She could not see a space for Marco.

'Perhaps we can clear these a bit and sit here?'

'He will go in here.' The guard moved aside some of the sacks and began to open a trap door in the floor of the carriage. 'He must be contained.'

Ethel bent over Marco and began to talk to him. She sniffed hard. 'I'm sorry, old boy,' she said.

'As you can see,' said the guard, standing back, 'there's quite a large space here.'

'What is it used for?'

He shrugged. 'It's just extra storage. Sometimes we use it for an animal, things that need to be kept cool. Now please.' He gestured that she should put Marco into the hole. 'There is no need to worry, Fraülein. He will be safe there.'

Ethel thought of the long hours of the journey ahead. 'We have to show endurance, both of us,' she said, trying to reassure Marco that to be shut in a dark space just above the rails was almost an everyday occurrence. 'Don't worry, I'll bring you something to eat in a little while.' She pushed him down, trying to ignore his expression. 'I shall be nearby, dear Marco.'

Ethel suppressed a sob. The guard pulled the cover over, muffling the dog's moans, and gestured for her to return to her compartment.

Ethel perched on the one foot of seat that was left for her, pressed hard against a snoring man and opposite an old woman who, now that Marco had gone, wanted to talk. Her accent was so broad, however, and the noise of the train so loud, that Ethel could hardly catch a word.

Deafened by misery too, she thought, trying to doze. Her body felt feverish, occasionally quaking with some inner turmoil. It wasn't just Marco's trusting eyes that plagued her. Pauline was gone, not just heading back to London but on to her marriage too. She was a wanderer once more, heading for the reassurance of home that would soon feel like prison again. She took out of her pocket the little missal that Pauline had left for her, and read for comfort some of the words of the Mass. A tune started in her head, shaping itself around the words of the Kyrie Eleison.

Every so often, Ethel roused herself and made her slow way along the train to the guard's van, and lay for a few minutes on the floor of the carriage talking to Marco. 'What a beautiful boy,' she murmured. 'We'll be out of here eventually. When we get home, Mabel will feed us both and look after us.' His moaning stopped, and she could picture him lying there, his big head cocked, listening to her.

On one journey back to her seat, she opened the window and threw the missal angrily out of the window onto the snowy tracks.

The train stopped for an hour at Stuttgart. Ethel demanded that the guard allow her to take Marco out of his prison, as she termed it. She fed him the last of the meat she had brought for him. It was dark already, and he ran up and down the platform, playing in the deep snow that had gathered where there was no roof. Ethel rubbed her arms and shoulders against the cold air. She had no desire or money for food, but she bought a bowl of hot chocolate in the buffet, and begged a couple of bones for Marco.

She looked longingly at the well-lit first-class carriages at the front of the train. She knew what they would be like – full of bustle as the stewards prepared the compartments for the night, making up beds for the travellers currently taking dinner in the restaurant, ready to see to their every need. How poor and miserable her carriage was in comparison. But at least it was emptier now. She moved into a corner and persuaded Marco to lie under her seat. She leant her heavy head against the hard wood of the panel. Such a long, hard journey.

17

LONDON 1890

The concert hall was full of chatter and excited laughter as people greeted each other and found their seats. Ethel, standing at the side of the stage watching the orchestra take their places, was flushed and faint. The rehearsals she had been invited to had not gone smoothly. She had frequently found herself at odds with August Manns, despite her respect for him, who made changes with no reference to her, speeding the piece up here and changing an emphasis there. Her reasonable suggestions were met with rows of men with instruments looking at her resentfully. Eventually, however, everything came together. Just yesterday the leader of the orchestra had nodded slightly at her; he had decided at last it was worth doing. The rest of the orchestra would fall in behind him.

She found her seat on the end of the side stalls and looked out. The audience was quietening down in the expectant way of people looking forward to a Saturday afternoon's entertainment. With a few exceptions, they had not come to hear her. Her *Serenade* was just a small part of a full programme. She spotted her family near the front, sitting in a long row – her father,

154

who had never been to a concert before, and proud mother, all her sisters and their husbands. Just Bob, Nell and Hugh were missing – far away in India. Alice looked at her and blew her an encouraging kiss.

She tried to listen to some of the music scheduled before her piece but found her body was shaking with nerves. Her mind was skittish and unfocussed. The overture from *Tannhaüser* was followed by some songs by Hubert Parry and Pergolesi – all beautifully done, she was sure. She tried to calm herself by thinking of the telegrams she had received. Even Herr Brahms had deigned to send her good wishes: *The chances to hear your own music are all too rare. Don't let anything spoil it for you.* And Pyotr Tchaikovsky had written: *When you hear the hall fill with the sound of the orchestra playing your music, you will be glad you met me.* Cheeky, arrogant man. She smiled joyously. Other Leipzig friends had written too: Papa Röntgen telling her to enjoy her *breakthrough in England*, as he termed it.

Herr Manns left the stage to loud applause at the end of the songs, then returned, changed the music on his stand and raised his baton. She leant forward as the opening strains of her *Serenade* filled the concert hall. How rich and resonant that cheerful and dramatic opening was, sounding so well in the hall full of people, so different from the rehearsal room. Oh my word, she thought, I did this. Her body straightened up to greet the high notes of the flute. The kick of fear in her chest gave way to excitement, tinged with relief. She began to relax, dared to look up, study the alert faces of the musicians, feel a sway in her body. In the pause between the first and second movements, there was a sigh from the audience; they were involved, happy to take a few breaths, waiting for the next section.

The applause at the end was warm and prolonged. Smiling, Herr Manns beckoned her to the stage. Was that a few cheers she could hear amongst the enthusiastic clapping? She bowed awkwardly. She looked over to where her family were watching her, smiling broadly. She wished she was down there amongst them, instead of stuck up here on the stage like an exhibit.

The final item on the programme was one of Tchaikovsky's piano concertos. She was sharing the programme with one of her heroes, but she did not hear much of its intricacy or thunder. Mary and Violet were still smiling and made small, triumphant gestures whenever they caught her eye. She noticed a man sitting on the end of the row. Some friend of Mary's, perhaps. He was looking at her with an intensity that drew her eyes again and again. She sat back in her seat and put her hand over her mouth. Her heart was racing in an uncomfortable way. She focussed on the stage, though she neither saw nor heard what was going on.

Harry! Harry Brewster! She stole another look. It was him, surely, though he looked different, a beard, perhaps; yes, that was it. He looked towards her, and before she could look away, their eyes locked. His face broke out into a broad smile, and while Ethel kept her hand over her mouth, she knew that she was responding.

The concert ended and Ethel went backstage to congratulate the players, who applauded her once more. Herr Manns came and kissed her, and promised to play more of her music in the future – her *Antony and Cleopatra*, perhaps. As she went towards the foyer, she could hardly bear to look, in case Harry had disappeared. Mary dashed forward and enveloped her in a big hug.

'That was amazing,' she said. 'We were so proud.' She released her and all the sisters and the brothers-in-law wanted to kiss her and congratulate her. Her mother looked as though she might faint with pleasure, and even Father looked proud.

'Well done, Ethel,' he said. 'You've made us all very happy this afternoon.'

'Guess what,' said Violet. 'He's already been out to send a telegram to Bob, to tell him how wonderful your concert was.'

'Yes,' said Nina. 'And at the end of each movement he kept getting up to go to the post office. We had to hold him down. He had no idea what was the end.'

As the noise and laughter calmed down, Ethel could see Harry at the back of the foyer. She gestured towards him, and he came towards her and bent low over her hand. The touch of his lips on her skin sparked through her.

'Harry,' she said, 'what a lovely surprise. What are you doing here?'

'I was just passing through London on business and saw the notice in the paper about the concert,' he said. 'I'm so happy for your success.'

'This is Harry Brewster, one of my friends from Florence,' said Ethel, unsure how to introduce him to so many people at once.

'We know,' said Alice. 'We've already done all our introductions.'

'How did you find my family in all that crowd?'

Harry laughed. 'I was getting my ticket and saw someone very like you standing there. I knew she must be related, so I couldn't resist asking.'

The family began to disperse, kissing and hugging each other, making arrangements for their next get-together.

'Mother,' said Ethel, 'I would love to hear news from Harry about my friends in Florence.'

'What's that, dear? I can't hear anything in this noise.'

Ethel repeated herself in a louder voice.

'Of course.' She turned to Harry. 'Would you like to come down to Frimhurst and stay for a day or two?'

'Thank you, Mrs Smyth. I would love to. Unfortunately, I have to get a train up to Liverpool tonight for my ship to America. But why don't you join me for some tea?'

'Thank you, Mr Brewster,' she said. 'But we must be getting back.'

'I'll come on a later train,' said Ethel, walking with her mother towards the waiting carriage and settling her in.

Her mother leaned forward and clasped her hand. 'This has

been the most wonderful afternoon of my life. I'm so happy for you.'

Ethel leaned over and kissed her. 'It was so good to have you all here. Bye for now. I'll be home for dinner.'

At last all the goodbyes were said, and there was just Harry standing beside her on the pavement.

The shop lights sparkled against the darkening sky. They were jostled as they walked up the street by people running final errands before the end of the day. Ethel felt Harry draw her arm into his own.

'My dearest Ethel,' he said, 'I thought I would burst with pride when you were up on the stage, looking so fine, and everybody applauding you like that. And your music, so very good.'

'I was pleased to see my family happy. I've put them through a lot. This was the first time they've been able to come and hear me.'

'Yes, I saw from the programme that this was your first performance in England. Not your last, I'm sure.'

Ethel felt dazed; so much hard work, so much excitement, and now this. She squeezed his arm against hers, turned her face to smell the warm woollen fabric of his coat.

'Shall we have some tea?' They were passing a hotel and stopped, attracted by the lights, the smells, the sounds of a busy dining room.

'I'm starving,' she said, laughing. 'I could eat a whole orchestra, and a choir too if there was one handy.'

'You do surprise me.' He turned to guide her up the steps, putting his arm across her back and looking at her beneath her hat. 'I am giddy with happiness, Ethel. Seeing the poster of your concert gave me such an unexpected delight, and now here you are. I'd forgotten what fun it is just to hear you talk.'

'I haven't really eaten for days,' she said, following the waiter across the room. 'It's been so hectic. Even the nicest conductors don't like being told, you know.'

'And you loved every minute?'

'I did.' They sat at a table at the very back of the dining room, where there were few other guests. 'D'you know, I did. Loved it and hated it. It was infuriating. It was brilliant. Disaster loomed large at times.'

The waiter started filling the table with hot buttered muffins, jams, cheese and ham, and poured their tea.

'How exciting,' said Harry, putting cheese and ham onto a muffin and giving it to her. 'My life seems so dry in comparison.'

'Don't be silly,' she said, tearing huge mouthfuls off. 'Mm, just what I needed. You're travelling to America tomorrow to talk about your new book, meeting with the best minds, no doubt. My life is very messy in comparison.'

She blotted butter off her lip.

'I would rather be here feeding you than at the best dinner in town.' He began to spread jam on another muffin.

'Now you're being silly.'

He caught her hand across the table and kissed it, continuing to hold on to it and stroke it. 'I feel silly. And preposterously happy. Please, Ethel, please tell me you're not going to banish me for another five years.'

She dropped her eyes, which for a long moment had been locked on to his, and took the muffin. She started to eat it more slowly, savouring the sweet strawberry taste.

'When I banished you, as you put it,' she said slowly, 'I couldn't see any other way out for us. I hoped I would regain Lisl's affection and share in her life. That hasn't happened. I know things are never going to be the same with her again.'

'Do you want it to be?'

'Oh, I would leap at it.' She shrugged. 'But too much time has passed. I do long for those happy times, of course I do, but they are gone. Really, I was little more than a child then.'

'You've become a beautiful woman.'

She shook her head. 'But presumably, you are still a married man. What would Julia say if she could see us now?'

Harry sat back and sighed, looking around the restaurant at the other diners.

'I'm not going to tell you what it's been like these last few years,' he said eventually. 'Florence with its endless gossip became intolerable to me, and we moved to Rome a few years ago. I do spend time there, to be with the children, and I still hold Julia in the highest regard. Then life becomes grey and I have to go, go anywhere. She knows that your brightness has never faded in my mind. Time has gone by. I don't think she would mind so much if we met now and then.'

'I would want her to know,' said Ethel.

Harry nodded and looked down. Then a broad smile spread across his face. 'My dear Ethel, did you just say we can meet now and then? And we will write to each other?'

Ethel didn't answer. She had forgotten the sheer deliciousness of being near him, the stormy reactions in her body. It was dangerous, what she had just done.

'Shh,' she said, aware of other diners nearby. 'People will hear us.' She took an Eccles cake from the stand and bit deeply into its sugary crustiness. After a couple of mouthfuls, she pushed her plate away. 'Wonderful! But I ought to go. Mother and Father want to have a little dinner celebration tonight.'

'Shall I arrange for a carriage, or shall we walk to the station?'

'Let's walk. It's not far.'

Harry beckoned to the waiter and paid the bill, and moments later they were out in the dark street. The shops were closed now, and the pavement shadowy under the gas lamps. Ethel tucked her arm into Harry's and leaned into him for a moment.

'You haven't told me what you're working on now,' he said.

'A Mass,' she said.

'A Mass? Goodness me. You don't mean Kyrie Eleison, Sanctus, the whole lot? A Bach, Beethoven sort of Mass?'

'Yes, that's it exactly.'

'But you've never been interested in religion. Where's that

come from?'

'A lovely woman I met in Munich,' she said slowly. 'A religious woman. Her belief was so strong, Harry, that she half convinced me there must be a God. More than just the God we sing to on Sunday. Something anyway. I feel its mystery.' She looked down at the pavement, trying to find some words. 'I want to bring some of that enormity into the concert hall. Look out there.' She waved her arms to take in the whole night sky.

'You know my thoughts about all of that.'

'I do, Mr Rational Man.' She laughed, remembering long discussions in Florence cafes. 'But it's so dramatic. And the singing, the magic of the voices. I feel so excited the way it's all coming together. I've never written for a choir before.'

'Sing me a bit.'

'What, here in the street?'

Her voice swung up and down on the syllables. *Gloria, Gloria, in excelsis deo.* People turned their heads at her resonant, loud voice, and Harry pulled her closer to him.

'How wonderful to be embarrassed by you again,' he said.

'It's very big. Sometimes I feel frightened by it.'

'What do you mean?'

'It's not just… well, how I can match those great men who've already expressed these ideas so perfectly? It's the bigness of the feelings themselves, the challenge of distilling that into something that can be performed.'

'You are big. Big enough to write a Mass or anything else you put your mind to. I'm sure you're not going to be put off by a few fusty-dusty old men, dead old men too. Are you properly daunted, or just a bit scared?'

'Both. And more. No, you know how I am, I'm happy to be grappling with it.'

He laughed. 'I'm sure you are. And after today, you know that people will want to hear you.'

'Not everyone sees it like that. Mother apparently said to

Mary the other day that if today's concert was successful, maybe I would be satisfied.'

'Aren't you?'

'Not in the way she means. She hopes that I'll feel I have proved my point and be happy to settle down and be a good daughter.'

'Are you tempted?'

'What do you think?'

They walked up the slope into Waterloo station, smoky under the dim lights. He drew her into the darkened doorway of a closed shop. Shielding her from passers-by, he put his hands on her shoulders.

'You have missed this, haven't you? A little?'

Ethel thought of that day in Halle, so many years ago. It had seemed so easy, and yet so much suffering had resulted. That must not happen again.

'Restraint is called for,' she said, looking up at him.

In the dim light of the station, she could see his eyes flash. 'Years of misery are worth it to hear you say that. Please promise me that nothing will be so arid and meaningless ever again.'

Ethel knew she should draw back. Their cheeks rubbed against each other gently, and as he moved his mouth to kiss her, it was like a caress.

'I must go,' she said. But instead of drawing back and away, her mouth had moved towards his again. Instead of a farewell kiss, their lips were touching in a little dance of longing, whilst waves of pleasure ran through her body, and her heart beat to a different rhythm.

After a few moments she pushed him away.

'Please show me to my train,' she said.

'Ah, I knew you would say that eventually. Can we not wait for the next one?'

It was an enticing idea. 'No. I must get home.'

He stroked her face for a moment, and then leaned forward and straightened her hat.

They walked along the platform, his hand on her back, and he settled her into a compartment.

'You're looking after me,' she said. 'Thank you.'

'That's what I want to do, if you give me the chance.'

There was a screeching as the engine began to gather steam. 'Don't say anything, just go,' she said.

'Shall I write to you from America?'

'You'd better.'

He laughed and jumped off the train as it began to move, waving and running alongside as it gathered speed.

18

FRIMLEY, SURREY 1891

Christmas was over, thank goodness; she could get on with her music. Father took up his political and charitable activities again, and Mother stayed in bed, exhausted. The house was cleaned, and everything restored to its drawer or cupboard.

She had loved having everyone here, though she and Mabel had survived a few hair-raising moments making sure everyone was fed, and that there was enough cutlery and crockery for the elaborate dinners they had held. There had been riding and hunting, and crazy races on the new-fangled bicycles they now owned, not to mention board games and charades and the children's variable dramatic output. There was even enough talent in the house for a half-decent musical evening. That talent had included for a few days George and Lilian Henschel, her mother's favourites of all her musical friends, who seemed able to draw her out of her deafness and isolation. The audience had included their new neighbour.

'Empress Eugénie has come to live in Farnborough,' her mother had said just a few weeks before. 'You'll love her, Ethel, really. She's not like our military friends at all.'

'That can only be good,' Ethel had replied. 'Do you mean Napoleon's widow?'

'Yes. Since he died, and their son, she's been in England. Exiled. Now the Queen has given her Farnborough Hill to live in.'

'Is she happy to socialise with the likes of us?'

'Of course. Your father and I and the brigadier had dinner there just a few days ago. You should see that fabulous house. She's said she'll come to our New Year dinner.'

Ethel had not seen her mother so animated for a long time.

It had been such fun, but now all she wanted to do was get on with her Mass. She had already been writing it for the best part of a year, trying to combine all she knew of those classic requiems and masses that she had feasted on in Germany with this new religious feeling – more, this actual belief in God – that Pauline had sparked into being.

Ethel went to fetch Marco, who bounded up to her room with delight. He regarded his banishment to the Frimhurst kennels as an insult. He was used, after all, to being in her room, asleep on her feet whilst she composed. That's what he had done all those months in Germany, and Ethel couldn't help but feel a pang of betrayal when she insisted he stay outside.

Settled at her table, the dog comfortably heavy on her feet, Ethel drew out a fresh sheet of paper. She sniffed it as if she herself was an animal who received a great deal of information through her nose. It smelt of luxury, and felt thick and solid, as if it would accept any amount of corrections. She smoothed it in front of her, creamy, pre-printed with its sets of five lines. Thank you, Harry, she breathed, picking up her pen. No chocolates, no flowers, no jewellery or scarves. Just a pack of thick paper, all ready for her to write her music on.

Ethel heard something fall. She looked up from her manuscript and saw that it was already beginning to get dark. She yawned and got up from her table and went out onto the landing. Through the open door of her mother's room, she could see an upturned glass of water on the floor and Mother lying awkwardly on the bed as if she had been stretching across for it.

'Are you all right, Mother?' she said.

As Ethel went in to help her back onto the pillow, she could see how white her face was. Her eyes were closed. Ethel's stomach lurched as she leaned over to touch her face. There was no response.

'Mother?' she said. 'Mother? Are you awake? Shall I make you a little more comfortable?'

Her mother's eyelids flickered, but she did not say anything. Ethel gently lifted her back onto the pillows and pushed her hair back where it had fallen out of her cap onto her face. How cold and clammy her skin was. Her breathing was almost imperceptible.

Ethel rang the bell furiously, and went to the door and shouted down the stairs. 'Mabel, Mabel. Go and find the major and tell him the doctor must be called at once.'

Mabel came in a few minutes later, and helped plump out the pillows and straighten the bedclothes. Ethel found herself studying her mother's every variable breath.

'I've sent for the doctor,' said her father, hurrying in a few moments later. He leant over the bed. 'Cathy? Cathy? Look at me.' He gave her shoulder a slight shake, but there was no response.

After his examination, the doctor talked vaguely of a seizure, and advised them to expect the worst. Ethel's father took to walking around the house, up and down the stairs, out into the yard, muttering about how well she had seemed, how she was hardly sixty years old. Ethel arranged for telegrams to be sent to the family, who had left only a couple of days before.

Ethel sat with her mother throughout the day, only getting some rest when Violet arrived to relieve her. She thought of her mother's bright radiance that had illuminated her childhood, and how that had changed to an endless bitter, miserable examination of herself and everyone else. She was glad that during this year at home, she had not found her mother irritating beyond bearing, as she had before, and not reacted to her so angrily.

The house filled up with the family again. Not a happy, festive family, but sad and thoughtful. Two days later, Mother was dead.

~

'I think you should go,' said Mary when Ethel told her about the invitation to stay with the Empress Eugénie on the Balmoral estate. 'You need a rest.'

'You know I can't leave Father,' said Ethel. This phrase had become a harsh reality over the months since her mother's death. He expected her to live with him and see to the household. She was the unmarried daughter and that is what unmarried daughters did.

She was doing her best to re-focus her life on Frimhurst. It wasn't so bad; there were friends living nearby, plenty of social events, sports, riding. Her father was well and busy; he didn't ask for much. He was happy enough for her to be in her room composing or trying things out on the new grand piano in the drawing room. She was free to come and go as she liked, spend days in London, invite people to stay.

And yet… she wasn't free, of course, anything but. The house had to be kept, dinner served, guests welcomed and cared for. It was his order that was imposed on the day, his routine that decided the pattern of each week. On some days, Ethel longed for the meanest of the lodgings she had stayed in: a few shovels of coal lying between her and a cold room, a bread roll and a bit of ham the only food in the cupboard. There she had worked, day or night, Marco warming her feet.

'How long does she want you to go for?' asked Mary.

'It's an awful long way. I think she's going to be there all summer, but of course I wouldn't stay that long. Three weeks, perhaps?'

'She's been very kind since Mother died, and she obviously enjoys your company. Do go. Alice will be coming to London during the summer, and I'm sure she'll be happy to stay with Father for a few days, as will all of us. Do you think you might get to see the Queen?'

'She's there, I expect, at Balmoral. If she's invited the Empress to stay on the estate, I would imagine they'll spend some time together. Whether any of that will include me, I've no idea.'

'She does appreciate music, though, doesn't she? She loves all those visiting Germans. Wasn't Mendelssohn a big buddy?'

'That's a long, long time ago, when she was a happy, young Queen. I don't think she does much now.'

'Hmm. Well, don't let any opportunity slip by. Not that you would. They might be old ladies now, but they're still very powerful. And Eugénie did love your Mass when you played it at her party.'

'If they can make that wretched Barnby put my Mass on, as he promised, I'd be happy as anything.'

~

The Empress was whisked away to dine with the Queen, and Ethel was shown into dinner with the ladies and gentlemen of the court. She would have enjoyed the sumptuous meal a lot more but for the task ahead, not to mention the need not to allow anything to drip on the delicate fabric of the black bodice that Eugénie had lent her. She couldn't help worrying about the bobbing decorations on the elaborate hat that had come along with the bodice, her own plain hat having been deemed inappropriate. She had certainly never had a coiled serpent on her head before.

Nerves rendered the game soup, one of her favourites, tasteless. There was course after course, fish and meat dishes, beautifully cooked in rich sauces, followed by creamy puddings and some fruits that Ethel had never seen before. It was all in gold and silver dishes, and metallic sounds rang out in the huge hall whenever anything was served.

Ethel tried to keep up with the conversation, but it was dreary. She enjoyed as much as anyone else a morsel of gossip about what this prince or that royal child was up to, but it seemed that these people, immersed in the life of the old Queen's court, had little curiosity about the wider world. Ethel longed for something a bit livelier, but whenever she voiced even the mildest contrary opinion, she was ignored.

All at once, everyone was on the move. The Queen had finished, and her ladies-in-waiting hurried to attend her. Ethel was told to stay where she was until called, and soon a footman came and led her up the marble staircase, his black patent shoes clicking as he went.

She was shown into a drawing room, the largest she had ever seen, full of people standing quietly. Her eyes were drawn to a figure, small and round: unmistakeably the Queen in her funereal black dress, sitting in an upright chair by the hearth with its roaring fire, talking with the Empress Eugénie. The princes and princesses stood nearby. All of those people who had been with Ethel at the dinner table were standing silently in rows leading away from the fireplace.

The footman disappeared, and Ethel was left alone in the doorway. She was to be presented, Eugénie had said, but how was that to be done? Was she just to sit at the piano; but if she did, who would tell her when to begin? She began to walk up between the rows of ladies and gentlemen towards the fireplace. A look of horror came over Eugénie's face when she saw her. One of the princesses stepped forward quickly and drew her aside.

'Just stand here with me until the Queen is ready,' said the princess quietly.

Ethel knew she had breached some arcane rule of etiquette and fought down her embarrassment by looking around the room. The dark wooden panelling glowed in the light of the many chandeliers and, away from the line of silent courtiers, the forbidding furniture looked comfortable with its tartan cushions, the fabric mirrored in the heavy, drawn curtains.

By the time Eugénie came forward and presented her to the Queen, Ethel could only curtsey and mutter the most formal of responses.

'Please,' said the Queen, 'we would like you to sing for us.'

She waved towards the shining piano standing to one side, and as Ethel turned towards it the row of ladies-in-waiting made way for her. She had never seen a piano like it. It was gold, and the sides were painted, or inset, she was unsure which, with mythical musical scenes, surrounded with leafy designs. Even the pedals were gold.

Ethel had a sense of foreboding. Maybe it was just a beautiful ornament with a ghastly sound. She could hardly keep her fingers off the keys, so much did she want to try it out. Instead she sat swallowing nervously whilst the footmen re-arranged the chairs so that the Queen and the Empress were sitting near to the piano, whilst the others sat in rows behind.

Ethel stood up and curtsied.

'I would like you to play some of your Mass,' said the Queen.

'Your Majesty,' Ethel curtsied again, 'the Mass is meant to be performed by a large orchestra and choir, as well as soloists. However, I shall try to give you a flavour of it.'

'The Queen would like you to play it exactly as you played it to me the other day,' said Eugénie.

Ethel sat back down at the piano, arranged the pages of her manuscript on the stand and started to play. Within seconds, she knew it was the finest instrument she had ever played, perfectly tuned with a rich, rounded tone.

She began with the Sanctus. It wasn't the beginning of the Mass, but she chose it because it was the easiest section to convey by one person on a piano. She played the simple accompaniment and started to sing the rich solo line, Sanctus, Sanctus, which she alternated with the voices of the women's choir. She tried to capture the strong voice of the alto in sharp contrast to the ethereal tone of the choir.

The sound of the piano resonated throughout the drawing room. Ethel put all her effort into the meaning behind the words. Her religious belief might have died away the minute she finished writing the Mass, but the music was still full of strong feelings which had their effect on her as well, she hoped, as on the people listening.

Ethel stood up at the end, turned towards the Queen and curtsied deeply. She was rewarded with enthusiastic clapping, and she began to relax a little.

'Please continue,' said the Queen.

Ethel had not meant to play the long and complex Gloria, but she found herself flicking past the Benedictus and Agnus Dei to find it. It was risky, but the Queen appeared to be ready for more, and Ethel could not resist the challenge when the room and the piano were so suited to a big piece.

The beginning of the Gloria could not have been more different from the Sanctus. It was dramatic, loud and fast. The piano, which had been able to convey so well the delicacy of the previous section, now proved that it was equal to the drama of the crashing chords. Her world began to shrink to a familiar space which contained only herself and the piano. The Queen, whom she could just see out of the corner of her eye, blurred and disappeared. The smooth, cool white and black keys seemed to invite speed from her fingers as she tried to get in as many notes as possible to cover the sounds of the orchestra. The clear tones of her voice might be singing a part, or imitating a flute or a clarinet. She felt a rush of excitement when she stamped her feet to create a drum-roll, and managed to clap her hands twice for the cymbals. Her whole body was lost in an ecstasy of sound and movement.

A few hairpins dropped onto the piano keys. Ethel had an image of the coils of the serpent on the feathery hat unravelling about her head and shoulders. She shut her mind to that possibility. It wasn't going to stop her now she had reached the final Amen sequence, loud and furious, and she drove on to the end.

Ethel sat for a moment, looking down at her hands, now quiet in her lap. She was hot; her face would be bright red. She could only hope that her clothes and the dreadful hat were more or less where they were meant to be. She coughed into the silence, unsure what to do, and then there was the sound of a person clapping, then two, then more and more. She stood and turned. The Queen was smiling broadly, her blue eyes warm and excited, applauding enthusiastically.

'Bravo, bravo,' she said. 'My dear Miss Smyth, that was quite exceptional. I have never heard such dramatic music in my drawing room.'

'Thank you so much, Ma'am.' Ethel stood up and curtsied deeply.

'Written and played by a woman too. I congratulate you. And thank you, Eugénie, for bringing me such a wonderful afternoon's entertainment.'

She nodded in dismissal and Ethel, dazed and with no idea what to do next, followed the gesturing princess out of the room.

19

Ethel found herself standing near Peter Barnsdale. They had not spoken to each other since their argument at the archbishop's dinner, and she had no intention of starting a conversation with him now. Not that he was going to talk to her either; that much was clear from the way he turned his back to her. He had the look of a man who was deeply offended that a woman should be invited to a luncheon at the Royal School of Music, unless of course she was the wife of one of the famous musicians.

What struck her again was the ease with which these men talked about their musical lives: how they shared their experiences, exuded confidence, were willing to give each other a helping hand. She was not included in this. In fact, even the few composers she knew quite well always seemed surprised and a little embarrassed that she knew the technical language to dissect the music just as they did, or that she might have well thought-out and original opinions – opinions which she felt obliged to voice in a way that brooked no argument. The few women students present on such evenings tended to say very little.

Ethel went to stand with a group by the hearth discussing the concerto they had heard that morning, written by one of their promising students.

'The German influence was very strong,' said Robert Lane, who had just returned from a short spell at the Berlin conservatoire. 'I enjoyed it.'

'I agree. I thought it was quite similar to von Herzogenberg's cello concerto,' said one of the others. 'Did you meet him in Berlin?'

'Sadly not. What do you think, Miss Smyth?' said Lane. 'Was it similar? He was your tutor when you lived in Germany, wasn't he? Poor man, he's not at all well.'

'Not well?' said Ethel.

'Yes, since his wife died, he's been distraught, apparently.'

Ethel turned slightly aside as waves of shock rocked through her body. Surely she had misheard.

'Excuse me,' she cut into the conversation as soon as she could speak. 'Did you say that his wife had died?'

'I'm sorry,' said Lane, seeing her face. 'Was she a friend of yours? I didn't mean to surprise you. I believe she died at the beginning of the month.'

Ethel pushed her way through the chattering men, uncaring of how rude her behaviour might seem. She ran down the stairs and out into the cool afternoon. Lisl dead? No, no, not dead. That could not be.

She turned off the busy street into the park, walking rapidly, trampling the snowdrops in the grass and dodging round the well-wrapped nannies wheeling their large prams up and down the paths. If Lisl was dead, surely someone would have told her.

Well, Harry would have told her, so it could not be true. But of course, he was in America, and may not even know himself yet. Magdi would let her know. Maybe there was a letter lying on the hall table at home; she must go immediately. For a few moments, she could not think where she was; all she could repeat to herself was station, train, home; station, train, home. In a daze she negotiated people, streets, the ticket office, money transactions, train timetables. It was as if she no longer quite belonged. The familiar landmarks on the journey to Farnborough were different, odd; time seemed stretched and contorted so she could hardly judge how long it took.

She ran in through the front door and sifted through the pile of letters on the hall table until she spotted the telegram. It was from Harry. She ran up to her room, ripping it open as she went.

On way back to Europe. Expect you know Lisl fell ill and died. So sorry. Will write when know more. Harry.

She held the telegram to her, her throat choking as sobs took away her breath. He would go to Berlin first, help Heinrich with funeral arrangements, comfort Julia. It would be a while before she heard just what had happened.

Ethel had no heart for anything but to lie in bed or wonder aimlessly around the gardens. She told her father she was not well, and he believed her entirely because the piano was silent and the horses unridden. Despite the endless years when she had heard nothing from her, there had always been thoughts of Lisl, the hope of Lisl, the possibility of Lisl. Now there was nothing but an aching blackness in her heart. The day would never come when they would smile and laugh over their years-long disagreement, when Lisl would say that she had been too harsh, and Ethel would say she had misunderstood the pull of her family. They would never remember old times affectionately or plan to see each other again. There could be no more sitting close together on the sofa, laughing at everybody who seemed a little odd, or planning their next party. The promise of those kisses would never be fulfilled.

Despite the bitterness I often felt, I never gave up hope that one day we would be friends again, she wrote to Harry, weeping over the page. *And now the years of our separation are as nothing, and I am filled with memories of the loveliest years of my life. All gone.*

The flickering out of that hope, held so secretly yet so passionately for so many years, hurt beyond measure. She fished out of the boxes in the attic a piece she had written for Lisl in those happy days, and sat at her piano, endlessly playing it, allowing images of those times to wash through her. The music was full of the yearning that had resulted in those passionate kisses, so quickly trampled on.

It's hideous here, wrote Harry at last. *Sadness, surprise and dismay. No-one seems to know quite what happened, definitely something to do with her heart. Heinrich is a poor old thing, and Julia distraught. I shall be with you soonest.*

Heinrich, a poor old thing – how could that be? He had always become vigorous and energetic the minute he held a baton in his hand, or when he tried to explain to her some fine point of composition. Memories flooded into her mind – Lisl popping into the library with morning coffee or an invitation to lunch, warm and smiling, whilst she began to understand how to get down on paper the music in her head; the triumphant musical evenings; lying on the bed with her, arms entwined, when she was ill. It was impossible that Lisl was dead, and that lively, interesting man so sickly.

She crawled into her music as if it was a shelter, a dark, warm space, a refuge. It was a fertile place, full of images and sound, grief and anger and love. Music flowed out of her fingers onto the lines, fat notes, thin notes, each fully formed before the next leapt from her pen; melodies, harmonies, percussion; songs, choruses, strange instrumental combinations. She could hear them so clearly in her head, the flute and the cello, the voice and the horn and the violin, the drumbeat and the cymbals, the bassoon. Lines and lines of ensemble spread over the page, topped by the sweetest or most jarring of melodies.

Other times, she took her bicycle out and rode through the Sussex lanes, a sandwich and a cake in the basket. Exhausted, she would sink under a tree, sleep a little or vaguely doze the afternoon away. She relived time and again the warm physical presence of Lisl, and tried to capture the sweetness of their intense kisses, to reduce the years between to nothing. Her body would shake with sobs, and she would jump up and run across the hillside, leap fallen trees and jump streams until she was ready to go home again.

20

LONDON 1893

Ethel sat at the corner of the stage and wished she was somewhere else; almost anywhere would do. The music was terrible. Mr Barnby had asked her to attend the final few rehearsals so they could discuss any last-minute adjustments, but the whole thing needed massively changing, or even scrapping.

Each part of the Mass was different, but she had thought there was a unifying vision running through it. Throughout this week, however, neither she nor Mr Barnby had been able to find it. It was bitty and piecemeal, the exuberant sections sat uncomfortably by the more reflective parts. It was a mere collection of interesting sounds.

She could tell that the orchestra didn't think it hung together either. The last two mornings they had been irritable, and today they were hardly putting any energy into it or trying to find solutions. It was painful to notice that when they played the parts of Haydn's *Creation* that would make up the other half of the programme, they relaxed and the whole sound was warmer, more responsive, more assured.

She rubbed her eyes. She was tired and exhausted, and she already had about thirty changes to make to the score – changes which had to be completed by late afternoon so the copyists could revise the instrumental parts ready for the next day's rehearsal. She had her pieces of manuscript paper cut up and ready, scissors, glue and pens to hand. It was work she enjoyed, all part of the transition from the music in her mind to the performed work. Even a thousand last-minute changes, however, could not make this a worthwhile venture.

How proud she had been when the letter came. *The Royal Choral Society is delighted to include in their spring programme a performance of your Mass. Mr Barnby will be in touch in due course about the rehearsal schedule.*

She knew she had the Empress Eugénie to thank, and Princess Christian, and Hermann Levi and the Duke of Edinburgh and who knows who else. She had received so many rejections from other choral societies that it was clear that no-one was going to give up half their programme to a work by a virtually unknown composer. She was becoming quite an expert on how these things worked, the patronage required, the money to be poured into buying tickets for important people to attend. It was only the Empress's assurance that she herself would come and, if not the Queen herself, at least a prince or princess or two, that had persuaded Mr Barnby to engage worthwhile soloists and muster a small amount of enthusiasm.

Now, she wished he had not bothered. She hated the music; the orchestra considered it chaotic, and the eminent and ordinary members of the audience would find it excruciating. Her family and friends and Harry would be there to witness her humiliation.

She turned to look into the dark auditorium, preferring it to remain empty.

George was waiting up for her when she finally got back. Not only were George and Lilian Henschel putting her up and looking after her, but they were a fountain of advice and support.

'You look tired, my dear,' he said as she came into his library. 'Tell me how it's going before I leave you to your supper.'

'I've had so little chance to hear my music played, George,' said Ethel, removing her hat and sinking into the easy chair. 'Honestly, I wonder if I have any style at all. I thought I did, but it just sounds a mess.'

'It's a common feeling in rehearsal,' he said. 'For all of us. You mustn't despair. And this is a completely new work, a huge one too. The musicians don't know it. They are struggling with the notes and the dynamics and the shape. Even Barnby has no idea yet what it will truly sound like. Believe me, it all comes together in the end in a quite marvellous way.'

'I thought it would be such an adventure to hear a large orchestra playing my music. But it's just hard grind with no cohesion.'

George laughed and passed her a generous glass of sherry. 'Welcome to the world of performance. What's tomorrow?'

'A few hundred singers enter stage left.' She laughed, and tipped the sherry down her throat. 'Hard work to heartbreak?'

'You might be surprised,' said George, getting up and tidying his papers. 'The choirs are often quite well rehearsed by this time. Now, I'll leave you to eat your supper. Have courage, my dear. I've been there many times, both as composer and conductor. Don't stop believing in your work now. This is your first major work, remember.'

Soothed by kind words and the warm fire. Ethel almost dropped off. Sleep, how good that would be. But first, she must eat and then have another look at that section of the Benedictus that still seemed awkward.

~

Ethel exchanged greetings with the doorman at the concert hall. On the first day, they had argued when he insisted that this entrance was for musicians only.

'Yes,' Ethel had said. 'I am one of those.'

He consulted his schedule. 'It's not choir day today. Come back on Friday.'

'I'm not in the choir,' she said. 'I'm the composer of one of the pieces, Ethel Smyth.'

He scrutinised his list again, eyebrows raised. 'E.M. Smyth – is that you?'

'Thank you,' she had said sarcastically. 'Can I go in now?'

They had since become good friends.

'They've already started,' he said.

'Really? I don't think I'm late. They're probably just warming up.'

'Ten o'clock they started,' he said.

'Oh, I thought it was eleven.'

Ethel started up the series of stairs and corridors that would take her into the auditorium. She could hear the beautiful sound of a soprano voice and behind it the mellow fullness of a large choir with the gentle support of massed instruments. She stopped for a moment, full of yearning. How lovely that was, how complete and assured. They must have started with the Haydn. That was the sort of sound she wanted, she thought sadly. How did he achieve that?

She let herself into the stalls and sat to wait until Mr Barnby was ready to move on. But as the melody repeated itself, she slammed a hand over her mouth. It was actually a part of her Credo, of her Mass. She had never heard it performed by the whole of the orchestra and the choir, with the soloist too. My goodness, it was beautiful. It was ethereal and yet robust, quiet but strong. The section came to an end, and Mr Barnby turned towards Ethel. He was grinning, and the players were buzzing. He beckoned her up.

'Well, Miss Smyth, what did you think?'

'You've worked the transformation I hoped for,' she said. She wanted to hug him, but he was too forbidding. 'The dull notes have been given life.'

'At last,' he said. 'I myself was wondering. Now we have the chance to create something wonderful. Let us not question how this magic has been achieved.' He turned back to the orchestra. 'Now, on to the Sanctus.'

Ethel greeted the soloists. She had heard them sing many times and had absolute faith in them. Back in her seat, she could tell that the orchestra had committed themselves, and there was a feeling of excitement and curiosity. The choir looked out confidently over the heads of the orchestra into the huge hall, and there was silence as Barnby held up his baton, ready to make a start.

Ethel felt curious herself now, excited. But as Miss Cole began to sing, she sat up startled. The sound, with just the soft brass in the background, was being swallowed up by the large hall. Without enough support, the voice of the soloist faltered and became distant. Ethel got up and walked to the stage as Barnby brought the orchestra to a halt.

'That hasn't translated into the concert hall,' he said. 'It's not strong enough.'

The soloist looked at the full score over his shoulder. 'There's not enough body to it. The horns are too thin.'

'I see,' said Ethel. 'You're right. It's not too late to change it, if you agree, Mr Barnby.'

She looked around, embarrassed. Sometimes, when changes had needed to be made, the players had looked impatient or disparaging. Today, however, they were either quietly waiting to hear what would happen or even calling out some suggestions.

'We can try a few things,' said Barnby to Ethel, 'if you're happy with that. There isn't going to be any more rehearsal time, so we need to have it done by the end of the morning.'

'Yes, that would be good. I'll make a few notes as we go, and then I can change the copies this afternoon.'

After a few minutes, a new balance was struck. Ethel scribbled furiously. She was exhilarated to be working with people who knew what they were doing, despite her tiredness and the prospect of an afternoon spent once more with glue and scissors instead of with Harry, just arrived in London.

'You wouldn't believe,' said Ethel to Harry, laying her spoon in the empty soup plate, 'how this world works. The only reason Barnby agreed to do this was because of royal patronage. Or perhaps I should say pressure. And money.'

'Maybe,' he said, 'but all the influence in the world wouldn't make him do it if the music was rubbish. His reputation is at stake here, too.'

'Fortunately, you love it,' said Mary. 'There's nothing you like better than flaunting your talents to all your wealthy friends.'

Everyone laughed and Ethel leant over to smell the fragrance of the roast pork the servant placed in front of her.

'It's hard work, believe me,' said Ethel. 'Not only do I have to write the damn stuff, but I have to work endlessly to get anything performed.'

'Don't swear, Ethel, please,' said her father. Ethel laughed. She had thought he had learnt to ignore her familiar complaints by now.

'Who exactly is going to turn up, Auntie?' asked Kitty. 'Will the Queen be there?'

'The Queen's already heard her Mass,' said Violet. Everyone laughed. The story of Ethel's performance to the Queen had enlivened many a dinner table.

'You never know, but it's unlikely. No, Princess Christian, I should think, maybe one or two others. And the Empress, of course.'

'You are going to be so famous,' said Kitty.

'I'm sure Ethel's more concerned with how her music will be received, than the royal family's attendance.' It was Harry.

Ethel smiled at him. How she loved to hear the slight European accent within his correct English words. She must be grateful that he had not voiced his usual scathing comments about royal patronage in front of her family.

'It'll be a triumph,' said George. 'Please, keep eating everyone. It's wonderful music, well worth playing to royalty, even to God himself. Believe me, you are in for a treat. Everyone who goes will love it.'

Ethel smiled gratefully at George. 'Even the critics?' she said.

'Especially the critics.'

Lilian signalled to the servants to refill everyone's plate and top up the wine glasses.

'D'you know what?' she said. 'I wish I was singing that soprano part.'

Ethel looked at her curiously. 'Do you miss your singing career?'

'I certainly do,' she said. 'I love my children, but oh my, is there something special about stepping out on that stage.'

'Maybe one day, women will be able to do both,' said Harry.

'I can't see how,' said Lilian. 'Anyway, I'm pretty sure there has never been a performance of a Mass by a woman composer in London before, so we shall all take the greatest pleasure in that.'

'I'll drink to that,' said George, raising his glass.

'Auntie Ethel is leading the way,' said Kitty, taking a sip out of her father's wine glass.

'Hold on,' said Charlie. 'You're much too young to be drinking wine, however special the day.'

'Mr Brewster,' said Ethel's father, 'I'm told that you have a new book published that has been well received?'

'Yes, it has. Thank you, Major. In a small way, of course. We're not exactly talking popular novels here.'

'Oh, I don't know,' said Violet. 'I particularly liked the bit where the ravishingly tall, dark, hero...'

'Very funny,' said Ethel. The whole table laughed.

~

Ethel's heart sang. There were thousands of people playing, singing or listening to her music. Barnby was doing a wonderful job, the orchestra was engaged and the choir was producing a particularly rounded sound. The soprano and mezzo soloists shimmered in their dresses, bright as jewels on a stage of dinner-suited men, and the voices of the tenor and bass were full and distinctive. In the boxes women with precious stones glittering on their décolleté chests sat by well-groomed men; all seemed to be alert and listening.

Ethel thought she must remember to tell Harry that he should cease his cruel mockery of her religious fervour if this was the result. She smiled at the memory of their furious arguments about it – arguments that had in no way spoiled the pleasure they had in their constant letter-writing. She allowed herself to lean against him. He immediately responded, and under cover of the semi-darkness put his hand over hers where they lay on her lap, adding to the surge in her stomach as the choir poised itself for the Gloria.

There were moments of silence at the end, and Ethel braced herself for a smattering of applause. As the sound broke out, she had to look around to make sure that it wasn't just her family and friends who were making such a noise. Then she saw Barnby turn to take his bow, his face smiling, moved, satisfied. He turned and flung out his arms to bring the orchestra to their feet, and then the choir, and she saw him shake hands enthusiastically with the soloists before leaving the stage. The audience continued to clap.

When Barnby returned, he bowed and put his hand to his brow, peering into the auditorium to spot Ethel. He applauded her, and then beckoned for her to come onto the stage. The crowd, realising that the composer was there, started calling for her.

'Go on, darling,' said Alice. 'They want to see you. Have your moment of glory.'

Ethel made her way to the front and up the stairs, grateful that Lilian had made sure she had a clean skirt and brushed hat.

Barnby came towards her, shook hands and led her to the centre of the stage, where he raised their joint hands to the cheering audience.

'Well done, Miss Smyth,' he said. 'It all came together wonderfully, don't you think?'

Ethel turned and applauded the choir and the orchestra, impressed at what they had done, and the soloists came to her and there was more hand-shaking and kisses and congratulations. They left the stage and, as the audience stopped clapping, a loud buzz rose as hundreds of people made their comments and tried to decide what they might do in the interval.

Ethel went backstage and thanked as many of the orchestra and choir as she could, only going back to her seat as they returned to the stage for the second half. She heard little of it, so distracted was her mind, so unable to take in that success. From the little she did hear, she found Haydn's *Creation* dull and old-fashioned. How strange; she normally loved it.

~

Ethel went to sit by her father, who looked tired and quiet, sitting on the sofa in the hotel lobby.

'I miss your mother,' he said. 'She loved it so much when everyone got together. And she understood your music, before she became so deaf anyway, but it's a mystery to me.'

'I miss her too,' said Ethel. 'I think she would have enjoyed the Mass last night.'

'At least she saw you on your way to being successful. She was proud, you know.'

'I caused her a good few worries,' said Ethel, smiling. How long ago it now seemed, that bitter struggle to follow her own path.

'I'm more than a bit hungry. Can't stand these late breakfast, early lunch things – they just upset the digestive system as far as I can see.'

'You know Mary,' said Ethel. 'She likes to try different things. And you must admit this is a beautiful hotel.' She looked appreciatively at the coloured windows and deep leather sofas.

'Cost her more than a few pounds, I'm sure.'

Mary came in with George and Harry.

'Come and sit at the table, everyone,' she said.

'Thank goodness for that,' said their father, leaning on Ethel heavily as they made their way to the dining room.

When all the family were sat down, Harry too and George and Lilian, Mary gestured to the waiters to stand back.

'Last night we drank to Ethel's amazing success, so we won't do that again, but there are a couple of telegrams to read out. George, please do the honours.'

He stood up and slit open the first. 'This is from Joseph Barnby: *Thank you, Miss Smyth, for bringing us some wonderful new music to perform. It was a great evening, and much enjoyed by singers and orchestra alike.*'

'And us,' said Kitty.

'This one is from Miss Cole. *Thank you for creating a great part for a mezzo-soprano. Congratulations on a successful evening.*'

'That's nice,' said Alice. 'She sang it beautifully.'

'Now, here is one to relish, as good as from the Almighty himself. It is from the wife of Archbishop Benson.' Ethel's head shot up. She had not seen them at the performance. She shut her eyes tight as George read it out. '*We enjoyed your music so much. Though the ArchB did wonder if you were commanding God to have mercy rather than beseeching him. I'm so happy for your success. Well done!*'

Everyone laughed, and banged on the table.

'Blessed archbishop,' whispered Ethel to Harry. 'Thinks he has a monopoly on what God thinks.'

'Now,' said Mary. 'Food is imminent, but we just have one newspaper review as yet. Here's what they had to say about our wonderful Ethel – *the vigour and rhythmic force of the score carried us all away...* Not bad, dear sister, not bad.'

There was clapping and cheering. Ethel got up and thanked everyone for coming to support her once more; it meant a lot to be able to rely on a dozen or so people in the audience who would cheer no matter what, and she hoped if she was lucky enough to put on another similar event, everyone would come again.

Food was now served, plenty of it, but when Ethel tried the kipper on her plate, she found she could not eat it. She kept wondering where the rest of the newspapers were, and why they were not being passed around as usual.

She got up and went out to the reception desk of the hotel. She was directed into the lounge, where several papers hung on their long wooden poles. Ethel took them down one by one, flicking over the pages to where the reports of the previous night's concerts were.

'No,' she said. 'No, that can't be. No. *Over-elaborate and complicated… inexperience of what soloists can offer.*' The bubbles of joy popped and a hole appeared to have been blown through her stomach. She tried to swallow to ease the sudden constriction in her throat and leant against the pillar for support.

'Ah, there you are.' Harry was at her side.

'It seems that it wasn't such a success, after all.'

'They are not all bad, not at all, but I know you'll spot the criticisms rather than the many bouquets. You have never taken any notice of these people, Ethel, and you must not start now.'

'You're right, of course. But they ask things like: *Is a great female composer possible?* With the implied answer that it is not. Despite the applause of a thousand people, it is their opinion that will sway that of others. Look at that, Harry.'

A blaze of anger was coming over her, and she was conscious that her voice was becoming loud in the quiet lobby.

Harry took her hands and led her away. 'The fact that they ask such a question is a big thing, even if they shouldn't have to. Come, let's stroll along the street a few minutes. No-one will miss us.'

'They don't want to give me a chance.'

'You are leading the way, Ethel. Not everyone likes that.'

Ethel became calmer with every footstep, with the feel of Harry's hand pressing on hers where it was linked into his arm.

'Thank you, Harry, I'm not going to shout anymore.'

After walking around for a while, they turned back into the hotel. 'I did love the audience reaction,' she said. 'But that's not the main thing. I want to be talked of in the same breath as the best composers of the day.'

'You've always known what you have to fight against,' he said. 'Don't let this surprise or stop you.'

'I'm so frustrated, I could scream.'

21

FRIMLEY, SURREY 1895

Harry, please save me from this, Ethel wrote. *I am torn in so many directions. The minute I sit down to write the fate of that idiot of Mantua, there is some disturbance. The nurses are wonderful and love Father, and are doing such a good job when he is so poorly, but even so there are queries all the time that it seems no-one but me can answer. When Mary or Violet come for a few days, it does lift the load a little, but the household still has to be run. I just can't find the stretches of time I need to mix that brew where ideas take shape.*

She could, if she was very efficient, get the kitchen and the house and the stables and the yard sorted out early in the day, ensuring everyone was clear about their schedule. She could sit with her father for a while, discuss things with the nurses and be in her room by mid-morning ready to play or write. However, her ears pricked at every sound, any hint that she might be disturbed.

'Come on, Marco,' she said, pressing the seal to the envelope. 'Let's go and post this letter and have a bit of a walk. I'm doing nothing but making myself miserable.'

They struck out through the wooded area behind the house. Marco flew off into the undergrowth, frightening every creature that happened to be there, barking at any fly that danced around his nose, joyfully returning to Ethel now and then before starting all over again.

'Marco, Marco,' murmured Ethel, bending to pick some sticky burrs off his coat. 'If only I could feel so free.'

They emerged from the woods onto the canal path. The occasional barges steaming past on the smooth water calmed her. Father was going to die quite soon, there could be no doubt about that. He was being his usual stubborn self, clinging to life, making tiny recoveries, strong despite everything. She was glad to be here with him, definitely. And yet, the opera must be done; the deadline was beginning to loom.

In the bright green grass, celandines and cowslips shone in the spring sunshine. She raised her face to receive its warmth too, and stretched up her arms to release the tension in her back.

'This is hard,' she said, 'blooming hard.'

Marco ran back to see if she was talking to him, and now they both wandered along the canal side. The dog's excess of energy was spent, and he trotted a little ahead of her, sniffing the ground and following wherever a scent took him. Ethel's mind ran over what she had been writing the last few days. It was meant to be a comic opera, but the music was too heavy. The princess's disappointment was too sad; those dark clouds would have to go. They were in the wrong work, that was the problem. The sadness belonged in a work where a much-loved father was slipping out of the world, rather than one where even if a lover was spurned, the happy outcome was secure. She started humming. The heaviness in her own heart was not going to disappear, so she would have to introduce a few musical jokes into the life of the court.

She had never thought she might write a comic opera, or want to. Perhaps it was after the seriousness of the Mass that it seemed such a good idea. One day when she was sitting in Hyde Park with Harry having tea, he had pulled the story of Fantasio from his bag and started reading it to her. Perhaps it was his funny mixture of

French and English that set her laughing, and caused the surge of a light music to rise within her. It comforted her that, however tortuous the plot, it came right in the end.

It was Hermann Levi who had suggested she write an opera in the first place. She was determined to use the opportunity of the opera competition whose details he had sent her. The prize was immense – money, publication, guaranteed performance. Slowly, with Harry's help, the music and words had begun to come together. She must ignore the requiem dragging in an undertow beneath.

She climbed over the stile that would lead her to the village, Marco squeezing his large body underneath. She forced herself to slow down, studying the gravel on the path beneath her feet, trying to make herself focus. What was it Arthur Sullivan had said?

'Don't make the mistake of thinking that just because something makes the audience laugh, it's frivolous and easy to write. I haven't sweated over scores of comic operas without learning that.'

She had been invited to his London hotel, where the porter had showed her into his private room, all piles of music and books. Ethel couldn't help looking at the enormous, white sideburns that framed his big square head.

'I suppose we're rather poking fun at people's strength of feeling rather than claiming they don't have it?'

'Exaggerate, exaggerate, exaggerate. Now come on, think of a time when you were deadly serious about something, whilst others looking on might have found quite amusing.'

'That seems to happen to me quite a bit,' said Ethel, thinking. 'All right, when I went to Leipzig conservatoire, I thought a treasure chest would open and I would learn all the arcane secrets of music composition, but in fact it was quite mundane. I was devastated. Especially when the famous Karl Reinecke had no time for me.'

'Good example. I remember the conservatoire well. Reinecke was just a boy tutor in my day. Very keen. Go on.'

'I felt let down, outraged, disappointed, that my dream was going to end before it had begun.'

'That could be quite a powerful drama. Now, what might others have seen?'

Ethel was silent for a moment, then started to laugh. 'A naïve girl who knew nothing? One who was very ill prepared to become a musician? A headstrong, you-can't-tell-me-anything type?'

'Lovely,' said Arthur. 'Now what about the conservatoire? Exaggerate its eminent, fusty-dusty musicians who've always done it this way, the studious, obedient students, their uninspired music...'

'I get it. It's still a mini-tragedy for our young woman, but it's also funny to watch.'

'The audience must still feel with the hero, however foolish. We can all be a bit ridiculous.'

'What about the music? All my music's been so serious so far.'

'You don't need me to tell you anything about music, Ethel. Really, you don't. Think of your story, and its two versions. The serious, naïve young musician in a venerable institution she can't fit into. Or the headstrong, vigorous girl in a rigid, male establishment. You know that the music needed is entirely different for each version.'

'Of course, of course. It's so obvious, isn't it? You've cleared my head after ten minutes of talking.'

'Bring me a bit when you get started,' said Arthur, rising to show her out. 'There's a few musical tricks I could mention might help.'

Now, walking through the field, hurrying to get back to Father, she wondered what those musical tricks might be. She would write to him asking for some more time with him. It infuriated her that Britain's composers learnt from each other all the time, went to the same clubs, met and exchanged ideas, solved each other's problems, recommended each other's work. Whereas she, continuously excluded, had to ask, in the time she managed to get, specific questions which merely demonstrated how much she still did not know.

She had a deep pang of longing for Leipzig. That was the nearest she had come to belonging, when she'd had lessons with Heinrich, and Lisl had been so loving; not to mention spending time at the Röntgens and meeting Brahms. Even later, when those best years were over, there had been Pyotr and Edvard Grieg, and she had talked music with them all, played it, listened to it, learnt it.

Well, those days were over, really over, long gone, and she must not hark back to it. She was on her own and had to take help where she could find it. She blew out of her mouth and started to run. 'Come on, Marco,' she said, who returned to her side and ran alongside her. 'We don't need them. Let's get this letter posted and get home.'

She must have been out for a while, and Father might be asking for her. His wasted body, his weakened mind, once so strong, reminded her that she was not done with grief and pain yet.

22

WOKING 1895

Ethel looked across the fireplace at Harry, sitting reading the newspaper as usual. She smiled broadly. Her hearth, her house.

'I've wanted this for so long,' she said.

'What's that?' he said, looking up.

'My own home. Running it how I like. My routines. I never realised how wonderful it would be. Father's death has brought me unexpected happiness.'

She had to resist the temptation to get up and go outside and come in through her own front door all over again.

Frimhurst had been sold. Father had threatened so many times to sell it as the only way out of the family's financial problems, that Ethel could hardly believe it was finally gone. Her mother had been ridiculously extravagant, he had grumbled, what with her parties and endless new furnishings, and Bob, ever since he had been posted to India, seemed unable to manage the sort of life expected of him on his salary. Not to mention Ethel, who must have an allowance since no-one had managed to persuade her to find a husband who would look after her. And there's you as well, Ethel would add under her breath. You with your huge staff keeping too many horses in tip-top shape, not to mention the grounds of the house with their beautiful, formal gardens, and the farm, and the number of people who no longer worked but were supported.

At last all the papers were sorted and signed. Her inheritance turned out to be enough for a small living, and to buy a sizeable enough cottage in Woking. Friends and sisters pitched in, not just offering their own gardeners and handymen to help her get it straight, but providing her with furniture and curtains and carpets. She had no idea so much was needed to make a house fit for living in.

'Does that delight in your very own house include me being here?' asked Harry.

'How am I going to complete *Fantasio* if you're not here to argue with?'

'You know that's not what I meant.' He came and stood behind her, his hand stroking her shoulder.

'Do you mean, will the day come when we're not thinking about when we'll have to part?'

'Yes.' He sat on the arm of her chair, stroking her hair and shoulder.

'But you still have to go home to Julia.'

'Yes. I thought it would be different when the children were grown up, but she's become even more isolated. I find I can't completely leave her. Is our cause hopeless?'

'Not at all. It's strange, isn't it, finding we still want to be together after all this time?' She leant against him.

'Whatever drew me to you in the beginning hasn't gone away – not one bit of it. I want to be with you despite all the limitations. Just because I must always return to her, does not mean there cannot be changes for us. She knows I can never stay with her for long.'

Ethel was silent. She knew exactly what he meant. He wanted to turn their love, their kisses, their longing for each other into something more intimate. All those reasons which had prevented her being with him – her promise to Lisl, the certain disapproval of her parents, any possible scandal – seemed to be disappearing one by one.

She wanted it too, yet she still held back. 'I need to get used to all that has changed in the last few months,' she said.

'Yes,' he said. 'The time must be right for you. It will be.'

Marco stirred on the carpet and began to get up. 'Blessed dog. I'll just let him out in the garden.'

~

'*Fantasio* sounds as though it might be great entertainment,' the Empress Eugénie said.

The Farnborough Hill dining room was huge, magnificent. Although there were only six guests, sitting three on each side of the Empress, the dinner was sumptuous, served as always in the porcelain dishes, with multiple candles enhancing the light.

Ethel was trying to explain how much she had loved writing it. 'Such a silly little story, and yet the music has to be brilliant, of course, not to mention great parts for the soloists.'

'A bit lighter than the Mass, perhaps?'

'Oh, goodness me, yes. And all the music has to fit with acting out this foolish situation. I have to actually write in when people move on and off the stage, not to mention the things that they do. I've never done anything like it before.'

'As usual, it sounds as though you've put your heart and soul into it.'

'I've hardly played golf for weeks.'

'Well, that is serious.' Eugénie laughed.

'Anyway, it's finished now. And yet, I can't stop fiddling with it.'

'Is it something that could be acted at my garden party – part of it, anyway? I'm looking for something new, and it might help.'

'That would be wonderful,' said Ethel. 'I could find two or three singers for the main parts, I'm sure.'

'My guests arrive at the weekend,' said Eugénie. 'We'll do it on Friday next week.'

Ethel gulped. 'Of course.'

What began as a short run-through with a piano and a couple of singers began to develop into a semi-performance. Some of the guests wanted to join in. They raided deserted far-flung rooms and attics to find suitable costumes, and a stage area was created. There were days of uproarious rehearsals from which the Empress was banished.

At last, about seventy people sat in the beautiful garden on a fine evening and watched, and laughed and clapped. Afterwards, there was universal praise. No-one doubted for a moment that Ethel would win first prize in the competition, and they could all go to Germany and have a wonderful time seeing it again.

For Ethel, it was merely useful. She was glad everyone had a lot of fun, but several bits did not work. The instructions for how the soloists should sing and act had not been enough; a lot of the music was still too dramatic for such a slight story. She drew on memories of all the dozens of operas she had seen, and made some more changes to it. Finally, although the closing date for the competition had been put back to the autumn, she sent it in, just to stop her endless tinkering. She longed to get on with something else.

Hermann Levi wrote to tell her that he was pretty sure he knew the work of everyone who might send in an entry, and none had her musical skill or power.

~

'Shall we walk to dinner?' said Harry. 'Or would you like me to hire a cab?'

'Oh, let's walk,' said Ethel, standing under the portico of the hotel entrance. She sniffed the evening air, the slight whiff of the Paris sewers mixed with the scent of flowers. The trees of the gardens across the street were just beginning to lose their definition in the dusk, and the songs of the birds were less frequent as the daylight faded.

'I could sing,' said Ethel.

Harry tucked her arm into his and turned into the avenue. 'How wonderful that would be, your voice ringing out over the sounds of Paris. What would you sing?'

'A bit of Schubert? Suitable for a late summer evening, but not very Paris. A French song, maybe? There aren't many songs about the city.'

'You should write some.'

'Don't talk about writing music. I'm on holiday, remember, from composing and every other dashed musical thing. I don't care if I never see another page full of sets of five lines.'

'They are indelibly scored across your mind.' He guided her through the gate into the gardens that ran alongside the river.

Ethel shuddered. 'Don't say things like that. It's like a life sentence. For the moment, I'm free. The need and desire to place dots on lines is dead.'

She shouted the last words and, freeing herself from Harry's arm ran down the path, across the grass and out onto the riverbank. She stood watching the river's flow catching the last glimmers of the sky. The boats already had their lanterns lit, swaying as they made their way up- and downriver.

Harry came and stood close by her, his arm across her back. 'You must feel a little lost. I always feel sad when I finish a book, and you have this unbroken silence to contend with.'

'That light and jolly opera was wrought out of pain and sheer hard work. Father was scarcely in his grave when I had to be saving the princess from that ghastly duke.'

She turned so she faced Harry. He drew her close and kissed her.

'All those experiences are in the mix that produces the music,' he said. She turned back to watch the river. 'Naturally, there are other potent ingredients in this smouldering potion – horses, for example, fine dinners, golf, loud arguments, expensive concerts.'

'Trips to Paris, good friends, the dark, glistening river,' she finished, laughing. 'You must remember that when you're doing one of your brilliant this-is-where-art-comes-from lectures.'

'And love?' He tucked her arm in his again and they started to walk along by the river. 'Is there a little love scattering its gold dust over all?'

'Harry,' she said after a while. 'When we get home tonight, back to the hotel, I mean, will you come to my room?'

'To your room? Of course. Is there something you want me to look at?'

'Yes,' she said quietly. 'Me.'

They stopped and turned towards each other. It was darker here despite the lamps flickering on the river. Ethel reached up and pulled him towards her. An excitement stirred deep within her.

'Dearest Ethel. Please don't tease me. Do you mean the time has come?'

'I do,' she said. 'Hold me tight, Harry. I've made up my mind now.' She was shaking all over. She leaned against him so he staggered back against the low river wall.

'Why don't we go back to the hotel now?' he said. 'We can send a message with some excuse for not turning up for dinner.'

'No, no. The Ambroses have come to Paris specially to see you.' She quietened herself, drawing away a little and beginning to straighten her hat, his collar, her hair. 'Let's go for dinner, and then we shall be free.'

'If you're sure,' he said, leaving his arm around her until the path opened into the lit streets.

'Oh, I'm sure,' she said. 'At last, after all this time, I'm sure.'

The dinner was a small affair, just a couple of Harry's friends from America and some from Rome. Ethel would have preferred a larger occasion when she might have been able to keep quiet with her own thoughts. That's what she wanted to do – to savour this moment when at last everything had become simple.

The obstacles had melted away. She could hardly recall how large they had seemed, how painful, over such a long time. She had kept Harry at bay in the hope of recovering Lisl's affection and regard, and had the solace of neither for many years. Then the need to protect her family from scandal had been so strong. There was still Julia, of course, but that marriage's story now seemed to have little to do with her. There was still the need to safeguard her reputation as a single woman and musician, though she thought that people hardly cared, as long as they were discreet.

She thanked the waiter for the beautifully dressed piece of fish he put on her plate, and started to eat with relish. Throughout it all, Harry had never wavered. He had gone away when she told him to, and come back into her life when she'd allowed it. He had accepted her intense feelings for her women friends, and committed himself to their strange life, with its many frustrations. She looked at him now, talking in his usual quietly determined way about… about what? She had completely lost the thread of the conversation. They had already dismissed God, she remembered that, dismantled the monarchy, which for once she hadn't hotly defended, dissected aesthetics. Now they seemed to be talking about something the President of America had done, she couldn't catch what.

He caught her glance, and looked at her, eyebrows raised, questioning her quietness, perhaps. She also caught a gleam in his eyes, much like the one that had sustained her so often at slightly tedious dinner tables, accompanied by a loving smile. Today, that look nearly made her choke. A surge of excitement swept through the inside of her body, and when it receded she felt like a washed beach, waiting for the next wave. Confused, she coughed into her serviette to try and regain a little poise.

Mrs Ambrose asked Ethel if she would sing for them. Usually she resented these invitations, grumbling to Harry or her sisters that she was only valued at people's dinner tables for her entertainment value. But tonight, before Harry could start to protest on her behalf, no doubt ready to plead that she was having time off music after the strain of finishing *Fantasio*, she was on her feet.

'I'd love to,' she said. If she couldn't concentrate on the serious discussions these people were having – and perhaps they were disappointed in her because they had probably been told that she always argued fiercely about everything – then at least she could sing.

As Ethel sat at the walnut, polished piano, she felt the power of that space. The dining room faded, as did the lights and conversation, the guests and even Harry himself, against the strong enveloping world of the instrument, her fingers on its creamy keys, ready for the marvel of sound. She explored it for a while, feeling the notes a bit like a friend or much-loved child not seen for a while. She could hear port being poured into glasses, cigars being lit, chairs being turned towards her.

'Although there are few songs about the city,' she said, making her voice just audible above the piano, 'there are thousands about the countryside. I started my musical life in Germany, so I'll begin with some of their songs.'

She sang of nightingales, the spread of trees and sun-kissed streams. She loved the silence that fell when people heard her powerful voice and knew the fluency of her fingers. And tonight, feeling the urgency of something new within herself, she exulted in those sounds and the resonance of the piano in that room.

'Bravo,' cheered her host when she paused to draw breath. 'Wonderful, thank you so much.'

'I shall end up loving German songs if I hear much more like this,' said one of the dinner guests who had put up a strong argument for the supremacy of French art. 'Well done,

Mademoiselle.'

Harry came over with a glass of port for her and, turning his back on the guests, said quietly, 'You are unbelievably beautiful tonight, Ethel. Your singing is glorious, but I hope you won't go on too long.'

Ethel let her hands play on the keys. She didn't dare look at him in case lightning flashed through the room.

'Thanks for the port,' she said. 'You know what it's like when I start singing. This could go on for hours.'

'I do believe there are other things to be done tonight.'

'You know music is always my priority,' she said.

Harry nearly choked on the explosion of laughter that broke in a bark from his mouth. He took out his handkerchief to provide some cover for his face as he went back to his seat.

'Finally,' she said, 'since we are in Paris, I will sing a few of the intriguing new songs of Gabriel Fauré, whom I'm just coming to love.'

When Ethel finished, she sat for a moment at the piano. Now she wanted everyone to just fade away and leave her and Harry alone. But there were more drinks, chocolate confections, cigars and talk to be had. She could see that Harry was restless too, and when he looked over at her, she yawned as if she hadn't slept for days.

'I think I should get Miss Smyth back to her hotel,' he said. 'She's been working hard for weeks, and it seems to have taken its toll.'

'I do apologise,' she said. 'I don't want to spoil the fun. This has been a quite lovely evening, thank you so much.'

At last their coats were fetched, suggestions of carriages were rejected, new meeting arrangements were made and farewells said, and they were out on the street.

'I need to walk,' said Ethel, breathing deeply of the cool, night air. 'All that yawning wasn't entirely fabricated.'

'You shall sleep soundly in my arms tonight,' said Harry.

A cavernous space opened up all at once where her stomach

had been. This wasn't a promise of some event in the unspecified future; it was not a flirtation; it was not about sparks in the eyes and in the air or the delight of a man's regard. It was not even about loving somebody and knowing how steadfastly that love is returned. It wasn't about playing, or composing tempestuous music or singing songs of love.

'I don't know what it is about,' she said, clutching Harry's arm. She cast about wildly in her mind. She was getting on for forty years old and she had very little idea of what was going to happen. Of course, she knew of the solitary pleasures of the body, but how was that to be replicated, if indeed it was meant to be? Might it hurt, as some women said, or bring great joy, as others hinted, or be what seemed to many a boring necessity?

'You must trust me,' said Harry. 'You know you can, don't you?' He put his arm around her as they walked slowly along.

Why on earth would she want to do this, anyway, she was thinking? She could deal with all those feelings in her own way – not that she was feeling anything just now. She yawned again. Wouldn't it be better if they did what they always did, kiss and go to their separate rooms?

That hand on her back seemed controlling rather than loving. She shook it off and tucked her hand into his arm, more for politeness than that she wanted to be near him.

'Ethel, Ethel,' murmured Harry. 'You have thrown yourself headlong into so many adventures, into so many situations that others would not even contemplate. Shall you draw back from this now?'

'No, I don't think so,' she said slowly. 'I like what we have, Harry. I must be growing old, scared of changing things in case they turn out worse.'

She was cross with herself now. Since when had she been so cautious, so scared, so nervous of events she may not be able to control? She straightened up and laughed.

'We shall have champagne,' said Harry.

Ethel nestled closer to him, and now she was not alarmed when he put his arm around her, and she stopped and turned towards him and drew his face towards her and kissed him. They turned into the hotel.

'Very well, Mr Brewster,' she said. 'Give me ten minutes.'

'Not one second longer,' he said.

Ethel opened the drawer of the little dressing table and took out a nightgown and jacket. She stroked the soft silk of the fabric. It had cost her a lot more than she could afford, that and the lacy new underwear. She had been shopping with Mary, who had offered to buy her a new dress for any posh events she might attend that autumn. As they wandered around the London stores, looking at fabrics and the styles of the best designers, she found herself going to look at the lingerie department. Her normal attitude to clothing was intensely utilitarian. She lacked the money or desire that others had for new clothes, but on this day she appeared to want something more luxurious.

'That's quite expensive for you,' said Mary, eyeing up the undergarments appreciatively.

'You know what I'm like,' said Ethel. 'All my underwear's falling apart. I'm ashamed to put it in the laundry basket! Time for something nice for my trip to Paris.'

'To Paris?' said Mary. 'Would you be meeting Mr B there by any chance?'

'These things are not connected, I assure you,' she had said.

Now, however, drawing the fine fabric over her head, she wondered.

It wasn't unknown for Harry to visit her in her hotel room at night. Long ago, they had got used to sharing a nightcap occasionally, and recently, when she had been unable to tear herself from *Fantasio*, he had been there, altering the words sometimes to match the music that she hummed or beat out for him. They would discuss whether the music suited that moment of comedy or that delicate situation – discussions that might turn to stubborn argument.

Those occasions had been intimate in their own way, but she still felt nervous when, after the quietest of knocks, he appeared in his dressing gown. Before she could feel how very strange this was, he covered the yards between them and took her hands.

'Come on,' he said. 'Let's have champagne.'

At the first sip, Ethel began to feel a sense of the drama of the night. By the second glass, she was ready to embark on an adventure, however it might turn out. They took off their gowns and sat against the head of the bed. She cuddled up to him, still sipping, whilst he told her a scandalous story about one of the dinner guests she had just sung to. He had certainly saved it for just this moment.

She took the empty glasses from him and they wriggled down until they were lying on the bed. Ethel giggled and turned towards him, beginning to feel excited as he teased her mouth with his tongue. His hands stroked her skin, and he bent over to kiss her breasts, which now seemed, under the silky fabric, sensitive in ways she had not expected. Kissing his neck, which was so soft compared to his cheeks, she was full of the desire to see, feel, experience the body that was still concealed beneath the soft pyjamas.

'Don't you think we should take our night clothes off?' she said. 'I can't see much sleeping going on.'

'I thought you were so tired,' said Harry, rolling her over and lifting the nightgown over her head. 'And now look at you.'

'Shall I order some breakfast?'

Ethel heard the words through a haze. Sweet, so sweet, she was thinking, tunes exploding in her mind. Songs of foolish, romantic love, simple country love, uncomplicated boy and girl love. She opened her eyes slowly, reluctant.

Harry was moving around the room. She looked at his part-clothed body. She had not expected to find it so beautiful. His chest and back were stronger, squarer, browner than she had imagined.

'You're quite strong and muscly for a man of fifty who spends his life talking and writing books,' she said.

He came and sat on the side of the bed and stroked her shoulder.

'I knew you'd be strong,' he said, bending over and laying little kisses on her face. 'All that tennis and golf and horse-riding, not to mention attacking the piano every day.'

She pulled him down, wanting to feel the weight of him on her.

'That wasn't just one night, was it?' she said happily. 'It wasn't just a great experience that becomes a sweet memory. How amazing.'

'I'm so glad,' he said.

'What?'

'We waited until it was the right time for you.'

'You must have wondered if that time would ever come.'

'I knew it would, eventually. The last few years have been miraculous anyway, since we started to meet again.'

'Shh,' she said, holding him tight. 'The bad years have gone. There will be many more happy times.'

23

WOKING 1896

Ethel almost wrenched the letters out of the postman's hand, flicking through them rapidly. Everyone's hand-writing was so easy to identify – George Henschel, Alice, the Empress – though why she should be getting a letter from her she didn't know, since she had only seen her two days ago – her niece Kitty. She faltered for a moment over an envelope with a Munich stamp – no, it was from Magdi, not the one she was hoping for. Come on, Mr Levi, she said, when are you going to let me know that *Fantasio* has won your competition, now that you've been drafted in as a judge? She did not really expect to hear yet; the closing date had only been a couple of weeks ago.

Her lips tightened and she took a sharp intake of breath. Nothing from Harry. What could have happened? In all the years since they had resumed writing to each other, surely a week had never gone by without a letter, certainly without knowing why. And since Paris – shorthand in her mind for all those hours spent together in her hotel room – there had been letters every day.

She went through to the drawing room and started tidying away the books of songs she had used the evening before at her little soirée. So all those stories were true, she thought, banging the books back onto the shelves. Once you've given yourself to a man, he has no further interest; he thought he loved you but he wasn't that bothered after all. Mother was right all along: wife or whore, those are the choices. She knew she was being ludicrous.

After two more weeks of nothing, in which Ethel varied between resignation that the friendship was over, an anger that almost had her booking a train ticket to Rome to demand an explanation, and schooling herself to patience, the letter arrived. Her heart gave an enormous jolt.

My dearest Ethel. You must be wondering what has happened, so here it is briefly. Julia had a short illness and unexpectedly died last week. There is much to do here. I will be in touch as soon as I can.

Ethel sank onto the chair, her heart beating wildly. Julia dead? How could that be? Yes, she was older, quite a bit older, sixty at least, but she had always had good health.

She couldn't know, of course. It must be over fifteen years since she had seen her. Harry didn't talk about her much, except to say how alone she was. Julia, dead. How Ethel had yearned for friendship and intimacy with that clever, aloof woman. She had a brief picture of her walking amongst the shady trees of her Florence garden, the two little children sedate at her side.

The past forced itself into her mind. She went into the loft and dug out letters from years ago, letters which discussed their relationships in all their intricacy. Could they, the three of them, Ethel, Julia and Harry, work it out somehow in a society that said 'no'? In the end, it hadn't been about Julia or even Harry. She had given them up for Lisl.

Now all those women were dead – the two daughters, so different, so attractive, and their fierce, protective mother. She had loved them all – Lisl incomparably more. Out of that muddle of longing, just she and Harry were left.

Ethel played golf, and accepted dinner invitations, and composed at the piano, and waited.

~

It was a lovely day. The smells of the finished harvest rested on the air flowing through the house. Humming quietly, Ethel went to answer the bell.

She screamed with surprise and delight. Harry was standing there, smiling.

'You're looking mighty pleased with yourself,' she said. She felt the broadest of grins spreading across her face and turned into the house.

'It's not every day I get to make you scream,' he said, following her.

'I didn't know you were in England. If you've written, I haven't received it. Marco, stop it.'

'Marco,' he said, ruffling the excited dog's ears. 'At least I know I will always get a warm welcome from you. I haven't written. I wanted to surprise you.'

'I could've been anywhere,' she scolded. 'Your journey would have been quite wasted.'

They stood in the hallway looking at each other and moved into each other's arms.

'I had a good feeling about it,' he said.

'Harry,' she said. 'Really, feelings. Whatever next?' She rubbed her cheek against his, breathing in the distinctive smell of his hair oil. 'I've missed you.'

'And I you. So much. I've never felt so confused. But now I'm here.'

She responded to his passionate kisses and led him up to the bedroom, their unbuttoning and unlacing quick and impatient.

She was surprised at how intense he was. Normally there was teasing and witty talk and laughter. But none of that today. She willingly accepted the slight strangeness of him.

'We've lost so much time,' he said. 'A house of death is a terrible place, Ethel. It sucks life away. I feared it was just a dream that we were ever together.'

She held him close and rocked him slightly. 'Do I feel like a dream?' she said.

'You do,' he said. 'And yet at the same time, most emphatically not.'

In time, Ethel fetched tea and cakes, and they sat on the bed, feeding each other and talking.

'Was it very bad?' she said.

'It was so unexpected. Just a few days of illness and then she died. It is a terrible thing not to feel as much as you should when your wife dies.' He got up and went to stare out of the window. 'And the children were devastated, of course. I feel so sad for them, especially Christopher. He loved to be with her most of all.'

'What about Clotilde?'

'Ah, well, now you are going to find me out for the fraud I am.' He came back to sit on the bed. 'I didn't come from Italy on the off chance of finding you home. She decided in the end she would continue with her plan to come and study at Cambridge, so I brought her over.'

'Is that where you've been?'

'Yes, I didn't write because I wasn't sure how long she would need me to be there. I'd forgotten what it's like to be young – after a few days she didn't want an ageing father anywhere near. I agreed to go away for three days and then come back and see how she was before going back home.'

'Is that what we have, three days?'

'Well, two and a bit now.'

~

Ethel held the letter in her hand, walking round and round the breakfast table.

'You keep peering at it,' said Harry, 'as if something might be written in code on the envelope. Have courage. Here, let me open it for you.'

She passed the letter to him, and he slit open the envelope with his little pocketknife. She took it back from him and walked around the table a few more times. Marco started barking, puzzled at what was happening.

Harry settled Marco down, then steered Ethel into a chair. He stood behind her, his hands on her shoulders. 'Now, read it,' he said.

Slowly she drew the paper out of the envelope. She felt hot, and her breath was short.

'I haven't won it,' she said. She sat looking at it. 'Read it for me, Harry.'

'No-one has won,' he said. 'The judges couldn't agree, it says. There are three "highly commended" operas, of which *Fantasio* is one. I'm so sorry, Ethel.'

'Three? Highly commended? What does that mean? Is there any prize at all?' She took the letter and read it again. 'Nothing. There's nothing, Harry. No performance, no publication, no award. It's worthless.' She threw the letter across the table. Harry sat down by her and poured some more coffee. He took her hand and stroked it gently, then gripped it as she started to shake.

'That damn Levi,' she said, her voice rising. 'He gave me assurances, Harry. He virtually guaranteed me first place.'

'It's such a shame,' he said, putting his arm around her. 'Perhaps he wasn't quite as powerful as he thought. In the end, he was just one of three judges, and each presumably had their own ideas. He shouldn't have given you that sort of hope.'

'I've wasted my time,' she was sobbing. 'Our time. Two years, that took. More. And I made myself write it even when Father was dying. How mean is that for no-one to win? It's like the judges all picked their favourite and then couldn't be bothered to fight it out to agree the winner. It's a hideous compromise.'

She got up and began walking furiously around the room, carrying dishes to the side-board and slamming plates together.

'It's sheer cowardice,' she continued. 'Now no-one has to take the risk of publishing or producing an opera by an unknown. I never would have thought it of Levi.'

'It doesn't matter,' said Harry, coming and putting his arms around her, forcing her to stand still. 'It's a disappointment, that's all. *Fantasio* was your first attempt at an opera, and even so it came in the top three of over a hundred entries. Now look at me and tell me that isn't some achievement.'

Ethel closed her eyes for a moment, leaning into him. 'I'm sorry. You've had a terrible time, and here I am making a fuss about a stupid competition. Your last day, too.'

'I'm glad I was here when the letter arrived. Very glad. It's a setback, but you already have another opera in the pipeline. And failing to win the competition doesn't mean there won't be other opportunities for *Fantasio*.'

'The prize was such a complete package,' said Ethel. 'Now I'll have to do the rounds in the hope someone will take it. Oh, I'm so cross about it. More than cross.'

She started piling the breakfast things together, so haphazardly that several plates fell to the floor.

'Leave that for now,' he said, taking the pots off her and steering her to a chair. 'Let's go out and enjoy the sunshine. We could take a walk across the fields to the inn by the lake and have some lunch there. Then I'll go on to the station and get the train. I so wish I could stay longer, but it's not the right time to let Clotilde down.'

'No, no, of course you must go. That's a good plan. Marco will be happy if all this clattering-about is finished, won't you, my beauty?'

Marco had been lying watching Ethel, his big face on his paws. Now he got up and started to lick her face.

'Stop it, you monster,' she said, pushing him down. 'Go and find your lead.'

24

WEIMAR 1898

Ethel made herself keep still so as not to wake Harry. She looked around the unfamiliar hotel room – expensive, but not to her taste with its heavy dark furniture and dull, plain drapes. Her stomach churned. At last, the day was here; *Fantasio* was to be staged. Although she had been dazzled at the dress rehearsal the day before, with everyone resplendent in their costumes, the set perfect, the music well produced, it could still go terribly wrong.

She needed both hands to count the number of opera houses she had visited in vain before coming to Weimar, but here the old Grand Duke himself decided what should be performed. Ethel had worked hard to get invitations to dinners and parties where she could play and sing a little of the opera. In time, people began to talk about how they would like to see the whole thing staged. The music was big and dramatic, they said, and the plot such a ridiculous comedy of manners, with princes in silly wigs and innocent girls singing the most beautiful songs – it would be great entertainment.

She had made herself ill more than once in those three years with the effort of going to each of those opera houses, of drawing on every musical contact as well as anyone with any cultural influence. She dreamt of seeing her work accepted at Covent Garden, but they would not put on any new opera until it had been staged abroad. It was hard, too hard.

She lay quietly. She wanted to get up, start the work of the day, but although the bright morning sun was trying to penetrate the thick curtains, she knew it was still early. She turned to watch Harry, still asleep after the long journey from Rome. She would wake him soon; he would want to get back to his room long before Clotilde might knock to see if he was ready for breakfast. In other beds in the hotel slept sisters, brothers-in-law, nephews and nieces, George Henschel and his daughter. How lucky she was that they had all come to support her again. They would enjoy their day in Weimar. She knew Mary had organised a tour for them all.

'It's going to be a great day.' Harry had woken up and was watching her.

'Oh, you're awake.' She raised her head so that he could slide his arm around her, and snuggled into his shoulder. 'I don't share your confidence. What if it's a disaster?'

'If this place is as you've led me to believe, with its old-fashioned Grand Duke in charge, everyone on that platform is going to perform to their very best. What could go wrong?' He put his hand over her mouth. 'That is not a question that needs an answer.'

Ethel kissed the soft skin of his neck. 'I shall blame the librettist if it goes wrong.'

'You would too. I plead guilty here and now.' He started to wriggle out of bed. 'I must get back to my room. Shall we find a little time later this afternoon?'

'I hope so. Yes, all being well, I'll come back here after the final checks. I'll have to get changed for the performance, anyway. You know Mary's organised a dinner party afterwards, don't you?'

'Of course. That's why I've come.'

Ethel threw the bedclothes back as Harry went to the door. If he had his way, they would be married and no-one would have the slightest interest in their bedroom arrangements. Ethel didn't properly understand it herself, why she was so adamant. Julia had been dead about a year, she supposed, when he had formally proposed to her. She had refused.

She had bored herself and all her friends to death with the subject. Her sisters had to be told to shut up, so often did they begin their sentences, 'When you and Harry are married…'

'It's just the way it is,' Ethel said to Mary, when pressed. 'You know what it's like; women give up any work they might have done when they get married. I don't know of any woman who manages to continue to write or compose in a serious way once they're married.'

'That's not true, surely. What about your Clara Schumann, or, let's see, George Eliot, for example?'

'See, you're really struggling to think of anyone.'

Mary had laughed. 'All right, I agree. But isn't it a worry that you and Harry can never be completely open about how things are between you?'

'It is a worry, yes, because unfortunately I need people of influence to help promote my work. But I must be as free and independent as possible. We seem to have done all right so far.'

'You're not that easy to live with, anyway. No, seriously, he's still crazy about you, but do you think he will be content?'

'I don't know,' said Ethel. 'I hope so. It's a risk I have to take.'

As Harry shut the bedroom door behind him, Ethel wondered again at how, even in middle age, convention tugged at her.

~

On the morning after the performance, Ethel was so tired it was as if she had not slept. When she walked into the breakfast room, she had to screw up her face against the light, and the noise scraped along the inside of her skull.

'Hurray, here's our favourite and very successful composer,' Violet called. They all cheered. It was hard to understand their energy and enthusiasm.

She stood hesitating in the doorway. 'Come and sit with us, darling,' said Violet, getting up. She put her arm around her and guided her to the table where she and Dick were sitting. She sat by her and held her hands.

'Dick, be a poppet and get Ethel some coffee,' she said.

Dick planted a kiss on Ethel's head as he went to the buffet. While he was there, he ordered for her the softest scrambled eggs they could make and a bread roll warm from the oven.

'Did you not sleep well?' asked Violet. 'I assumed you might, since you would be so happy with the performance.'

'It did go well, didn't it?' said Ethel, rubbing her face. 'But as soon as I shut my eyes there was Danila singing her ballad again, and again, or the chorus being so much louder than they should have been, or the orchestra playing the overture over and over.' She yawned and shook her head. 'I feel as if I've run a hundred miles.'

'You're exhausted, and no wonder,' said Violet, stirring another spoonful of sugar into the coffee and handing it to her. 'Drink that, sweetheart, then we'll get some food into you. You'll feel better in a minute.'

'I can't imagine how it must feel,' said Dick, buttering the roll for her, 'waiting to see what the audience's reaction is going to be. But you must be pleased, surely. I thought the applause was never going to stop.'

Ethel shook her head but nevertheless began to scoop up the scrambled egg on her fork. Its buttery-ness was a delight in her stale mouth.

'Come on, now, admit that it was a great success. You certainly didn't dream that, it really was.'

Harry came into the breakfast room and stood behind Ethel, his hand on her shoulder.

'Good morning, Harry. Come and sit with us.' Violet cleared a space for him. 'She looked wonderful standing on the platform whilst everyone cheered, didn't she?'

He put his hand briefly over Ethel's. 'She has no idea how proud we all are. Or what an achievement that was.'

'You're kind,' said Ethel, who could still hardly understand what was being said. 'But I can't rest until I see what the press says. You know how cruel they can be. This is what we thought after the Mass, and look what happened.'

'It was just a couple of critics who were so harsh,' said Harry. 'You mustn't think about them so much.'

'Everyone who was there last night enjoyed it enormously,' said Dick. 'Isn't that the main thing, that you have given hundreds of people a great night at the theatre?'

Ethel felt within herself a little smile. 'It is something, certainly.'

She began to feel hungry, and asked Harry if he would get her a couple more rolls and some of that smoked ham she could smell even at this distance.

Mary came over and gave Ethel a hug. 'George has told us about a lake in the forest not so far away, and the girls are thinking they might like to swim there. Are you game?'

Ethel looked over to where George was sitting with his daughter, Helen, Clotilde and Kitty too. She must spend some time with him before he went home; his comments would certainly help with the next performance.

'Brrr,' said Ethel. 'Even I think it's a bit early in the year for swimming in the lake. I'm not sure I'll be very good company today.'

'We could just walk in the forest,' said Harry, 'if you want to be quiet.'

Tears stung the back of Ethel's eyes. Here was a whole dining room of people who loved her and had come to support her.

Of course, they were happy to be in Weimar with its wonderful culture and social circles, and to have the chance of a day in the forest. But they were here first of all for her, and her best chance of surviving this hideous, anti-climactic day was to let them take care of everything.

She looked over at George, who smiled warmly at her. 'Is it the same lake?' she called.

He knew immediately that she was thinking of the summer they had swum every day with Thekla and Gustchen.

'Probably not,' he said. 'But similar. Shall we play leapfrog again afterwards?'

'I hardly think my poor knees can cope with that now.'

'Oh yes, Auntie Ethel. Leapfrog it is.'

'Now look what you've done,' she said.

'All right,' said Alice. 'I shall go and talk to the landlord about a picnic.'

'And I shall charm the housekeeper into giving us a stack of towels to take,' said Violet.

Dick stood up. 'Shall we get some carriages ordered, Harry?' he said. He banged on the table and said in his best drill-ground voice, 'We leave in one hour exactly. Be there.'

~

After the day by and in the lake, they made short work of the sandwiches and cakes set out for them in their dining room. The party was breaking up early next morning. Only Harry would stay for the entire week with her, to hear the next performances. Then they would head south to Rome.

Second and third performances! That had never happened before.

'What are you thinking about your opera, darling, now that a day has gone by?' asked Alice, pressing another slice of apple tart on her, covered in thick cream.

'Well, I've got at least three pages of notes for Stavenhagen,' she said.

'Poor man,' said Mary. 'I'm sure no other composer makes his life so difficult.'

'I'm not,' said Ethel. 'It's just a few points…'

Everyone laughed. 'Exactly,' said Mary. 'Look.'

Dick put a basket of letters on the table.

'I don't want to read them,' said Ethel, nervous. 'I'll have a look at them tomorrow when you've all gone.'

'Allow me,' said Harry, standing up and banging a spoon on his tea cup.

He started to read. There were little notes of congratulation from people who had attended the opera; also from people who had not, like the telegrams from Bob in India, and from Nina and Nell at home. There were brief letters from Herr Stavenhagen, saying how much he had enjoyed conducting it, as well as from the soloists. In a thick, creamy, gold-embossed envelope there was a card from the Grand Duke himself, and less ostentations ones from other people at the Court.

'Goodness me,' said Ethel. 'The Grand Duke himself.' The letters were passed around for everyone to comment on. Ethel felt giddy with delight, despite knowing it was merely the custom for such notes to be sent. It means nothing, she kept saying to herself.

When the letters were finished, Harry pulled out some newspapers from under the table. Ethel felt her face flush, and a ringing came into her head. This was the real test. She could hardly hear him.

The composer is skilful and demonstrates a rich musical creative talent. Harry was turning the pages of another one – *her musical development since Leipzig is extraordinary…* Well, she hoped so, it was, after all, more than ten years since her music had been performed there. *Thoroughly enjoyed the orchestra's part in the opera.*

'Somebody's following your progress with interest, Auntie,' said Kitty.

'So they should,' said George. 'You have had to overcome more hurdles than most, Ethel. I'm so proud. And from what I hear, we might all be gathered to hear a new opera soon. I do hope so.'

'Well, at least so far no-one's said it's not too bad for a woman,' said Ethel, shaking her head to clear the tension. 'That's a step forward.'

25

BERLIN 1902

A smile of excitement spread across Ethel's face as her train came into the station. Here, right here, in the centre of German power and influence – though perhaps not of musical innovation – was to be staged the premiere of *Der Wald*. Her bag bulged with scores: a revised version for the conductor, parts for each section of the orchestra, copies for the singers and soloists. The Empress Eugénie had once more put her hand in her pocket – a deep pocket, but nevertheless – to pay for all these copies to be made. She also had plans for the stage settings, and designs for the clothes of the wood spirits and the young lover Röschen and the wicked Lady. She patted its bulk: an opera in a bag. She had a new sequined bodice and skirt for the first night which her sisters had given her at Christmas, together with a hotel reservation for as long as she needed it.

The porter led her out of the station to hail a cab. Brrr, it was cold, too cold even for snow, perhaps. The streets were full of people hurrying. No-one would want to wander along the street looking in the richly lit windows for long in this chill wind. Ethel pulled her collar more closely around her neck as she settled into the carriage, hoping she might be able to afford one of the snug hats she could see other women wearing.

As soon as she got to her hotel, a modest place in a side street near to the opera house, she sat at the little table in her room by the fire and wrote to Herr Pierson, who would be producing her opera.

Ich bin hier. Shall I meet you at the opera house tomorrow?
I await your instructions.

The young lad who had brought up her luggage ran off to deliver the note, and Ethel unpacked her trunk, carefully smoothing out the creases in her dresses, and laying out all the paraphernalia of a composer on the move – manuscript paper, pens, nibs, scissors, ink, paste.

Twice she went down to the hotel foyer to see if the boy had returned. The second time, she sat in one of the deep leather chairs and took a look at a newspaper over a cup of tea. Finally, the boy ran in, his face and hands red and raw from the cold.

'Fraülein,' he said, coming to a halt in front of her and handing her a note. 'There was no-one at the opera house, and I had to go to the gentleman's house.'

'Thank you,' she said, tipping him a few pfennig. 'That was kind of you.'

Sehr geehrtes Fraülein, she read. *I'm so glad that you have arrived safely in Berlin, but I'm afraid your opera won't be staged at the end of the month as planned. I am not at all well, and we have not been able to make any preparations. The opera house will be in touch with you as soon as possible.*

The excitement and energy drained out of her. Her heart beat wildly with disappointment on top of the long, difficult journey. She ran up to her room for fear of anyone trying to talk to her, and stood at the window, hugging herself, barely noting how bright the street glowed as the lamps were lit to fend off the winter darkness. She would have liked the feel of Marco, now too old to travel, pressing against her knees.

~

Ethel was not exactly lonely in Berlin, but she had come expecting a short stay with a triumphant production and swift return home. Now the weeks were becoming months. Poor Herr Pierson died and new dates had to be arranged with Karl Muck, who would come in to conduct the opera once it was ready. The person nominated to produce it was, Ethel quickly realised, purely an administrator. Maybe he was an able one, but when it came to putting music together with story, orchestra with chorus or stage with setting, he was neither effective nor respected. When Ethel tried to take a more active part herself, directing the stagehands in building the set, for example, he did not welcome it. She endured his stubbornness and drove the preparations as much as she was able.

Although she was made welcome and found new friends in Berlin's drawing rooms and over its dinner tables, she found the main topic of conversation was what the British were doing in South Africa. She had never experienced any hostility in Germany before. She considered herself part of a rich, cultural exchange that had, now she was forced to think about it, been going on for a few hundred years. Had not Haydn, Mendelssohn and Clara Schumann been almost as at home in England as in Germany? Had hopeful musicians like herself not been coming to study at the German conservatoires since they were first instituted? Didn't they all love Goethe and Shakespeare and Schiller and Jane Austen? And wasn't the Kaiser the grandson of the dead Queen?

Yet none of that seemed to matter now. Germany had decided that England was being barbaric in pursuit of its war in South Africa. Only a few days after her arrival, she found everyone scandalised by 'photos' in the paper of an English soldier holding a baby aloft on a bayonet. Even those not taken in by such cartoons, felt dismay and unease at the herding together of Afrikaner women and children into camps.

Her family's close relationship with the army stirred in her blood. Until this Boer War, as it was being called, it had always seemed a relatively safe occupation. Now Bob and Nell's husband Hugh were to be sent out there. Soldiers were dying in large numbers. It had never struck Ethel that the British position might not be supported.

She felt under attack at dinner parties where these things were discussed. She had always loved to argue, never sat silent, as many women did, at the dinner table, whilst politics and matters of state were discussed, never felt worried if she was a single voice. This was different, however; it was not an issue that could be debated calmly. When a group of young men smashed the window of the British Embassy, she cancelled a dinner invitation and wept that the country she loved so much seemed so inhospitable.

Ethel went into the hotel after another day of frustration at the opera house and found Harry sitting in the foyer.

'I was worried,' he said, as she rushed towards him, surprised and happy. He drew her into a darker corner of the foyer, signalling to the waiter to bring tea, and put his arm around her. 'I kept waiting for you to tell me the opera was to be staged, and I should come. But from your letters, I could see that the exciting adventure had become a hideous ordeal. I decided to come anyway.'

'It's awful. Worse than you could imagine.' She settled onto the sofa and leaned into him, resisting the desire to simply sob. 'Nothing is being resolved. We are scheduled for two weeks, and I fear utter humiliation. Your lovely libretto is being murdered, too.'

Harry poured tea. 'Would it be such a terrible thing to walk away? After all, they have hardly honoured their part of the contract.'

'It's too late now. Maybe I should have done that when poor old Pierson died, and I could see what sort of person was in charge. But now I must see it through. It's sure to improve when Karl Muck arrives.'

Ethel could feel Harry's eye on her. She put a hand to her hair, feeling how, beneath her hat, strands had escaped from the pins. She couldn't remember when she had last washed it, or brushed her dress and coat. 'This isn't how I wanted to welcome you. I'm a mess.'

'That doesn't matter,' he said. 'What does is that you're overwrought and exhausted.'

She leaned back against the sofa and yawned, pressing her hands to her forehead. 'If I relax for a moment, I shall sleep for a fortnight.'

'Tomorrow, we're going to take a tram out of the city and walk around Wannsee. There is a little hotel by the lake where we can stay. Then you will be ready for battle again on Monday.'

'It's a lovely idea,' said Ethel, sighing. 'But I've already arranged—'

'Cancel it,' said Harry. 'You need a day or two away from all of this. Then I'll be on my way again and leave you to the fight.'

She put out her hand for him to pull her up. 'Take me to my room, before I become incapable of further movement.'

~

Ethel popped her head in at the office of the opera house to check that Karl Muck had arrived.

'You could say so,' said the secretary. 'He has had quite a morning. We all have. He's shouted at everyone, insulted the orchestra and driven the stagehands crazy, not to mention—'

'Sounds as though he means business,' said Ethel, trying to hide her pleasure.

'I think he's down by the stage,' she said. 'Good luck.'

Ethel made her way into the auditorium, busier than she had ever seen it.

'Well, Fraülein,' he said, hardly greeting her, 'we have been very badly let down here. There has been no shaping; there's no story-telling. The stage is not properly prepared, and soloists are wandering around not knowing how this is to be made ready. Now we must see what we can do.'

The man, who had seemed so urbane at her sister's dinner party when he had decided to stage *Der Wald*, who had decades of experience behind him, was angry, very angry. Ethel would have liked to throw her arms around him.

'Just tell me how I can help,' she said.

'Please, spend time with the chorus, and get those overfed singers to think of themselves as woodland spirits. That would help enormously.'

There was no way this mess could be brought to anything but a shabby first performance, but at last here was someone who wanted to try. Perhaps, in the end, thought Ethel, the spirits of the forest would be able to close tranquilly over the strange, frantic activity of the human race.

~

Ethel had not told her family and friends when the opera would be performed. She could not bear for them to spend a lot of money to come, only to be sad and disappointed. She told them she had received good news from Convent Garden, and that she was confident they would be able to see the opera in London very soon.

Apprehensive and embarrassed, she sat with her wealthy friends in their box and endured a performance that showed only a fraction of the charm and coherence she knew lay within it. Nevertheless, the audience didn't seem to find it so terrible; there was warm applause between the sections, and if some of the acting was unsure and haphazard, and bits of the set still unpainted, the glory of the soloists singing her strong music was there for everyone to enjoy.

Several curtain calls were taken. When Karl Muck gestured towards her to show the audience the composer was present, she was glad she had made the time to go back to her hotel and get changed into her bright sequinned bodice. She stood up, ready for him to welcome her down onto the stage, but stopped short as hisses and boos broke out from a section of the crowd. The jeering grew louder. She could hear words like 'British barbarism', 'Go home', 'No British wanted'.

Ethel looked at Muck for guidance. He was applauding her, as were the cast, but she understood from his manner that she was not to go onto the stage. Recovering herself, she curtsied, smiled and added her applause to that of the crowd for the performers before sitting down again. Later he reassured her that it wasn't the music or even the stumbling staging that had caused that reaction; it was simply an unfortunate day for a British person to be in the Berlin spotlight.

~

Ethel walked along the streets to the opera house, familiar now and pretty with their spring blossom. She recalled how thrilled she had been when asked to take the cutting rehearsal. Muck had left to see to other engagements and would not be back until the day before the second night. She was to review the first performance and make decisions with the orchestra and singers on what needed to be cut or changed. What had seemed an honour, however, was now a terrible burden. All those people had witnessed the jeers – maybe they shared those anti-British sentiments. Maybe they would not bother to turn up. Her stomach was in turmoil, and her eyes sore from another restless night. She had to talk severely to herself, calling for courage to salvage her opera.

The theatre had its usual morning quietness about it. It seemed to be recovering from the crowds of the night before, as well as awaiting the next event. The smell of extinguished candles hung in the air. She was surprised to see the orchestra pit full, and rows of singers sitting on the stage. As she walked towards the conductor's stand, swallowing heavily, they started to applaud.

'Thank you,' she said, astonished.

The leader of the orchestra stood up. 'Fraülein, we would like to apologise for the rudeness of a section of the audience last night. We do not believe it was a reflection of your music or, indeed, what most people thought of your music. We were ashamed.'

'Thank you,' said Ethel. 'I really do appreciate that. Let's forget about it, shall we, and focus on what we need to do now.'

But he had not finished. 'We have been very upset at the way this whole performance has gone. We loved Herr Pierson, and after losing him and having no direction, perhaps we did not work hard enough to achieve a satisfactory standard. With your help, we want to change this for next time. *Der Wald* is well worth the effort.'

Bows tapped on stands, the triangle rang out its little cheer, singers clapped and flowers were brought. They're serious, she thought, overwhelmed.

'Thank you. It's nobody's fault, what happened. Let's have a look, shall we? We'll start with the peaceful forest.'

Ethel raised her hands. The situation may have become more forgiving, but it was nevertheless a terrifying moment. They would soon find out that she had never conducted a full orchestra before, never mind one that was combined with over a hundred singers. Within a few bars of the start, however, she was surprised that she could see what was needed. She stopped to ask the woodwind to play more prominently, and the violins to take a background role. The support of the musicians warmed her and restored the belief in her own music. Soon, she was able with a small gesture to convey her wishes, even to change the tempo. It was extraordinary how they, and the chorus too, responded.

Every now and then she stopped, asked for opinions, cut repetitious passages and found better ways of acting out a scene. She began to get a hint of the power of the conductor. She had observed so many; some conducted with the widest, most exaggerated gestures, others, like Karl Muck, with just the barest movement of the baton. What she had not known was that her vision of the music was translated into the movements of her hands, and that it was a language the musicians knew and responded to.

'We have worked so hard this morning,' she said at the end of the session. 'I will have the parts changed ready for the return of Herr Muck. Many things will still be imperfect at the second performance, but at least we are now a little surer. Thank you.'

As Ethel crossed the Kurfürstendamm, she started humming Röschen's love song. She would have a look in Wertheim, the new department store everyone was talking about, and treat herself to afternoon tea.

26

'It was perfect, wasn't it?' Ethel knew she was being boring and repetitive, but she seemed unable to stop. She kept moving around her sitting room, touching ornaments and re-arranging the delicate carnations in the vase.

'It was wonderful,' said Harry, looking up from the table, where he was writing in his notebook. 'Just like you always hoped for.'

'Francis Nielson, who'd have thought it? I never expected such a sure touch. He had everyone eating out of his hand.'

'You are a success, at last, as we always thought you would be. Covent Garden loved you. Did you see the latest review? I left it on your desk. I'll get it for you.'

'Oh, look,' she said, taking it from him and reading it, 'they're talking about how well the music reflected the Lady's destructive passion. Oh, I like that.'

'You really are a proper opera-writer now,' he said. 'Perhaps you were wrong; perhaps England is more ready for opera, for your music, than you thought.'

There was a shout from outside the cottage. It was so hot that all the doors were wide open to allow any breath of air through.

'Post, I think,' said Ethel, getting up and going to the door.

Ethel stood in the tiny hallway looking through the pile of letters handed to her. She was still getting several a day from people who had seen *Der Wald*, congratulating her. Here was one with an American postmark; who could that be from? It was not Thekla's writing.

Ethel opened the envelope and scanned the letter. Her breath came quicker. She put a hand to her mouth.

'Harry, it's from New York.' She rushed back into the sitting room. 'Guess what, they want to stage *Der Wald* at the Metropolitan Opera House. Oh, my goodness.' She sat down with a plump on the sofa and read the letter again.

'I'm so happy for you,' he said, coming to sit by her. 'Let me see.'

'Look, they want me to go and help set it up. A big fee and all reasonable expenses paid.'

'You won't go, though, will you?'

'Of course I'll go,' she said. 'Imagine, what an adventure!'

'Think about it, Ethel,' said Harry. 'America's not like Europe. I'm not sure they are ready for anything quite so unusual and dramatic as your music. They're not as adventurous as you think.'

'It's good, surely, that they don't have all those hidebound traditions. They stage all kinds of operas at the Met. Perhaps they'll take my other work, too.'

'Don't go, please. You know how taxing you find all this. And you'll be all alone out there.'

'I'm used to coping with disappointment,' she said. 'Aren't you pleased?'

'Of course, but you don't have to go. Why not send them the opera, and let them put it on without you being there?'

'I'd be crazy to turn this down,' she said.

Ethel was thinking about money as well as her opera, but she was not going to mention that to Harry. Like all wealthy people, he found financial considerations crude and embarrassing.

He would 'solve' any problem by insisting on giving her a large gift of money. The money from her inheritance was just about enough if she stayed at home or spent time with her friends and sisters. Whenever she went abroad, however, unless with Harry or as a guest of Eugénie or a friend, her funds disappeared at a frightening rate. So far, she had made virtually nothing from the handful of performances of her operas, had barely covered her expenses. Here was an opportunity to make some real money in a country with a different musical tradition, which was hungry for European music to perform. Surely, once they had staged *Der Wald*, they would also want *Fantasio* and perhaps even her Mass.

'Think about it, at least. They're not as innovative as they like to think, as I've discovered on my lecture tours.'

'No, Harry, don't try and talk me out of it. I'm going.'

'Don't expect me to go with you.'

'I don't.'

~

Why don't I come with you? wrote Mary when she heard the news. *I promised John Singer Sargent I'd go over and see his frescos in Boston. This would be a good time, and I'll pay the extra so we can travel first class and enjoy some good hotels. It's a great opportunity for you. What do you think?*

'Please don't go,' said Harry again. 'You've heard too many stories of people finding their fortune in America, but so many more don't. Wouldn't it be better to build on your success here?'

She kissed him to hush him. 'I'm not going to turn down an offer like that, am I?'

'Mary will interfere; you know she will. She always drives you to distraction after a few days.'

'For heaven's sake, Harry. Stop going on.'

She didn't like it. They hardly made up before she left.

Ethel stood at the railings of the steamer with Mary and waved madly at Violet and Alice. Slowly, they became just two more dots amongst the crowds on the Liverpool quayside. Mary turned and hugged Ethel, and they went off to find their cabin.

'How shall we ever find our way around this enormous ship?' said Ethel. She had to shout to make herself heard above the horns sounding, as great flumes of steam shot into the air. 'I've never seen anything like it. I thought the Empress's yachts were huge, but this is entirely different.'

'We're going to have such fun,' said Mary, checking with a steward which staircase would lead to their cabin. 'Three weeks on board with nothing to do except enjoy ourselves.'

Ethel did not share her sister's delight at the length of time stretching out ahead, with such a limited range of activity. There would be games to play, of course, but also endless after-dinner entertainments. A lot of time would be spent in gossipy get-togethers over tea. Only the fact that the music was said to be excellent on these ships was going to make the journey pass quickly enough.

'You go ahead,' she said to Mary as they came to the stairs. 'I'm going to stay up here until England has quite disappeared.'

She stood watching the land slowly recede, shivering a little as the quiet, sunny day which had warmed her skin turned into a cold bluster, and the water churned up by the engine left an ever longer, whiter plume. She had made numerous sea journeys, but none that had taken her so far from home.

'Someone called Barnsdale's in charge of music on the ship,' said Mary, hunting through the cupboards to find where the steward had put her stockings. 'Do you know him?'

'Oh no, did you say Barnsdale. Peter Barnsdale?'

'Yes, that's the chap.'

'Damn. He hates me. I was hoping to drum up some support for *Der Wald* before we get to New York,' she said.

They were preparing for dinner. Mary had already tried on and discarded three dresses, each more glamorous than anything Ethel possessed. 'If I put myself forward, he'll probably ignore me.'

'I don't know how you managed to get on the wrong side of him,' said Mary. 'He's probably quite harmless. I expect you were rude to him.'

'He's always extremely rude to me,' said Ethel. She had finished dressing and was sitting on the side of her bed. The room was large, hardly a cabin at all, and yet Mary seemed to have taken up all the space. 'Every single time I've sat at a dinner table with him, he has trotted out the same old garbage about how women are only suited to writing drawing-room songs.'

'I expect he's a failed composer,' said Mary. 'I've certainly never heard anyone speak about his music. And being a musical director on board a ship, even one as beautiful as this, is not such a great achievement, after all.'

'You really are becoming the most awful snob.' Ethel laughed.

Mary started to put on the golden hairpiece she had taken to wearing. 'Are you sure you want to work during the journey? You could just enjoy yourself, you know.'

'I intend to do both if at all possible,' said Ethel. 'There are influential people on board, and they have friends and acquaintances in New York who love a night at the opera. I'm hoping to build an audience.'

'Leave it to me,' said Mary, tucking in the last wisps of her hair. 'There are quite a few people who will insist to your Mr Barnsdale that they would love to hear some music by Miss Smyth, who happens to be on board.'

Ethel smiled when, two nights later, Peter Barnsdale, looking resentful, announced that at the weekend the ship's orchestra would be playing extracts from *Der Wald*, hot from its very successful performance at Covent Garden. Ethel had found a couple of soloists amongst the passengers, so some of the arias were sung too, to great applause.

Afterwards, she stood on the deck, blowing away the heat of the dining room before going to bed, when Peter Barnsdale came and joined her.

'I suppose you think you're a success,' he said. 'Bored people on a ship will applaud anything.'

Ethel looked at him. He was drunk. 'You really are a very sour man,' she said.

'Well, perhaps I wouldn't be if you showed me some appreciation,' he said. He stepped nearer to her and put his hand across her back, pulling her towards him. He put his other hand on her breast.

Ethel slapped him. 'Get off me, you creep,' she shouted. She pushed him hard, so he stumbled.

'Ooh, very feisty,' he said. 'Just like they all say.'

'Don't you ever touch me again,' said Ethel.

He gave a drunken laugh as she hurried to her cabin.

Ethel began to coach other singers she found. Bored passengers started sewing dresses and painting trees to create a magical forest on the sea. The night before the boat docked in New York, a scaled-down version of the opera was performed to the delight of everyone. Ethel took a bow, standing well away from the conductor, Peter Barnsdale.

~

Ethel sat in the stalls and waited for the orchestra to finish its warming up. She thought that even a composer who had been celebrated and performed much more often than she had would find the Metropolitan Opera House forbidding. It was bigger, more plush, better lit than any of its European counterparts. The overwhelming impression was of red and gold, relieved only by the musical scenes painted around the ceiling.

The business, however, was the same as in any other opera house. For the first time, soloists, chorus and orchestra had come together with the conductor for the final preparations of *Der Wald*. It was exciting. She knew the chorus would be fine, as she had been coaching them herself for the past few days, and the set was in place, looking almost as she had requested. The first section went well; there were a few stops whilst the conductor explained to the orchestra how they should interpret some parts. She herself went up on stage several times to suggest the orchestra restrain themselves and become as ethereal as the chorus of wood spirits in the primeval forest. Their tendency to melodrama would be more welcome in the second part.

When Röschen started to sing Ethel thought the soloist must be joking. She could not see why, but perhaps it was a quirk of the American mentality. No-one laughed, however; the conductor congratulated the singer on the first aria and signalled for the orchestra to continue.

Ethel stayed in her seat, unsure what to do. Let it unfold, she said to herself, though she could barely contain herself. It was soon apparent that the soloist was little more than a music-hall artiste, untrained and unable to get her voice around the delicate arias, or to reach the high notes, or control the runs of sound. Her acting was blunt and sentimental. She could see now from the embarrassed faces of the other soloists that this was neither a joke nor a misunderstanding. The conductor had appointed her, knowing this.

When Ethel tried to broach it with him, she came to realise that her opera was simply an item in a grand gala performance. Her objections were disregarded. It was to be a night of glitz and glamour, rather than of art and opera. The dramatic sections became melodrama in the hands of the orchestra. She was being discussed in the press as a novelty. She would have withdrawn, if she had not been so tied into the contract.

'I can't believe you actually thought that was a great evening,' Ethel said to Mary over breakfast the day after the performance.

'Come on, Ethel,' said Mary, 'I know you want to control every detail of every second of your music, and it's true it was very different from Covent Garden, but the audience and the press went crazy for it. How many curtain calls did you have?'

'They just made a big melodramatic show out of it,' said Ethel. 'That's not what it's meant to be.'

'You must have enjoyed everyone's comments at the dinner afterward, surely. The ambassador is a very cultured man. He was so pleased that a British composer had received such acclaim.'

'It was a wonderful dinner. You really do host the most marvellous parties. And your New York friends were all very enthusiastic. Thank you.'

She turned away. There was no point arguing.

You were right, she wrote to Harry that night. *Our lovely opera has been packaged into a commercial product, and I'm no more than the monkey on the barrel organ, dressed by Mary. She loves this role she has adopted of patron of the arts, yet really all she cares about is status and ostentation. The reviews should make my heart swell with pride, they sing my praises so, not to mention that there has never been an opera by a woman performed at the Met before. And yet because they show no sign of artistic sensibility, I would rather they had never been written. Even the Berlin performance was more true.*

After three pages of precise description interspersed with angry outbreaks, Ethel still had not begun to find the words for the torment within her. Most of her performances had been achieved despite enormous problems, but she had always felt the music had been respected, and she herself too as its creator.

The only lovely thing to happen is that amongst the ex-pat musicians invited to the Banquet, there was Thekla! As soon as we could, we headed for the ladies' room. We had a little weep. 'Even after ten years away from the stage,' she said, 'I could have done better than that.' Wouldn't that have been lovely if she had sung? She thought it was a beautiful opera, despite the terrible performance. It was worth it for those few precious minutes. I shall see her again when we get to Boston.

Ethel's dreams unravelled. There was no-one she met to whom she could entrust her Mass or *Fantasio.* She waited impatiently for the Boston performances to be over, delighting only in the time she spent with Thekla and her family, and felt nothing but relief when she boarded the ship and set off back to England.

She thanked the heavens daily that Peter Barnsdale was not on the return journey, and she pleaded sickness and exhaustion if she was asked to take part in anything. Whenever she could, she lay on the deck and listened to the music of the sea and of the wind.

27

PARIS 1903

Ethel looked around, her gaze caught by the opulence of the room. She had been a guest in the homes of an empress, a queen, an archbishop, of lords, ladies and aristocrats of all types, but she had never seen such luxury. This music room, as it was called, appeared to have a full-scale organ built into its wall, and two vast grand pianos stood at one end, on a raised area. Brocaded, velvet sofas, filled with chattering people, stood on the richly coloured rugs scattered around the parquet floor. Bright, modern paintings – she was pretty sure more than one of them was a Manet – relieved the golden oak panelling.

It wasn't just the details of the décor or the intriguing musky perfume of the candles that made her content to look out from the window seat. Her French was good enough day to day, but when there were so many people laughing and talking excitedly, she struggled to join in. Her companion, John Singer Sargent, who had helped her bear Mary's imperiousness in Boston, was amusing enough anyway, with his comments about the many people in the room.

'You'll love that man there, the one with the enormous white moustache,' he said, pointing to a man sitting on a sofa nearby.

'Gabriel Fauré. He plays all his new music here first, and the man opening up the piano is Reynaldo Hahn. We're in for something special if he's going to play.'

How exciting to have the chance to meet Fauré, whose music she had loved for a while. Later, perhaps. Some women drew her gaze, talking excitedly at one end of the room. They were dressed in ways Ethel had never seen before, in trousers and shirts and cravats.

'Who are they?' she asked.

'Oh, a couple of crazy Rumanian princesses, poets, that sort of thing. Winnaretta,' he called to the woman walking by, 'let me introduce to you Miss Ethel Smyth. Miss Smyth is a composer of some fame, especially in England and Germany. Ethel, this is our hostess, the Princesse de Polignac. She runs a music salon here on a Friday.'

'Welcome, welcome,' said the Princesse. 'John has sung your praises many times.'

'Thank you. It's wonderful to be here.'

Ethel took in the fine fabric of the sage green dress the Princesse was wearing, the jewels studding her dark hair, the elaborate stole thrown around her shoulders. For all the ostentation, Ethel took comfort in the plainness of her face – she must be about the same age as herself, she thought – and that accent! John had told her that Winnaretta was an American heiress as well as a French princess, and yet she talked like they were in Devon.

'You must forgive me for not stopping to talk now,' she said. 'But people are restless for some music. Why not come to my Bach supper on Friday, and we can talk afterwards? Bring something to play.'

She moved on towards the pianos.

'She spent a lot of her childhood in Torquay,' said John in answer to Ethel's query. 'It was her American father who invented the sewing machine.'

'Goodness me. What did she mean, Bach supper?' asked Ethel.

'She plays Bach better than anyone in France,' he said. 'She absolutely adores him. She'll sit at the organ for hours and play. You'll see.'

Ethel felt the air get even more charged. Bach in Paris. Bach played by that strong-faced woman on the ornate organ whose pipes filled one side of the room.

Before she could ask more, the Princesse was standing by the piano, calling for quiet whilst the footmen went around refilling glasses, and making sure that by every sofa there was a dish of tiny cakes.

'Thank you, thank you. Our very own Reynaldo Hahn.' She gestured towards him and waited whilst the applause and whistling died down. 'Reynaldo will entertain us with some of his songs – enthral us, I should say. Then – and I tell you this now so that you can be thinking about it – we shall have another of our opera performances. Everyone is to sing what they can and anyone can come forward to perform an aria or take a role. And tonight, our opera is to be... *Cosi fan Tutte.*'

The room fell silent as Monsieur Hahn ran his fingers up and down the keys and started to sing.

Oh, how beautiful, thought Ethel, as his baritone voice soared. And the acoustic in this room...

She did not know the songs, which were in the French style, yet they had the same intense blend of music and words as a Schubert song.

As if to break the spell he had woven, Hahn broke into the overture to the Mozart opera, and people began to get up – it seemed as though four men might take the part of Alfonso, and a group of women were discussing which of the female parts they might sing. The pianist went on, regardless, singers joining in or dropping out as they wished to much laughter and applause.

'*O soave sia il ventro...*' sang Ethel from her seat. The smile on her face arose from a deep well of pleasure in her body.

'I think Miss Smyth is feeling quite at home,' murmured John in her ear. He had got his notepad out and was making sketches of people in the room.

~

Ethel stepped from the house onto the Avenue Henri-Martin, surprised to feel the cool rain on her hot face. She hardly noticed the horses clattering by on the street, some pulling carriages whose enormous wheels threatened to soak her with the dirty water that ran in shallow runnels by the pavement. Despite holding her skirt up, it was already wet.

'Oh, my Lord,' she muttered. 'I love her. I've only known her a week, but I love her. What a woman. She must love me, surely, just a little bit?'

The Princesse was surrounded by elegant women, some so beautiful that they filled Ethel with despair. Anna, Hélène, Justine and many more – brilliant women, artists, poets, intellectuals. There was no idea here that women were less fit to speak, or have an opinion, or be expert in their work. Men too, whose names were already legend, wanted nothing more than to sit in Winnaretta's lounge and exercise their wit, and display their formidable artistic talent.

Ethel walked rapidly down the road, almost laughing out loud with the delight that bubbled up in her, just from being in that house for a while and sitting close to perfection. There were musicians too, some of whose names she had known throughout her life. How silly that she had been so snobbish about them because they weren't German or Austrian – white-haired Gabriel Fauré and Claude Debussy, to name just two.

Even by the time she reached her hotel, soaking wet, the smile had hardly faded. It made her almost delirious to be with these people, the women especially, not just because of their outrageous manners and elaborate dress, or the ridiculous amount of talent gathered in one room. No, it was the ideas, more modern and challenging than anything she had met before, their independence.

Ethel knew that they were hardly as excited about her as she was about them. She might feel delightfully at home, but they, the Princesse and her friends, regularly collected new, 'interesting' people, and then spat them out if they weren't prepared to be radical and brave in their thinking, accomplished and confident in their art.

Her smile wasn't just about her invitation to the most sought-after musical salon in the whole of Paris. No, it was the touch of Winnaretta, and a look in her eye which had made Ethel arch her back and blush deeply.

~

Ethel raised her face to the warmth of the winter sun. The Canale Grande was blue, alive, studded with little boats, traghetti and gondolas going about their daily work. On the opposite side, the ornate facades of the Palazzi were dark in morning shadow.

It was early, but she had been sitting at the window for some time, putting the finishing touches to the song she had been writing for Winnie's birthday. She still had not quite captured what she had seen the day before on the lagoon – the glimmers on the water, the light as it glanced off the ripples, the silhouetted fisherman holding his line, waiting, waiting. She tried to imitate his patience, his belief that if he sat long enough, connected by his line to the depths of the water, what he hoped for would emerge. She was experimenting, fragmenting the sounds in the French fashion to create a lighter flow. But that word, oh, it wasn't right at all, hardly fitted the notes; a scratch, a dip of the pen, yes, that was better.

It was a song of love.

'Ah, here you are.' The voice of Justine interrupted the dreamy yearning that arose within her whenever she thought of Winnie. 'Anna's going to rehearse some of the poems she's written for this evening. She won't start unless you're there. We're in the morning room.'

Ethel pulled her shawl around her shoulders as she followed Justine down the corridor. A Palazzo in Venice could be very cold in January, and she hoped the fire had been lit long enough to warm the room.

'Found her,' said Justine as they went into the room. 'Listening to the sounds of the canal out there.'

'Come and sit down, darling,' said Hélène. 'You must be freezing. As you can see, Anna is arranging herself on the sofa ready to declaim.'

'Well, I would,' said Anna, 'if I could only get these bits of paper in the right order. And find something to tie back my hair.' As usual, Anna was not dressed properly. Her long brown hair fell over her shoulders, and she seemed to have on any number of gowns and shawls under an embroidered cape.

'How many writing books have I given you?' scolded Justine, trying to help set the scattered pages in order. 'Made by the best Venice paper manufacturers, covered in finest leather, both plain and lined? If only you'd use them, we wouldn't have this fuss every day.'

'Save me from practical people, Ethel,' said Anna. 'They have no idea what it's like to be a poet.'

Ethel leant over and kissed her. 'The chaos of creation. Is Winnie likely to arrive in the middle of this?'

'Who knows? She left last night with that magnificent young Italian contessa and we haven't seen her since. This afternoon, maybe.'

'Having an early birthday treat, perhaps.' Hélène laughed.

Ethel could not join in the laughter for the tightness in her chest.

'Right, we're ready. Justine, please sit by me and try and keep my papers in order. I promise I'll try out one of your notebooks sometime soon.'

Ethel sat in a chair nearby and felt herself relax. She could never tire of hearing Anna's poetry, especially when, as today, she seemed well and cheerful. It was so provocative, so witty, so wise; the words and images so fresh, and yet so apposite that people wondered why they had not thought of them themselves. The sing-song flow of her voice delivered the words in her heavily accented French, delicate yet robust as steel.

'No, no,' said Anna, breaking off and shocking them all back into the everyday world. 'That's complete rubbish. For heaven's sake, Winnie's going to hate it.'

She made as if to tear up the pages, which Justine managed to rescue. 'Darling, don't be like that. It's beautiful, wonderful. Don't judge yourself so.'

Eventually, she calmed down and read on for a while longer. Coffee was called for, and the women started to talk about the evening that was to come.

'Now, Ethel,' said Hélène, 'it's your turn. What will you sing tonight?'

'I've got a new song,' said Ethel. 'But it's not quite ready yet. I still haven't found the ending. So don't include me in any plans for this afternoon.'

'Hmm, a little love song, perhaps,' said Hélène, 'for our birthday girl?'

Ethel felt herself flush.

'All right,' said Anna, still full of the energy of her poems. 'But you are going to play a bit of *The Wreckers* too, aren't you? I know it's not finished yet, but please, darling, give us a taste now. When you sit at that piano, you're like a tiger in a cage at the zoo, eating his red meat so savagely, so tenderly. I can hardly bear it.'

The women laughed and Ethel got up to go to the piano. As she played, she became aware of a movement at the doorway. It was Winnie with a look on her face that made Ethel smile and attack the piano with greater fervour to counterbalance the melting in her body.

Ethel eyes widened as she looked across the dinner table at Harry. The restaurant was full of Parisians enjoying an evening out, but he looked sad and irritated. He had withdrawn from her. It was as if she had swept all the candles onto the floor in one cold moment, extinguishing the golden light.

'Harry?' she said at last, quietly. 'I'm sorry.' She screwed up her face. She had been telling him how at home she felt in Winnaretta's salon, how commanding and wonderful Winnaretta was, how much she loved her. She was used to telling him everything.

'I don't want you to be humiliated,' he said, looking across at her at last. 'They are interested in their own pleasure, that's all.'

'Is there anything so terrible about that? But it's not fair, either. Where would Manet be, for example, without the Princesse's help? And all those others, artist of all kinds. France can be so difficult with its forbidding Académies and Sociétès.'

'I hate all those stuffy institutions, too, as you well know; I always have. Artists' reputations are made and broken by them, and they are intensely conservative. Of course, it's great that de Polignac offers something different. I know you are always going to seek out people who will help you promote your music.'

'So what's the problem? You've always wanted me to be less Germanic in my style. Now I've met people who can help me with that.'

Harry took a few mouthfuls of the guinea fowl on his plate, and put his knife and fork down. He pushed his plate away, swallowing heavily.

'I'm glad of these new influences in your life and in your music. Of course I am. That is not the issue. It is their behaviour, and the fact that you have decided to become a part of it.'

'Come on, Harry. Whenever has the unconventional been an issue for you?'

'Now you are insulting me,' he said. He signalled to the waiter for the bill. 'I'm sorry. The food is making me sick.'

Ethel looked at him in surprise. They loved to argue. Occasionally, they made each other unhappy, but she had never seen him upset like this.

'Harry?'

'It's not about their behaviour. I don't like it, but you know I don't care about that. It's the way you debase yourself in front of Winnaretta. I had never seen you like that until tonight. You are making yourself look foolish, and me too. Please do not include me again.'

He threw notes onto the table and pushed his way out of the restaurant. Retrieving her coat, Ethel struggled to catch up with him as he strode along the river path.

'Are you actually running away from me?' she called. 'If you are, then please just say so.'

He halted and turned to face her. 'Why do you do this, pretend it's all about your music? You've always had your big relationships with women. Sometimes it hasn't been easy for me to share your love and attention. But now, I feel that you have nothing for me. In fact, you are content to leave me sitting in a corner whilst you try to get near to her.'

Ethel gasped. He knew all about her longing for the Princesse. What a fool she had been to think she could chat about this as if it were the same as getting to know any other exciting person. He would know, she thought, that she had longed for Winnaretta's hands on her body, even as she had turned towards his caresses.

'You talk as though you were completely faultless,' she said. 'You've never hidden the fact that there are sometimes women in Rome whose company you seek out. All right, let's say it straight – whose bed you seek out. I have always been utterly faithful to you in that way.'

She could hardly bear the miserable anger on his face, caught in the flickering lamps alongside the river.

'That's not worthy, Ethel. Do you want to have a conversation about what constitutes fidelity and what doesn't? At least I have never flaunted any desire for another woman in front of you. But these women's husbands are pure tokens, screens behind which they do whatever they wish. Fine, I don't have a problem with that. But I'm not your husband, although I would have liked to be, and I certainly will not be your token.'

'I'm sorry, Harry. It is true that this is more intense than my usual silly crushes, but I certainly don't want to hurt you.'

'Are you sure about that? Well, I'm sorry too. I wish I could be more generous about what you are experiencing, but I find I can't.'

They had come to their hotel. His face was grey and wretched in the light from the portico lamp.

'I shall return to Rome tomorrow.' He leant over and kissed her. 'Goodbye, Ethel.'

Ethel stared at him as he turned away, her heart wrenching. She did not know how to disentangle this. She was unsure whether she wanted to. Even now, with him striding away from her, she thought of being on Winnie's sofa, perhaps with Anna too, their limbs entwined whilst they read poetry and laughed at the antics of visitors. Somewhere inside herself she was glad that Harry was leaving.

She turned away from the hotel and headed for the Avenue Henri-Martin.

28

Ethel could hardly get the notes down fast enough, so much was fizzing and sparking in her mind. New ideas, more flowing lines. She stood the better to lean over the large manuscript page, dipping the pen frantically into the inkwell so that spots fell onto the page, occasionally obscuring what she was writing.

Power ran through her, the excitement of new experience, of Winnie's creamy skin as they lay in bed, the sparks of two strong bodies seeking pleasure. She was drunk with the sweetness of it, edged with danger.

Each time she spoke of the future, Winnie put her hand to her lips.

'Now,' she murmured. 'It's about now. Enjoy it.'

Music swirled like a turmoil within her. She had come home to try and write it down.

Ethel closed her eyes, the better to call on those times when she had heard the sea singing its tempestuous song so clearly. On a holiday in Cornwall she had lain amongst the pink thrift and tufty grass on the cliff top, listening to the relentless ebb and flow of the waves below, the water throwing itself onto the rocks, whilst gulls screeched in the clear air. Then she had visited the underwater caves on the Scilly Isles and heard stories of how even the most upright characters in the old fishing community had stretched their thin living by enticing boats onto the rocks to profit from their cargo. She must have been told at some point of the suffering of the young woman 'Thirza' and her lover who wanted to live a different, lawful life. The morality fascinated her.

Everyone in this story has their own justified point of view, she had written to Harry when she had first outlined the story to him. *There's no right or wrong. Can you write a libretto based on that?*

How exciting those early exchanges had been, how intense the discussions of how the words and music might fit. *The Wreckers* – a great story of a time not so long ago in her own country. None of the opera conventions held here. That's what she wanted, strong women, no dukes or princesses, no fantasy figures or fairy-tale lovers. This opera would be rooted in reality, an English reality of love and danger and hard living.

As they had worked at it, creating the lines for the chorus and for the arias, the beautiful love songs and the shouts of the vengeful villagers, it had grown and grown until it had become longer and bigger and more precious than anything she had written before.

Now Ethel exulted in the power and pleasure of filling out the music for all of these themes and characters. Day after day, she worked at them. She began to pour passion into the songs of love between Mark and Thirza. She wanted to show that love can take you to the very edge of the world.

She tried not to think too much about Harry. He had become passive since the argument over her attachment to Winnaretta. They did not see each other. Letters went to and fro. He re-wrote the words when she asked and then revised them if she changed her mind. She missed the robust dialogue, the opposition, the resistance that had always been part of their correspondence. She missed him.

Ethel almost ran out of Winnaretta's house and back to the shelter of her hotel. It was over, she knew that, had been over for a while. Winnie had new lovers. She had not exactly rejected Ethel. No, worse, she thought, she was still warm and friendly towards her, and gave space to her music in the salon, but...

Oh, must she describe it? She could neither think nor say the words that had to be thought and said. Winnie did not love her; she probably never had. There, that was it.

Ethel rushed along by the river. How could it be so cheerful, flowing and glistening in the spring sunlight, with its laden boats, its oarsmen always ready with a greeting, its sumptuous, curved bridges? She was excluded from happy, daily life, fighting her way along a corridor of pain.

She felt faint and ill at what she had seen – Winnie putting her hand so tenderly on that young woman's shoulder, her playful muttering in her ear. She had wanted to march up to them, slap Winnaretta's hand away, and show that young madame the door. Instead, she had turned away as calmly as she could, collected her coat and left.

In her hotel room, she tried to settle herself by the ritual of taking her manuscript from its drawer, setting it out on the table, and preparing her pens and inks. She inserted a new page into the first act. She would re-write Avis's aria, pour this scoured longing into her song, and gather together the forces of the strong wind and the sea on the rocks to help her.

My heart is sore, so sore.
Pit-pat, hear it beating, madly beating
As stricken heart ne'er beat before.

How mild the music was that she had written before. Had she forgotten about love gone sour? Now she must find the notes for it.

~

Poison washed through Ethel's veins. She wanted to hurt Winnie.

'She's gone out, just like that, without saying anything?'

'She's moved on, darling,' said Anna.

Ethel paced the room. Backwards and forwards. Vengefulness seeped out of her pores.

'She can't,' shouted Ethel. 'She loves me.'

'She loves us all. But not like you want. You should know that.'

'But it was so very special between us, is so very special.'

'She still wants you here. But not if you keep on raging.'

'Is she so shallow, Anna? She can't just pick people up and throw them down.' Ethel hated the petulance she could hear in her voice.

'She doesn't mean to hurt you. You just want different things.'

'I don't know how you put up with her. She's despicable. I think it would be best if I went home.'

'That's a good idea. Give yourself some time to recover, then come back to us.'

29

ROME 1904

Ethel grew afraid as the train made its determined way south. It was a couple of years since she last travelled to Rome, years spent in a turmoil of desire, musical inspiration and rage. Her stomach clenched and her breath came short at the thought that those lovely times with Harry might be past, that she might no longer be the honorary mistress of his home, or ever see him smiling at her from the other end of the table.

As the train came into the station, she realised she could not just turn up at his villa. She booked herself into a small hotel in a back street, all she could afford, and wrote to him.

The smells of the breakfast table – eggs, meats, kippers – turned her stomach. Overwrought and tired, she had hardly finished a cup of black coffee when the porter brought a letter to her. It was from Harry and said simply: *The carriage will wait outside the hotel until you are ready to come.* Leaving her coffee half-drunk, she rushed upstairs for her coat and almost ran out of the lobby. The driver, who stood feeding his horses, greeted Ethel and helped her into the carriage before taking his seat at the front.

Harry was standing in the courtyard of the villa. How familiar it was, the sound of the horses' hooves as they went through the archway into that enclosed space, the great pots of grasses rustling in the slight breeze, the venerable, stone faces of the statues looking out. She almost stumbled as she stepped out of the carriage, and paused, too scared to look at what might be in his face. Anger, perhaps, or irritation that she had turned up out of the blue, or that terrible sadness when they had said goodbye in Paris.

When she looked up his arms were stretched out, and there was a broad smile on his face.

'Ethel, Ethel,' he said. 'Impulsive yet.'

'It was so cold, Harry, so cold,' she said, relief flooding through her as she felt his arms around her back, and as hers wound around him.

'Long days that were hardly worth getting up for,' he murmured. 'I feared this day would never come.'

'I hurt you,' she said. 'I'm sorry, so sorry.'

'I thought I loved everything about you, and then I discovered that your whole-heartedness might not always be so palatable.'

'I asked too much.'

'I had forgotten your enormous appetite, and then I missed it so much. I always believed that we should follow where love leads, but I couldn't live up to it. Can you forgive the things I said?'

'It is I who must ask for forgiveness.'

'We should go in,' he said at last, ushering her towards the door. 'I'm sure any passers-by are enjoying this immensely.'

Ethel laughed. It was so delicious to feel his arms holding her, the tickle of his beard as he bent to kiss her. There was much to talk about. A kiss and even a deeply meant apology couldn't disperse so quickly the cloud that had blackened between them.

In the evening, after a day of talk, Ethel took out *The Wreckers*.

'I'm longing to hear some,' said Harry. 'You write these ferocious and detailed letters about all the things you do and don't like. I've missed a lot, and I'd love to hear how it fits together now.'

Ethel played and sang some of the sections they had recently been exchanging letters about, and Harry made notes. That early scene did seem too long, but on the other hand, they needed to establish clearly the odd morality of the village and its minister. And yes, the tension was rising nicely there.

Their discussions took them through the evening and the early part of the night. When at last it became clear that Thirza must die, they curled up together on the sofa, murmuring and dozing.

After a while, Ethel got up and stretched her arms out, twisting her head to relieve her shoulders.

'I'm falling asleep,' she said. 'I'd forgotten how wonderful it is to work together. To be together. Thank you.'

Harry got up and put his arms around her. 'Thank you so much for coming. I know how much courage that must have taken. I feared this day might never come.' She felt him lay his cheek on her head.

'I'm ashamed that I was so mean,' she said. 'I've put you through too much.'

'Shh. No more. Tomorrow, you shall sleep late. Then if you wish, we could take the carriage into the hills and walk a little.'

30

PARIS 1905

Winnaretta's music room was already buzzing with people talking and drinking wine, and selecting tiny things to eat from the mountainous trays continuously circulated by the footmen. Ethel could still only understand a part of what was being said, but it didn't bother her. Everyone was at ease in the salon. There were as many poor artists as there were aristocrats; as many, like Ethel, in their workaday clothes as in elaborate, bejewelled evening dresses; as many not speaking French as speaking it.

She breathed in strongly, laughed loud at a very feeble joke out of sheer happiness. She greeted, and was greeted by, numerous artists, musicians, writers, philosophers. She kissed Winnaretta warmly. She would never stop loving her, and she hated herself for her jealousy and anger. How she hoped that now, at last, the poison had leached out of her system.

Ethel spotted Emma Calvé and went over to check that she was still happy to sing. A few days earlier, at an informal evening, Emma had enthusiastically started singing Thirza's songs as soon as she heard them. Calvé, world-renowned opera singer! They had sealed their bond by exchanging painful anecdotes about the Metropolitan Opera House in New York.

Anna began the evening by reading some of her poetry, the images almost impossible to capture, so delicate were they. Then the Princesse introduced Ethel as someone who had just completed her third opera, *The Wreckers*, and wanted to share some of it, with Mlle Calvé taking the main female role.

Ethel was delighted with how Emma interpreted the strong, feisty character of Thirza, but otherwise she was happy to present the whole opera herself, singing the other parts, and the chorus, as well as suggesting different orchestral sounds. After a while, she felt the moulding of herself with the music, with her vision of the piece, with its emotions as much as the notes. She was dimly aware of the quietening in the room, the absolute stillness, the little sighs and murmurs as she ended a chorus or described a piece of action. Then cheers and applause broke out as she ended.

~

'I have written to Monte Carlo,' Emma Calvé said. 'I had a great season there a couple of years ago, and I've offered to sing Thirza if they take up the opera.'

They were in Winnaretta's library, talking about how *The Wreckers* could find a stage.

'Monte Carlo?' said Ethel. 'Thank you, that would be wonderful.'

'I'm hopeful. I just want to get on a big stage and sing those arias.'

'I wondered if you would contact your old colleague the director there? He's going to guest conduct at Covent Garden next year, and I'm hoping he might like to put on *Wreckers* since it's written in French.'

'Ugh, no. Don't ask me.' Emma tossed her head, which, even at this time of day, was done up in elaborate swirls and braids. 'I shall never sing with him again. Never. The man thinks just because he's director, he can be an absolute tyrant. I've made his shows successful and did everything he asked of me, but he just trampled on me. I'm done with him.'

She turned to Anna, who put an arm around her and hugged her. 'It's all right, darling. Ethel didn't know you had such problems with him.'

Ethel dropped her head in dismay. Despite the success of *Der Wald*, Covent Garden was as adamant as ever that it would not stage *The Wreckers* until it had been successful in a European opera house. She had hoped to bypass that.

'I'm sorry, Emma,' she said. 'We wouldn't struggle so much if occasionally women were in these top positions.'

'May that day come soon.'

Good ideas became distinct possibilities, and then nothing. Anna and Hélène wrote to the few Eastern European opera houses to recommend they consider it, with no success. Winnaretta had high hopes of the Brussels opera house, where she had influential friends. She was desolate when they finally decided that it was too big, too Cornish and, unfortunately, written by a woman.

~

Ethel felt Leipzig greet her like an old friend as she got off the train. It was one of the last places on her list. She had thought that Dresden, Munich, Weimar – all those cities and many more – were more likely to stage *The Wreckers*, but they had come to nothing. Leipzig had always been snobbish about opera. To the musical minds of that city, which had included Lisl and Frau Frege in days gone by, opera was a dilution of the pure musical form, over-dramatic, frivolous even. But there were new people in charge now; the opera house would never have half the weight of the Gewandhaus and its orchestra, but nevertheless it had a full programme each year.

Ethel greeted Artur Nikisch enthusiastically.

'I'm so thrilled,' she said. 'Last time I was here you were second at the Gewandhaus, and now look at you, director of the opera.' His shock of hair and immense moustache were still there, even if a little grey.

'And I've been following your progress,' he said. 'New York, hey? Not bad. I'm so much looking forward to hearing a little of your opera.'

Ethel sat at the piano and performed a few sections of *The Wreckers*, dramatically, tenderly or threateningly, as the story demanded. Nikisch listened attentively and got up several times to look at the score as she played, even attempting part of one of the duets.

'It's wonderful,' he said. 'Yes, of course, there are a few refinements needed. I would love to put it on.'

'And do you think the powers that be will agree?'

'Yes, I have no doubt about that. They are happy on the whole to leave the programming to me. My only concern is that they won't accept an opera with a French libretto. It will have to be translated into German. Is that possible?'

Ethel thought of the long hours that Harry had spent carving the French language to fit the music. 'It's a shame,' she said. 'But of course it can be done.'

'Come back on Thursday, and we will have the contract ready.'

Despite the celebratory party Joanne Röntgen and her few remaining Leipzig friends held for her, Ethel was deeply disappointed. After six months of travelling, she had only this one contract for her opera, despite everyone acknowledging it was her best work by far. And she must arrange for its translation. There was a tinge of bitterness in her stomach. She had no champion to do this work for her; each time she had to go through this sickening process, this begging game, this drawing on every known contact.

~

Ethel was in the middle of checking the latest tortured translation of preacher Pascoe's bloodthirsty arias, when the two letters arrived.

I want you to come and meet me in France or Belgium, wrote Harry. *You are working too hard, overseeing the translation, not to mention preparing all the orchestral parts. I can tell from your letters that you're worn out, and everything has become grey and dreary. I was thinking of somewhere that is well away from all the people we know. We can spend a few days just walking the streets and riding out into the countryside and eating at village inns. You need a break from work and people and being so busy all the time. I would happily come to England but doubt you would really rest if I did.*

Ethel put the letter down, smiling. Dear Harry. But the whole idea was preposterous. She despaired of being ready as it was, especially since the translator had turned out to be so poor at meeting deadlines. She absolutely could not afford to take a couple of weeks out. It was true, she needed it. Every day there was fatigue, aching joints, a sick stomach and sore eyes. She slept badly wondering where, if anywhere, she might find a home for her opera after Leipzig. And what about the Mass, and *Fantasio* and *Der Wald*, sitting unrequested on her shelf? She longed for Harry; his thoughts mingling with and softening hers, walking, lovely food. And if she managed to relax, there was fun and making love and sleeping safe. Not yet, though. She must wait a while.

The other letter told her that Artur Nikisch had been asked to leave Leipzig for plunging the opera house into debt. The opera house would still honour her contract, of course, and would be in touch shortly when whoever was appointed was in place.

She stretched for a piece of paper, scrawling on it in anger and dismay. *I can meet you wherever you say, Harry, at the end of next week.*

Ethel breathed in the Christmas-infused air of Rouen. It was cold, much more cold than they had anticipated, and they had spent a pleasant afternoon poking round the market stalls buying hats and gloves, with a warm scarf for Harry and a wool jacket for her. Now, as it became dark, candles on the stalls created a warm glow, and the cold in their fingers was dispersed by goblets of hot, spicy wine. Ethel sank her nose into the steam coming off the cup, as much for the warmth as for the fragrance.

At one end of the market was a little covered area where young men dressed as elves or similar woodland folk sang cheerful songs accompanied by pipes and strange string instruments, whilst youngsters danced nearby.

'That wouldn't fit into *Wreckers*,' said Harry.

'We're a long way from sea songs here. It's fascinating, isn't it, how different each locality's songs are? Art has its own *terroire*, like the grape.'

'There speaks the international artist.'

'Let's sit down and listen.'

They sat on a bench in a little park to the side.

'Do you know who that cross commemorates?'

'What, that ugly thing there?'

'Yes. It's Joan of Arc. In whose mould you were made.'

'What? Joan of Arc? She was just a witch, as far as I know. Burnt to death, quite right too.'

'My goodness. Where did you learn your history?'

'Mrs Wotsit's school on the edge of nowhere?'

They burst out laughing.

'The French prize her highly, you know. She's a rare example of a strong, defiant woman.'

'Go on then. Show me how ignorant I am.'

'She broke with her family and fought hard to achieve what she did in a world of resistant men. Sound familiar? After successfully leading the French army in various battles, she was burnt at the stake right there by the English occupiers. The cross was erected when her innocence was proved decades later.'

'What a great subject for an opera.'

'You would not be the first to try. Didn't your friend Pyotr do it?'

'Who, Tchaikovsky? Did he? Poor Pyotr, I miss him so much. He was the loneliest of men, despite his success. I'd give a lot to be sitting at a piano with him right now. He was just being honoured in his country, you know, when he died, but his mind was too troubled to enjoy it.'

Ethel and Harry were lying in bed, chatting sleepily and sharing random thoughts, when Ethel turned on her stomach and looked at him.

'Thank you so much for these few days,' she said. 'This translation's turned out to be a nightmare. I didn't realise how much I needed a break.'

'I didn't just lure you here to make love to you, you know,' he said, stroking hair back from her face.

'Oh, that's a shame. Why then?'

'I'm worried about you, and I want you to make me a promise,' said Harry. 'We have to hope that Leipzig will do their best for *Wreckers*. When you're happy with the arrangements, I want you to leave the conductor to do what he's paid for. Spend the summer quietly at home. Or on holiday with your friends. Or come to a spa with me. Being there only leads to more stress for you, and you really aren't well enough at the moment to do everything. Do you promise?'

'We don't know yet who will put it on,' said Ethel.

'You're not such a young woman now. Your alarming energy still shines out, of course, when you're not worn out. You mustn't lose that.'

'All right,' she said. 'If, and only if, I'm happy with who they get to put on *Wreckers*, I promise I'll leave them to it. I shall enjoy the early summer with you as usual, and then go home and play lots of golf and tennis with everyone I know. Would that do?'

'Very good. Then we will turn up just for the performances.'

'I think we should drink to that. Is there any cognac left in that bottle?'

31

LEIPZIG 1906

Ethel almost ran through the portico of the Hotel Hauffe. White and shaking, she went straight up to Mary and Nina, who were having tea in the lobby.

'I'm going home,' she said. 'Straight away. I'm sorry I've dragged you all the way to Leipzig under the impression that my opera would be worth seeing. It's not. It's an abomination.'

'For heaven's sake,' said Mary. 'Whatever has happened?'

'He promised, and he's broken every promise. Now, it's ruined.' She turned away to go up to her room.

Nina jumped up and caught her. 'Wait a minute, darling, come and sit down. Tell us what's going on. I'm sure there is something that can be done to help.'

'It's been butchered. It's my opera, not his. Oh my! We had an agreement – no changes. That dreadful, conniving man has altered it so much it's a complete mess.'

'Oh gosh,' said Nina, 'that's not fair. Is this Hagel we're talking about?'

'I'm going to pack my bag and go. I absolutely cannot bear to see it. I'm afraid you're all going to be horribly disappointed after your long journey.'

'Don't think about us,' said Mary. 'That's not important. Look, let's have a think about this. You can't get a train at this time of day, anyway, so why not have a little rest, and then we can talk over dinner?'

Ethel was unable to eat much. She kept on breaking out into different incidents that had offended her, banging on the table or pacing the floor, shaking.

'Ethel,' said Violet, coming to put her arm around her, 'darling. Please calm down. You must tell us what actually happened.'

Eventually, she was able to tell them. The orchestra, the chorus and the singers were not bad at all; the staging was perfect and she had to admit that the first two acts were all she could have wished for.

'That's why it was such a shock,' she said. 'I was actually feeling very happy. This was the first time I'd seen it on stage, and it was marvellous. Dramatic and exciting. Poignant too, just as I wanted. I thought everyone was doing a great job.'

'And then what?' said Dick gently.

'We started Act Three all right, and then I began to think I must be going crazy. It was a complete mess. Scenes had been changed around, and even parts redistributed. It made absolutely no sense as a story, or as a piece of music. Of course, I stood up and pointed these things out, and Hagel just blanked me. Said he had decided to do it that way, and he couldn't see any problem with it. We had a bit of an argument, but he was adamant, so I left. I told him I wasn't coming back until it was put back together properly.'

'What did he say?'

'He just shrugged and said there would be no more changes. That's it as far as I'm concerned.'

'Quite right too,' said Nina. 'We shall all pack up and leave with you in the morning.'

'Hang on a minute,' said Violet. 'Surely we're not just going to give up like that? Could you threaten to withdraw the opera? Might that work?'

'I did. He simply reminded me of the contract.'

'A contract which he has broken.'

'Unfortunately, our agreement that he would not make any changes without consulting with me was not in the contract.'

'Ethel,' said Nina, 'am I right in thinking that after the first performance there's some kind of discussion as to what needs changing before the next one? I'm sure I've heard you talk about that.'

'Yes, that's what happens.'

'Well, obviously nothing is going to change before tomorrow night, but surely there's a chance of doing it afterwards?'

'That's a good idea,' said Dick. 'Please, don't throw it all away without another try. It really does sound like your best opera yet.'

There was a pause whilst the waiters cleared away the meat and vegetable dishes, and prepared the table for dessert.

'What do you think, Ethel?' said Violet.

'Don't ask me to go. I've told Hagel I'm not going and that's that.'

'You don't need to go,' said Mary. 'We'll go and tell you what happens. A lot of your friends will be there, and I'm sure if nice letters are written to whoever runs the theatre, or to the local press or whatever...'

Ethel looked around the table. She knew that if she insisted, her whole family would leave with her in the morning. But her opera was to be staged, she couldn't prevent that, and their idea was not such a bad one. How she wished Harry was here, that a stomach problem had not prevented him from travelling.

She nodded.

'I'll stay with you, Ethel,' said Charlie. 'We'll take the carriage and go and have the best dinner miles away. How about that?'

~

Ethel could hardly bear to watch her sisters gather in the foyer. They were beautiful and glamorous in their swirling, low-cut evening gowns, part-covered now in capes and stoles. They were quiet, compared to the usual chatter, giving Ethel warm hugs as they stepped out onto the snowy pavement and into the carriage.

Ethel watched them, dry-eyed, with a hollow feeling where her rage had been. It was the first night of her opera, of a work that she had sweated over for years, argued with Harry about, filled with the joy of Winnaretta. She had plagued all her musical colleagues for their opinions and advice and traipsed from city to city, her hopes raised and dashed time and again, made herself ill. And now she was not to hear it at its first performance.

'Shall we go?' said Charlie, coming away from the door where he had been watching for the next carriage to pull up. 'We can drive along by the river; it'll be lovely on this snowy night.'

'I'm sorry,' said Ethel. 'I can't bear not to go. I'm going to sit in the stalls so no-one will see me. I have to see what happens.' She looked up at him. 'You don't look cross or surprised.'

'I'm not,' he said. 'But we can still go off in the carriage if you want to.' Ethel shook her head. 'Shall I come with you?'

'No, there's no need,' said Ethel. 'You go and sit with the others.'

'Are you sure?' She nodded. 'We'll all meet for supper at the hotel.'

Ethel felt rather like she had when she was seventeen and used to escape to London and sit in the cheapest seats at a concert. People were packed together tightly, excited at the prospect of a new opera by a woman who, apparently, had years ago studied at their own conservatoire. As the first notes of the overture were played, Ethel sat back. She was no longer the composer, just one of many waiting to be enthralled.

She found herself being swept along by the people around her. They were quite prepared to laugh or cry as the story and the music demanded, to sigh at the sweetness of Mark's love or gasp at the perfidy of Avis. It seemed, as the opera came to an end, that they hardly cared that the story had become quite incomprehensible, so out of order were the scenes, and that the finale was not what she had intended. In fact, the finale was so weak, that when the orchestra finished, there was a momentary silence of puzzlement, rather than the murmurs which greet a satisfactory end.

Then the applause began. Ethel experienced it far more immediately than she would have done in the box. It was loud and protracted. There were cheers and whistles. The soloists took bow after bow, including the chorus and the orchestra, until the conductor climbed up on the stage, grinning from ear to ear. A surge of anger swept through her. He had butchered her work but was taking all the applause.

She dashed out of her seat, through the auditorium doors and ran along the corridor around the side. From the wings, she called to Hagel, who quickly covered the shock on his face by gesturing that she should come onto the stage and stand with him. As the audience understood who she was, there was more applause and cheering. Ethel stood there, grim-faced, defiant. Hagel should not think she was content.

At a late supper in the elegant dining room of the Hotel Hauffe, the conversation was muted. Ethel could tell that everyone had loved the evening, and they were not too bothered by the opera's mangled ending. At the same time, they could see how upset she was, and so they kissed and hugged her close, and wished her the best of luck when she got up from the table before dessert was served.

First-night parties were always held at the Hotel de Bavière, and though it was late now, she thought Hagel and the director would still be there. Celebrating, she thought bitterly as she walked in to a wall of chatter and laughter – a sound which suddenly went completely dead. Then someone clapped, and everyone followed.

'The audience loved it, Fraülein Smyth, don't you think?' said Herr Hagel tentatively, coming towards her as the conversations restarted.

'They did, I have to agree,' said Ethel. 'But do you not think they would have loved it more if you had kept your promise and produced it as it was written?'

He shrugged. 'We can't know that. You can't just dismiss all those curtain calls.'

'Look,' said Ethel, 'I'm not asking for anything difficult, just that you keep to the score as written. You had no right to make those changes, none at all, without contacting me. That is what we agreed.'

Hagel flushed and looked at the director. Neither said anything.

'If you agree to revert to what I wrote, which will make a lot more sense, then I will undertake to get the scores updated for the next performance at my own expense.'

'Fraülein Smyth, it's very late now.' The director turned back to the table. 'Let's have a drink together. Come to the office at the theatre tomorrow morning, and we will talk some more.'

'Ten o'clock,' she said, walking out.

~

Ethel, having said goodbye to her family as they continued on their various travels, set out for the opera house in good time for the meeting. The side door used on no-performance days was locked. There was no doorman, and Ethel's loud banging met with no response. She went round the building, trying every door, large or small, that she came across, hammering on each one with increasing fury. No-one answered.

She walked around once more, thinking she might have missed a door, then walked blindly through the streets, through the busy markets that were impervious to her pain. Down to the new conservatoire and Gewandhaus she strode, passing the Thomaskirche and other utterly dear and familiar places. She hardly noticed them. She even found herself in the Humboldtstrasse where Lisl had lived, and choked unexpectedly as she walked by that house. 'Oh, Lisl, Lisl,' she muttered. 'What am I to do?'

Eventually, tiredness and hunger drove her back to the hotel.

The clerk handed her a letter, marked from Hagel, which she ripped open standing there at the desk. *On reflection*, he wrote, *it would be foolish to change one note of an opera that met with such a huge success on its first night. Surely, now you have had a chance to think about it, you must be thrilled. We don't feel there is any point in having a meeting. The director and myself looked forward to seeing you at the second performance.*

She sat at the table in her room and spent the rest of the day writing letters. She wrote to Hagel demanding he meet her the next morning and had the hotel's post boy take it to his home at once. She wrote to Harry, a long letter during which she found herself scrawling her disappointment on page after page. How she wished for him to be here now. She wrote to the editor of the Leipzig daily *Allgemeiner Zeitung*, wondering if Leipzig's opera house had adopted a new policy of ignoring promises made to its composers. Then she walked down to the station and bought a train ticket to Rome for the next day.

Ethel walked along the city streets, which were cheerful to her this morning with their usual busy merchants, market smells and women out shopping. The door to the theatre was open and Ethel found her way to where the offices were. Perhaps everything would work out well, after all.

The secretary, with whom Ethel had regularly corresponded over the past year, welcomed her with embarrassment rather than his usual warmth.

'Fraülein Smyth,' he said, 'congratulations on your successful first night. I'm so pleased everyone liked the opera so much.'

'Thank you,' said Ethel. 'I have an appointment with Herr Hagel.'

'I'm afraid he's not here. He sent his apologies and said that he would not be available for a meeting with you until after the next performance.'

'Did he give any reason for not meeting with me?'

The secretary shrugged. 'I'm sorry. I don't even know if he is coming into the theatre today.'

Ethel walked back out of the door into the corridor. She paused, her body tense and her face stiff with fury. Instead of heading for the exit, she made her way along to the auditorium. It was empty, eerily quiet, asleep, almost dark without its lamps and candles. She marched down to the stage, her feet making no sound on the richly carpeted floor. Only as she went into the orchestra pit did she have to quieten her heels on the wooden boards.

The deserted area had an abandoned look. The music sat any which way on the stands, or even on the floor, just as the players had left it, and their chairs were higgledy-piggledy. A cover had been carelessly thrown over the timpani and cymbals. Above, the stage looked enormous, the dark cave and the sea almost real in the dimness, ready to be brought to life by sound. Ethel shivered.

She gave herself a little shake and moved steadily around the pit. Every time her elbow or skirt caught on a music stand or chair back, she jumped at the noise, but still she collected up every page of the music left there. She piled it up on a chair, then began to push it into her bag. There was too much of it, it was heavy, it wouldn't all go in. Finally, she managed to close the clasp. She hesitated before picking up the conductor's score. No, she was not going to leave one page of her opera here to be further mangled. She tucked it under her arm, and walked quickly and quietly out into the crisp winter air.

Back at Hotel Hauffe, whilst waiting for the carriage that would take her to the station, she finished off the letters she had written the afternoon before and gave them to the hotel clerk. *Unlike in New York*, she ended her letter to Harry, *I have not remained passive in the face of this attack on the integrity of my opera.*

32

LONDON 1908

My dear Miss Smyth, I am so pleased to have got a post in London conducting the Symphony Orchestra, as I expect you know already. I feel I owe you something for the way I had to quit Leipzig, leaving your marvellous opera to the whims of young Hagel. I can't put on your opera but I would like to promote your music here if I can. Please come and see me. Artur Nikisch.

Ethel kissed the page and kissed it again. A saviour! What a dull year it had been. She had nowhere to go with *The Wreckers*. The few that loved it were not in a position to stage it. No-one in Germany would touch it, or any of her work, after the Leipzig episode. Covent Garden prevaricated.

She had still been busy, of course. She had spent time with Winnaretta in France, playing in her salon and dissecting the different sounds of the music being written by their French composer friends. Out of this had come some complex new songs, and some experiments with accompaniments by various instruments. Hélène and Justine wanted to arrange a concert in Paris to celebrate English music, with her songs prominent.

The songs found favour with the Empress, who hired some musicians to perform them at one of her posh dinners. They had been sung and played again in a short recital at Queen's Hall and had received some surprisingly good press.

Ethel enjoyed it all, but only twenty minutes of her music in a proper concert hall in a whole year was poor pickings. She read Artur Nikisch's letter again. A conductor she respected greatly, now with one of London's best orchestras, was asking her what he could put on.

Ethel wondered at the feeling in her stomach. Yes, it was excitement, of course it was. She had almost forgotten, so dull and flat had she become, how exciting it was to sit and wait for her music to be played. She was sure Nikisch would do her proud. His orchestra couldn't stage her opera, but she would hear a little of it, the Prelude to Act II. It was redolent with the dramatic play of the sea against the cliffs.

Mary had hired a box for the family, who were happy to hear her music played again after the Leipzig business. Ethel watched entranced as the huge hall filled up. The people had not come specifically to hear her music, of course, though many of her friends had. No, this is what it should be like, her music taking its place as part of a programme, sitting happily alongside other musicians, both old and new.

She wished Harry was here to enjoy this evening after all their disappointments. When she had been with him in the autumn, she had noticed that he tired easily, and his appetite was not good. His hair was full of grey, and he complained of feeling old. The cycling holiday they had talked of had been put off. He had not improved much over the winter, though friends who went to Rome found him in good spirits.

~

'Now,' said Ethel, 'your marvellous orchestra has already learnt a very tricky bit of my opera. Do you think it went well enough to go ahead with the whole thing – well, not the whole thing, of course? Everything but the acting.'

Ethel was sitting in Artur Nikisch's office. There were congratulations to share, press reports to ponder over, plans to make.

'Yes, indeed,' he said. 'I've put it to the orchestra, and if you can find the singers, they would love to do it. It's disappointing for them if they learn to play something well, and it doesn't have another outing. We can't schedule it, unfortunately, so they will need paying.'

'Amazingly, we have money and a hall,' said Ethel. 'Moreover, Madame Marchesi is offering herself without a fee for Thirza's part. And she has ideas for collecting a chorus together too. What do you think?'

'She's a wonderful, dramatic singer. I'm sure she'll rise to the challenge. Is she available?'

Ethel nodded.

'Then we can start planning rehearsal time immediately. I have some ideas for the other lead singers, too.'

'That's wonderful. I'm hoping so much that this will be enough to persuade Covent Garden to stage the full opera.'

~

Hélène wrote with a date for the English music concert in Paris – it would be just a few days after *The Wreckers*' concert performance. Ethel smiled ruefully. All those months she had suffered when nothing at all had happened. She wrote back to ask for a new date; she would not be able to get to rehearsals or see to any of the preparations. Hélène insisted. Surely she did not want to lose Louis Fleury, who had played the flute so beautifully when her songs had been performed at the Queen's Hall, and Gabriel Fauré was involved, too. And was it not such fun to have two concerts in two countries within a few days? She only had to come for the final rehearsal, and she would find everything in order. Courage!

Ethel laughed out loud. They were determined, and she would have to go with it. She did not mind getting a taste of the life of a sought-after musician.

~

Father would be very angry if he knew I was writing to you, she read. She looked at the signature: Christopher Brewster. *But I thought you should know that he is quite poorly. I have arranged for him to see one of the best physicians in Rome, because his symptoms are so worrying. Of course, he insists that all is well. He is absolutely determined to come to your concert in London at the end of the month, but I do not know that he will be well enough. I will be in touch after the physician's visit.*

Ethel held the letter to her pounding heart. It must be serious then. She thought of Harry's letters over recent months, sometimes complaining of 'kitten claws' in his stomach. She had tended to put it down to his usual heartburn and indigestion.

Harry's letter, arriving the next day, was very cheerful; yes, he was quite poorly, nothing a trip to Karlsbad wouldn't cure, if she had time to come with him after the concerts. He was determined to come to London. He wanted to show his new play to a couple of friends, and of course he could consult some of the famous London doctors if she insisted.

A week later, Christopher wrote that the physician had diagnosed cancer of the liver, inoperable.

~

Ethel was frightened to look at Harry, and she focussed on the stage ahead of her. It should have been a wonderful night: a great orchestra conducted by someone who believed in *The Wreckers*, with celebrated singers creating magic out of her arias. Hundreds of people were absorbed in it, not just her ever-supportive friends and family.

She leaned across and took Harry's hand. She had to remember not to squeeze it, as she usually would, to convey to him her happiness and excitement at the music unfolding. At that signal, he would normally hold her hand hard, happy too that she was satisfied. But his hand was cool, the skin papery and dry. Where was its muscularity, the strong fingers, the energy of his usual response? She softened her touch and enfolded the weak, thin hand as if it were her most treasured possession.

She sensed how rigidly he sat there and started to caress his hand. She was too shocked to look at a face that had been transformed in a matter of weeks from that of a vigorous, curious, healthy man into something so pale, so thin, so weary. He probably should not have stirred from his bed in Rome. He had done that for her. Feeling the energy of her music flowing through her, she tried to channel it through her large, strong hands into that slight, sick, dying man beside her.

There, she had said it, not aloud, not yet, but inside herself. Harry was dying. It had been obvious the moment she met him off the train. A terrible disease was at this very moment eating away at his body, laying a suffocating blanket over his life organs, poisoning the blood in his veins, leaving him weak, sad, in pain. Leaving her desolate.

The first half was coming to an end, and when it did, and the applause started, she looked at him. He nodded his head slowly and smiled at her. She knew that smile, weak as it now was. It said: my goodness, Ethel, you really are very good!

The other people in the box, Mary, Violet, Dick and Alice, all got up to go to the lounge, but Harry and Ethel continued to sit there. Christopher, who had never come to hear Ethel's music before, leaned over to smooth the blanket on his father's knees and asked what he might get for them.

'Just a little water,' Harry said. His voice was scarcely audible. 'And a glass of champagne for Ethel. Thank you.'

The two were left in the box, watching as beneath them people filed out to stretch their legs, get a drink and chat with friends.

'It's a great buzz, isn't it?' said Ethel. 'I think people are enjoying it.'

'Ethel,' said Harry. She leaned in and kissed him on the cheek. 'Promise me, you won't stop.'

'There's no stopping me—' started Ethel.

'No, when I'm not here. Promise me.'

'No, Harry, no. I'm not talking about that. It's not going to happen. Please let us just enjoy this wonderful evening.'

'On the brink,' he said, stopping to cough. 'On the brink of all you've worked for.' His breath was very short.

'Please, darling, don't talk. I know what you want to say.'

'All you've dreamed of—'

'That we have dreamed of, dearest. I couldn't have done any of this without you...'

Ethel couldn't talk through the constriction in her throat. She wanted to feel his arms around her, teasing her for being so dramatic. But it was him that was being dramatic; surely it was just one of his games.

'Promise me,' he said.

'You know I will always write music,' she said. 'But that's not at all important just now. Please rest.'

She looked up gratefully as Christopher came in with their drinks. Harry took his water and tipped the glass towards Ethel before taking the tiniest sip.

Ethel thrilled, as always, at how in moments a concert hall could go from a bustling place, full of sound and movement, to a carefully ordered quietness, where everyone sat primly in rows, their hands in their laps, their faces pointing in one direction. And tonight it was her music they were looking forward to. How lovely they were, too, those smartly dressed men on the stage with their horn, or their oboe, or their violin resting so lightly in their hands, the chorus in silent rows behind, waiting for the soloists to return to the stage. There came the women in their elaborate gowns and sparkling jewellery, followed by the men in their long-tail jackets. Ethel could hardly contain her delight, her pride.

It was true, what Harry had said. On the brink, that's where she was, of all that she had dreamed. She turned to Harry, her face alive with love and gratitude for all the many ways in which he had helped her. How beautiful he was, despite his pallor. His eyes were shut, but as she leaned over to take his hand again, she felt the slight press of his fingers.

33

1 9 1 0

I can hardly bear to live in England anymore, wrote Ethel to Lady Lytton. *One is constantly being asked one's position on the suffrage question, and nothing is talked about at the dinner table but the latest self-dramatising actions of the suffragettes. As far as I can see, they are making the very people they wish to influence so angry that women will never get the vote. Thank you for congratulating me on receiving the honour of Doctor of Music, but I promise you I will never join the women's cause. I don't want the vote, and should not use it if I had it. Britain has been well-governed, on the whole, and it's not necessary to turn upside down all the structures that are in place. Do not write to me again.*

Ethel folded the page furiously and jammed the hot seal onto it so that it smeared.

'Honestly, Pan,' she said to the dog sleeping under her writing table. He stood and shook himself, putting his front paws on her knee. 'These women, they never stop. In their eyes, all we have ever wanted to do is go into a polling booth. You can tell they don't have a living to earn. Now, find your lead and let's go and see what Hanni has for our dinner tonight.'

She pulled a cape around her shoulders and stepped out into the soft evening air. 'Mm, lovely Vienna,' she murmured, admiring as she always did the wide boulevards with their trees in full summer leaf, and the solid, square buildings with their evenly spaced windows.

'Oh, Harry.'

The lurch of grief had become familiar. It would have been so much better to walk the streets with him, pointing out who had designed what house, and who lived where. He would have had a lot to say about those campaigning women, of that she was sure. He would have been especially curious to understand what was making wealthy, well-educated, influential women take to the streets to smash windows and make such a nuisance of themselves. Why wasn't he here? Her face screwed up to dispel the longing.

He would have loved Helmut and Hanni, Conrad and Magdi's daughter, too, even if he might have joked in his slightly mocking way about their serious approach to life. He would have admired their tiny household, and the way they organised their lives. He would have enjoyed sparring with another writer, fighting out the value of Helmut's novel against his own philosophical works. She and Hanni would have joined in when they took a break from their musical conversations. If only she had known her when she was writing *The Wreckers*; they could have talked about how to develop the strongest songs for Thirza. It was too late now.

All that was over, the composing. She still promoted her work, but she would not be writing any more. Her musical inspiration had died along with Harry. She missed it terribly, those sounds in her head demanding to be turned into notes on a page, the task of trying to transfer the vision in her mind, the agony of it never quite happening. She missed the absorption of composition, the way time flowed by, the satisfaction of it.

'I had a letter from Lady Lytton today,' she said to her hosts, as they sat at supper around the kitchen table. She leaned forward the better to breathe in the rich meatiness on her plate. 'Mm, this is a wonderful pie, Helmut. Congratulations. She's a marvellous woman and all that, but it doesn't mean I'm going to join her blessed suffragettes.'

'Is that what she was asking you?' said Helmut. 'Aren't they just the women you'd find common cause with? Fighting like anything just to get somewhere.'

'Good heavens, no,' said Ethel. 'I've got absolutely nothing in common with them. Constance Lytton made herself look ridiculous getting herself arrested posing as an ordinary woman. And why? Just to show that the prison authorities treat common women more harshly than wealthy women. Well, of course they do.'

'It's hardly right, though, is it?' said Hanni, spooning another piece of pie onto Ethel's plate. 'And she more than proved her point. Didn't she compromise her health too? Women are going through hell just to get basic citizenship rights, and your government is playing tricks with them. It's no better in Austria, mind you.'

Ethel thought uncomfortably about the letter on her desk. She hadn't even acknowledged what Constance Lytton had done. 'All right, all right. Some of them are brave and courageous, of course they are. Why Asquith should be so thuggish as to order force-feeding, I don't know. It's a brutal way to go on. But more and more illegal acts isn't the right way.'

'Have you heard Emmeline Pankhurst speak?' asked Helmut.

'Good Lord, no. I avoid those ghastly Pankhurst women at all costs.'

'You should go and hear her next time you're in London. She is astounding! The most sensible, logical, rational speaker I've ever heard. Really, she makes her political opponents look like idiots. And she's right, isn't she? If the government won't act when huge numbers of people demand their rights in perfectly legitimate ways, what is left but militancy?'

Ethel held up her hands, laughing. 'Hear the converts! No, really, it's not for me. I've got to give all my attention to getting Thomas Beacham to turn up and put on a decent performance of *The Wreckers* at Covent Garden.'

'Think about it,' said Helmut. 'It really is your fight, too. It's about opportunities for talented women like you just as much as those working in the hideous factories. You have to support it – surely you don't want to be classed alongside those dreadful women who prefer to leave everything to the menfolk.'

Ethel blew out her cheeks. 'Hardly.' She turned to Hanni, laughing. 'Why is he so passionate all of a sudden?'

'He's probably putting it in his next novel.'

'No,' said Helmut, getting up and piling the plates together noisily. 'That's not the reason. It's true I am trying to capture something of this entirely new spirit in my book. But it's because of you, Hanni, and millions of women like you.'

'Me?' said Hanni. 'What do you mean?'

'You want to carry on singing and you should. Everyone agrees you're one of the best in the world at the moment. But you also want children, we both do, but that's not allowed for an opera singer, is it? Well, not a woman opera singer. Of course, men just carry on as normal if there is a new baby in the house. These ridiculous cultural traditions have to be challenged. They cause such pain, and as far as I can see, the suffragettes are showing the way. The moderates have tried their best but got nowhere.'

A pang of loneliness shot through Ethel as she saw how Hanni put her hand on Helmut's. If Harry had been here, would he have been nodding in agreement or arguing in his elegant way? For once, she wasn't sure.

'It's true,' she said. 'Think about my friend Thekla, one of the best singers of the '70s and '80s. She loved her husband, and her family, and her new country, but boy, was she angry with life when she could no longer sing in public? Perhaps you're right, Helmut; it's scandalous that a whole generation later, Hanni's facing the same thing.'

Helmut went to the larder and put an elaborate cream dessert on the table.

'Goodness me,' said Ethel. 'You didn't make that too, surely?'

'Sadly, this is not my creation,' he said. 'Hanni's the pudding-maker, but the patisserie's a good standby when she's in rehearsal. You will think about it, won't you, Ethel?'

'All right, I'll go and hear your Mrs Pankhurst when I'm next in London. Then I'll decide. Is that fair?'

'Yes, yes,' said Hanni, giving Ethel a large slice of the lemon posset. 'I know what. My sister knows people who are close to Mrs Pankhurst. Shall I get an introduction for you to one of her drawing-room meetings?'

'Excellent,' said Helmut. 'You won't be disappointed, believe me.'

'I had no idea when Magdi suggested I look you up, that this would happen,' said Ethel, tackling the dessert.

'You mean the pudding or the suffragettes?' said Hanni.

~

Emmeline Pankhurst was elegant and beautiful; Ethel decided that within two seconds of seeing her. More – she was warm, vivid, lit up by deep conviction. All of that was obvious when she stood up to speak. She was totally at ease with herself, in command, confident that the thirty or so women in the ornate drawing room would lay down their tea cups and turn to listen to her, as they did.

They were of a similar age, Ethel supposed, but against her, she felt ordinary, workaday, plain. Mrs Pankhurst was dressed in a green dress in some soft, silky material, with a delicate lace collar, and her hair was scooped up on top of her head. Ethel wished that she had made more of an effort. Uncaring of her appearance at the best of times, she had bothered even less since Harry had died. She found herself wishing that at the very least her boots were clean, and she had gone to the effort of getting a fresh pair of gloves out of the drawer.

Ethel could also see that behind the energy radiating from Mrs Pankhurst, there was tiredness, thinness. Ethel recognised that, the exhaustion of a woman who has thrown all of herself into a project, extending herself beyond everything she might have thought herself capable of.

'Here I am again, dear friends,' she was saying. 'How good to be far from the narrow stone walls of Holloway and the cruel attentions of its warders. Hunger is a terrible thing – we must never forget that so many go hungry each day for lack of food. But this was my choice, a choice forced on me by the refusal of our government to grant us what is our right. Even so, to resist the food, however unappetising, which is pushed in front of you each day, twice in each day, calls for such strength and belief in the rightness of our cause, as you might never have expected. But my suffering was nothing compared to that of our sisters who, having refused that food day after day, are forced to have those vile tubes pushed into their bodies and a hideous liquid poured into their unwilling stomachs. It is an assault, my friends. It is a grievous bodily harm, which, if not imposed by the government of this country, a country of which we used to be proud, would be a prosecutable offence. But you know these things. For two years Herbert Asquith and his government have preferred to torture women rather than concede their basic rights of citizenship.'

Ethel felt a flush of shame but a certain resistance too. She had sat at dinner tables with some of these men – not Asquith himself, it was true, nor his powerful, anti-suffrage wife – and they seemed well-wishing, knowledgeable, wise even. Did they really have such black hearts, those charming conversationalists? Surely this beautiful, strong woman must be exaggerating. Nothing quite so sordid could be going on.

'There are still many women,' went on Mrs Pankhurst, 'who cannot believe what is happening – that this country of ours, with its fine values of human decency, is carrying out this torture with impunity. I understand that – it is incredible, but it is time for those women to wake up.'

Ethel raised her eyes to find Mrs Pankhurst looking directly at her. In fact, she felt sure that it was well known to her that she had been running away from the message of the suffragettes for a long time, had spurned all that Agnes Garrett and Maeve Parry had said to her all those years ago.

'Women can never succeed,' the words were gentle, spoken as if to Ethel herself, 'unless they work together for equality. Only the vote can deliver that equality, and that is why we must now...'

Ethel was not listening anymore, though that strong, melodious voice formed the backdrop to her thoughts. Her mind was ridiculing what Mrs Pankhurst said – it was crazy, wasn't it, all this sacrifice, all this time wasted on planning what to do next to get the government to sit up and take notice, all this resistance to the slow-turning wheels of power. And yet, deep within her, there was a nub of excitement. Mrs Pankhurst would certainly have something to say about the stern, male gatekeepers of the music world. And here was a beautiful, eloquent woman inviting her to step out of the greyness that had fallen on her when Harry died. Another shining thread was weaving itself into her life.

Ethel was introduced to Mrs Pankhurst over tea.

'Oh yes,' said Mrs Pankhurst, scarcely smiling. 'Dr Smyth. Pleased to meet you.'

Ethel felt as if she had been left out in the cold street, whilst everyone else enjoyed mulled wine around the fire. None of the passion, the inclusiveness that had charmed her so much, was directed at her.

'Your speech was wonderful,' Ethel said. Mrs Pankhurst was nodding and smiling, but her eyes were looking to see who else wanted to talk to her.

'I don't think I've seen you at one of our meetings before. Or in the streets at our demonstrations.'

'I'm afraid my musical activities keep me busy in Europe much of the time,' said Ethel. It sounded pompous.

'Excuse me a moment,' she said. 'I must speak to the general before she goes. Everyone's skills are needed in the campaign, you know.'

A rustle of silk, a trail of perfume and Ethel was left watching Mrs Pankhurst warmly greet and kiss a friend, and engage in lively discussion and laughter.

Ethel turned to the woman who had introduced her. 'Thank you,' she said. 'I've got a lot of thinking to do.'

There were other acquaintances in the room whom she could have spoken to, but she did not feel at all sociable and took her leave.

If I had known, she wrote to Mrs Pankhurst a few days later, *when Agnes Garrett regaled me with reasons why I should join the fight for the vote, that fifteen years later that fight would still be going on, would have become bitter and even tragic, I would perhaps have made a different decision. Instead, I chose to focus on forging a career as a composer for myself, a path which has been long and often lonely, despite moderate success. Perhaps I could give two years to the cause, and do what I can to work with you towards the success that must come?*

Two days later, she opened the reply. *We welcome all women to work for suffrage in whatever way they can. Please call in at our offices in Clement's Inn.*

Ethel turned the page over and over. Was that all? She had barely slept all week wondering what she might contribute. Was that all the thanks she got?

~

'Are you crazy?' said Mary. 'Those women have lost their minds. It's preposterous what they are doing, and extremely unlikely to win them the vote.'

Ethel looked around the dinner table at her sisters, their husbands and the young folks who had been able to come to see Mary and Charlie off on their latest travels. On most faces there was an expression of disdain, disgust, even fury.

'Darling,' said Alice, whose face showed nothing but concern, 'surely you're not going to be out on the streets with those women? It's full of danger. There are injuries, assaults, all sorts.'

'I think I am,' said Ethel with relish. 'I'm really taken by this idea that if we don't fight in whatever way necessary, we will never get the vote.'

'Please,' said Nell, 'don't give us a lecture on how long the campaign has gone on for, and all its different forms. We've been watching it for years whilst you've been swanning around Europe.'

'Why not? Why should men keep on denying women a legitimate right?'

'Good old Ethel,' said Dick, shaking his head admiringly. 'Always up for a fight.'

'Be quiet, Dick,' said Violet. 'It's good you've decided to do something, Ethel. I know how sad you've been since Harry died. But why do you have to join the Pankhurst gang? Millicent Fawcett is doing a grand job too, though she doesn't get half the publicity. If you really feel that strongly, you can agitate for it without bringing shame on us all, surely?'

'This suits you perfectly, Auntie,' said Kitty. 'I would love to join you.'

'Don't you even think about it,' said Mary. 'Look what you're doing, Ethel. Do you want to draw your nieces into danger?'

'You talk as if the Pankhursts have created this situation. They haven't. The government could end it tomorrow by doing what they have actually said many times they would do, and enfranchise women, or some of us anyway. Come on, now, I appreciate your concern, but it is so that our children, my lovely, clever nieces, can play a full part in society.'

'God help us,' said Dick.

'I'd lay a considerable amount of money,' said Charlie laughing, 'on you getting arrested within the next few months.'

'For God's sake,' said Mary. 'Don't provoke her.'

'She has already been provoked,' he said.

34

LONDON 1910

Ethel stood with Mrs Pankhurst and several other women in the shelter of a doorway to Parliament. One of them she recognised as the Princess Sophia Duleep Singh, daughter of the exiled maharaja, whom she had met in various drawing rooms over the years. The others, all older than her, she did not know. Three policemen stood in front of them to stop them going any further forward.

'I would like to come through,' said Mrs Pankhurst in a sharp voice, her northern accent more pronounced than Ethel had heard before. 'The rest of the procession has arrived now.'

'You stay here, little ladies,' said the one of the three who appeared to be in charge. 'You're too old to be part of this mayhem. You're safe here.'

'Excuse me,' said the princess, 'I am certainly no older than you. So please, let us through.'

The policeman looked at her disdainfully. 'I am here to protect you,' he said.

'I certainly do not wish to be kept safe by you,' replied Mrs Pankhurst. 'These are my women who your officers are pushing about. Let me through. I am entitled to ask the Prime Minister to hear our deputation.'

Beyond the policemen, Ethel could see hundreds of women, all pushing towards Parliament. Many were holding banners: 'Votes for Women Now', or 'Deeds not Words'. Policemen were wrenching the banners out of women's hands, when they got the chance, breaking the poles into two and throwing them back. In some places, Ethel could see women being pulled out of the procession and thrust into the crowd on the pavement. Above all, there was noise, the chanting of the women against the shouts of the police, the jeers of the onlookers against the occasional yelp and howls of outrage as someone got hurt.

Mrs Pankhurst pushed her way between the policemen, with Ethel and the others close behind. 'Either arrest me or let me through,' she said. 'We have many matters to discuss with the Prime Minister.'

Before she had gone more than three paces, Ethel saw a new surge of movement amongst the women packed into Parliament Square. Police on horseback pushed slowly through the crowd, making space for the rows and rows of police who walked behind them.

'Go home, go home, ladies,' shouted the officer at the front. 'There is nothing for you here. The Prime Minister does not wish to receive your deputations. Now go home, or risk being arrested.'

'We demand to see Mr Asquith.' Mrs Pankhurst's voice cut across the noise.

'The vote; we demand the vote; let Parliament decide,' chanted the women.

'Posh cow.' Ethel could hear the taunts from the crowd on the pavements. 'Go home and make your husband's dinner,' 'No vote for women, no vote for women,' 'Want the vote 'cos you can't get a husband, is that it?'

'The Prime Minister will not see you today,' repeated the officer on the horse. 'Move along, please. I've warned you and you will be arrested if you don't leave.'

Quietness fell over the square. 'We shall not go away.' It was the clear voice of Mrs Pankhurst again. 'Women will never go away until we have the vote. Come on now, let's have a song.'

Despite the singing, Ethel could see the increasing nervousness of the women, holding themselves tense and linking arms as they moved forward. She struggled to keep up with Mrs Pankhurst.

'Very well, charge!' said the policeman on the horse.

The police on the ground drew out their truncheons and started lashing out. Men from the crowd on the pavements started to get in amongst the women.

'Look at this one,' Ethel heard one shout, and saw a young man put his hand over the shoulder of one of the women, tear open her coat and stick his hand down the front of her bodice. 'Oh, very nice. That's a nice handful.' Others followed suit, some pushing up women's skirts, others pinning them against the railings and pressing into them with their bodies.

Ethel turned away, her face flushed with shame and horror. 'Hey, look, you gormless policeman,' she shouted. 'Look what those men are doing. Aren't you going to stop them?'

The policeman turned and looked at her, laughing. 'It wouldn't be happening if you women had done as you were told.'

'Look, they're assaulting the women – you can't just look on.'

'Can't see anything, myself.'

Ethel could hear the insistent voice of Mrs Pankhurst further ahead and pushed forward. As she did so, there was another surge in the crowd. Women were being thrown through the air to shouts of, 'Bloody bitch, that's what you deserve,' and, 'Oho, let's see your legs then.' Ethel spotted a woman in a bath chair ahead of her. The chair lurched and fell despite the efforts of those by her to keep it stable. The woman fell onto the ground and tried to gather her skirts about her. Ethel lowered her head and butted through to get to her side.

'Out of my way,' she shouted in her most determined voice.

'You're monsters,' shouted someone else. 'How could you let a disabled woman lie in the street like that? Do you really not care who gets hurt here?'

'Shame on you,' chorused others.

Ethel bent down and lifted the woman back into her bath chair.

'Shall I take you out of here?'

'No. This is the vilest crowd I've been in, and I've been in a few,' she said. 'No surrender! Can you see my hat anywhere? Come on, my friends. Push me forward to Parliament.'

~

Ethel processed slowly down the centre aisle of the Albert Hall by the side of Emmeline Pankhurst, whilst hundreds, many hundreds if not thousands of women stood to cheer them. For the first time since becoming a Doctor of Music, she was wearing her black academic robes. Their heavy weight on her shoulders and the funny little cap pinned at the back of her head made her look, according to Emmeline, serious and professional. Ethel liked the contrast between them – Emmeline, as always, was elegant and assured in her long cream coat and wide-brimmed hat.

Her newly composed *March of the Women* had been played and sung as they entered the hall. The singers she had trained had not let her down, conveying the idea of women marching confidently into the future to the strong beat of the music. Now the applause was passionate, the clapping protracted.

When Ethel had joined Mrs Pankhurst, she had not known what might happen. She might just be another body on a demonstration. Maybe she could bring in wealthy and influential people from her social contacts. The music that began to form in her head was unexpected. It had always happened whenever she encountered something new, but that was before Harry died. Emmeline had sparked it in her.

How naïve she had been that day in November when she set off for the Houses of Parliament alongside Emmeline. She had thought that they, along with the thousands behind her, might be forced to wait in the street for a while, then Mr Asquith would receive the leaders. He would hear them speak and then make some reasonable argument about why he had dissolved Parliament with no suffrage bill, promising to do more in the next session. Instead, there was violence and brutality. No-one had been called to account, despite the detailed statements of many women.

Ethel was quite pleased when she wrote *Outside Parliament*. It was full of drama and threat, and captured the stubborn persistence of the campaigners, as well as the marvel of her strong feeling for Emmeline. But when she played a section to Mrs Pankhurst, she had shown little interest.

'Ethel, I'm sure you are a great composer, but please, give me a song that people can sing.'

Ethel had pondered this for a few weeks. She had always seen her music as art and, if she thought about it, written for an audience of a certain kind. Now she was being asked to write something very different.

All the suffrage organisations had songs for demonstrations and protests, full of strong, fighting words that were sung to old, well-known tunes. The *Women's Marseillaise* was the current favourite. But Mrs Pankhurst wanted a song written entirely by women, for women.

Ethel puzzled over it. She missed Harry keenly. She longed to talk over with him all these new ideas crowding into her mind, the pros and cons of militancy, the extraordinary Pankhurst family, the brutality of the various confrontations, what it could mean for her music. Thinking about him set off a tune in her mind. Once when walking in the hills of Tuscany, they had heard a young shepherdess singing in the clearest, truest voice, a simple tune they had later hummed as they walked. It was perfect, if only she could find some words. Mrs Pankhurst asked the playwright Cecily Hamilton to work on it with her, and eventually the *March of the Women* came together.

Tonight, it was having its first outing.

The applause died down, and the little orchestra played the tune quietly as Ethel and Mrs Pankhurst ended their procession. Turning to the audience, Mrs Pankhurst raised her hand.

'That might be our anthem, don't you think?' she said. 'Ethel Smyth's *March of the Women*.'

Ethel wondered again at that fine voice which, though quiet, could be heard by everyone in the enormous hall.

'Everyone must learn it. And to thank Dr Smyth, one of the most eminent British composers of our time, both for joining us and for giving us her music, I would like to present to her this conductor's baton. The day will come soon when women are equal in the music world, as all other areas of life, and no-one is surprised to see a woman take the baton.'

Ethel opened the box, which was festooned with green, purple and white ribbons. She took out the little white baton with a gold, engraved collar. Wonder and surprise ran through her body. Unable to speak, she handed the box back to Mrs Pankhurst and, turning her back on the cheering audience, raised the baton.

'Let the music speak,' she said, signalling to the players and singers to be ready.

She beat out a faster speed than before: one, two, three, four. As she brought the baton down, women all over the hall sang, 'Shout, Shout, Up with your song. Cry with the wind, for the dawn is breaking.'

35

LONDON 1911

'Hey, Auntie Ethel,' said a cheery voice, 'this is amazing, isn't it? I'm sure there must be easier ways to avoid filling in the census form, but this is good fun, don't you agree?'

'Norah!' said Ethel, kissing her. 'What a lovely surprise. I agree, I'm sure Trafalgar Square doesn't often see such crowds at midnight. I didn't know you were part of the campaign?'

'No, and you must keep it secret,' said Norah. 'I've been longing to come to one of these events for ages. I'm staying with a friend, but Mother and Father would have a fit if they knew I was here.' She turned to her friend. 'Betty, this is my spectacular Auntie Ethel. Is Mrs Pankhurst in the Square?'

Ethel shook hands with Betty. 'No. Emmeline's gone on to Aldwych to make sure everything is OK there. Are you coming?'

'Skating in the middle of the night? That's not to be missed.'

Betty had a poster in her hand and turned towards Nelson's column, thinking to stick it on the plinth. Before she could take more than a couple of paces, two policemen were standing in front of her. She turned away, laughing.

'Oh boy, they're tetchy tonight.'

'They don't know what's happening,' said Ethel. 'In fact, they can't cope with the fact that nothing is happening. It's the middle of the night, and the Square is full of women wandering about, chatting. They're waiting for a group to break away and do something terrible. As far as I know, that's not the plan. Shall we get a cup of tea?'

They joined the queue in front of the little tea kiosk, where some women were having a heated debate.

'I still can't see how refusing to fill in the census form is going to get us the vote,' a middle-aged woman was saying. 'We're getting too far away from the main thing with actions like this.'

'Well, what is going to get us the vote?' said another. 'We don't know. Even women in prison being forcibly fed doesn't seem to be doing it. We have to try everything.'

'At least tonight we're out here enjoying ourselves, not starving to death. I've done a bit of that and believe me, it's not pleasant.'

'That's true, it shouldn't be us doing all the suffering. Here, it's your turn to get a cuppa.'

The lukewarm tea didn't take long to drink, and Ethel said goodbye to the two young women and set off for the skating rink. She chuckled as she walked along. How lovely, how unexpected to have another suffragette in the family. Kitty supported the cause, but she hadn't quite managed to persuade her out onto the streets yet.

The skating rink was almost unrecognisable. Multi-coloured, beautifully sewn banners hung from the walls, and the railings surrounding the rink were hung with ribbons of all colours. Huge bowls of flowers sat on the ends of the table, behind which Emmeline stood speaking. She was flanked by her two daughters, who, Ethel had learnt, were never far away, Christabel and Sylvia.

Ethel felt herself relax. All she had to do tonight was conduct her March whenever Christabel gave her the signal – and enjoy herself, of course. Her concert had been held the night before at

Queen's Hall – a whole programme of her own music, conducted by herself with a small orchestra made up of women. Even Emmeline, who did not enjoy music very much, had been happy, very happy, with the all-woman orchestra, surely never seen before.

Ethel could not get enough of Emmeline's speeches. There was something utterly thrilling about watching that small, graceful woman talking with so much passion, about observing the attention and intensity of the other women listening, about feeling her own heart beating faster with inspiration and love. It was exciting to see a woman so in charge, not just of herself, but of all the women in the room, and the supportive men too. She had never seen that before. Even Winnie, despite her fiery support of all that women might achieve in the arts, did not lead like this. Ethel's body throbbed to Emmeline's tune, describing a world so different, bringing it every day nearer to reality.

'Every principle of liberty,' she was saying in that powerful voice, 'enacted in any modern country on earth, has been intended entirely for the benefit of men. When women have tried to put these into practice for women, they have met with nothing but opposition. We have to be strong enough to fight for a different order.'

Ethel, standing in the roller-skating rink at three in the morning, felt scalded, as if layers of what she had always believed were peeling away. It wasn't just about getting the vote, it wasn't just about improving the lives of impoverished women and children: it was so much more than that. What would the world be like if women were equal, if they had a proper say? Emmeline challenged everyone there to think about it.

Ethel could hardly begin to grasp the scope of that. But it was something to do with those gatekeepers, wasn't it? Something about who made the rules.

Reeling slightly, Ethel hardly noticed that Emmeline had finished talking and Christabel was announcing the March.

Quickly she stepped into the rink, searching her pocket for her baton, and brought her singers to their feet. As the piano struck up, the big space with its wooden walls and high-domed roof came alive with sound. The singers sang in the classical style she had taught them, some blossoming into fine singers under her tuition. When the rest of the people joined in, the raw fervour of their voices added a drama she could never have anticipated.

'Wonderful,' said Christabel when the chorus had been sung yet once more. Christabel's voice was just as clear and assured as her mother's, but cold as ice. 'Here we are. There are several hours to go until it is safe to go home, so hitch up your skirts, fasten on some skates and let's rink the night away.'

'Come on.' Ethel held her hand out to Emmeline. 'Let's go and get you fitted out with some skates.'

'Goodness me, no. You should know by now that I never do anything the least bit sporty, so please don't ask me.'

'It's very easy,' said Ethel. 'I'll teach you and make sure you don't fall.'

'It's not easy for me,' said Emmeline, 'and not fun either. You love this kind of thing, so don't let me hold you back. Go on, off you go. I'm going to sit and chat and drink tea. Constance Lytton is usually game for a round or two of whist, and who knows, I might even have a little doze.'

Several of the younger women had organised a rota to play the piano to help the skating along. Some were tucking their skirts up as best they could, whilst a few had turned out in harem skirts that Ethel eyed enviously. They might be rather good on the golf course. At first, she found roller-skating a very poor substitute for the ice, but nevertheless she soon began to enjoy the whirling and twirling, the sensation of her breath coming faster to the varying rhythms of the music. When the skaters grew bored, they played games, a few rounds of statues or hokey-cokey, followed by some sprint races and even a three-legged one on skates.

Ethel emerged onto the street with a sleepy Emmeline on her arm. It was five in the morning and the streets were quiet and cool after the pandemonium within the rink. Christabel and several others went off to the Gardenia for an early breakfast, and Ethel would happily have joined them if she hadn't undertaken to get Emmeline back to her hotel.

'You are so full of life and energy, Ethel,' she said. 'Whereas I'm a sleepy sack of potatoes.'

'Yes, but then I'm not organising one of the most important political movements ever.'

Emmeline laughed. 'Oh, Christabel does most of it. I'm just its public face.'

Ethel looked at her, expecting her to laugh at her own joke, and was surprised to see that she was serious.

Dawn was not far off, but the night had hardly released its grip. The rain had stopped, but thick, low cloud prevented any early signs of morning breaking through. And yet there was increasing activity in the streets: buses rumbled by, workmen briskly walked along at the start of the new working week and the lights of an occasional motor car passed them by.

'Remember we're going in the back way,' said Emmeline as they approached her hotel. 'Mrs Rossler is an absolute darling, but I can't rely on her not to put me on the hotel form, even though I've given her the strictest instructions not to. She's more frightened of the census enumerator than me.'

'I doubt that,' said Ethel. 'You'll have to show me where the back door is. I suppose this is an entrance you use now and then when avoiding the police?'

'It has been very useful. Look, it's that door with the blue paint. It's never locked because of the little courtyard where the staff's privy is. Now, keep quiet until we get to my room.'

Ethel could hardly prevent herself giggling as they slipped in through the door, circumnavigating the kitchen where cooks were already preparing breakfast, sending bacon and sausage smells up the back stairs. Even when they were safely in the room, Emmeline held her fingers to Ethel's mouth to make sure she stayed silent, before turning away to take off her coat and dress.

As she was buttoning up her dressing gown, Emmeline said quietly, 'It's not often we get to enjoy ourselves in this business.'

'Well, not the sort of enjoyment we had tonight, it's true. Though I'm surprised at the fun we do have sometimes.'

'I wasn't that keen on this census boycott at first, but it's good to have a big action that people all over the country can take part in. It'll strengthen our hearts for what's to come.'

'What do you mean, for what's to come?' Ethel pushed her thick stockings off and spread her toes.

'Please don't make the mistake of thinking that tonight's protest, no matter how successful, no matter how many women refuse to fill in their forms or spend the night in dusty old halls, or even beautifully decorated skating rinks, is going to deliver us the vote.'

'The government can't continue to ignore such mass actions.'

'Now you are revealing what a newcomer you are. This isn't one of your sports with rules in which the winner emerges and everyone accepts it. The government has shown that there are no rules in this game; they break their own solemn promises with impunity. If they don't balk at forcibly feeding our sisters, despite how horrified the general public is, they are not going to climb down over a peaceful and relatively harmless protest like tonight's.'

Ethel swallowed. 'But they can't keep on blocking what is, after all, a reasonable demand.'

'They can, they have and they will. But of course, we will continue to play the game. We'll have all the usual processions this summer, and make our representations to Parliament and put our evidence to any new Conciliation Committee that's formed. We'll chain ourselves to railings and smash windows, and starve ourselves half to death in prison. It's important to get public support and prepare women for greater participation.

But Asquith will never give way, not unless he's driven into the tightest corner, perhaps not even then.'

'You're tired, darling,' said Ethel, moving to the window. 'No government can stand long against all this.'

'There will need to be something stupendous to make them give way. I don't know what it is yet.' She joined Ethel at the window.

'Look,' said Ethel, wishing to break the sombre mood, 'see how the morning light is chasing back the clouds now? Perhaps we're going to have a better day.'

'I hope you're not trying to make some hideous symbolic point,' said Emmeline, tucking her arm into Ethel's.

'Well, you know, the dawn always does break eventually.' She waved an arm dramatically at the merest glimmer of sun touching the river.

'Now I know why I keep you close to me.' Emmeline pressed her face to the glass.

A silence grew between the women as the sun continued to dispel the night. Ethel could smell the remnants of Emmeline's perfume and was aware of the slender body standing so close to her. She put her arm around her, and Emmeline lay her head on her shoulder. This is a huge moment in history, Ethel thought. There are going to be terrible things happen for women, and wonderful ones too. And this is the path.

'It's a long path,' said Emmeline, as if Ethel had spoken aloud, 'with great suffering but a greater reward. It stretches far into the future, way beyond our lifetimes.'

The two women turned and hugged each other.

'Come on,' said Ethel. 'Let's get you to bed. No-one mentions how important sleep is when you're trying to change the course of history.'

'Thank you. Thank you so much for looking after me,' said Emmeline, pulling back the bed covers. 'Three hours at the most, and then breakfast.'

Ethel helped Emmeline into bed. Just a short while ago, she would have longed to climb in with her. Now, she simply kissed her and made sure the covers were straight.

'Don't worry, I'll wake you,' she said, taking off her own dressing gown and climbing into the other bed. 'I never sleep much in London, and besides, my head is still whirling around the skating rink.'

36

WOKING 1912

They waited until it was dark before leaving Ethel's cottage. Pan offered a good enough reason for them to be out, but they did not want anyone to see what they were doing. Emmeline clung to Ethel's arm, trying to keep warm.

'This is spooky,' she said, as they picked their way through the woods on the edge of the golf course. 'How can you bear it, all this darkness and shadows?' She tripped over a fallen branch. 'It's more dangerous than crossing Piccadilly Circus.'

Ethel laughed. 'Did you always live in the town?'

'I certainly did. Look, there's not a person or a light to be seen.'

'Well, that why we're having a practice here rather than in the centre of London. When we get through the trees, there'll be enough light.'

After a few more trips and curses from Emmeline, they emerged into the open spaces of the golf course. Unobstructed by trees, the moon shone brightly and the expanse of grass with its dips and hillocks and bushes lay in a curious grey light.

'Isn't it lovely?' said Ethel.

'Lovely? I suppose so. I can understand why some of the girls like to come out at night and dig their slogans into the turf.'

Ethel shuddered. It was one of the more innocuous protests, out of all the damage the suffragettes caused to property. It was annoying for the players and arduous for the groundsmen who had to restore greens where 'No Votes No Golf' had been burnt in during the night, but it caused no harm to anyone. Ethel knew it was simple and effective, but golf courses were precious to her.

'It's so easy, Ethel,' said Emmeline, 'and causes so much annoyance. I'm almost tempted to—'

'Absolutely not,' Ethel said fiercely. 'The powers that be know perfectly well that a suffragette lives on their doorstep. I'd be arrested in no time.' She didn't care so much about that as the thought of being banned from the golf course.

Emmeline laughed. 'I knew that would alarm you,' she said. 'Now come on, we're here to practice something a lot more important.'

Ethel chose a particularly broad-trunked oak tree, stark in its winter nakedness. She marked out a line a few yards away from it and collected a small pile of fir cones and stones.

'All right,' she said. 'Aim for about eye level. That is the window of the Prime Minister's house. We'll try a few cones first so we don't make too much noise.' She handed a cone to Emmeline.

'No, you go first. You've got to show me what to do.'

Ethel stepped forward and, with a light underarm throw, produced a satisfying thud on the tree.

'That looks easy enough.' Emmeline picked up a cone and made the same throwing motion. The cone went a foot or two in the air before falling at their feet.

'Whoops!' said Emmeline. 'What went wrong there?'

'Let's try again. Give it a bit more welly.'

This time Emmeline swung her arm harder, and the fir cone fell to the ground behind her.

'What?' she said. 'How on earth did that happen?'

'I'm guessing you haven't played many ball games in your life,' said Ethel.

'I haven't played any.'

'Just remember what you did as a child.'

'I didn't. I never played ball games. Little girls didn't.'

Ethel thought of herself chasing through the woods at Frimhurst, closely followed by Violet and Bob to get to the lawn where they'd play rounders, or cricket, or tennis, or some made-up game that involved throwing chestnuts into the trees.

'But surely… Never mind. Let me teach you. Are you sure you need to do this?'

'Oh yes, absolutely.' Emmeline moved about, replenishing the little pile of cones. 'We always get better publicity if I'm involved in the action, and there is something powerful about it being me that smashes the Prime Minister's window. Besides, the girls always tell me what a great feeling it is when they hear the sound of the stone hit the window and the glass shatter and fall. I'm looking forward to it.'

It was another hour before Ethel felt vaguely satisfied that Emmeline had a chance of hitting a window, though she wasn't sure that her throw would be strong enough to break it. Twice she had collapsed in a laughing heap at her friend's throwing, and Emmeline's face took on a determined, cross look. Two of her best shots were when she threw cones directly at Ethel.

'I'm not your Mr Asquith,' yelped Ethel, rubbing her arm.

'You are exactly the same as him, pretending to help when in fact you're just mocking.'

'All right, let's get serious.' She took Pan behind a tree to the side and told him to sit down. His yelping and chasing the cones was not helping. She handed a stone to Emmeline. 'Just keep your eye on the target as you throw, and you'll be fine.'

At last, Emmeline was satisfied, or too cold to make any further improvement. Ethel whistled to Pan and they started to walk home.

'You will come with me to Downing Street, won't you?'

'I think the general will want to be with you,' said Ethel. 'No, I want to go to Lewis Harcourt's Colonial Office. His wife is a friend of mine, and he keeps saying stupid things about women's abilities.'

They walked along in silence for a while, Pan by their side, tired now.

'I'm going to pull the action forward by a day or two.'

'What do you mean?'

'Last week, I said we would react to the latest parliamentary tricks on March 4th. They'll be bringing in masses of police to the West End. After all this, I don't want to be arrested before I get the chance to throw my stone! But what if instead, we went the day before, or two days before? The streets would be full of office workers and shoppers, but very few police.'

'I see what you mean, but how will you get the word round?'

'I'll go back to London tomorrow and work it out with the others.'

Ethel put her arm around Emmeline and hugged her. 'You don't allow yourself much time to rest, do you?'

'We can rest when we've put our voting paper into the ballot box,' said Emmeline. 'You are prepared, aren't you, dearest? I keep forgetting you haven't done this sort of thing before. It's not like the processions. You could end up in court. I don't want you to feel later that you were caught up in a swirl of activity you couldn't get out of.'

'Absolutely not,' said Ethel. 'I would never have thought the British establishment could be so stubborn and stupid. I want to stand up against them. It's not just ignorance, as I'd thought, is it?'

'No, those with power never give it up easily.'

They crossed the silent lane and went through the gate of Ethel's house and into the porch. 'Do you think your amazing housekeeper would make us a bowl of hot chocolate?'

'I would imagine she already has the pot on the stove,' said Ethel, kicking off her muddy boots.

~

The streets were full of people going home after work or making last-minute purchases before the shops shut. Ethel pulled her stole closer round her neck.

At every step, she was aware of the heavy weight on her left side. There was no reason to think that any of the police mingling with the crowds were on the look-out for suffragettes. Nevertheless, she felt sure the bag holding her stones was visible to any policeman she passed, despite them being completely hidden within her coat. Surely, her intention was written all over her face.

Ethel made herself slow down, look in a few shop windows and have a walk around a department store, where the clock showed there was more than enough time to get to her post. She started to rehearse the arguments. Prime Minister Asquith has reneged on all his promises. He has decided to hear a bill that could give the few remaining men the vote, without any mention at all of women getting the vote. Even the most law-abiding suffragist is outraged, betrayed. He's making fools of us all. Trying to. She allowed the stones to bang against her leg.

None of her sisters or friends knew what she was going to do tonight. How cross they would be. Ethel did not want to hear their arguments. They were simply excuses which allowed them to do nothing more than write the occasional letter to the newspaper or brighten up the dinner table with an argument.

She left the busy street and turned into a quieter area. She liked the idea that now, ten minutes before the designated time, women all over Central London would be moving towards their selected targets, one moment scared and doubtful, the next determined, excited.

As she turned into the little street, Ethel started to hum the *March of the Women* for courage but fell silent as she saw two policemen standing at the other end. Her stomach started to sing its own confused chorus. Nerves, well, she was used to those, that tightening before the baton fell to end the music, before the audience cheered; or before the final putt, before the serve for match point; or at the moment when a woman's eyes flashed and she did not turn away, that instant when she had no idea what might happen.

The policemen started to move towards her. Any woman alone around these houses was seen as a possible suffragette law-breaker. Ethel stood directly under the streetlamp, drew out a cool stone from her bag and held it high in the air.

'Oy, you there. Stop. Stop this instant.'

The policemen were running as fast as they could down the street towards her. One was shouting, and one was blowing his whistle. As Big Ben struck out its six chimes, Ethel thought of all the women in the streets of London, raising their stones at this very moment. Many, like herself, had never done anything like this before, and would never have thought to do so. She pulled her arm back and swung it vigorously forward. 'Lewis Harcourt,' she shouted, 'respect women and give us the vote!'

The stone disappeared from her hand and was lost in the darkness. A beat later, there was the sweet sound of a glass window plumb hit, shattering into a thousand pieces. Her ear registered the music as shards of glass of all sizes cascaded to the ground.

She turned to the police. 'What a great sound,' she said. 'Don't you think? Now, I'm not going to run away so there's no need to push me about. My name is Dr Ethel Smyth, suffragette and composer of music. You may take me to the police station.'

As she was marched towards the end of the street, she wondered about Emmeline. She suspected the Prime Minister's window remained intact.

~

'What a successful action,' said Emmeline. She looked subdued and strange in the grey, prison dress, pale in the weak light of the corridor where they were sitting. 'I'm so proud of those women, Ethel – over 180 arrested. No matter how much support we give, every single one of them has to make that decision themselves, whether to take action, how to conduct themselves, whether to risk imprisonment. We've completely bunged up the court system.'

Ethel was exhilarated, proud of her defiance in the court room. Yet even so, she could feel the bleakness of this place suck her energy away. The tea in her hand was weak and tasted foul. 'The government must surely see now how determined we are. Soon we shall have the vote, I'm sure of it.'

'I hope so,' said Emmeline. 'It often seems we must, and yet we don't. We have to carry on regardless. It's a success in many ways, so much publicity, so much pressure on the authorities. Yet at the same time that ghastly Asquith must be rubbing his hands with glee.'

'How so?' said Ethel, fingering the thin blanket and wondering how she was to keep warm at night.

'I didn't expect two months, Ethel, I really didn't. Two months, that's harsh. For not breaking a window? That's two months when I'm out of the way.'

'We'll appeal, of course. And Christabel and Sylvia will make sure the publicity doesn't die down, won't they?'

'Yes, naturally. They won't let us be forgotten, and they'll keep the momentum going. And now, we must make the most of these hideous mugs of tea, because this is as good as it gets.'

37

Ethel held her hand over her nose until she was clear of the foul smell of the toilets. Only then did she notice the commotion at the end of the passage. Women and wardresses were jostling and shouting, and then there was the sound of glass smashing and Emmeline's commanding voice.

'Don't you dare touch those women. They're just protesting at the filth you serve them under the name of food. Leave them be.'

Ethel raced up the corridor, but before she could get there, Emmeline's cell door had been opened and she was being dragged away. She was so slight to the wardresses' strength, and yet she fought and shouted.

'Where are you taking her? Let her go.' Ethel herself was overwhelmed as other wardresses grabbed her and held her arms up her back. 'She's not well, you know.'

The women corralled into a corner of the landing were also shouting for Emmeline to be freed. Their protests rang around the lofty arches of the ceiling.

Emmeline was bent over double, coughing. Before she could say more, Ethel was pushed roughly into her cell, so she fell onto the narrow bed, and the door slammed to.

'Let me out. What's happened? Open the door. You can't just lock me up like that.'

Ethel hammered on the door and the little glass viewing window. How on earth Emmeline had broken hers, weak and ill as she was, Ethel couldn't imagine.

She could see Emmeline being dragged down the stairs, and there was the noise of the other women being pushed roughly into their cells, and the doors being locked by the huge jangling keys.

'Is everyone all right?' shouted Ethel as soon as the noise had died down, and the call came back: 'All right.'

'Bit bruised. Where will they have taken Mrs Pankhurst, do you think?'

'I do hope she won't be punished. She was only trying to defend us.'

All the women adored Emmeline. They said it was a privilege for them even to be in the same prison as her. Some of that love rubbed off on her, Ethel knew, just by virtue of her being Emmeline's friend.

~

The women near to Ethel were quiet, locked in their bleak cells for twenty-four hours as a punishment for what had happened. Ethel made a number of threats to the wardresses, hoping they would tell her where Emmeline was, but for once no-one was saying. As the day wore on, she wondered how she could raise her own, never mind anyone else's, spirits.

She went to the window and clattered on it with her tin mug. 'Women,' she called, 'come to your windows. Let's talk. Mrs Pankhurst would not want us to be miserable.'

The windows all overlooked the exercise yard below, and faces appeared behind the bars. They started calling to each other, encouraging each other and exchanging bits of news.

'I've been thinking,' shouted one. 'They don't care if they break our bodies in here. Some of our sisters have suffered starvation and force-feeding, and even now we don't know what's happening to our dear Mrs Pankhurst. But remember, it is their cruelty, not ours. We do not try to destroy bodies, only property.'

'True. And who will fare worst on the scales of justice?'

All the women clapped and cheered, rattling the bars with whatever they could find.

Another waved her hands to speak. 'We are used to suffering,' she said. 'We give the best part of a year every time to create a child. So we can certainly allow a few months to give birth to the idea of women's equality.'

Even more cheering met this, and banging on the window bars. There were shouts of, 'May that day come soon,' and, 'Well, at least we won't get pregnant in here.'

~

When she was let out of her cell to exercise, Ethel demanded to be taken to see Emmeline.

'Prisoners are not allowed to visit the hospital.'

'Look,' said Ethel, trying to keep her voice reasonable, 'you know as well as I do that if anything happens to Mrs Pankhurst there will be uproar in here, never mind outside.'

'Move along to the yard, or you'll be locked in again,' said the wardress.

'Please go and tell the governor right now to allow me to visit her. The women must be reassured of her safety.' She put as much determination as she could into her voice.

A few hours dragged by and, just as she was wondering what to do next, she was fetched and led along dark, airless corridors. Countless gates were unlocked and locked, until she entered the hospital.

She rushed up to Emmeline's bed and gathered her into her arms. 'Oh my dear. I'm so glad to have found you.'

Emmeline gave a brief laugh, which became a rough, chesty cough. Her face was thinner, older, paler. 'Thank goodness you've come.'

'What happened?'

'I don't know what they think they're doing,' she said as angrily as her breath permitted. 'I was shoved into a hideous hole. I've never seen anything like it before, a basement cell beneath even the exercise yard. It was damp and so dark, despite the lamps. There was some sort of drain running through there. Huge cockroaches too, and who knows what else.'

Ethel held her close, murmuring comfort.

'I was afraid, Ethel, but my chest wasn't too bad at first. When I demanded to see the governor they told me he would see me when he was ready. They must have forgotten I had to go to court, because quite suddenly, they brought me up here and gave me proper food and let me have a good hot bath, and the doctor came to see me.'

'So you still had to go to court, despite everything?'

'Yes, I was glad to. I made sure the judge knew what was happening, I can tell you, and that I had not had any chance to prepare my defence. He wasn't a bit pleased, went on about how prisoners are entitled to be treated with respect, and ordered that I should be given time and facilities to prepare my case, and talk to lawyers. Look, I've got paper and pens. Law books too.'

'That's something, anyway. We must make sure they keep to it.' Ethel found a brush on the little table and started to brush through Emmeline's hair.

'That's nice,' she said. She turned and buried her face in Ethel's shoulder. 'They're closing in, Ethel. However concerned the judge might be about my rights, this is the most serious charge by far that I've ever faced. Incitement. It carries years of imprisonment. I'm so glad Christabel managed to get away.'

'Did you find out where she's gone?'

'Sylvia whispered Paris to me, but I don't know. I couldn't bear to see her defeated.'

Ethel carried on brushing. 'Shush, shush. No-one's being defeated. This can't go on much longer.'

'Come on, now, Dr Smyth,' said the wardress, hurrying into the room. 'Back to the cell with you.'

'Just five more minutes,' said Ethel.

'No, now. Come on.'

Ethel bent down to kiss Emmeline, who whispered, 'Please try and get me back to the cells. I shall die of loneliness and my miserable thoughts if I have to spend every day on my own in here.'

The wardress took hold of Ethel's arm. 'Don't you touch me,' she said, standing up and shaking her off.

~

'Tell the governor I must see him today,' said Ethel to the wardress who brought the thin mix that passed for porridge.

'I will put in your request. He will send for you when he is ready.'

'Please,' she said. 'It's for Mrs Pankhurst's sake.' Ethel had discovered by now that many of the wardresses admired Emmeline just as much as did the prisoners.

'I'll do my best,' she said, with a slight smile.

A little later, Ethel found herself being led along the many corridors. She had found the governor pleasant enough on the four occasions she had seen him so far, making complaints, as did all the women, about the conditions they had to put up with, the lack of nutritious food, the cold nights and spasmodic exercise. As she was pushed into his office, however, she reminded herself that this was not a nice man – only two weeks ago women were being forcibly fed on his watch.

'What is it, Dr Smyth?' The governor looked up from the

other side of the large desk where he sat. His office was so full of light that she blinked.

'Mrs Pankhurst must be returned to the cells where we are,' she said in a voice she hoped had the right mix of determination and deference. 'You know how much all the women love her – they need to see that she's all right.'

'Thank you for your representation, Dr Smyth,' he said. 'However, Mrs Pankhurst has been unwell and needs the care of the hospital.' He picked up his pen dismissively.

'We will take care of her. She is facing a very serious charge in a new court case and has no-one to support her.' She glared at him.

'She hasn't completed her punishment yet for breaking the glass on her cell door so unnecessarily,' he said. 'Even when she is well enough to leave the hospital, she will not be returned to the landing for quite a while.'

'There are a lot of women in here who wish to be able to see Mrs Pankhurst and ensure she is being properly treated. Not allowing her to come back to the cells could result in many of them becoming ill and needing hospital care.'

'I hope you are not threatening me,' said the governor, rising from his seat. 'Until this episode the prisoners had exceptional allowances, which they abused.'

Ethel paused. She wanted to argue fiercely, but she must be careful not to make things worse.

'Well,' she said cheerfully, 'however generous the privileges, for which we are very grateful, of course, not every day in prison can go smoothly. But I can assure you that if Mrs Pankhurst is restored to us, the days will pass more quietly than might otherwise be the case.'

The governor flushed and made as if to come round the desk, then stopped. 'Thank you, Dr Smyth. You may go now. Your representations will, of course, be considered.'

Ethel hurried to pick up her few belongings as instructed and was led up the metal stairway to a cell on the top floor. It was slightly roomier, with a larger window. Three times she demanded to know why she was being moved, with no answer forthcoming. An hour or two later she saw two wardresses supporting Emmeline along the corridor.

'Oh, my dear,' breathed Ethel, shocked at the blank, pale face. 'Emmeline, Emmeline. Welcome back,' she shouted.

'Is that you, Ethel?' There was still a smile, though the voice was weak. 'Thank goodness, I'm out of that hideous hospital at last.'

After taking Emmeline into the cell next door, the wardress came and unlocked Ethel's door. 'You can go and sit with her until after lunch,' she said.

Ethel rushed into the cell and drew Emmeline, who was sitting on the bed, to her.

'There is something about this place that utterly kills the spirit,' she said. 'I couldn't feel worse if I'd been on hunger strike for a fortnight.'

'Nothing can kill your spirit,' said Ethel. 'We'll look after you now.'

'Let the women know I'm back on the wing, if you can, and I'll try and come down to the yard at exercise time. Are they in good heart?'

'We've had our ups and downs. But today will be a good one for all of us.'

The wardresses allowed Ethel to take Emmeline down to the exercise yard. Every step was an ordeal, but Ethel felt her straighten up as they came through the doorway and breathed in the fresh air. It was brighter in the yard, despite the towering buildings all around. A great roar went up from the twenty or so women who were exercising, stamped out immediately by the wardresses with threats of a return to the cells. They could not silence so quickly the shouts of welcome and the songs that came from the women at their windows. All at once, pieces of cloth were unfurled, makeshift banners bearing the familiar 'Deeds not Words', or just strips of cloth they had somehow managed to dye shades of purple, green and white, depending on what was to hand.

Emmeline stood smiling by Ethel's side, leaning still on her, clapping and waving to the women. 'We shall never be defeated,' she said. Despite her weakness, her voice rang out clearly across the exercise yard. 'Neither the prison authorities nor the government shall ever stamp out the demand of women for the vote, or their hunger for equality. Stay strong, stay strong.'

Three wardresses strode towards her, and Ethel stepped into their path. 'There's no need,' she said forcefully. 'We shall simply take a few turns around the yard without saying another word.'

To her surprise, the wardresses stood aside, and Ethel and Emmeline made a slow circle around the yard. Women walking past came up to Emmeline and touched her, and gave a silent greeting, their faces alight with love and relief that she was back with them.

'Can you hear that, Emmeline?' murmured Ethel. The sound of the *Women's Marseillaise* came floating to them from outside the prison.

'I thought the police had cleared the area around the prison of women.'

'They have. But my niece told me that someone has rented a house nearby. Every day, when they think we might be in the yard, women go there and sing for us.'

Several of the walking women were now humming the tune under their breath.

'Isn't that the most wonderful thing?' said Emmeline.

Ethel was not able to write music in here; she was not allowed her pens or music paper. She longed for a piano – she couldn't remember any time in her life when she had not been able to play for so long. She dreamt of the white and black notes, of bending forward and kissing each one, hearing its own sweet tone. The lack of any real exercise created a restlessness and tumult in her body that sometimes almost overwhelmed her. It made it more bearable to challenge the rules. She trained everyone she could find who could sing, and at random moments, on a hidden signal, a few bars of an opera or a protest song or a hymn would break out in the exercise yard or from open windows, sung in perfect harmony. It could be over before a wardress could even see who was singing.

Other women poured their creative powers into brightening the dreary yard. A new banner or placard was hung from a window, even if just for two or three minutes. One woman found a piece of chalk and bent down quickly to create a little hopscotch pitch. All day long the women whose turn it was to exercise jumped and hopped in ways they had not done for years, until the wardresses managed to erase the lines, and the chalk was confiscated. The women weren't allowed to run in the yard, but occasionally there might be a bit of a lining up and half a dozen women would make a mad dash from one side to the other in an impromptu race. Punishments became less and less frequent.

They were still locked up for much of the day, but sometimes they were allowed to sit at their open cell doors, getting on with their sewing. When it rained and they couldn't go outside, they walked around on the landing. They might recite poetry as they walked, and one day Letty, a trained dancer, cleared a little space and gave a short routine to the enthralled women, who kept walking around her to keep the wardresses' suspicions at bay. She had made herself a flowing skirt in green, purple and white, which flashed bright against the stained walls and iron railings.

~

Ethel was unwell. It was one of those long days when the fear of being forgotten, the feeling that perhaps no-one cared about her being locked in a cell, utter boredom and poor food reduced her completely. Everything was silent, beyond silence. She would die in this dreadful place.

Late afternoon she heard women humming her March and climbed on the chair to see what was happening out of the high window. The women in the yard below cheered when they saw her and started again.

Ethel laughed, shaken out of her despondency. She waved her arms at them and looked around her cell for something to conduct with – there was nothing. Then she spotted her toothbrush and, climbing back onto the chair, had them start again whilst she conducted furiously through the bars, using her toothbrush as a baton, singing lustily. The wardresses stood by, doing nothing.

~

Ethel and Emmeline were released on appeal along with dozens of others, and hugged each other at the gates in the bright, early morning sunshine.

'No Christabel,' said Emmeline sadly, as Annie Kenney ran towards them. 'But at least she's safe.'

A crowd of friends whisked them off in a carriage to Lincoln's Inn, where a sumptuous celebration breakfast had been prepared. Emmeline had to go to court before it was finished for another day of ludicrous legal argument. Ethel went with her; the unaccustomed noise and rich food made her head ring.

Next morning, Ethel kissed Emmeline goodbye and caught the train to Woking. She delighted in the sheer ordinariness of the countryside that sped by. She craved the safety of home, the open fields and fresh air.

Violet and Dick were at the station to meet her. Lunch was ready, but first she was given flowers and presents from all the family. Best of all, there was Pan, who leapt at her with all his force and covered her face with licks, just like when she returned from any of her travels.

'I love you, dog,' she said, glimpsing for a moment the possibility of a return to normality and routine. Music, golf and dog-walking, that was all she wanted.

After Violet and Dick left, she walked around the house, touching things, running her hands up and down the piano, looking at piles of books to check the titles. It was not like returning from her other travels at all. She kept looking around to see who might step out of the shadows to stop her enjoying herself, to shut her away in gloom and darkness, to say she must not. It would take a bit of getting used to, this freedom.

38

WOKING 1912

'They're still there,' Ethel said to Emmeline, watching the men moving about in the lane from her dining-room window. At first it had been amusing to see the police camped out, trying to hide themselves behind the gorse bushes on the edge of the golf course. Now it was serious. Emmeline was a prisoner in her home, and the minute she stepped outside the garden gate, she would be re-arrested.

Emmeline sat at the breakfast table reading the newspapers, and Ethel went over and filled her plate with eggs and toast. 'Try and eat some more, dearest.'

She thought Emmeline looked a little better today. It was six days since she had arrived, weak and thin, shrunk and yellow, deposited at speed in the night in the hope that the police would not know where she was. Her eyes had sunk deep into their sockets, and there was a horrible odour about her – one that Ethel knew came from long periods of refusing food. It was terrifying. The rest away from prison and the demands of London, however, together with the country air and robust food had begun to restore a little flesh beneath the hanging, see-through skin. Ethel stopped fearing that she was going to die.

Every day of her two years of protest had been worthwhile, but all the time the demands of her music kept biting at her heels. She had turned down several invitations to conduct or attend concerts in Germany and France, and had not been available to build on what performances there were of her music. She had certainly been too distracted to compose much.

The time had been right for her to leave active protest behind. She loved Emmeline, and the admiration she felt for her was unchanged, but she could not support the way the campaign was going. It was entirely Christabel's fault; many of the most radical suffragettes thought so too. Rather than face the incitement trial, she had escaped to France to run the campaign from there. It seemed a reasonable thing to do, though how she could leave her mother to suffer as she was doing, Ethel did not know. But in fact, removed from the brutality of what was happening on the ground, only getting news through letters, newspapers and occasional visits, Christabel had kept urging ever-greater militancy. Ethel wanted to support Emmeline, but surely it wasn't right to agree to send her other, equally committed daughter Sylvia packing, together with some of their very best friends and supporters who dared to disagree. Ethel had decided to limit herself to supporting Emmeline as much as she could.

'I shall go back today or tomorrow,' said Emmeline, breaking into Ethel's thoughts, 'and leave you to get on.'

'Back to London? How are you going to do that with all these police on the doorstep? Adept as you are at disguise, I'm not sure how we could make that work.'

'It won't,' said Emmeline. 'I know we managed it a few months ago when you managed to smuggle me into a car to go to Paris, but they're wise to those tricks now.'

Ethel could see no easy escape. They could hide themselves in the countryside if they managed to leave the house after dark, but

Emmeline was too weak to go far and was surprisingly nervous when there was no light. Since the new act came in, police numbers had soared. They had new powers too and, having tracked Emmeline down to Woking, they were not going to be easily tricked.

'If we asked Norah to bring a car to Maybury, could we meet her there at night?' wondered Ethel.

'It's possible. But the fact is that whilst I'm under this obscene licence, there is no escape unless I go out of the country. And I can't keep you from your work any longer. No, I'm determined to call an end to this now.'

'What do you mean?'

'No more hiding! They've passed this stupid act to wear us down completely. We shall see if they dare to carry it to its logical conclusion.'

'Please, Emmeline, you're making me scared.' Ethel swallowed loudly. 'You're not a young woman anymore to keep putting your health at risk like this.'

'No, that's true. It's obvious that the government would rather do anything than give women the vote. Well, let's see if they do actually dare to kill me.'

'Is that what you mean to do?' Ethel could hardly keep the anger out of her voice. 'To allow that hideous government to take your life? Not just yours, but Sylvia and the others? No, Emmeline, no. They might just call your bluff. It's not worth it.'

'Come on now, dearest. No tears. There are casualties in any war, as your father would have said. The government will have to learn eventually that it can't hold power over women for ever. For some reason, people look to me to lead, and that is what I must continue to do. I can't hide out any longer. Today, I shall go back to prison.'

'What, and then Nurse Pine and the general and myself will find you even weaker in a few days' time?'

Emmeline got up from her chair. 'Now, let me sit and listen to you play once more, and then we shall smarten ourselves up and go and make those policemen very happy.' She went over to the window and waved at the vigilant men. 'Oh, good, it's raining quite hard. Well, we'll wait for that to go off anyway. I don't suppose they like this any more than we do.'

The two women moved into the drawing room and Emmeline lay in her usual place on the sofa.

'Sing me some songs,' she said. 'Your voice is so beautiful. Some of the old ones about trees and streams and young love.'

Emmeline was not at all musical, and yet in recent months, the weaker she became, the more she had been soothed by the songs and music of long ago. Ethel sang to her the songs of Handel and Schubert and Brahms, some of her own songs, too. She played on as Emmeline drifted into sleep – a Beethoven sonata, a Mendelssohn Song Without Words, a Chopin Prelude. Almost in a dream-like state herself, mesmerised by the familiar tunes, Ethel thought of Lisl, of how they would play to each other in those days which were so full of love and fun and simplicity.

39

VIENNA 1912

Ethel breathed in the cool air of the November day. At mid-morning, the streets were not particularly busy. A number of horses and carts or carriages made their noisy way across the cobbles, with an occasional car tooting imperiously at anyone in the way. People were going about their business on foot too, men tipping their hats in greeting or women turning towards the cafes to have coffee together or an early lunch.

Ethel had come here to work: to meet with contacts, talk about *The Wreckers*, consider ideas for a new opera. She could still do her bit for the campaign too, and later on that day she was going to talk to the Vienna Women's Suffrage Committee. She loved the fact that the fight for the vote was going on in so many countries. She looked forward to hearing more about how the women of Austria were fighting for a say in political life, since many had actually lost their right to vote only a few years ago. They would be eager for news of the much more militant campaign she had just left behind. There was sure to be talk about tactics, and the best way to achieve their goal.

No-one knew what that way was. Every country had their own type of campaign; each was struggling to persuade men to give up some of their power to women. Few had embraced the militancy of Emmeline and Christabel, a strategy that still caused Ethel endless worry, sleepless nights and fearful anger as she continued to watch her friend suffer.

She hated herself for not being with her. At the same time, it was wonderful to walk freely through the streets, not being brave or watchful – just a visitor in a beautiful city on her way to a rehearsal with one of the best conductors in the world. Well, that's how she regarded Bruno Walter anyway. She thought of the boyish enthusiast who had loved her *Wreckers* from the first time she had played it to him – what, best part of ten years ago? He had never wavered from his desire to produce it when he had the power to do so. That moment had not quite come yet, he had said in his recent letter, but now he was at the Vienna Philharmonic and in a position to programme her orchestral work, how did she feel about a joint billing with Gustav Mahler?

At first, she had written back to him and said yes, well, that was wonderful, but she was not able to come because she was still tied up with the suffrage fight. She had got used to missing concerts of her own works over recent months, but this time she blinked back tears as she wrote.

Emmeline, released from prison once again through weakness, had been angry.

'Don't think you are the only person who can look after me when I'm poorly,' she had said, lying on the sofa in Ethel's sitting room.

'Oh! I thought you liked coming here.'

'I do, of course I do, but I hate the thought that I'm holding you back. It's important for you, and also that people can see that a woman can compete. I do know that what Christabel and I are doing is not the only way to fight this campaign.'

'I can't leave you, so let's not talk about it.'

'This is what I'm thinking, anyway. As soon as I'm well enough to travel, I'm going to try and get to Paris to talk with Christabel, and then I shall go on to America. Those weeks on the ship provide such precious recovery time and it is very pleasing that the government gets so taxed about my giving lectures to American women. There are some splendid suffragettes there. Best of all, I will be able to walk freely in the streets again.'

'You're making it easier for me to begin to get back to my music,' said Ethel.

'Good,' said Emmeline. 'Get your pen out and write another letter to that Walter chap.'

~

Ethel looked at the programme, the audience, the rich décor of the concert hall. It was such an honour, more than she had ever experienced, to be on the same programme as Gustav Mahler. The people of Vienna, the people in this audience, adored him. He had been their musical director for years, made important the city's music and, though two years dead, was talked of as if he was still there. Her music was going to precede his. She hoped the audience would like it.

Bruno Walter strode onto the stage, to wild applause. He was Mahler's faithful pupil and assistant, after all, and the audience was transferring their affection to him. Ethel clung on to her seat in fearful anticipation as he raised his baton. She felt tears sting her eyes as he started 'On the Cliffs of Cornwall', the rippling harp and the cellos so suggestive of the movement of the sea.

She wondered at the orchestra: saw how the skilled musicians responded to the baton of an energetic conductor just finding his power. And the audience, so perfectly turned out for their evening in the concert hall, jewels, and well-groomed hair and moustaches in abundance, listened carefully. It was home, of course it was. She had been away for a while, but now she was back. Now this knowledgeable audience was listening carefully to her music.

And yet, and yet... it was spoiled, wasn't it? There were no women there, proud with their violins, bows poised to play, or a flute placed just under female lips. Alma, for example, she could have been here. She was good enough; she could have competed with any of these players. Others too, if they had received even a fraction of the training and opportunity that these men had – May or Catherine, perhaps, if they had not spent their whole lives listening to people say they could not.

Oh, but this was good. Bruno had always understood *The Wreckers*, long before it had ever been performed, and now she was hearing the intensity of the Act II Prelude just as it had formed in her mind. She had heard many terrible, under-rehearsed performances, when she wondered if she had written it right. Tonight she knew that she had.

The applause was whole-hearted. Vienna was a conservative place, but they had embraced it.

~

Helmut asked Ethel if she would like to look after their apartment for a while, as Hanni had been asked to fill in the part of Isolde at short notice in Munich. Ethel was thrilled to be in the same city as Bruno, part of his circle of musical contacts, meeting guest performers and composers at his home. It reminded her a little of the close musical world of Leipzig.

She was restless, however. When people asked her what she was writing, she had nothing to say. Apart from a few suffrage pieces, she had written nothing since Harry died. She was embarrassed – her reputation could hardly stand on a Covent Garden performance six years ago.

She started to think about another opera, looking for a story, turning possibilities over in her mind. It had to be something dramatic and compelling, something that would engage her over many months.

Several nights she woke sweating and feverish under the covers. She had lost so much time. She was a composer in her mid-fifties with no ideas. As soon as she knew what she was doing, she must write undisturbed. No meetings, no interviews, no musical suppers, no worrying about Emmeline and the campaign. Music, work, music must be her life now.

40

1913

Ethel turned out of Winnie's house along the Avenue Henri-Martin, smiling. A wonderful lunch had been laid on for her and she was full of the good wishes of her friends for her trip to Egypt. She was excited at the prospect of several weeks far away from the turmoil of suffragette activities and their toll on Emmeline. She almost hopped and skipped along the pavement. She had an idea for her new opera, and that was what she was going to write. Tomorrow she would catch the train south.

The billboard on the corner caught her eye: '*Suffragette lutte jusqu'à la mort.*' She almost dropped her bag as a wave of panic swept over her. She had only left Emmeline a couple of days ago, and though she was continuously weak and ill, in and out of prison, hardly able to stand, there was no reason to believe that she was dying. Emmeline loved the game, even if it was a deadly game, where the authorities, the police, the government, all the power lay on one side, and weakened women's bodies, imagination, defiance and unbelievable courage lay on the other.

We've formed a bodyguard for Emmeline and Sylvia and the others, Norah had written to her shortly before her last visit.

Hundreds of us are getting self-defence training, and if the police do manage to find out where one of them is appearing, we form a barrier so they can't get to her. We've learned how to break their grip, and even to bring them down. You should see the look on their faces. It's a marvellous feeling, I can tell you.

She ran from newspaper shop to newspaper shop, seeking fuller news, different news, pictures. It wasn't Emmeline, thank goodness! She reproached herself, but there was a momentary relief that it was Emily Wilding Davidson whose tangled body graced the front pages, her body kicked by the King's horse at the Derby. What on earth had happened? No well-trained horse would kick a person. It must have been terrified, startled at her running out. What was she thinking of?

Tears started to fall down her cheeks. Strange, impetuous, brave Emily. Had she martyred herself, as the papers were suggesting, or was it one of her brave but foolish stunts gone wrong?

A summons from Christabel awaited Ethel at her hotel. Every time Ethel saw her, and compared her young, healthy, confident face with the yellowing, gaunt eyes of Emmeline, she felt a surge of dislike. It was she who kept pressing those women to do more, whilst enjoying all the delights of Parisian life, including the company of Ethel's dear friends; it was she who had caused the split with so many who had fought so hard and loyally, including her own sister, Sylvia; it was she who encouraged her supporters to more and more extreme actions. Ethel liked to think that Emmeline would not have allowed it if she had not been so weak, but she would never hear a word against Christabel.

Ethel knocked on the door. She knew what would happen. Christabel would make it impossible for her to refuse to go back to England. She would be given a sheaf of papers to take to her loyal leaders back home with instructions on how to get the maximum publicity and advantage out of the situation. She would also have to face Christabel's contempt because she had abandoned her active role in the movement, as well as the scarcely hidden jealousy that Ethel spent so much more time with her mother than she had.

'Right, Ethel,' said Christabel before she had even had time to stir sugar into her tea, 'it's looking like Emily will die. I want you to go to England and talk to Grace Roe about the sort of funeral she's to organise – more or less a state funeral, I should think, with everyone in white. Can you travel tonight?'

'Emily's not dead yet, thank goodness,' said Ethel. 'I've been saying my farewells today as I start for Egypt tomorrow. I won't be back in England until the spring.' She had decided that she would return to England to be part of whatever happened to Emily, but she wasn't going to tell Christabel that. 'Perhaps you should go back yourself?'

'You're being ridiculous,' said Christabel. 'I've still got conspiracy charges hanging over me. I would go straight to prison if I appeared in England. What use would that be? Someone has to lead the campaign.'

'Does it have to be you? From here?' said Ethel. She could feel hot blood rising to her face. 'Your mother has undergone at least six hunger strikes whilst you've been here, and your sister has to be carried around on a stretcher. They could both die. You could exchange places with them.'

'Now you're being foolish,' said Christabel. 'This is what Mother and I decided, as you well know, and we're not going to change our tactics now, just because the going's got tough.'

'Got tough for her, you mean,' said Ethel.

'I would have thought that you of all people would recognise what has to be done to succeed. It's not always pretty. Well, are you going to take these or not?' Christabel glared at her and pushed the papers across the table. 'If you're so worried about the women on the ground in England, then the least you can do is save Grace Roe a journey.'

'Yes, of course,' said Ethel. 'You know I'll do anything to help your mother.'

~

Ethel suppressed a sob as she put her arms around Emmeline. She felt as though her arms might be able to go round that tiny, thin body several times.

'Oh, my dear,' she exclaimed, holding her close so she would not have to look into those too-large eyes. Was she even more fragile than when she had left her little more than a week ago?

'I'm so glad you came,' said Emmeline, leaning against her. 'I need your good cheer now, and your strength. This is a half-life, Ethel, if that. I have to stay free until Emily's funeral. It's so tragic, I can't bear it. This is what they're forcing on us.'

Ethel stood back a little and smoothed some stray hairs from her face. 'These licences are a joke. Even the staunchest supporter of the act would be shocked at how little time you're given to recover before you have to return to prison.'

'One week, they gave me. One week! Two have already gone by, and look at me.'

'Please promise me you won't refuse water as well next time,' said Ethel. 'Why put yourself through another ordeal that hurts only yourself?'

'Shh!' Emmeline put a finger to Ethel's lips. 'Don't deter me, dearest. This is the way it has to be. But less of that. I'm bored to tears with it. Now tell me about Christabel and what she's up to. And your new opera, and when you're leaving for Egypt. Come on, have some tea and take my mind off this misery for a while.'

Ethel was continuously at Emmeline's side over the next few days. All the leading suffragettes were either in prison, or out on licence, weak and ill, or, like Grace, hiding out somewhere. Only once did a few of them manage to get together to remember Emily. Brave Emily, who thought nothing of throwing herself over the railings on a prison landing to force some concession. Imaginative Emily, who spent census night in the broom cupboard in the House of Commons.

Ethel found herself carrying messages between people who could not be seen outside for fear of being arrested, getting used herself to playing cat and mouse with the police to avoid being followed. It was a responsibility which she found both exhilarating and exhausting. She feared she herself might be arrested sometimes, so loosely were the laws applied – any suffragette might be arrested at any moment for conspiracy, or withholding information, or planning a forbidden act. Ethel could taste the reality of what Emmeline had said, that the government was now using all its powers not to find a solution but to break the women. The chain of message-bearers like Ethel lengthened and shortened and changed direction, as seemed best.

~

Ethel left her hotel by a back door and walked by a new circuitous route to where Emmeline had been moved for the night. She needed help to be washed and dressed. In the past year, she had hunger struck countless times, and on two of these occasions, she had taken no drink either. No wonder she was hardly able to stand.

'I certainly don't need this corset,' said Emmeline, as Ethel started to lace her up.

'You're not thinking of going out without it?' said Ethel.

'Would that be so shocking? Do we or anyone else really care? But carry on, it might help me sit up straight, if nothing else. Now, be careful with that dress. I shall be quite worn out by the time I get all these clothes on.'

Emmeline lay down for a few minutes whilst Ethel pulled on her stockings. 'Pass me my powder bag, dear. I want people to see that I'm still strong and defiant, whatever the government might do to me.'

Norah came in. 'Auntie,' she said, kissing Ethel, 'I'm so glad you're back. Mrs Pankhurst, the closed cab is waiting around the corner from the garden gate. There are no police anywhere nearby, but I will drive the decoy car, just in case. Are you ready to go?'

'Yes, I'm ready. Oh, Ethel, what a sad day this is.' Ethel helped her put on a hat and coat. 'Goodness, these are horrible. Am I changing into something a bit more fashionable later?'

'Yes, darling. This is your disguise. You are going to be dressed in a beautiful white wool coat with a marvellous hat at the next stop. I'll see you there.'

Ethel helped Emmeline out to the cab and, after a few minutes, let herself out of the front door. She had chosen a route that led her up and down alleys, across parks and along broad, busy streets, before she dashed down the lane that would bring her to where Emmeline was waiting for Sylvia. As she approached the house, she could see some sort of skirmish and quickened her pace. Emmeline was standing by the door, supported by Nurse Pine and the Princess Sophia, surrounded by Norah and two or three of her bodyguard. Three policemen were talking to them.

'Oh no,' said Ethel, breaking into a run, hitching up her long dress the better to do so. This was meant to be a safe house, and yet the number of police vehicles in the street indicated that they were well prepared.

As she approached, she could hear the loud voice of the police inspector telling Emmeline that she was only out of prison on licence under the Cat and Mouse Act – even the police called it that. The licence had run out several days ago, and she had not reported to the police station as she had been required to, so now she must come with them.

'She won't be giving you any trouble,' shouted Nurse Pine. 'I'm sure even a dolt like you can see that she's not fit to go back to prison.'

'That is not my concern,' said the inspector. 'Mrs Pankhurst will see a doctor as soon as she returns to prison, as she always does, and it will be for him to decide if she's fit to stay.'

'Look,' said Ethel, hardly able to contain her fury, 'you must know that this Cat and Mouse Act is an absolute abuse of power. Does it make you feel better that you're causing the death of one of Britain's finest women? Does it? And for what? The crime of wanting to vote.' She pushed herself under the policeman's nose.

Ethel thought he had the grace to look uncomfortable. 'That is not for me to say. I am here to carry out my duties under the law.'

'Oh, don't be so damned pompous.' Ethel felt Emmeline's restraining hand on her shoulder. 'Look, please don't do this on such a sad day for us all. Allow Mrs Pankhurst to go to Miss Davidson's funeral, and then I'm sure she will do the honourable thing and come down to the police station.' She turned to Emmeline for confirmation but could only see how pale she was and how strongly Nurse Pine had to support her.

'I can't allow that,' said the inspector.

Emmeline stepped forward. 'No, Ethel. I will go with the policeman now. It is cruel what it being done here, but there must be no fuss on the day of Emily's funeral. You go and tell the others. The state is over-bearing, even on a day like today, but it shall not grind us down.'

She stepped forward and virtually fell into the inspector's arms. In moments, she was in the back of the police car. 'Let my carriage ride empty in the procession, Ethel.'

Ethel linked arms with Nurse Pine as they turned into the house, stifling their sobs. Sylvia would be here soon, and she would take charge. Ethel needed to get to her place in the procession, to lead the musicians who were to play the Funeral March as they walked in front of the coffin. Emmeline would not be there; how very bitter that was.

41

EGYPT 1913

It was impossible to settle down to work. Ethel longed for the streets of London with all their dangers and excitement, where she was active, feted and loved. What she had instead was an old-fashioned British-style hotel in a near-desert village near Cairo, with nothing but the hot sun, the sand, a blank page and a silent piano to keep her company.

No sooner had she sat down than she had to get up for a drink of water or a new pen, or to kick the gravel alongside the veranda. She waited for the quiet and the stark beauty of the place to work their magic on her musical spirit. She must get used to being nowhere near Emmeline, not supporting her or fearing for her. She must become less impatient for her letters, days old by the time they arrived, and weeks-old editions of *The Suffragette*.

The day meandered along, interminable. At least she had made a decision as to what to write. The interesting stories she had gathered over the last few months had failed to ignite any musical spark. When her mind was so full of the intransigence of the British Government and the possibility of women dying in the prisons of England, opera's extreme drama seemed absurd. No, she must do something lighter. She wanted to write something for all those women who never had the chance to learn music or appreciate it; for those who had found a love of it under her tuition and responded to the baton.

She turned to a story she had read recently which had made her laugh, it was so ridiculous: *The Boatswain's Mate*. She could make a strong woman character out of the landlady of that pub, and the people would be able to sing brilliant choruses. The British were ready for new comic opera, now Gilbert and Sullivan had given up writing, and she would be happy to deliver it. She sketched a few outlines.

As often happened, she had just managed to write a few lines when the sun set, and the remote hillside hotel came to life. Every English-speaking person for miles around was going to arrive for a pre-dinner drink at the very least, if not a full evening in the dining room. There were the foreign office men from the Coastguard stationed nearby, including her nephew, Robert, wealthy families going south, travellers of all kinds, golfers, nature-lovers, new faces every evening. They weren't all unknown to her; many she had met previously in the large community of English people abroad. Several were friends of friends and acquaintances. She put her pens away, irritated and relieved.

There was always talk of the heat and the food and the flies; of the places they had visited and which hotels were better value, but Ethel never had to wait long before 'the woman question' was mentioned. It made her feel less distant from the campaign if she could fight about it at dinner.

'You'll see,' an older woman declared. 'Once that ridiculous Pankhurst woman is dead, and surely it can't be long now, all this nonsense will be forgotten, and we can talk about something else.'

Ethel had to put her hand over her mouth to stop herself from choking on the mouthful of lamb she had just taken.

'Well, it's not just a one-woman campaign,' she said mildly. 'We must sincerely hope that Mrs Pankhurst will not die, or the government will have the blood of a truly heroic and courageous woman on its hands. And it certainly would not be the end of it.'

'Heroic,' the other woman spat. 'In what way is it heroic to break the law and cause such destruction to houses where people are living? The woman's unhinged, anyone can see that.'

'Anyone might be a little unhinged if they suffered such persecution, don't you think? Being dragged around when you're so weak and ill you can hardly stand. But in fact, she remains resolute and clear-thinking. Have you any idea what it's like in Holloway prison?'

'Well, she must be used to it by now.'

'You never get used to it,' said Ethel angrily. 'I can absolutely assure you of that. Do not think for a minute the campaign would be over if she were to die. Women have been asking for the vote for nearly half a century, remember, and they will never give up until it is granted.'

One of the men sitting nearby said, 'It's her choice, entirely. If she ate and drank, she'd soon be well enough to get her sentence served and be a free woman again.'

'She's never going to accept a brutal sentence for fighting for a basic right. The best way for this to be over is for all of you to put pressure on the government to do the right thing and give women the vote. Until then, she and all of the rest of us will continue to fight as best we can.'

Ethel felt sick. She brushed aside her nephew, who was trying to divert her with dishes full of vegetables with unknown names. For all she knew, these people might have their wish, and Emmeline might already be dead.

Ethel tossed and turned in bed, searching for a cooler spot. However hard she might defend Emmeline and the campaign, the fact was that she was not there. She had virtually abandoned her at a time when she needed all her friends. Yes, her music was important to her, of course it was, but what was it in comparison to supporting Emmeline? Wasn't that what the women meant when they defended their destruction of great artworks? You make such a fuss about us destroying property, they said, but you are happy to destroy the most beautiful of living women. Wasn't that precisely what she was doing, putting her art before the life of one of her dearest friends?

She was bored with the arguments churning around in her head. She had made her decision, right or wrong, and she must stick with it. She must work hard to ensure a good result. And she could still do her bit, even from this distant, hot corner of Egypt. She could write letters to *The Times* and articles for *The Suffragette* that she hoped would provide some comfort to the women, and discomfort to the wretched Prime Minister.

~

'Auntie Ethel, we're going south to buy camels as soon as Christmas is done,' said Robert as they sat sipping sherry on the veranda which she had made into her composing room. 'Do you want to come? The director-general has specifically told me to insist.'

Ethel gestured at the stack of manuscript paper on her table. 'I've still got so much to do.'

'That's what I said to him – until that piano goes quiet at night, you won't be going anywhere.'

'Cheek,' she said. 'I'm always very careful not to play when people might be sleeping.'

'You mean, between 2 and 5am? I thought if you came with us to the camel fair, we could give these good people a rest.'

'They don't deserve a rest,' said Ethel. 'They do absolutely nothing between dawn and midnight except gossip, eat and drink. There's hardly one that will even come out on the golf course with me.'

'Ah, the ultimate crime...'

'Why on earth does he want me to go anywhere with you?'

'Beats me. He thinks you are absolutely wonderful. Apparently, he's never known anything quite so entertaining as your dinner conversation. He says the whole place has come alight since you arrived. For some reason, he adores you. As do I.'

'Don't be foolish. The place needs a bit of livening up. It's like being put into a nineteenth-century drawing-room drama here. So what is the camel fair?'

His face broke out into a boyish grin. 'I told him you wouldn't be able to resist the idea.'

'Just a minute, I haven't said yes yet.'

'I'm not going to tell you. It's the most amazing and exciting thing. You'll love it, but you have to trust me.'

'Trust you? I've travelled a good deal, you know, seen a lot. If it's just a few people selling chickpeas and four old camels in a pen, I'm not interested.'

'All right, you stay and talk to these ghastly people if you want. I'll tell the DG your days as an adventurer are over. Shame! Mother said you would love it.'

'Your mother? Nell? Well, she does know a bit about what I like.'

'It's spectacular, I assure you.'

Ethel looked down at her manuscript. It was flowing well, at last. She still seemed to lack the fluency she had experienced when she would end every day with a letter to Harry, telling him about it, which of his suggestions she was using or ignoring, and why. It had become lonely work, but it was getting written.

'Did you say right after Christmas?'

'Yes, 1ˢᵗ or 2ⁿᵈ of January.'

A deadline would surely help her.

'Yes, all right. Why not?'

The boy bent down and hugged her. 'I'm so glad, Auntie. It will be much more fun with you there. Everything is.'

The sun was hardly up when the truck arrived to take Ethel to Cairo. Yawning still, she joined Robert and the DG and a handful of others from the Coastguard and the hotel for the long train journey south. As she had suspected, the draw of an exciting event had spurred her on, and now she felt she deserved something different. The first Act was done; Benn and Travers were well on their way with their tortuous plan to win Mrs Water's love, and she was turning out to be deliciously independent. The music was stupendous, though there were still a few problems to solve. She had forgotten the delight of having a work underway, not just the writing but all the decisions about the story and the choruses and the staging.

She read again the letter she had received from Emmeline. Weaker with every spell in prison, she had decided to use the licence period to escape to Paris for a while. It seemed to Ethel, reading between the lines, that Emmeline had decided that she did not want to die in prison after all. Nor, it seemed, did the government want to have to handle that eventuality, since she seemed to be able to get away with suspicious ease. She would stay with Christabel for a while, until the need to be part of the action drew her back again.

There was little time to recover from the hot, dusty train journey before they were led down a precarious landing stage onto a little cruiser that took them down the coast of the Red Sea. Hanging over the side, Ethel could see coral reefs through the clear water, and fish of astounding colour. She would have liked the journey to go on much longer, but all too soon they pulled in to a tiny port full of fishing boats.

Once again, there was hardly time to draw breath. This was a work trip, Robert kept saying; there was no time to stop to enjoy all the sights and smells. Despite his warning, Ethel hardly kept her balance as her camel lurched to its feet and started the day's journey, across sand and more sand, the soft, golden hills going up and down, ever nearer to the mountains ahead.

'I love it,' Ethel shouted across to Robert. Her face might well split from the smile of pleasure, of deep excitement at the sheer, wonderful novelty of this journey.

'I knew you would,' he called. 'And this is just the start.'

The ungainly animal strode confidently and smoothly into the desert. Hour after hour it kept up its pace, until they arrived at their camp – or the place that would become their camp. At the moment it had no distinguishing feature at all. Ethel staggered and tumbled onto the sand as she dismounted.

In no time, the soldier escorts had set up their tents, including a kitchen and a shelter that would serve as a dining room and sitting room.

Ethel looked around. 'Where are the camels to buy?' she asked. 'Where's the fair? Nice as this camp is, it's not exactly what you promised.'

'Auntie, Auntie,' said Robert, 'you always were extremely impatient. Now just settle yourself in and enjoy the scenery.'

'You did put the golf clubs in, didn't you?'

'Of course.'

'Then if you can lend me one of your men for the afternoon, I shall set us up a golf course.'

'What, here?'

'Indeed. Don't look so doubtful. You are talking to the woman who put a golf course onto Queen Victoria's front lawn, you know.'

Robert laughed. 'How could I have doubted you? Besides, it will give us something to do whilst the DG and the others shoot gazelle.'

'Even I find that unnecessary and quite barbaric.'

~

Ethel had no desire to get out of her warm bedclothes. Nights in the desert were cold. She just wanted to snuggle down again, try to ignore the hardness and narrowness of the little camp bed, and go back to sleep until someone brought her the local approximation of morning tea. It was not to be; the pressure on her bladder was too great, so eventually she wriggled out of the bedclothes, leaving them intact in the hope that they would hold in the heat whilst she was gone, and stepped out of the tent, pulling a shawl around her shoulders on top of her pyjamas.

It was hours still until dawn, she guessed, but the night was light enough for her to find her way easily to the covered trench they called a toilet. Stepping out again, more comfortable now and a lot more awake, she started to notice where the light was coming from. The sky was alive with stars. Points of light, some tiny, some larger, some sparkling, some still, all standing proud against the navy-blue sky behind and around.

Ethel gasped. She had never seen such brightness, so many stars, those patterns. She lay on the cold sand to look more comfortably. My goodness, she did not recognise that sky. She was unable to find the few constellations she did know. It was astonishing.

She was being shaken awake, and Robert was asking if she was all right. The stars had dimmed or disappeared in the cold glow of the dawn.

'Oh, oh, Robert, that was so beautiful.'

'I was wondering if you wanted a game of golf before it gets ridiculously hot again.'

Ethel struggled to her feet. 'What, now?'

'Yes, I'm going to be busy later. The camels will start arriving today.'

'All right. I'll just go and get dressed.'

'You really don't need to. The DG won't be up for hours yet.'

Ethel laughed. The idea of playing golf in her pyjamas rather than her stiff cotton skirt was enticing.

'Only if you promise not to tell your mother.'

'Oh, I won't. It's small beer against me telling her how you took your underwear off when you were playing tennis the other day.'

Ethel's eyes opened wide. 'How on earth do you know about that? No, don't answer.' The story had presumably been all over the hotel. 'All right, let's go then. I obviously have a reputation to uphold.'

~

Ethel had not been much interested in the talk of the camels arriving, or rather not arriving. The life they had created in their camp was so interesting and different, especially when the spectacular show of stars each night was added to it, that she had almost forgotten about the fair and why they had come. However, camels were arriving, as the word got about that the British Coastguard had arrived for its annual purchase. Almost overnight, the whole area just a couple of hundred yards from her tent was full of camels, their smells, their snorts and occasional shrieks, as well as of the men dressed in flowing robes and headdresses who cared for them. Their clothing seemed to form no impediment as they flung themselves onto the beasts and rode them about.

Once or twice, Ethel had to stand over her golf course when the camels came too near. Soon she began to recognise some of the riders and exchange good-natured banter with them that neither could understand. Several times she asked the DG to arrange for her to ride. It was so different from a horse, but she soon came to appreciate the camel's intelligence and compliance, speed and delicacy.

Late afternoon, as the heat began to disperse, the drivers put on a show. There were breakneck races across the sand, or acrobatic displays done on the camel's hump, mock battles, breath-taking leaps from back to back. Sometimes, the show went on into the night, and involved fire-throwing and fire-jumping. Ethel sat by the campfire, enthralled, breathing deep of the cinnamon coffee in her mug.

During the night, Ethel watched the stars, and at dawn played golf. It was hard to imagine that, just a few days' journey away, women were starving themselves in prison – perhaps Emmeline too if she had returned from Paris and been captured. There were concert halls where men and women, dressed in their most glamorous outfits, sat and listened to opera or a great symphony. But here she was, in an ecstasy of new experience, with a story about a strong woman in her drawer at home half set to music.

~

'We're leaving tomorrow,' said Robert as Ethel attacked the ninth hole.

'What, just like that?'

'Yes. The DG's selected the camels we need and managed to haggle the price down to something we can afford. They'll be taken up to Cairo as soon as possible. Our job is done.'

'Oh, I could stay here a lot longer.'

The camp was packed up, and the journey home prepared. Ethel was desolate.

As Cairo came nearer, she became nervous, with a sick feeling in her stomach. What if... What if Emmeline...? She had abandoned her to get on with her music, when she was so weak and ill that she could die. Then she had taken herself off to where she couldn't even be reached. She wouldn't have heard if anything had changed.

The DG was sitting by her on the train as it shuddered its way up the coast.

'You're very quiet, Dr Smyth. It's not an easy place to leave behind, is it?'

'It's been wonderful, thank you so much for taking me. A completely different experience. Now I find myself worrying about Mrs Pankhurst and what the news might be.'

'Do you think she wants to sacrifice herself completely?' he asked.

'I don't know. I used to think so. She would talk of it after Christabel went to Paris, that the battle would be fought out over women's bodies and she must be the first to put herself in that position. But in the end, I think she decided not to go so far.' Ethel smiled. 'She probably wasn't going to let the government off the hook that easily.'

'Mm. I'm sure the government is anxious for her not to die. She does have the most extraordinary following, as well as personal strength – that has certainly been a surprise to them. They are driving her to the edge, but I don't think they would want to risk the consequences of her dying.'

'That's small comfort,' said Ethel, trying to smile. 'They should give us the vote and then it would be over. She's very resilient, but it's like playing Russian roulette. Besides which, she can be very intense and do unwise things.'

'Let's hope not,' he said. 'If it's any comfort, I think I would have heard in my dispatches if anything much had changed.'

It was, a small comfort.

42

1914

Once she knew that Emmeline was safe, Ethel could not make up her mind to leave. Spring came, and every European who was able to move on to a cooler place, did so. Ethel kept on saying she must go but did not. Robert had arranged for a telescope to be installed on the roof of the hotel, and every night, at whatever hour the constellations were to be clearest, she got out of bed, put on her dressing gown and climbed the rickety iron staircase on the side of the hotel, until she was half-lying, searching the skies for what could be seen. There were always new revelations. Sometimes, she just lay there on the mat, not focussing at all, allowing the stars, which seemed to hang unsupported in the vast blackness of space, to create a deep peace within her.

In the day, she wrote angry articles for *The Suffragette*, accusing the government of attempted murder and wilful blindness. She wrote to musical contacts about the *Boatswain's Mate* and continued with the final sections of the opera.

~

I am so happy, wrote Bruno Walter. *Now that I have started work at the Munich Opera House, I can fulfil the pledge I made to you all those years ago, to produce* The Wreckers *as soon as I was able. That day has come at last. Please come so we can make arrangements.*

'Bruno,' breathed Ethel. 'You darling!' She almost packed her bags on the spot, then managed to quell her excitement. If she could finish *Boatswain*, then she could get his comments on it, and perhaps secure a performance of that too.

The rains came. The stars were obscured. Her mind refocussed, and within a couple of weeks the basics of the whole opera were in place.

~

Ethel looked up at Bruno Walter and knew a broad smile was on her face, mirroring his. They had just completed the discussions which would lead to several performances of *The Wreckers* next season.

'I was wondering if you would like to hear a bit of my new opera, *The Boatswain's Mate*. It couldn't be more different, but I think you will like it.'

'With the greatest pleasure,' he said.

She went and sat at the grand piano that filled at least a half of his study, and pulled the music out of her bag. The score was in a terrible state, full of corrections. It was, in fact, two scores, as only the first part had been orchestrated – the second half was still just songs and arias, with possible instrument combinations sketched in but not yet fully realised.

It was quite a while since she had done this – played a whole opera on the piano whilst singing the parts and, sometimes, making the sounds of the instruments or stamping her feet – but she knew exactly what she wanted. It was as exhilarating as ever.

'It's very good,' said Bruno. 'It's what's you might call "comic", but it does have some very powerful emotional scenes in it. I can see how much you've developed musically, despite all the distractions you allow yourself to have. There's just a couple of suggestions, if you want to hear them.'

This was exactly what Ethel did want. It was no good someone like Bruno Walter just nodding and saying it was good. She needed his knowledge and expertise to build on what she had done. Not that she necessarily accepted all his comments – he did not really like the folk songs she had put in, for example, but she would not give way on that. The argument was all part of the fun.

'Thank you, Bruno,' she said at last.

'It's such a pleasure to see you writing again. Right, so it's agreed we'll put on *Wreckers* during the next season. I'm looking forward to working on that so much. I'll have a contract drawn up before you leave. As for *Boatswain*, well, I love it, but I'm too new here to propose a comic opera. I'll give you a letter for Frankfurt if you're heading that way. Hans is always looking for something new.'

'I'm definitely going that way now you mention it,' said Ethel, laughing. 'My publisher has said that if I can get a contract, he'll publish the opera for me, parts and all. That's never happened before.'

A few days later, Ethel was back on the train. How strange it was to be picking up again this wandering musician's life, looking for those in charge to love and produce her work. She hadn't done that since Harry died.

Ethel lay on her bed clutching two thick parchment contracts to her chest. After all this time, twenty years, if not thirty, of hard work, she had two definite commitments for her operas to be performed – in big, continental opera houses, too. Never mind the manoeuvring at Weimar or the humiliations of Berlin; never mind the betrayals of Leipzig. Germany had welcomed her back.

She had not had to ask her aristocratic friends to pull any strings, or made artistically doubtful compromises. She had not had to pay anyone out of her own pocket.

On the contrary, she was going to be paid, and quite handsomely at that, and have *The Boatswain's Mate* published by a reputable printer, so that it would be available whenever anyone wanted to perform it. Two honourable, proper artistic directors had promised to perform her music, just weeks apart. This time next year, her career would be properly relaunched. Covent Garden would certainly follow suit.

'I love you, Germany,' she said aloud. 'I always have. We've had our ups and downs, more than enough of them, but here we are again. Lisl would be proud of you.'

43

ST MALO 1914

Ethel stood on the harbour-side waiting for the boat to tie up. It was taking an eternity. The sailors kept jumping on and off the quay, winding and rewinding the huge ropes on the capstans whilst the captain manoeuvred it into its exact berth, steam exploding out of its funnels.

Ethel scrutinised the passengers. There were dozens of them standing by the gate where the gangway would go down – mainly holiday-makers, she thought, from the number of families dressed in their summer outfits with a profusion of bags and sunhats and coloured balls, ready to enjoy St Malo's sandy beaches. There were businessmen too, smart with black hats and small cases, keen to stride through the ancient, towering archways into the city.

There was no sign of Emmeline. She could not see everyone clearly, but even when the crowd thinned into a line as people made their precarious way down the landing-board, there was no-one who looked like her. Ethel sighed, resigned to waiting until the last person had come off the boat, and bracing herself for the disappointment of having to wait, once more, for the next boat three days ahead.

She must not expect so much. Of course, Emmeline was not

free to travel whenever she wanted to, however lax the authorities seemed at times. It had not been that long since she had tried to come to France, and been apprehended on the train to Dover and manhandled through the carriage window onto the platform by brutal policemen. Another debilitating spell of starvation had resulted.

'Come on, Emmeline, come on,' she murmured. 'Where are you?'

She remained on the quay, watching the very last people and luggage and goods unloading. It was so very long since they had met.

She was just beginning to tell herself not to be so disappointed – she would return for the next boat, and the next, if necessary – when a small group appeared by the landing-board. A sailor and a young woman were supporting an old woman who could hardly walk unaided. The old woman waved in Ethel's direction.

'Emmeline,' breathed Ethel, before shouting it in her loudest voice. It came out almost as a scream, and she ran towards the boat, where two sailors were now creating a chair out of their hands so that Emmeline could be carried off the boat. The younger woman, who Ethel could now see was Norah, followed behind, trying to keep hold of numerous pieces of baggage.

'Give us a hand, Auntie,' shouted Norah.

Ethel caught Emmeline as she tried to steady herself on the quay. She felt the thinness of her, caught again that strange smell of the starved body, saw the yellowish skin, the dulled eyes, the attempt at cheerfulness.

'I hope you're going to look after me again and make me better,' said Emmeline.

'That is precisely what I'm going to do,' said Ethel, trying to sound brisk and everyday. 'Look, one of my golfing admirers has sent a car for us. The air here is magic, you'll see.'

Supported by Ethel on one side and Norah on the other, they made their slow path to the car waiting a few yards away.

~

Emmeline lay on a sofa on the veranda of the hotel, reading, chatting quietly, sleeping. A wheeled chair was found so that she could be taken to the most shaded parts of the beautiful gardens, where Ethel would often find her dozing or listening to Norah as she read the papers to her. The countries of Europe were in turmoil. The shooting of an archduke had become an international incident with countries lining up against each other, mobilising their forces along borders, questioning their alliances.

~

'I'm so bored,' Emmeline said, 'now Norah has gone back. I know you're busy with your opera, but this is worse than exile here, it's so quiet. I've already walked around the gardens twice.'

Ethel smiled. Emmeline was making one of her remarkable recoveries.

'I know I told you that I'd go to Paris when I'm strong enough, but I've decided to ask Christabel to come here. Do you mind?'

Ethel swallowed hard. 'Of course not. Why the change of plan?' At least she would not lose Emmeline again so soon, even if she had to put up with Christabel.

'I don't feel very confident about going to Paris just now.'

'You normally love it there.'

'I do, of course. It's just that… well, who knows what might happen?'

'Nothing's going to happen,' said Ethel. 'It's just sabre-rattling, as it always is. You don't think anyone wants to break up Europe, do you? All these alliances that have held so long.'

'You're being over-optimistic, Ethel. There's an awful lot of gathering together of troops and arms going on, not to mention threats to break treaties.'

'I only came back from Germany a couple of weeks ago,' said Ethel. 'No-one's that worried. All right, so the Kaiser's got a big mouth and an even bigger chip on his shoulder. The allies will face him down, you'll see.'

Nevertheless, a cold numbness settled into her stomach. She must write around again, asking her friends in all the countries she could think of what their opinion was.

~

Ethel excused herself from Emmeline and Christabel's company. Strategy and tactics had never interested her much, and she found their endless conversations tedious. She must concentrate on her opera and its fast-approaching deadlines.

Deep in the grounds of the hotel she found an abandoned summer house. It must have been grand once, intricate in shape with beautifully carved wood. The trees around had been allowed to grow over, providing shade, but she could glimpse the sea beneath, and the beach, vast at low tide. There were still old garden tables and chairs scattered around and, after she had begged a tablecloth and cushions from the hotel staff, she had a pleasant working space.

She loved creating the orchestra's lines, choosing the different instruments to illustrate her story, merging them into luscious or dramatic or shocking bursts of sound. The tunes only came alive as that depth and richness were added. Now the silly plot of two men's game to win the hand of the landlady having been exposed, she could concentrate on Mrs Waters and Travers reaching out to each other. There were some lovely songs in the opera – she thought so anyway – funny songs, folk songs, technically perfect songs, and now, finally, a love song: *In the woods the paths are strips of velvet, fairy green/Edged with silver where a tiny brook gleams/ Up through the ferns.* Strings, she thought, scribbling furiously, simple at first and then more interwoven and complex... *Goodbye then, until this evening.*

Ethel felt numb. Germany was poised to start fighting France, violating neutral Belgium to do so. Her Germany, wonderful, musical Germany, was behaving dishonourably, scrapping for domination of Europe.

At dinner, Emmeline and Christabel were pale-faced.

'We've made some big decisions today,' said Emmeline. 'Perhaps I've seen the last of my prison cell.'

'What? Has the government given in at last?' She looked at their faces, but they did not break into laughter. 'No, it's not that, or we'd be celebrating. What is it?'

'If only we could. No, dearest, we've been talking all day, and if England comes into this horrible conflict, which surely it must, we're going to call off the campaign.'

'Call it off?'

'Yes, we can't carry on if Britain is at war. We would have to get behind the government, not fight it. It will be very strange, Ethel, but Christabel is right to see it that way. I've been arguing against her all day, but it is the only thing to do.'

Ethel looked from one to the other. 'You mean everything will stop? No protest, no militancy, no hunger-striking?'

Emmeline stretched across the table and covered Ethel's hand.

'All of us are going to need a bit of time to get used to the idea,' she said.

'It's the right thing to do,' said Christabel. 'But also, it gives us a chance to re-set the argument. We're at a stalemate right now. But surely, if we throw ourselves behind the government on this, it will change how they regard our demands.'

How Ethel hated that crystal-clear voice, that brook-no-argument tone.

'If necessary, the campaign will pick up again in a few months' time,' said Emmeline. 'We'll have lost some momentum, but we can think of some new tactics. Don't look so upset, darling, it's just the way it has to be right now.'

~

Ethel wanted to go home immediately, but Christabel was waiting for the most perfect time for her plan to work. Emmeline must not be re-arrested when they returned. They were writing to people to plant in their minds the idea of what the suffragettes would do if England joined the war.

Ethel hated the whole idea and struggled to accept that Germany's aggression must be halted. She mourned the decades of links that were being destroyed – political links, cultural links, family links. She could think of a never-ending stream of German people, not just her friends, who would hate what was happening, who would be deeply unhappy. Who created these situations? Who wanted them? Were they really all now meant to think of the Germans as their enemies, the Austrians too? They were the people of countries in which she had been made so welcome and been so happy.

'Darling,' Emmeline said at dinner, covering Ethel's hand with her own, 'make sure you are ready to go home. Christabel went down to the port today and was told all the larger boats have been called in by the Navy. She's managed to find a fisherman who will take us over, but we need to be ready at a moment's notice.'

'When do you think that might be?'

'I don't know. Tomorrow or the day after. We won't be able to take all our luggage.'

That night Ethel considered all the possessions in her room, gathered over so many months of travel. She began to see what she could cram into her travel bag. Slowly, she put the mementos and the little gifts for her nieces and her favourite jackets back on the shelves, ready for the maids to pack into the trunks that would be forwarded to England as soon as this was over.

She would not need any of that. She placed her performance contracts and the manuscripts for her two new operas into her bag. That was all that she needed. She was ready to go.

EPILOGUE

LONDON 1933

Ethel talked long and hard to herself as she got ready to go out. It might be in her honour, this concert, but that didn't mean she was going to get all grateful and weepy about it. It was wonderful, as everyone kept telling her, that her achievements were being celebrated – 'At long last,' she muttered under her breath – but, but… She struggled for the words she might use to describe it in the next instalment of her memoirs. It was no more than a flurry of sparks at the end of a firework show, in which seconds of glory had been preceded, and followed, by long stretches of darkness. That was it.

Thirty-three musicians – eminent composers, conductors, players and singers – might have written to invite her to this festival, this series of three concerts of her work, organised to celebrate her seemingly endless life – they hadn't used that exact phrase – but that didn't fool her into thinking she had become part of the musical establishment. She had made a bit of a dent, that's all, become a tiny wheel in the English music machine. Perhaps her music would have a place in the programmes of the future, but nothing was guaranteed. She knew that now.

So it was going to be lovely; she would see many friends, old and new, but that was that.

'Come on, Norah,' she called to her niece, 'don't forget your camera. Time to go and be feted.'

Their taxi was met by some young men and women, students of the Royal College of Music, perhaps. Ethel wasn't sure who they were because she could not hear their introductions, no matter how loud they repeated them, in the noise and bustle around the Royal Albert Hall on a Sunday afternoon. Never mind, Norah would cover for her. Chattering away, they led her inside the Hall, slowly leading her up the many stairs, along the curved corridors and into the box where she was to sit. A large, ornate chair with shining wooden arms indicated this was the Royal Box. Several people were already there, and she was led to a seat near where an old man was already sitting. He stood to greet her, and then she recognised him, underneath all the white hair and whiskers.

'George Henschel, my goodness,' she cried, gasping with pleasure. 'Sir George.'

'Dame Ethel.' He grinned and bent over her hand, kissing it, and drawing her to him for a hug. He was still a very handsome man.

'What a wonderful surprise,' she said. 'Have you moved back from America?'

She couldn't hear his reply, but they smiled at each other happily. He introduced the person sitting next to him, his daughter, perhaps, and she introduced her niece. As Ethel turned to lower herself into her seat, she could see how full the Hall already was. Several people were waiting for her to look down so that they could wave at her. Despite her resolve, tears stung her eyes. She waved madly.

Darling George, Thekla and Gustchen had called him, shy, full of musical fervour – he had been there at so many of the best musical times in her life, and she at his. She had a glimpse of long legs and lean bodies jumping into the cold Thuringian lake.

'We've shared some good times, haven't we?' she said, stretching for his hand. It was thin and bony with arthritis, and she lifted it to her lips and kissed it. 'Thanks for everything.' She couldn't remember saying such a thing before, and he looked at her quizzically. She set her face to stern lest he think she was going soft in her old age.

She sat back in the comfortable seat and looked around the Hall. It was nearly full. How could that be, when so many of the best people in her life were dead? But apparently not everyone. In the boxes around her sat wealthy friends, some of the musicians who had organised this event, others she did not recognise. Scanning the circle, she spotted Bob and her remaining sisters, nephews and nieces. Christabel gave her an abrupt wave – Emmeline should be here, of course, but she had died just as the vote was finally won for them all.

The choir filed in and sat sedately, waiting for the orchestra to settle itself down and tune up. Ethel counted the women – yes, nearly a third of the players were women, standing out from the dark-suited men, their bare arms shining in the bright lights and their hair clasps and necklaces sparkling. She could take some credit for that. She felt a surge of energy at the thought of the tough battles she had fought. And she had been proved right, so right. The women were proud to be there, focussed, concentrated, adding a richness of tone that warmed the music. They had certainly taught those complacent chaps a thing or two.

'We've sat in an awful lot of concert halls in our lives,' she said to George. 'Hundreds of them, in lots of countries.'

She thought he said, 'Loved every minute,' but before she could check a hush came over the hall and everyone stood up as the Queen was escorted into the box. Ethel curtsied deeply as the Queen greeted her. She hoped she looked reasonably respectable and her hair wasn't falling out of its pleat, or her bodice dropping too low. How kind the Queen's face was, how warm and welcoming.

No sooner had the Queen and her entourage settled down than Thomas Beacham came onto the stage and, with his usual casual wave of the baton, had the concert underway. The energy of the musicians crackled as the choir launched into the *Gloria* of her Mass. She could not resist raising her arm to try and speed the violins up, grinning broadly at George sitting by her. The acoustic of the Hall delivered a mere fraction of the sound to her deaf ears, and there was far too much buzz to enjoy it.

Nevertheless, it was triumphant.

AUTHOR'S NOTE

There is a lot of factual information available about Dr Ethel Smyth. She wrote several memoirs, complete with pen pictures of some of her friends, and there are biographies too, She appears in the writing of and about other composers and in suffragette stories. Musicologists, particularly those who study the music of women composers, have taken an interest in her in recent years, and her music has started to be performed more regularly. Because of her bisexuality, she has begun to be included in studies by LGBTQ+ historians.

This novel has been carved out of, and alongside, this information. I have tried to keep to the facts as known, though occasionally times, places, names and characters might differ slightly. However, the interpretation of the facts is my own, and the whole book is the product of my novelistic imagination.

Many of the characters in *Shining Threads* are based on the real people of the time – her family, composers, musicians, wealthy people, royalty, protesters. Some have a major role in her life and in the novel; others touch on her only briefly. I have tried to be true to what I have come to know of them, and take full responsibility for my interpretations. Just occasionally, I have invented a character to serve a specific purpose in the novel (Peter Barnsdale being the most notable example of this).

Ethel fought to be recognised in the male-dominated society of the time, and to create change where she could. Over a hundred years later, women continue to struggle to achieve equality.

ACKNOWLEDGEMENTS

Writing a historical novel requires the input of many different kinds of information, research and understanding. Each small piece could come from a book or article, a knowledgeable or inspirational person, a building, a song or a sonata, a chance encounter, an object and much else. It would be impossible to thank all of these sources, and I apologise to anybody whose contribution I have failed to acknowledge.

As always, I'm indebted to some wonderful libraries and their librarians – I would particularly like to mention The Women's Library at LSE, the Westminster Music Library, Surrey History Centre, and some in Leipzig too.

Many people have helped shape this book. Thank you so much to Lynne Goddard, Barbara Paterson, Suzanne High and Tarja Moles for reading the book (sometimes more than once) and offering such valuable suggestions. I'm also grateful to Steve Dixon, who sadly died in 2021. Professional editors/mentors too at TLC, Jericho Writers and Curtis Brown - thank you also for your critiques and support. Special thanks to Bridget Holding at Wild Words, who mentored me for a year and helped me develop the style of the book. Most memorable was a Wild Words retreat in the South of France, where participants acted out some of the scenes which was both fun and illuminating.

A morning's conversation with the composer, Gordon Crosse, who sadly died a couple of years ago, provided much to think about on composition, musical ideas and influences, and helped me see how Ethel might have got started on composing. Thanks too to Thomas Croft of the charity ATD Fourth World UK, which now owns what was the Smyth family home, Frimhurst, and runs it as a resource to support families particularly affected by poverty. Tom Croft generously showed me around the house giving me a lot of information about it in the time of the Smyths, and signposted other resources too.

I have enjoyed working with The Book Guild in bringing my novel out for people to read, and have appreciated their enthusiasm and professionalism.

I couldn't end of course without expressing gratitude for the support of my son, Leif Dixon, who always makes me feel that what I'm doing is worthwhile and, as an academic historian, provides invaluable historical perspective and context.